What Would Mary Berry Do?

What Would Mary Berry Do?

Claire Sandy

PAN BOOKS

First published in 2014 by Pan Books
an imprint of Pan Macmillan, a division of Macmillan Publishers Limited
Pan Macmillan, 20 New Wharf Road, London N1 9RR
Basingstoke and Oxford
Associated companies throughout the world
www.panmacmillan.com

ISBN 978-1-4472-5349-5

1 3 5 7 9 8 6 4 2

A CIP catalogue record for this book is available from the British Library.

Typeset by Palimpsest Book Production Ltd, Falkirk, Stirlingshire
Printed and bound by CPI Group (UK) Ltd, Croydon, CR0 4YY

Visit www.panmacmillan.com to read more about all our books
and to buy them. You will also find features, author interviews and
news of any author events, and you can sign up for e-newsletters
so that you're always first to hear about our new releases.

This book is for Caroline Hogg;
friend, editor, heroine

Prologue

Marie Dunwoody loved her children, all three of them, with a ferocity beyond understanding. But every once in a while she would gladly sell them to a passing gypsy. And that Friday morning, the morning of St Ethelred's school fete, was one of those once-in-a-whiles.

'Mum,' said Iris, lavishing the last of the milk on her cereal, 'I did tell you that you need to bake something for today's cake stall, didn't I? It's got to be a . . . um . . . what was it? Oh, yeah. It's got to be a *show-stopper*.'

JULY

School Fete

Show-Stopper

Dear Iris and Rose's mum

Thank you so much for agreeing to bake the show-stopper for the school fete. Every penny made by the fete will go to the PSA and will directly benefit our pupils.

Best regards

The PSA

Their shoes squeaking on the gym's waxed floor, hordes of parents rifled bric-a-brac, lucky-dipped and bought one-eyed hunchback teddies from the craft stand.

Over at the cake stall the show-stopper was attracting attention. Of the wrong kind.

'I'm sorry, girls.' Marie took in her daughters' crestfallen faces, both so perfectly alike, with their ski-slope noses, their confetti freckles, their grave brown eyes just like their dad's. 'Next year . . .' she began, but went no further. She'd made the same speech last year: her annual promise to be the mum they deserved.

Angus – video camera, as ever, grafted to his hand – zoomed in on his mother's contribution.

'Darling, *don't*,' pleaded Marie. The world didn't need footage of her show-stopper. With minutes to spare she had had to rely on the petrol-station minimart. The realisation that just-on-their-sell-by-date French Fancies were as good as it would get had made her want to lie down among the chilled wraps and weep. She'd bought the lot, hoping to make them look . . . well, *abundant*; but, huddled bleakly on a tiered cake stand, the dozen battered fancies looked . . . well, *shop-bought.*

'It doesn't matter, Mum,' said Rose.

'Nah,' said Iris.

But they kept sneaking looks at Lucy's cake.

Lucy Gray. Mild-mannered mum of one, neighbour and nemesis. As if constructed especially to shame Marie, the woman was birdlike, a petite and neat counterpoint to Marie's more-than-adequate bosom/bottom arrangement. Her house, the largest on Caraway Close, boasted hanging baskets, gleaming windows and a perfect front lawn of neon emerald; across the way, Marie's house number hung upside down (transforming them from number nineteen to sixty-one) and the twins' bikes copulated in the porch, tripping her up each and every morning.

Lucy baked show-stoppers every other day, 'just for fun'.

Wearing a flowery tea-dress, without a speck of make-up on her wholesome face, and simpering with false modesty at the compliments raining down around her, Lucy stood proudly by her cake.

And what a cake it was!

It was a supermodel of cakes, an Alfa Romeo, a Crufts Best in Show. A multi-storey sponge high-rise, plastered with the softest buttercream and festooned with hand-made fondant roses that could deceive a bee, it came complete with its own theme tune of tinkling harps.

Or maybe, thought Marie, *that last bit is just in my head.* 'Go on, girls,' she sighed, defeated, handing over a pound coin as a donation. 'Ask Mrs Gray for a slice. Politely!'

She was jealous. It was not a nice thing to admit, but Marie was frank about her own faults. She freely admitted she was rubbish at Monopoly, that her boisterous hair needed a cut, that she should visit the gym more often (or at all), and that she was deeply envious not only of Lucy's baking prowess, but of the general air of homespun domestication that surrounded the woman like a pastel pea-souper. Hard to imagine Lucy snarling at her husband to 'get out of the damn way or, so help me God, I'll mow you down', as Marie had at poor Robert that morning.

In her defence, Robert should have known better than to shrug when told of the twins' bombshell. 'Sorry, love – your department. You don't expect *me* to bake, do you?' he'd said, as if the notion of him making a cake was as absurd as juggling with fire. She'd answered with a loud un-Lucy-like 'Why expect *me* to bake? Because I have ovaries?' and had jumped into the car.

Robert was lovely. He was her best mate. He made her laugh and still fancied her, despite stretch marks, greying hair and even greyer pants. (She fancied him right back. No longer the black-haired, brown-eyed skinny guy she'd first lusted after, Robert now had a spiky salt-and-pepper thatch that was, in her opinion, every bit as gorgeous; she simply didn't see the lines around his eyes, or the useful little shelf around his middle.) And what's more, Mr and Mrs Robert Dunwoody were a team, securely yoked together in harness as they shouldered the burdens of raising a family. But it peeved Marie that the kitchen was 'her' domain simply because of her gender.

Lucy had no such qualms. Lucy *loved* the kitchen. She

pickled things. She preserved other things. She candied peel. She froze gluts. She even – and Marie could work up a ten-minute rant about this – *potted shrimps*. Lucy's kitchen (the literal opposite of Marie's; the Grays faced the Dunwoodys on their circular cul-de-sac) boasted a walk-in larder. Marie's boasted a sofa and the UK's largest private collection of Pop-Tarts.

'Hello there!'

Oh Christ, Lucy was talking to her.

'Hi,' said Marie.

'Nice to see you here. I thought maybe, you know, what with work and everything, you might not make it.'

Always a little barb. Some little insinuation. *Some of us have to work*, thought Marie, going further with a heartfelt *Some of us love our work*. 'I make it to most of the school stuff,' she said, keeping any defensive briskness out of her voice. She didn't want Lucy to know she was rattled. Marie nodded at the cake, looming over them like a sugary Nelson's Column. 'Amazing cake!' It was true, and Marie had been brought up to be polite, even to a nemesis.

'Oh well, I try,' said Lucy. She even worked up a blush.

Beside her neighbour, Marie felt seven feet tall and almost as wide. A Boden ad come to life, Lucy had the pearlescent skin of the clichéd English rose and the matching, almost transparent, fine fair hair, always pulled back into a careless yet charming ponytail. A few fronds escaped to dangle around her face, a style that semaphored *I am not vain enough to fuss with my hair*.

For the first time Marie noticed the boniness of the

knees sticking out of the flowery dress, the tiny circumference of the wrists. How could a woman who baked every day be so skinny? 'How's Tod?' she asked conversationally, aware of an oppressive awkwardness.

'He's great, thanks. Working hard. You know.' Lucy smiled, wobbled her head, also at a loss for conversation. 'And how's . . . um?'

Typical, thought Marie. 'Robert,' she said slowly and clearly.

'Yes, Robert,' repeated Lucy, as if congratulating Marie on knowing her own husband's name.

'He's fine, thanks!'

And the awkwardness descended like a toxic cloud.

The gulf between them was too wide to cross. Marie, with her untidy hair and her pretty, animated face always ready to break into a hooting laugh or exasperated gurn, could never find common ground with this geisha who kissed her husband goodbye every day on the doorstep, having filled him with home-made muesli and freshly squeezed orange juice. Marie thought with hot shame of the careful way in which she carved out the jade dots of mould before throwing toast at her brood. And just last week Robert had gone commando to work because laundry duties had clashed with water-pistol-battle-with-the-twins duties. 'Anyway . . .' Marie began to back away, over-smiling, 'must get on.' She lost her basic social skills around this woman. 'Congratulations on the cake!'

'Take a slice with you.' Lucy deftly cut a triangle of gateau. 'I owe it all to Delia!'

Escaping outside to the grounds wrapped around the

low-rise sprawl of the school, Marie thought *That figures.* Delia Smith, head girl of the TV chefs, was Lucy's natural leader.

The sunshine was shockingly bright after the gym's cool institutional interior. Wandering, paper plate in hand, her epic culinary fail firmly on her mind, Marie recognised representatives of other foodie tribes milling about the stalls erected on the tennis court, or chatting in little knots by the adventure playground.

Presiding over the raffle, Miss Harper was undoubtedly a devotee of Nigella. A luscious hourglass, the teacher's pouting air of posh wantonness ensured that Robert took in nothing at parents' evening. Like the original domestic goddess, she could kill a man by slowly licking a spoon.

Over by the car park, marshalling the twins and their nine-year-old classmates for the country-dancing display, the new teaching assistant's swooping eyeliner and vintage sundress gave her away as a Rachel Khoo. Dinner at her place would be all mismatched china and vodka in teacups.

Warming to her theme, Marie picked out Angus's floppy-fringed art teacher, who was sketching caricatures for fifty pence, as a Raymond Blanc. Although not French (he was Welsh, probably as un-French as it's possible to be), he had the requisite passion and style and floppy hair and . . . Marie conceded that she rather fancied Angus's art teacher and moved swiftly on, gravitating towards the second-hand bookstall.

A familiar figure caught her eye. Far from the action, in the shadow cast by a large oak, sat her son. *On his own*, thought Marie. *Again.* She quelled an impulse to go and sit by him. A clump of teenage boys passed her, shouting and pushing, a messy, laughing amoeba.

And there was Angus, head down as ever, camera by his side, fingers flying over his iPhone. Marie felt exasperated: *Why is he emailing some girl he's never met, when he's surrounded by flesh-and-blood people?*

TO: stargazinggirl247@gmail.com
FROM: geeksrus39@gmail.com
26.07.13
15.03
SUBJECT: Me again

Hi Soulmate

Yeah I know my family are always mad but today they're madder than usual. (Should that be 'more mad'? Go on. Correct me, Grammar Freek, u know u want to.) Mum threatened to murder Dad this morning reversing out over the gravel at 300 mph in that stupid little car of her's. And right now my worst nightmare is coming true. MY MUM IS IN MY SCHOOL. Bet she drools over Mr Rosen again and thinks nobody notices. The twins are giggling in that special evil way. It's not looking good, Soulmate.

Which is why you should be here. It's so selfish of you to live in Scotland. Tell me what's going on at your house. Your Mum and Dad still giving each other shit? Don't let it get to you. Wish you could come to this party with me tonight. Gonna be awesome. Amazed I'm even invited. I'm not one of that trendy crowd. I could never be a Clone. They all look the same and they all sound the same but I'm a geek and proud of it! Like you.

Will we ever meet up? Can't believe I found a best mate on an indie film forum. I know what films you like but I don't know what your voice sounds like. Mad.

EVERYTHING is mad.

laters

Angus

Marie, staring at her son, popped a plastic forkful of cake in her mouth.

Stopped in her tracks by the ambrosial taste, she almost groaned. Lucy's cake was exquisite, like being French-kissed by angels. It was buttery, it was light, it tasted like Mother used to make (if Mother was a genius).

In that instant, Marie suddenly got it.

She got why people make such a fuss about cooking. She got why there are foodie tribes, and why people worship the ones who show them how. This cake was more than the sum of its parts; it couldn't be reduced to butter, eggs, flour. It was life-affirming, it was joy-bringing; it was simple and complex all at the same time.

I want to be able to do this! she thought with sudden vehemence.

Chasing crumbs round the plate with a forefinger, Marie froze. As if placed on the bookstall by a celestial hand, a hardback book, its edges worn by loving overuse, sat at an angle atop the rubble of novels and TV tie-ins and self-help manuals. Clever blue eyes stared out and found

Marie's from a tanned and handsomely lined face, framed by a genteel blonde bob.

Here I am! that wise, friendly face said.

Marie picked up the book reverentially, as if it might explode.

'That one's a pound,' said the head of the PSA, a hoity-toity woman with a regrettable fringe, who was a Hairy Bikers disciple if her moustache was anything to go by.

Paying up, Marie knew she was changing her life. In a flash she saw her new existence. She saw her family gathered around the table. Angus wasn't peering down a viewfinder; the twins weren't arguing about what they'd call the cow that they planned to own one day; Robert wasn't repeating mind-numbingly dull office gossip; they were all saying *Mmmm, Mother dearest, that smells good!* as Marie sliced into something heavenly that she'd made earlier. Their faces were rosy, their eyes were bright and the kitchen seemed to have been miraculously redecorated.

Placing her hand on the book as if it was a Bible, Marie whispered the vow she'd abandoned earlier. 'This time next year,' she said, eyes closed, heart a-flutter, 'I'll make a show-stopper for the school fete. I swear, on the *Mary Berry Complete Baking Bible*.'

It was a long time since Marie had read a book walking along the road. She remembered the summer of her first Jilly Cooper novel, banging into lamp posts on the way home from school. This was like that, but more so. Meandering down wide and winding suburban avenues beneath early-evening lilac skies, she devoured the *Basic Equipment* section in her new *Mary Berry Complete Baking Bible*.

Hmm, she thought, eyes narrowing, *my whisk doesn't look like that*. Robert had used it to stir emulsion and it hadn't been the same since. 'Wait for me at the kerb, girls!' she shouted, and the twins obediently stalled.

She caught the glance they gave each other. She knew they were humouring her; some nine-year-olds may need their mum to guide them across the road, but not ones who could retool the UK economy while brushing their Barbies' hair. She looked behind to see Angus tailing her, with his camera to his eye.

'Not from behind!' squawked Marie, covering her bottom with the *Baking Bible*. 'Give your poor old mother a break.'

'You don't look that old from behind,' said Angus, with that special teenage-boy gallantry that makes a woman feel 104.

'Look,' said Marie, pointing. 'Somebody's calling your name.'

Scuttling along in St Ethelred's wine-and-blue livery, Chloe shouted 'Hey! Angus! Wait up!'

Chloe Gray was goth Ying to Lucy Gray's blonde Yang – one of the reasons Marie liked her so much. The other reason was how vividly Marie remembered being fifteen and totes in love with a boy who barely noticed you.

Presumably Chloe had also clocked the faint slump of Angus's shoulders when he saw her, and had noted the mechanical nature of his barely there smile.

Be nice, Marie willed her son, recognising from her own youth Chloe's desperate-for-a-welcome-but-expecting-a-knock-back expression and her hyper-casual conversation opener.

'Saw you tootling along. Thought I'd – you know – say hello, kind of thing.'

'Right. Cool.'

For Angus, this was Noël Coward-style repartee; since he'd finally saved up enough for his Sony HDR-AS15 camera, he spoke less than a child raised by orang-utans.

They'd caught up with Iris and Rose. 'Look straight ahead and cross, ladies,' said Marie, bonking both girls gently on the head with her new Mary Berry, confident that this translated as *Stop staring at Chloe!* Her daughters were obsessed with Chloe's obsession with their brother, and loved to watch her watch him.

'Why,' they often marvelled to their mother, 'would anybody look at Angus like that?'

'Because,' Marie would answer, 'your brother is handsome.'

Despite the retching sounds this always provoked, it was true. Angus had wayward chestnut hair that curled forward like Caesar's, and wide blue eyes. Perhaps Marie was prejudiced (he'd inherited her colouring), but she saw her gauche son, teetering on the cusp of manhood, as poetic-looking.

It wasn't all poetry. There were pimples, of course, those pus-filled pressies from Mother Nature, and his feet had already grown to canoe-like dimensions. Marie had had to pointedly leave anti-perspirant at eye level in his room before he got with the whole showering-every-day programme and eradicated the whiff of musky compost that warns of approaching man-child. But Angus was a bit of a looker – if only he'd ever look up.

You should have more confidence, she told him endlessly.

You're biased, Mum, he'd laugh. True enough, and it was also true that all teenagers looked gorgeous to a woman wading through her forties. It was the bright whites of the eyes, the untroubled brow, the resilient glow of almost-new skin; even Chloe, who sought to obliterate her distinctive features beneath Cleopatra eyeliner, black lipstick and Elvis hair dye, couldn't dull that bloom. Marie winced with feminine empathy as she watched the girl swim upstream against Angus's lack of interest.

'I saved you some of my mother's cake.' Chloe held out a Tupperware box.

'Not hungry, thanks.' Angus fiddled with his zoom.

'We are,' said the twins.

Disloyal beasts, thought Marie, as the fruit of her loins grabbed the plastic container and fell upon Lucy's handiwork like dingoes.

Feeling for Chloe, Marie took up the conversational baton dropped so charmlessly by Angus. 'Do you cook, Chloe?' With the *Baking Bible* throbbing in her hand, Marie longed to be alone with her new mentor.

'Nope.' Chloe wound a lock of raven hair around a finger. 'With my mother in the house, who needs to?'

'Why do you always call her "my mother" and not "Mum"?' Iris was happy to ask the un-askable.

'Because Lucy's not her mum, stupid,' said Rose, a skilled eavesdropper who knew more or less everything about everybody. 'Lucy's her stepmum.' She looked to Chloe for verification. 'That's right, isn't it?'

'Sorry about these two,' said Marie. 'I'll beat them soundly when I get them home.'

'She always says that,' said Iris.

'She never does it,' said Rose.

'She usually cuddles us,' said Iris.

'Shut *up*!' said Angus, who had never – not for one millisecond – found his sisters cute.

'I don't mind.' Chloe's smile revealed black lipstick smudges on her front teeth. 'It's true. Lucy isn't my real mother.'

'Where's your real—'

Marie put a hand over Iris's mouth. 'None of your beeswax.'

'Nobody knows. Too far away to cuddle, that's for sure.'

They were at the corner of Caraway Close, where the road veered away on either side to form a large circle around the green in the middle. Marie's heart filled for brave pretty little gothy Chloe, with no Mummy – just a Mother with a capital M, who spent more time perfecting her Genoese sponge than she did noticing the troubled young woman under her roof.

'Why don't you and Angus walk to the party together tonight?' she asked. 'The one everybody's talking about. The *cool* one.' Marie enjoyed her son's squirming at her double whammy of pimping him out *and* using the word 'cool'.

'I'm not invited.'

'Oh.' *Damn*. 'Well, me neither!' Marie could have kicked herself, but not before she'd kicked Angus for failing to hide his obvious relief.

'See you, Mrs Dunwoody. See you, Iris, Rose.' Chloe ambled off round the far curve of the cul-de-sac. 'See you, Angus.'

'Yeah.' Angus had forgotten her already, racing the girls to the gate of number nineteen (or was it sixty-one?)

'Bye, Chloe. Come over in the holidays, yeah?' Marie watched her go, then turned and raced after her children, beating them to the door, eager for her one-on-one with Mary.

'Robert,' Marie said gently, about midnight. Then, louder, but still gently, 'Ro-bert!'

'Uh? Wha—' Robert shot upright on the lumpy old red sofa, the novel he hadn't been reading plunging to the floor. 'Wassenazleep,' he slurred.

'Darling, go to bed. Don't wait for me.'

'I don't like going up on my own.' He scratched his head, sending his hair haywire above his sleep-creased face. 'No nice bottom to snuggle up to.' He yawned. 'Just one of the many advantages of having a wife built along traditional lines.'

'Just say "fat", for God's sake,' muttered Marie, propping her glasses back on her nose, leaning again over the book spreadeagled on the pine kitchen table. A half-drained tumbler of white wine stood to attention, its glassy depths sparkling in the kindly light shed by the lamps dotted around the kitchen. Marie had long ago decreed that the fluorescent lights beneath the cream-painted wall units were too harsh on a mature complexion. '"Curvy. Ample. In-and-outy." All your different little ways of telling me I need to lose a few pounds.'

'If I meant fat, I'd say "fat".' Robert was on his feet now. 'And don't you dare lose a few pounds. I love each and every one of your pounds. Especially, you know, the ones in this area.' He pointed to his chest. 'Oh, go on, *laugh*, Marie! You've been like the school swot preparing for an exam all evening.'

'This is fascinating,' she murmured, lost in her book again.

'You don't have to be a domestic wonder, darling. And besides, no woman your age, living in a suburban cul-de-sac, has a nemesis.' Robert seemed to think it was all about rivalry. 'I mean, does Lucy have an underground lair? Is she planning to take over the world one cupcake at a time?'

'Hmm?' Deep in Mary-love, Marie was gone again, beyond even Robert's reach. '*Oven thermometer . . .*' she read out, wonderingly.

'Goodnight.' Robert, beaten, headed for the stairs.

'Night, love.' Busy scribbling, Marie didn't look up. The list of things to buy in order to bring her equipment up to scratch was daunting. The cake tins and measuring cups she'd hauled out were dented and scratched or too damn old. She'd recognised a prehistoric loaf tin from her granny's kitchen and been overwhelmed with a sensory memory of that beaming old lady enveloped by an aromatic fug of lemon-drizzle cake. Perhaps, Marie thought soppily, her granny was beaming down at her now, proud of her granddaughter's (rather late) culinary aspirations.

Or perhaps, she thought as she put aside the tin and wrote *Silicone loaf-thingy*, her granny was looking for her glasses and complaining about Terry Wogan, just as she had most of the time down here on Earth.

Rarely up this late – dentistry is, as she often said with

feeling, *knackering* – Marie savoured the quiet, looking contentedly around the tranquil room, but aware that the mellow lighting hid a multitude of sins. She saw everything now through the prism of Mary Berry's expectations.

The kitchen would have to shape up. It would have to get real. The rusted cheese grater would be chucked out; the microwave would be cleaned; she would learn how to switch on the cooker hood. It was as if, over the years, the kitchen had realised Marie didn't take it seriously and had morphed into a room with far more emphasis on the eating of food than the preparation of it.

Poor kitchen, thought Marie. It never stood a chance. She was drawn to recipes that proclaimed in bold print 'express' or 'easy' or 'for the beginner' at the top. She was a doyenne of the ready-meal, a devotee of the frozen pea, and believed the takeaway to be more beneficial to modern humanity than penicillin.

Despite this, the kitchen was her favourite room in the house. As Mary said, it was the heart of the home. The Dunwoodys had had many lively debates in here over microwaved pie. They'd argued over fish and chips, sung songs from the shows over boil-in-the-bag curry and laughed until their Arctic roll came out of their noses.

Learning to bake at Mary Berry's knee would change all that. For the better. Her brood would become a family who 'dined' together, as opposed to sitting over pasta with the TV chummily butting in. The love she felt for them – sometimes hard to express in the hurly-burly of daily life – would blossom in her cakes and soufflés and flans and tarts and muffins and whoopie pies.

Ironic, really, that tonight she'd slung burnt fish fingers at them in order to bury her nose in Berry. She'd packed the girls off to bed an hour later than normal, as befitted the first night of the summer hols, apologising for the lack of a bedtime chapter of *Mallory Towers* and appealing to their honour to undo each other's plaits without supervision.

After a decent interval, Robert had refilled her glass and murmured something about not wasting the peace and quiet – what with the twins in bed, and Angus out till God knows when – and did she remember what they did on the kitchen sofa that time after his nephew's wedding?

Marie did remember, and it was tempting (even though Iris had found her mother's Spanx down the back of the cushions the next day while looking for a nit-comb), but she'd declined. 'Mary's my date tonight,' she'd insisted, dashing her husband's saucy hopes and surprising herself by eschewing a good seeing-to in favour of an appendix on egg size.

Far away, a church bell tolled two. Never audible in the day, it was crisp in the silent middle of the night.

Partway through a recipe for *millefeuille*, which thrilled and terrified her in equal measure, Marie rose and went to the window.

Beneath the table a snuffly heap, like an abandoned bath mat, stood, shook itself and followed her. Prinny was a rescue dog and there was no way of knowing his age. He was a mixture of many breeds, having cleverly bagged the scruffiest attributes of each. His ears didn't match, and he loped like a jackal, but his heart was full to bursting with love for his owners, whose patting and stroking and adoration had done much to undo the damage left by the unguessable cruelties of his past. Greyish, brownish and terrible at fetching, he never liked to be far from a Dunwoody, so he couldn't stay under the table while Marie was at the window.

'*Prinny*,' Marie cooed with the special soft voice she saved for their daft dog. His true title was Princess Mister Coochycoo – as good an illustration as any of why six-year-olds should never be allowed to name pets.

The kitchen, part of a side extension, looked out on to Caraway Close. The lady of the house stared at the boxy modern shapes of her neighbours' homes; like the Dunwoodys, most neighbours had added a room or two, or had carved windows into the roof. There was a basic similarity to each tidy dwelling, yet the owners had stamped their individuality on each property, from the peonies that turned number two into a riot of purple and pink, to the crazy-paving number twelve was so proud of, and the LA modernism of number nine, where every surface was arctic white and there was no evidence of human existence.

Marie and Robert had moved here when she was just about to pop with Angus. She'd had cravings for cheese and clotted cream. Robert had asked to be excused the duty of carrying her over the threshold 'in case I put my back out'. The kitchen had been a galley at the back, over-looking a playing field, which was now another estate of similar homes.

The Close's daytime technicolour was now toned down

to night-time's nostalgic black-and-white. Marie shooed away a jabbing finger of anxiety. Yes, sure, 2 a.m. *was* late for a fifteen-year-old to be out. But fifteen-year-olds were different these days: at that age she'd never tasted alcohol, been on a plane or cheeked her dad. And her own fifteen-year-old was particularly different. Angus was trustworthy, steady and – it could be admitted in the dead of night – a little *odd*.

When Angus had announced (or muttered, rather) that he'd been invited to Lauren's party, his parents had been surprised. They knew Lauren by sight; everybody did. The wild-child niece of a school governor, she ruled the roost at St Ethelred's and managed to get away with a nosestud, a tattoo and a skirt rolled up so high it could double as a belt.

Despite all the usual party fears – booze, cigarettes and worse – Marie was glad. So long a nerdy outsider, Angus was going to a party. No, *the party of the year*. And, she'd said to Robert as they chewed it over, *things can't get that out of hand at the home of a school governor.*

Marie was that rare creature: a mum who wished her teenager would get out more. She worried that Angus was too much of a loner. That he was too studious, too introverted, too wrapped up in the small world he composed carefully through his viewfinder. She also worried that he wasn't getting enough vitamin C, that he had his granny's legs and that the world might end in nuclear Armageddon before he reached twenty-one. In short, Marie worried about Angus (and the twins) more or less non-stop, with the occasional break to worry about Robert. She'd started worrying the moment her period had failed to materialise sixteen years ago; it was what mothers did. But right now she refused to fixate on the fact that Angus was late home, and resisted images of police cells, hospital beds and ditches.

Wrapping her baggy, only-around-the-house cardi tighter, she wandered back to the table and picked up her glass. Life was approaching a phase that she dreaded.

Bonds must be loosened.

Chicks must be drop-kicked out of the nest.

Just thinking this made her want to tug on her coat and rush off to locate Angus and squeeze him to her. Marie took a reassuring glug of wine. You let them go – so said those who'd already done it – and they do a big, wide circle and, eventually, come back.

But how, how, *how* do you stand and watch the back of their head as they walk away?

Marie put down the wine. *You are a false friend*, she told it sternly. One more sip and there would be tears. She was racing to meet her troubles halfway, a habit that always made Robert roll his eyes. If he was here instead of snoring upstairs, he would remind her that Angus was a sensible boy, a trustworthy boy – *their* boy.

Yawning, stretching, Marie knew it was time for bed. She should slip between the covers and drop off to sleep, without neurotically listening for a key in the door.

Just another page or two with Mary and she'd retire.

TO: stargazinggirl247@gmail.com
FROM: geeksrus39@gmail.com
27.07.13
3.09
SUBJECT: oh no

U awake? Bet youre not. I hope u r having nice dreams. Just gotin. Bit pised. God. Tonight. shit. Sorrry for swering. House is mad. Mum asleep at kitchen table. Dad asleep with rose between teeth. Twins asleep with plaits still in which is STTRICTLY AGAINST THE LAW.
Glad Mum's asleep cos of the pissed thing but also cos I don't want to talk to anybody about what happened tonight except you. Why is life so difficult, Soulmate? especially love is hard and sex. Do you mind me saying this stuff? you are the only person i can say it to.
my life is officially over. Tonight will come back to haunt me. The Clones will get me.
laters
Angus

AUGUST

Sunday Lunch

Victoria Sponge

Dear Granny Gaynor,

I am good. How are you? Rose says hello. Shes at piano. I am not at piano because I don't go to piano. Mum said you are coming to lunch next sunday and I am glad because ~~you always give us money~~ I miss you. Rose and me are top in English and almost top in maths and french. Mum is making a victorian sponge for sunday. Dad says when he divorces Mum he will name Mary Berry as the other man. I don't think he means it. Do you really drink falling down water or was that a joke when Dad said it?

lots of love Iris xoxoxoxoxo

'A little wider, Mrs Blyton.' Marie was peering into the open mouth of a librarian, but all she could think of was cake. 'Lovely. Your gums have settled down nicely. Using an electric brush at last?'

'Gnnn uf boom.' Mrs Blyton waggled her eyebrows for emphasis.

'Good, good,' murmured Marie, thinking of cake. 'Aileen!' Her assistant was staring into space, shaking her bottom to the Michael Bublé track oozing out of the radio.

'What? I'm ready.' Dubliner Aileen waved her pencil, affronted. A spherical five-foot-nothing in her white overall, she was broad of accent and narrow of mind. Sarcasm flowed in her veins and she saw no reason – ever – to hold back. An excellent assistant, she had been with the clinic since Marie had opened Smile! a decade back; Marie loved her dearly, but sometimes it could be tough to recall why.

'Cavity upper-six distal,' said Marie, thinking of cake.

'Ooh, a cavity.' Aileen loved cavities. 'Naughty-naughty, Mrs B. Somebody's been at the sweetie jar.'

'Ignore her, Mrs Blyton,' said Marie. Thinking of cake. 'Cavity lower-one-four mesial.'

'We'll have you in dentures if this carries on,' giggled Aileen.

'Have a rinse,' said Marie, thinking of cake.

'How's the baking going?' Aileen approved of little, but she approved of cake.

'It's . . . not as easy as I thought.' Marie selected a slender instrument with a hook on the end.

Mrs Blyton gulped.

'Open wide,' said Marie, thinking of her first attempt at cake, the night before.

Eager to get cracking, she had ignored one of Mary's mantras; she was not prepared. A shopping blitz was scheduled for the weekend – the list had grown until it curled to the floor like Rapunzel's hair – but Marie's fingers twitched with the desire to create cakey splendour. Her path to next year's show-stopper started here.

And stopped here, when she realised she didn't own the requisite loose-bottomed twenty-centimetre tins.

'Damn,' she said, as Robert leaned against the fridge, making sundry poor jokes about loose bottoms. 'You!' She pointed at the nearest twin. 'Iris! Go and ask Mrs Gray if she's got two I can borrow.'

'Ooh,' said Robert, opening the fridge and extracting a friendly little bottle of sauvignon. 'Sending your poor, de-fenceless daughter into the enemy camp.'

Marie, trying to look as if she was washing up, watched Iris pick her way along the winding front path (Iris never, ever walked on the grass, literally or metaphorically) and trot over to the Gray house.

'Why is Chloe's house the enemy camp?' Rose, sitting beneath the table with Prinny, made Robert jump and spill some of his precious Daddy Evening Juice.

'That was just a silly joke, darling.' Marie flashed Robert a punitive *pas devant les enfants* look – a look that *les enfants* had understood since before they could *parler*.

Soon Iris was back, cradling two shiny tins and chewing 'the most gorgeousest fudge ever – and Mrs Gray made it!'

Mrs Gray can fudge off, thought Marie, as she waved her thanks from her kitchen window to Lucy's house. 'Right.' She put her hands on her hips.

'Somebody means business,' said Robert, happily settling down at the table as if front row at a show.

'Are you going to make stupid comments the whole time?' asked Marie, running a finger down the ingredients list and stopping, with a start, at margarine.

'Probably.'

'Robbie,' wheedled Marie, using the nickname she used only when begging a favour or eliciting sex. 'Could you pop to the corner shop for me?'

'It's hardly popping,' said Robert, holding the tube of Pringles he'd just opened to his chest like a baby. 'It's not really on the corner. It's three streets away. We just *call* it the corner shop. And it probably isn't open this late.'

'It's always open. Go on. Please. I went through the pain of childbirth – the least you can do is go out for marge.'

By the time Robert returned, the twins had wandered off, bored, to lie upside down on the sofa watching *Toy*

Story 3 for the hundredth time. Marie met him at the door. 'I need eggs, too. Somebody used the last one and *put the empty box back in the fridge.*'

Marie knew that Robert couldn't wriggle out of that one. She knew he'd boiled eggs that morning for the twins, and they both knew he was a repeat offender at putting back empty packets.

The second time she met him at the door, however, her coy expression didn't work. Neither did upping the ante and calling him Robbie-Wobbie. He was adamant. 'I'm *not* going back to that bloody corner shop. The bloke in there will think I fancy him. I don't care if you need parchment paper – and what *is* parchment paper?'

Marie had no idea, and neither did the (flattered) man in the corner shop. Robert returned, like a valiant warrior home from the wars, waving a roll of parchment paper like a spear, having been all the way to 'the big Sainsbury's'. 'Have you got *everything*?' he asked pointedly, settling down with his drink and his savoury snacks.

'You're safe,' smiled Marie. It felt kind of sexy that such a big hairy man, with all the trappings of an alpha male, would do her bidding. 'Right.' She tied her apron tight and squared her shoulders. She tuned the radio to some idiotic dance music. She took a deep breath.

Step one was more like one of the twins' art projects than cake-making. Lining the tin entailed drawing around it on the parchment (which had turned out to be, basically, tracing paper) and then bollocksing it into the greased tin: Marie's language, not Mary's. A few goes and it was fine. Wonky, but good enough.

'Is that how it's supposed to look?' asked Robert.

'Are you reading from *A Handbook of Irritating Phrases?*'

'No. I'm a natural.'

'Right,' said Marie again, retying her apron and leaving margarine fingerprints on it. 'Now it begins.'

She had never creamed before. Such a soft, billowing word didn't do justice to the task. Without an electric mixer, Marie had to use her wooden spoon to combine the margarine and caster sugar. Round and round her spoon dashed, and up and down her elbow leapt, but the margarine and caster sugar refused to combine; they were the Israel and Palestine of cake ingredients.

Bored with their film, the twins returned and draped themselves over Robert, watching their sweating mother wordlessly, in identical outfits of spotted dresses and gravely nodding deely boppers. Marie had assiduously dressed Iris and Rose differently during their babyhood, careful to treat each daughter as an individual, castigating little Angus when he called them both 'Twin', and refusing to stifle their individuality. But as soon as their pudgy hands could do up buttons, they'd dressed the same, relishing the confusion it caused.

Of course, their parents could tell them apart. Iris had a birthmark, tiny and shaped like a toaster (according to Angus), just above the arch of her left eyebrow; Rose's front teeth were slightly larger than her sister's. Apart from that, they were identical, right down to the air of superiority.

'Why . . . won't . . . it . . . *combine?*' Marie stopped to take a few deep breaths.

'If at first you don't succeed . . .' began Iris.

'Try, try again,' said Rose.

'So young,' said Robert, 'and yet so wise.'

'Shuddup.' Marie was succinct: she had to save her energy for defeating the pale slop.

'Mum,' said Iris, peering at the recipe. '*Mum!* You should be beating the eggs as well.'

'And the flour,' said Rose.

'And the baking powder,' they said, in creepy unison.

'What? Let me see.' Goddamnit, they were right. How had she managed to misread two lines of type? She could carry out a root-canal treatment while discussing *East-Enders* with Aileen, yet she'd already veered dangerously off-piste with a cake recipe. She upended the flour into the bowl and a pale mushroom cloud dusted them all with a fine coating, turning the twins into cute zombies.

'You've ruined my wine,' grizzled Robert, drinking it anyway. They both knew there was no such thing as ruined wine in this house.

Plop. Plop. Plop-plop. Marie dropped in the four eggs, enjoying the rude sound-effects as they landed.

'Mu-um,' said Iris, noting the old-fashioned font on the baking powder. 'What's its sell-by date?'

'Can't read it,' said Marie. The baking powder had moved house with them in 1998 and had lived a simple monastic life ever since, at the back of a shelf snuggled up to some geriatric lentils.

Further vicious arm actions forced the belligerent ingredients to finally combine; time now for dividing and levelling.

'Mum, you need a . . . erm . . . spatula.' Rose stumbled over the pronunciation.

'What's a spatula?' asked Iris.

'It's an exotic pet that lives in your ear and eats only Camembert.' Robert enjoyed the twins' disgusted squeal.

'It's a thingy – sort of plastic and bendy,' said Marie, desperate to divide and level, but seeing nothing like a spatula in the drawer and resorting to using her hands. It was a messy business, grimaced at by the girls, relished by Robert. 'Right. Into the pre-heated oven.' Marie realised she'd forgotten something and whispered, '*Damn*'.

The batter sat, divided unevenly and resolutely unlevel, while the oven warmed up. Marie used the time to dance with Iris and Rose, something she rarely did, but which scored considerable Groovy Mum points. They requested, as they always did, 'All the Single Ladies', and Marie wanted, as she always did, to lie down and die during the second chorus.

'That Beyoncé earns her money,' she gasped as she ferried the tins to the oven, setting her mobile phone to alert her when twenty-five minutes were up.

Those twenty-five minutes would live on in Marie's memory. She would recall them as a happy time, a sunlit time, a time of tea-drinking and the prospect of a glorious future full of cake. 'Let's have your mum over next Sunday,' she'd said at some point during the twenty-five rose-tinted minutes. 'I'll make a Victoria sponge for afters.'

'Um, yeah, OK,' Robert had said, double-checking her for signs of a stroke. 'If you want.' After a moment or two, he asked, 'Are you sure, love?'

'Of course. It'll be nice to see her.' *And wipe her beak of a nose in my incredible home-making skills.*

Gaynor Dunwoody had a history of bad behaviour towards her daughter-in-law. At the wedding, drowning her sorrows at losing her son to 'an older woman' (Marie was five weeks Robert's senior), Gaynor, resplendent in a mint-green coat dress, disrupted the speeches by *whee!*-ing repeatedly down the children's slide outside the marquee. She'd loudly given it six months. She'd told Robert he'd broken his mother's heart. And she'd picked apart every plate of food Marie had put in front of her since.

Phone call made, invitation accepted – 'I'll only come if Robert collects me and drives me home. My legs have been playing me up. And my stomach. And my eyes. I've been downright queer for a week now. You're not doing your lamb, are you dear? No? Good. And don't forget my allergies: peanuts, cheese and Lucozade' – the twenty-five minutes were up.

'Is it springing away from the sides?' asked Iris, reading Mary's notes.

'Hard to say . . .' Marie pressed the sponge gingerly, then poked it hard. 'It feels a bit gooey.'

'Mary says,' commented Iris, 'that you should put a cocktail stick in and, if it comes out clean, it's ready.'

A cocktail stick was duly poked in and studied.

'Robert, would you say that's clean?'

'Well, yes,' said Robert uncertainly. 'And no.'

None of them could tell if the cocktail stick was clean. Rose discerned a tiny dot of yellowy sludge, and that was enough to send the cake back into the oven.

A few minutes more and Marie was still uncertain. 'It looks very pale.'

'It's done,' said Iris with certainty.

'It's not,' said Robert, enjoying being so definite on a subject he knew exactly nothing about.

Back into the oven.

After double the amount of cooking time specified by Mary, Marie said, with a rasp to her voice, that surely it *must* be done.

Regret swept through her like a forest fire as she surveyed the cake. Why hadn't she realised? It was *over-done*. The edges didn't 'spring back', they cringed. 'There are crunchy bits,' she noted.

'They're always the best bits.' Robert was optimistic, but then all he'd done was drink wine, eat Pringles and make remarks; he hadn't put his heart and soul into the strange thing in his wife's hands.

'That only applies to roast potatoes,' growled Marie. Wielding a palette knife (amazingly, already part of her *batterie de cuisine*), she removed the cake and watched it bellyflop onto a wire rack that she'd found in the garage behind the mower. Impatiently she began to peel off the parchment and found it clingier than her sixth-form boy-friend. Wisps of it remained embedded in the sponge.

Mary's next instruction was to choose the best sponge to form the top tier.

'Not sure that *best* applies here.' Robert looked over her shoulder at the dejected berets.

'That one,' said Marie, pointing, 'is the least horrible. Jam!' she stated imperiously, holding out a hand. Rose put a jar in it. An almost-empty jar. Without the energy for the usual witch-hunt to discover who'd done it *again*, Marie eked out every gory speck. Unable to spread it as directed, she dotted it along the edges of the bottom sponge and then, with immense ceremony, topped it with the other sad disc.

'*Voilà*,' said Marie, very quietly.

Another day, another mouth. Jonas Handler, the wrong side of eighty, always dapper as if perpetually ready to get married, sat back in the chair, his gob obediently open.

' . . . so I sez to him, I sez . . .' Aileen was in mid-flow, bringing Marie up to date with her life. Marie could have stormed *Mastermind* with *The Minutiae of Aileen Doyle* as her specialist subject. 'I sez, look here, you – I know your type.' She handed Marie a dental mirror, knowing from the tiny change in her boss's expression that she needed one. 'I sez, stop undressing me with your eyes, ya raving perv, or I'll separate you from your knackers with one swoop of me nail file. Sorry, Jonas. Don't mind me.'

Jonas, luckily, was rather deaf.

'Periodontal probe, Aileen,' said Marie, who knew better than to stem the flow.

'Here y'are. Now, where was I? Oh. Yeah. So he sez, excooose me, I'm a married man; and, sez I, they're the worst, and I set off me attack alarm.' Aileen dabbed at Jonas's lips with a swab loaded with Vaseline, careful to keep the old man's mouth moist while Marie investigated his gums. 'If it saves just one other woman from his clutches, I'll have done me job.'

'In his defence,' said Marie, holding out her hand for the mirror again, 'he did just ask you for directions to Asda.'

'It was the *way* he asked,' said Aileen, the plaited buns coiled on either side of her head bristling.

Marie was treated to daily bulletins about her assistant's battle against the perverts: the man in the post office; bus drivers; their local MP – they'd all undressed Aileen with their eyes. One intrepid degenerate had managed it over the phone. 'There. All done. Your teeth are in fine fettle, Jonas.' Marie carefully removed the bib from around the old man's neck and righted the chair. 'No need to see us again for six months.'

'Excellent.' Jonas looked at the floor. 'Marvellous.'

'Although . . .' Aileen winked at her boss.

'On second thoughts, we need to keep an eye on that incisor. So make an appointment with Lynda on reception, for a fortnight's time.'

'Bless him,' said Lynda, cradling a mug of tea in both hands. 'Most people put off coming to the dentist, but Jonas loves it here.'

'He's lonely.' Marie slumped in her turquoise scrubs, crinkly fresh this morning, but now as creased as their wearer. She liked this time of day, when all the patients had gone and it was just the little Smile! family together in the reception area. Lynda's desk sat in the window, and bright plastic seats sat politely around the margins of the room. It was a clean, calm space, with no posters of decaying teeth to jar the mood.

'Jonas is a gent,' said Aileen, raising her Coke Zero in a toast, burly knees a mile apart in white tights.

'Surely he's undressed you with his eyes?' Lynda looked archly into her tea.

Intervening, Marie said, 'Now, ladies, please. It's too late in the day to squabble.' Both her employees could bicker at Olympic levels. 'Start a nice fresh one in the morning.' Stretching her arms over her head, she let out a yeti-yawn that startled them all.

'You need a nice evening on the sofa.' Lynda was motherly, despite her boss's twenty-year head start. 'No baking for you tonight!' She lowered her chin, her slanted dark eyes stern. Possibly too beautiful to be a dental receptionist, Lynda wore her looks lightly, as if having skin the colour of burnt sugar, eyes that came complete with natural kohl and a smile that could charm even Aileen was a meaningless fluke. 'I'm taking Barrington to that wedding fayre in the town hall.'

'Lucky Barrington.' Aileen was allergic to wedding talk. Which was a shame, because since Barrington had popped the question, Lynda had just the one topic in her repertoire: her New Year's Day wedding of the decade.

'Is there any point going to a fayre?' asked Marie, putting her legs up awkwardly along two of the padded plastic seats bolted to the wall. 'Surely you've organised everything already.'

'Are you kidding?' Lynda was scandalised. 'I haven't even nailed down the bridesmaids' thongs.' She scowled, disappointed. 'Do you two even listen when I talk?'

'Of course we do,' said Marie.

'Obviously not,' said Aileen. 'And, just for the record, I refuse to wear a thong.' It had surprised both Aileen and Marie when Lynda had asked her co-worker to be a bridesmaid. 'I'm a bridesmaid, not a lap-dancer.' Evidently, beneath the day-to-day scrapping and the ceaseless bickering, some sort of bond had formed between Marie's staff.

'Let us know if you find a nice bridesmaid's thong at the town hall.' Marie was certain she'd never said that sentence before. 'As for me, I'm afraid I *have* to bake. The Victoria sponge needs to be perfected by Sunday. Robert's mother is coming over.'

Crossing herself – she'd met Gaynor – Aileen's eyes narrowed. 'Make Robert bake the feckin' cake. She's *his* ma.'

'That's not the point. I'm on a journey.' Marie turned her head to the side in an enigmatic pose, to show she was joking. (She wasn't joking.)

'Journey, my arse,' said Aileen, with all the poetry for which the Irish are famed. 'A cake's a cake.'

'Not when it's a home-made cake.' Marie pitied Aileen, marooned in the land of the ready-made and the shop-bought – a land from which Marie herself had only just emigrated. Half an hour in a locked room with Mary Berry would sort her out. 'Love is the added ingredient.'

'She's right.' Lynda was inspecting the back of her hair using two hand-mirrors and a great deal of bobbing and weaving. The impressive Afro needed so much care and attention it qualified as a pet. 'I mean, I'm looking for somebody to bake my wedding cake, because I want to know what goes into it. And I want it made with love.'

Aileen had an idea. This rarely happened, and when it did, nothing good ever came of it. 'Get this eejit here to make your cake,' she suggested, gesturing with her thumb in the direction of the woman who paid her wages.

'Oh, er . . . well . . .' Marie sat up, startled.

'Don't be silly,' said Lynda, patting her hair fondly one last time before slipping the mirrors into her bag. 'I want a proper baker. No offence,' she said, as an after-thought.

'None taken. I'm only a beginner. I couldn't tackle a wedding cake.' Especially for the type of perfectionist bride who had demanded a menstrual forecast from her maid of honour. 'At the moment I'm baking for the family. Well . . .' She recalled the kids' robust refusal to taste last night's effort. 'For Robert, really.'

'Why bother baking for him, when any minute now he'll have an affair and break your heart?' Aileen was sorry to break the news. 'It's a fact: 102 per cent of married men leave their wives for a younger woman.'

The cheep of her mobile interrupted Marie's defence of her husband's morals. She read out a message from him: *Won't be home until 9.*

'See? Having an affair.' Aileen was smug.

'He's at his monthly staff meeting.'

'Having an affair at his monthly staff meeting.'

Another cheep. 'Eh?' Puzzled, Marie read out: *Good God! Caroline is sucking*

'Having an affair and live-messaging it.' Even Aileen was taken aback at how low men could sink.

*

42

'Who are you texting?' Despite Caroline's statement shoulders, strong perfume and really big Big Hair, she'd somehow managed to sneak up behind Robert as they took their seats in the meeting room.

'Just the wife.' Robert hoped his colleague hadn't read her own name. Watching her suck up to the Chief Buyer yet again had made him forget that he needed to keep his wits about him in the meeting room: it was a jungle, and he was a hunter. Or maybe he was a wounded gnu. He'd forgotten which. (Robert tended to over-dramatise his job.)

'*The wife?*' Caroline repeated it loudly, making sure all the buyers and buyers' assistants heard. 'You'll be calling her "the little woman" next.'

'Her indoors!' laughed Jerry, the linens buyer, who had a stye and had disliked Robert since they'd been tied together in the sports day three-legged race and lost to two work-experience girls.

'The ball and chain!' said the new cosmetics buyer, who was straightforwardly beautiful and was fancied by all the men and distrusted by all the women.

'Settle down, guys.' Magda, Chief Buyer and Empress of All (not her official job title, but clearly how she saw herself), tapped on the long, pale table with her pencil. 'Let's get down to business.'

The chirrup of a mobile phone broke the respectful silence. 'Sorry!' Robert silenced it and read: *Forgive me for asking but just WHAT is Caroline sucking?* His giggle earned one of the Empress's glares.

'Perhaps you can start, Robert. How's the new Danish line doing?'

Relieved to have good news to share, Robert launched into the facts and figures of his recently launched cutlery range. The reputable, established chain of department stores they all worked for was well loved, but suffering an image crisis: consumers saw Campbell & Carle as 'fuddy-duddy'. As silverware buyer, commissioning a new cutlery design from a 'happening' Danish design firm was Robert's baby; had it bombed, it would have been his fault. He knew Magda well enough to realise that she'd take the lion's share of his success, but that went with the territory. Concluding his spiel with 'And of course we've had plenty of press and mentions in the style mags', he nodded to the junior in charge of the PowerPoint slide show, who clicked through an impressive number of articles featuring the sinuous new cutlery.

'Nice,' murmured Magda. From the Empress, this was high praise; she would describe a shrieking orgasm as 'acceptable'.

As the childrenswear buyer riffed on dungarees, Robert relaxed, sinking a little in his seat, looking around and wondering, as he often did these days, just how he came to be here.

The 1993 version of Robert Dunwoody had arrived in London wearing ripped jeans, fresh from wild years in college (well, he'd once ridden a supermarket trolley down a hill) and on the brink of a bohemian free-spirited romance with a clever brunette named Marie (well, they rode a train to the South of France and he was sick out of the window). That young gun was light years away from the sober-suited gent smelling gently of citrus aftershave with blinding-white collar and cuffs who was presently nodding with faux interest as the discussion moved on to the future of table mats.

The room, like Magda – like the stores' new advertising campaign – was modern, bland, clean. White walls bounced the sunlight off blond wood and nude leather. Robert recalled this room pre-refurbishment: dark panelling, a dented kettle balanced on a filing cabinet, squeaky chairs with missing wheels.

The new look boiled down to modern fabric thrown over the scarred and pitted old structure; the same was true of the staff. Despite Campbell & Carle's politically correct openness and accountability, the bosses still called the shots; despite the open-plan layout and the team-building weekends, the staff still formed gossipy cliques. Robert indulged in tittle-tattle now and then, but he never sharpened his elbows to compete. It wasn't his style; he had no killer instinct.

It was hard to admit that he felt out of step. There was no room for negativity under Magda's rule; she rooted out non-team-players and moved them on.

'Robert!'

For a millisecond he panicked that Magda could read his mind. 'Yes?' From the corner of his eye he saw Caroline slip out of the room: she'd be in trouble if Magda noticed her absence.

'There was a dip in silver frames last quarter? What do you attribute that to?'

Surfing confidently through his analysis of the problem with the old stock, and the steps he'd taken to source new products, Robert felt properly engaged at last. He knew his stuff. He loved working with silver – the feel of it, its weighty presence, the timeless processes that went into the making of it. He loved collaborating with venerable old firms such as Godley & Sons, their main supplier and his collaborators on the new range. A career history going back fifteen years with the store meant that Robert knew his job backwards and, despite his hankerings for his ripped-jean younger self with a guitar and no responsibilities, he would enjoy his work, if he wasn't so bored by office politics.

Or, it occurred to him, as Caroline returned with a trolley laden high with cupcakes, might it be truer to say that office politics scared him because he was so inept at them?

'HAPPY BIRTHDAY TO YOU!' Caroline's vibrato started the room singing.

Oh, shitty-shit shitsville.

As they sang, the other buyers produced cards and fussily wrapped little somethings from beneath the table. Magda, hands to her flushed face, looked delighted.

Who'd have thought, marvelled Robert, singing along limply, *that such a ball-breaker could be reduced to teary-eyed Disney-style euphoria by friggin' cupcakes?*

'Wow!'

'Amazing!'

'Look at them!'

The staff, each one a graduate, were jumping up and down over cupcakes.

Cup. Cakes.

The toiletries buyer, who spoke four languages, clapped her hands excitedly and squeaked, 'Glitter!'

The glitter baffled Robert. Was that a thing now? Wouldn't it choke him?

'Caroline made them *herself*,' said the lighting buyer, with a degree of awe Robert would have considered appropriate if Caroline had also made the plate and the trolley and the napkins. 'Right down to the little number thirty on each cake!'

Robert accepted a pink, glittery dollop, and for the first time it occurred to him that he was twelve years older than his boss.

Once more elbow-deep in flour – Prinny sported a continual fine coating of the stuff these days, like a ghost dog in a low-budget horror film – Marie irritated Robert when her only reaction to his tale of The Worst Staff Meeting of All Time was to ask 'How did the cupcakes taste?'

She in turn was irritated when Robert had no answer to this, or to 'What kind of icing did Caroline use?'

'Hang on,' said Robert, opening a beer, with what he realised was a touch too much enthusiasm. 'Are you rolling your eyes at me because I can't tell fondant icing from royal icing? I'm still a bloke, you know. I do have balls and stuff. It's a medical fact – you can't differentiate between icings if you own a willy.' He scowled and stuck his head in the fridge. 'Dare I ask if there'll be any actual dinner tonight?'

Biting her lip, Marie held back a smart retort. This was

so unlike Robert that it had to be a reaction to his bad day. She counted to ten and said, 'So. Magda?'

'Yeah.' Robert sat heavily at the kitchen table, sweeping aside the twins' drawings, Angus's photography magazines, Marie's glasses and some week-old unopened bills. 'Sorry, love.' He watched his wife's back as she stirred – very vigorously – whatever was in the mixing bowl. It was a little fatter than the back he'd married, and the bottom beneath it sat a little lower. But he loved that back very much. He loved how well he knew it; how he would be able to pick it out in a crowd of a thousand backs, just by the way her heavy hair fell onto her shoulders and by the shape of her head. 'Actually . . .' He'd been reluctant to verbalise his conflicted new feelings about life, work, the universe. Saying it out loud would make them real: cats let out of bags are infamously hard to force back in. But Marie would understand. 'Actually, I've been thinking and—'

The gormless sing-song of the doorbell intruded.

Marie ushered Chloe into the kitchen, applauding the girl's latest inventive ruse for insinuating herself into Angus's presence. 'A sponsored silence? Of course we'll sponsor you.' She signed up for fifty pence an hour. 'Angus should try it. Somebody may as well make money out of his natural talent. Which charity is it for? ANGUS!' Marie's sudden roar, employing the trademark change in volume common to all mums, made Chloe jump in her black jeans, black top, black make-up and black glittery scarf, wound round her slender neck like a bandage.

'PeTA.' Chloe produced a poster. 'People for the Ethical Treatment of Animals.'

Materialising wherever there was a sniff of brother-based romantic embarrassment, the twins gaped at the mutilated mink and the rabbits with ulcerated eyes. In their pastel-striped sundresses they were the polar fashion opposite to Chloe.

'No!' gasped Iris.

'Oh, look at that poor bear!' screamed Rose.

Anticipating nightmares, Marie deftly folded the poster and handed it back to Chloe. 'ANG— Oh, there you are. Make our visitor a drink, love.' She turned to Robert. 'What was that you were saying?'

But he was gone, out on the patio with his beer, sharing a bag of crisps with Prinny.

Accepting a mug of warm Coke from Angus, Chloe settled down on a stool and so, reluctantly, did he.

'My mother sent this over for you.' Chloe fished in her huge (black) bag and handed over a beribboned jar of marshmallows. In curly lettering the label proclaimed them to be *Hand-made with love in Lucy's kitchen*.

'They look professional,' said Marie, impressed that her teeth barely sounded gritted at all. 'Do thank her for me.' She'd been unaware that marshmallows were makeable; she assumed they were put together in factory vats using chemicals and voodoo.

'Wow! Your mum's brilliant,' said Iris, who presumably had been taking lessons in How to Annoy Your Own Mother.

'You're so lucky,' breathed Rose, as if she and her siblings were thrashed nightly and fed only dust.

'So, Angus,' said Chloe, eyeing him sideways from

beneath her flicked eyeliner and coloured-in brows. 'What's up?'

'Nothing,' said Angus. He lifted his camera. 'Doing this. And stuff.'

'He's making a film about . . . What *is* it about, darling?' Marie knew she sounded like an overbearing, interfering mother, but couldn't stop herself.

'Life – you know,' said Angus.

'Yeah,' nodded Chloe.

'That kind of thing,' said Angus.

Rose, already on her third marshmallow, asked, 'Is there a proper dinner tonight? Or are we just having *bits* again, because you're too busy making stupid cakes?'

This was Dunwoody code for leftovers: 'bits' could be wonderful (leftover roast chicken with leftover potato salad); and 'bits' could be not so wonderful (leftover sardines with leftover other sardines).

'You *like* bits,' said Marie, wounded.

'Not every day,' replied Rose.

'It's not bits tonight.' Marie reached for the Dragon Paradise menu on top of the fridge. Shamefaced in front of Chloe, who came from a family who never ever ate takeaways, she said, 'We don't do this often,' while fixing each twin with a *Say nothing!* glare.

'Can I stay for dinner?' Chloe bounced on her seat. 'I *love* Chinese food, but my mother makes it herself and it's just not the same.'

There is, thought Marie, with a quickly suppressed pang of empathy for Lucy, *no pleasing teenagers*.

'She's doing steaks tonight.'

Robert, wandering through en route to watch the news, muttered, 'Wonder if she wants a lodger?'

'But, Chloe, you support PeTA,' said Angus.

'Yeah. Exactly. I'll text her.'

The light was on across the way in Lucy's kitchen and, as Marie continued to cream her mix, she saw Lucy pick up the phone. The woman's shoulders slumped a little, before she looked over at the Dunwoody house. For a moment something flashed across her indistinct face, then she waved, and Marie made out a wide smile.

No probs! Enjoy yourself and be good, darling, read Marie over Chloe's shoulder.

August was in a good mood.

Even at 10 p.m. it was warm enough to sit out on the patio. The twins, sharing a deckchair, were being very, very quiet, under the mistaken impression that their parents hadn't noticed how much past their bedtime it was.

In fact their father was too tipsy and their mother too tired to care.

'Oh, Prinny,' said Marie sadly, as the dog turned up its nose at a wedge of freshly baked sponge. 'Seriously?' When a creature that licks its lips at a snotty tissue refuses your cooking, it hurts. 'Look at those two,' she whispered to Robert, beside her on the bench.

'Chloe's giving it her all.' Robert smiled at Angus and their guest, sitting on a blanket on the scrappy grass, outlined in the violet twilight. 'But himself's not having any of it.'

Angus's body language – cross-legged, hunched over,

head down – screamed *Leave me alone*; Chloe's – legs stretched out, head back, leaning on her splayed hands, – screamed *Come and get me*.

Marie laid her head on Robert's shoulder. It fitted and felt comfortable there. It always had. It was one of the reasons she'd married him. 'Are we relying on our boy too much?' Since the start of the summer break, Marie had happened upon another maternal worry. This was the first year that she (Marie could have said 'they', but in truth this was her domain) hadn't arranged a complex network of other mums, family members and childminders. At fifteen, Angus was deemed old enough to be in charge of two nine-year-olds, and it was working out just fine in some ways: the girls were happy, fed, safe from prowling mass murderers. And yet . . . Marie wondered if it was too much to demand of a young man. 'Are we clipping his wings?'

'What's the alternative, love?' Robert was practical.

Like so many parental problems, there seemed no perfect solution. Marie was already taking Mondays off; another day was unthinkable. Patients disliked being treated by a locum, and every Tuesday Lynda and Aileen were a-twitter, like doves after a fox has been in the coop, full of tales of the locum disrespecting the instruments, or dropping a Pot Noodle in reception. The current arrangement would have to do, but Marie was keeping a closer eye on Angus than usual. All the while, of course, pretending not to keep an eye on him at all.

'Is it me, or is our son even quieter than normal these past couple of weeks?'

'Maybe.' Robert nodded. 'It's since the party. Definitely a girl involved.'

'Not drugs?'

'Darling, I think he'd have to occasionally leave his room to work up a drug habit.'

'He'd have to leave his room to have a girlfriend.'

'I think it's girl *trouble*. That's why he groans when his phone rings and refuses the call. Some poor girl can't read the signals, and he's avoiding her.'

'Another Chloe, in other words?' Marie looked fondly at Angus, destined to be pursued by women who liked him more than he liked them. Not the worst fate in the world. 'I feel for Chloe. She tries so hard.'

'I used to think she was shy.' Robert shifted and put his arm around Marie. 'Not any more. She hardly stopped talking over dinner.'

'Maybe Lucy doesn't listen to her at home.'

'Claws in, Kitty,' said Robert. 'We've no way of knowing that.'

It was a hunch, and Marie trusted her hunches (even though they sometimes let her down; she'd had a hunch that she still looked good in shorts, and that had been memorably disproved on their last trip to the coast).

A nosy question from Iris over the crispy duck had loosened Chloe's tongue, despite Marie's hasty 'You don't have to answer that'.

'No, I don't mind talking about my real mum,' Chloe had said, ferrying rice greedily to her mouth. 'She and Dad split up when I was small – about two. Dad was brilliant. He fought for me. It's really unusual for a man to get custody of a child, but he was so passionate that the judge agreed.'

'Your poor mum.' That had slipped out; Marie couldn't help herself.

'Well, no, not really.' Chloe's unlined face had creased in puzzlement. 'She can't have been *that* bothered. She visited a few times and then . . .' Her hands, with their pale, tapering fingers that ended in bitten, black-varnished nails, had spread to illustrate her bewilderment. 'I get a birthday card some years. She was in Scotland for a while. Dad reckons she's in the States.'

'I want to go to America,' Rose had said, with the flinty self-absorption of childhood.

'Sshh,' Angus had chided his sister. 'God, Chloe . . .' He'd used up all his words then and had said no more, but Marie had been proud of his obvious compassion.

'Dad's brilliant about it.'

'You're close to him, aren't you?' Marie had smiled.

'Yeah. He's like a friend. He's so . . . you know?' Chloe had shrugged happily, with the same enraptured glow of the twins talking about their latest pop-star crush, or Robert whenever Carol Vorderman won an award for her bottom.

Tod Gray was obviously quite a guy. He was a hard-working man (and a successful one, judging by the cars on the Gray drive and the oak-framed conservatory that Marie had watched grow on the side of their house) and handsome with it.

She'd mentioned Tod's good looks once to Robert and had tried not to smile when he'd replied, 'Yeah, I suppose he's good-looking, if you like that sort of thing.' When that sort of thing was a cared-for bod, thick blond hair, sea-green eyes and a chin copyrighted to Mills & Boon, it was hard not to like it. With foolish prejudice, Marie had assumed that a man that attractive couldn't also be nice. Ashamed now, she revised her opinion: if Chloe loved him so passionately, Tod must be a good egg.

'It was just me and Dad until I was eight,' Chloe had gone on, the rate of rice-to-mouth traffic slowing as she said, 'then Lucy came along. And everything sort of changed.'

Subject closed.

Now Chloe reluctantly clambered up from the blanket on the grass, after a chivvying text from Lucy. Robert whispered in Marie's ear, 'No taking Chloe under your wing, OK? I know what you're like with lame ducks. We shouldn't get involved.'

'I know.' *Nicely non-committal, that*, thought Marie, as she shook the twins awake. 'One each?' she said to Robert, heaving Iris from the deckchair into her arms.

Angus's phone lit up as he and Chloe reached them on the terrace.

'You've got a text,' said Chloe.

'Whatever!' Angus deleted it with a jab of his thumb.

See? mouthed Robert at his wife, as he made for the house with Rose slumped over his shoulder. *Girl trouble.*

The kitchen was a different place at 6 a.m. There was birdsong. There was tranquillity. There was a lack of Dunwoodys.

In a few hours the kettle would be boiling, the grill would be lit, the radio tuned to Radio 4 would be competing with the other radio tuned to Radio 1, and people who shared her surname would be looking to Marie to satisfy their toast/orange juice/plaiting needs.

For now, it was a sanctuary. Marie yawned. She was glad she'd agreed when her sloshed other half had raised an eyebrow and asked, 'Early night, wench?' They'd had a memorable half-hour on the floor of their bedroom; she wrapped her arms around herself, smiling a secretive, interior smile at the memory, surprised and glad that they could still go from nought to sixty after all this time.

But she was paying for it this morning. Every bone in her body rebelled at the earliness of the hour. She caught Mary Berry's eye, twinkling up at her from the cover of the *Complete Baking Bible*.

'Yes, Mary, you're right.' Marie did a Pilates stretch that almost killed her. 'To work!'

It was time to go back to basics. To follow her instructions to the letter. To *focus*. This was what Mary advised at the front of the book, and Mary was right.

Mary was always right.

Like an alchemist, Marie weighed her ingredients with neurotic care. She put the oven on in good time. She creamed without complaint. She didn't forget the baking powder. She lined the tins as if lining for her life. She watched a YouTube video about how to test sponges for doneness and finally grasped the proper use of a cocktail stick. She didn't constantly open and close the oven door. She remained calm throughout, and only swore when

Prinny yawned suddenly from his bed in the utility room and startled her.

With the sponge safely in the oven, Marie fixed herself a coffee and felt drawn to the window. Outside, Caraway Close was shaking itself and coming to life.

Erika at number fourteen was on her porch with her poodle, picking up the newspaper. Even first thing, Erika was camera-ready in a magnificent negligee.

Marie pondered that word: *negligee*. She'd assumed nobody still wore them, but there was no other word for Erika's floaty chiffon creation. As Robert pointed out, every self-respecting suburban road had its sexpot; and their example, a well-preserved fifty-something, was a particularly fine one.

Erika had a facelift and a poodle, and a devotion to uplift bras that delighted her many gentleman callers. A divorcee, she liked to quote Zsa Zsa Gabor: 'I'm a marvellous housekeeper – I always keep the house!' Gaudily dressed as if to match her decor – if Marie squinted, she could make out swirly wallpaper and big mirrors through the windows – Erika was satsuma-skinned, with eyebrows arched in constant surprise. Marie had never before seen her without make-up. Erika looked tired today, as well she might after three husbands, but she also looked more approachable. The poodle darted out and Erika ran girlishly after it in her high-heeled slippers, scooping up the mangy little beast before it reached the gate.

A *Good morning!* floated in the early morning air as Erika's immediate neighbour – their houses divided by a white picket fence – stepped out in a tracksuit.

Free of vanity, Hattie was a holistic masseur. Not, to Marie's disappointment, the sort who uses aromatic oils and plays whale music, but the sort who pummels you remorselessly and bangs on about your endocrine system. With a shining innocent face, round and Land Girlish, she was a leading light in the Residents' Association. After a few stretches against the fence, Hattie popped her earphones in and was off through her squeaking gate to thump around the Close.

The timer sang and Marie approached the oven with reverence. She looked down at Mary, beaming reassuringly from the worktop. 'Wish me luck!'

Robert pondered the alternative universe that women inhabited. It was a place where they had room in their brains for muffin recipes, and time in their day to make the things.

Biting into Caroline's latest offering, he admitted it was good. Almost as good as the cheapo ones available at any supermarket. There was nothing special about Caroline's cooking; the muffins, like their creator, were all style and no substance. Year-on-year clock-department sales figures had nosedived since Caroline's appointment: her assistant was demotivated, her shop-floor staff ignored.

Yet there she was, kneeling by Magda's armchair in the staff lounge, the two of them thick as thieves, just because she could bang out an indifferent muffin.

Sauntering over, Robert put on his breezy face. (Marie insisted it was his serial-killer face, but he was pretty sure it was breezy.) 'Nice muffins,' he said and regretted it. Not quite a double entendre, but definitely getting that way.

'Thanks,' said Caroline.

'How does she find the time?' Magda shook her head in awe.

Maybe because she makes small baked goods WHEN SHE SHOULD BE DOING HER BLOODY JOB. Robert didn't say this; he chose instead to underline his credentials as a serious-minded elder. 'There was a brilliant interview in this month's *Buyers Today* with the chair of the Ethical Trading Initiative. Some interesting stuff about the global buying chain.'

'I saw that,' nodded Magda. 'Very thought-provoking.'

'Oh, come on!' Caroline prodded Magda. Robert could that see she'd ever so slightly overstepped the mark. Magda drew back, an Empress once more. 'Who'd bother with that boring interview when *your* piece is on the back page?'

Magda relaxed and Robert stiffened. He hadn't reached as far as the back page – *Buyers Today* was such a boring publication that there was an urban myth that it had killed a buyer in Liverpool who'd read it from cover to cover – and so he said with a rictus smile, 'Oh yeah, that was *great*!'

'You liked it?' Magda seemed both pleased and taken aback. With her head to one side, she reminded Robert of Prinny when droppable food was being eaten. Magda, however, had sharper teeth. 'What did you make of my basic premise?'

'I . . .' Robert would have liked the staff lounge to burst into flames at that point, but when it didn't happen, he said slowly, groping from word to word, 'I thought . . . you . . . made a very . . . good point.'

'Thank you.' Magda narrowed her eyes. Why, thought Robert wildly, didn't the woman ever listen this attentively when he talked sense. 'So you agree with it?'

'I do,' said Robert adamantly.

'Robert, you've surprised me.' Magda stood and squeezed his arm. 'I'm impressed.' She stalked away to her office, to make important calls, or possibly eat a baby.

'You've surprised me too,' said Caroline. 'Muffin?'

'Ta.' Robert took one and sat down, reaching for the copy of *Buyers Today* on the staffroom coffee table. While Caroline wandered off to spread the muffin love, he flicked hastily to the last page, to find four columns of type under a flatteringly soft-focus Magda (she looked about eight years old) and the headline 'Tough Times Call for Tough Measures'. He read, with mounting dismay, the ideas he'd just praised.

Like a hot knife through butter, today's executives must be unafraid of reducing their staffing levels, it began, in the uncompromising style typical of the Empress. One paragraph in particular leapt out at him. *One answer is to merge buying departments. Can the industry afford the luxury of two salaries, where one may suffice? There are some obvious bedfellows. It might be possible, for example, to combine gifts and stationery, or even silverware and clocks.*

Robert ate the muffin mechanically, its blueberries exploding – *pfff!* – in his mouth without tasting of anything. He'd just tightened a noose around his own neck.

Time to get back to his desk for a conference call with Godley's about production problems with the new spoon design. Caroline ambushed him at the door, holding out the plate.

'Last one, Rob!'

'No, thanks.' Robert paused. 'Don't worry, by the way,' he said conspiratorially, 'I'm not after your job. Magda couldn't merge us. I know sod-all about clocks.'

'Really?' Caroline's perfume at this proximity was suffocating. 'Have you ever noticed my surname, Rob?'

Pointless to tell her, for the umpty-fifth time, that nobody called him Rob. 'Godley,' he said, and then, with dawning horror that he tried too late to hide, '*that* Godley?'

'My family's been in silverware for – ooh, a hundred years now.' Caroline stuck the plate under his nose. 'Go on!' she sang. 'It's your last chance!'

TO: stargazinggirl247@gmail.com
FROM: geeksrus39@gmail.com
02.08.13
14.09
SUBJECT: Stuff

Hi Soulmate
I really do not ever want a girlfriend. What we have is better. This is a meeting of minds!! Laugh if you want but it is.
Love is over rated. And sex is a whole pile of stuff. Sometimes I wish I was a kid again like my little sisters and got my kicks dressing Prinny in a scarf. Sex makes everything too complicated.
Why don't we talk on the phone? It's weard that we don't. We could skype. We should.
For all I know you could have a boyfriend! ha ha!
laters
Angus
P.S. Do you have a boyfriend?

Mary was right. Mary was *always* right. *Go back to basics*, she'd advised, *and all will be well.*

'This is fecking good,' spluttered Aileen. Her white tunic was covered in moist crumbs, as was her chin. 'Jaysus, I could be walled up in this and eat me way out.'

'Delicious,' agreed Lynda, daintily picking apart a slice of Marie's Victoria sponge. 'Really light. The perfect amount of jam. Not too sweet. Bravo, boss lady!'

Fighting back the urge to do a lap of victory in the cramped reception area, Marie sighed with satisfaction. 'It *is* good, isn't it?' She revelled in her victory against – well, *herself*, the slapdash old-style Marie. No longer a woman who chucked in a handful of this and a handful of that and hoped for the best, she was now a baker.

'I've eaten so many cake samples in the last few weeks.' Lynda's pretty mouth turned down. 'Dry. Uninspired. No bounce. I've been exposed to unorganic eggs!'

Feeling that a shocked *You haven't!* was called for, Marie supplied it.

'And preservatives!' Lynda was cranking up another wedding rant. Marie tuned out, picking up only the highlights – 'E-numbers'; 'dirty apron'; 'eyebrows that met in the middle' – until her attention was grabbed by Lynda's sudden cry of 'Hang on! Aileen was right, for once. *You* can make my wedding cake!'

Gabbling, Marie sought to apply the brakes to Lynda's runaway bus. 'Hang on, wait a sec. I've only baked one edible item in my life. Don't go—'

'But you wanted to be involved with the wedding? Remember?'

'Um . . .' Marie had said so, and meant it, but this was *too* involved.

'Since . . .' Lynda slowed. 'Since . . .'

Sparing her from having to refer out loud to losing her mum, Marie said, 'We know what you mean, Lynda.'

'Since *that*, you've done so much for me. You're not just my boss, Marie. I trust you.'

'Just to be clear,' Aileen butted in, 'I don't.'

'I'd love to bake your cake, but it's not a good idea.' Marie hated to ruffle those serene features, but Lynda was wrong to rely on her for this. Emotional support: yes. Shoulder to cry on: always. A willing ear for troubles large and small: went without saying. But cooking the focal point of the biggest day of Lynda's life: madness! 'You need somebody with experience. A track record. You need somebody—'

Lynda interrupted. 'I need somebody who loves me,' she said.

And with that, Marie's case fell apart. She bowed her head and said feebly, 'What kind of cake do you want?'

'A croquembouche!'

Aileen scowled and stole Lynda's plate. 'A what-now?'

'I don't even know what that is.' Marie was nervous. It sounded French. As a rule Marie approved of the French – Gérard Depardieu, champagne, eating your own weight in baguettes, these were all undeniably good things – but cake-wise, the French liked things *fancy*. 'What is a crock . . . crocky . . . ?'

'Look it up,' growled Lynda. Lynda the receptionist/friend was adorable, but Lynda the bride was a tricky beast who could tear down buildings with her bare, manicured hands. 'It's just a cake. If you can do *this*,' she gestured at the sponge, 'you can do a croquembouche.'

'She's right,' said Aileen, who was, Marie knew, taking Lynda's side for the heck of it.

All modern women are stretched. Marie, like every one of her compadres, had insufficient time to meet the daily million-and-three demands made of her. She had to work, cook, clean, travel, wipe noses, soothe feelings, listen, yell, gauge symptoms, feed the dog, have sex. And all this while retaining in her head the best way to boil an egg, along with how many sugars everybody took in their tea, who couldn't stand radishes, and how to work the battalion of remote controls that stood between her and a quick *Escape to the Country*. So she knew, with a certainty that couldn't be doubted, that she had neither the time nor the brain space to make Lynda's cake.

Always best, Marie felt, to be honest. So she looked Lynda square in the eye and said, 'Of course I'll make your crockyboosh.'

Close up, Lynda's Afro smelled great, which was just as

well, as Marie's face spent a full minute in there while she was hugged by a woman who really knew how to hug.

'Thank you, thank you, thank you!' Lynda's freeform dance of joy was interrupted by a beep from the switchboard. 'Hello, Smile!' she beamed into the mouthpiece.

'Biiig mistake,' whispered Aileen happily to her boss.

'Yeah. I know.'

Lynda's recent history, all there in her face as she'd waited for Marie's answer, had overridden common sense.

Marie and Aileen had been through the diagnosis of Lynda's mother with her. They'd celebrated the periods of hope, and had weathered the decline. Marie had managed not to cry at the funeral, her arm around a hopelessly sobbing Aileen, and afterwards there were countless minor kindnesses – a Bounty bar waiting on Lynda's desk in the morning, an arm-rub when her expression turned inwards – as Lynda 'got over it'.

As if, Marie often thought, *we get over such things*.

Marie had been with Lynda in a changing room and had stood back, gasping, at how lovely the girl looked in her white gown; and then Marie *had* cried, because they both knew somebody else should be there, doing the gasping.

In short, somebody with a heart as soft as Marie's couldn't possibly say no.

'Yes . . . yes . . . no problem,' Lynda was saying into her headpiece, once again calm and professional. 'Just come in straight away.' She looked at Marie. 'Mr Blake. Sudden excruciating pain. Probably that tooth you advised him to have the nerve removed from.' She pulled a face. 'Gonna be a late one.'

'Right. Darn!' Marie whipped out her phone. 'Robert? Listen, love, you'll have to start dinner tonight . . . Pop into Sainsbury's and pick up some . . . You're already there? Why? Never mind, buy sausages and fry them and aim them at the kids, and I'll be home as soon as I can.' She went to scrub up, puzzled. 'My husband's never set foot in Sainsbury's without a list from me and explicit instructions.'

'He's having an affair,' said Aileen, scuttling after her. 'With some bitch who works in Sainsbury's.'

A smell hung in the hallway as Marie finally stepped over her own threshold that evening. She discerned burnt sausage and something else – something yeasty. 'Guys?' she queried, dumping her bag and coat and going through to the kitchen. The twins lay on and around Prinny, watching the small television and sending a delighted 'Mummee!' her way. Beyond the patio doors Angus toiled up and down with the lawnmower, headphones on, body present, but mind elsewhere, judging by the wobbly lines in the grass.

And Robert.

'Hello, love.' Marie stopped, looked him up and down. 'You're wearing an apron.'

'If you can't join them,' said Robert grimly, 'bloody well join the bloody bastards.'

'Swears!' cried Iris from the rug.

'Sorry.' Robert padded off to the utility room, returning with a large bowl covered with a teacloth. 'We kept you a horrible sausage, if you're interested.'

Marie picked up a flour-spattered open book, noticing that Mary had been moved to the top of the fridge and bridling briefly at her mentor's demotion. '*Paul Hollywood's Bread.*' Blimey. 'Is this cos of Caroline and her cupcakes of doom?'

'It's about me fighting back at last.' Robert rolled up his shirt sleeves. 'It's about me waking up to smell the coffee, and admitting that experience counts for nothing in my job.' He persuaded the cellulite-ridden dollop of dough onto a floured board and punched it. 'Like my knowledge counts for nothing.' Punch. 'And my loyalty and diligence, and being on time every morning for years on end, count for bloody nothing.' Punch. Punch. Punch.

'Swears!' shouted Iris, Rose and Marie.

'Sorry.' Robert peered at the pages. 'Is this how you knead?' he asked.

'Couldn't tell you.'

He pummelled and pushed, and the dough flopped forward and fell back, like a drunk. 'I'm up against it at work, Marie. More than you know.'

That stung. What hadn't he told her? 'Really? Want to talk about it?'

'No. I want to make some Cheddar and rosemary rolls that will blow Magda's knickers off.' Robert turned the dough and slapped it, rather camply.

As Marie lay in a hot bath (interrupted only eight times by a twin asking urgent questions like *Can flies go to heaven?* and *When I was in your tummy, could I see out?*) she wondered if there was such a thing as being too blithe about a marriage. She trusted Robert absolutely; left alone on a desert island with a Playboy Playmate, he'd bore the poor girl with his family photograph album. And yet . . . Was cooking for another woman a kind of culinary adultery?

It was beyond the bath gel's powers to soothe away this troubling new thought entirely, but Marie kept it at bay, relishing her sacred half-hour among the suds. She thought instead of Robert's choice of foodie tribe leader.

Not for Robert Mary's grave and gentle ways, or Delia's schoolmarm demeanour. The pictures of Nigella beside her recipes would distract him, and Lorraine Pascale's sexy gap-toothed smile would render him useless. Robert needed a man, but not Gordon Ramsay. Too abrasive, too loud. Raymond Blanc's food would be too ambitious. John Torode was too smooth.

No, Robert and Paul Hollywood were a match made in heaven. Not only did Paul bake bread – classic, unfussy, the nutritional backbone of humanity – but he was built along similar sturdy lines to Robert. They were both silver foxes, with a touch of naughtiness in their eyes.

She could hear cupboard doors slamming, and muttered oaths from downstairs. Robert was a perfectionist. When he set his mind to do something, he did it properly.

Once upon a time he'd set his mind on Marie. She'd run, not too fast, with frequent looks over her shoulder, and then he'd got her. It had taken a while to truly know the young man with the ripped jeans and the irreverent line in girlfriend-teasing. For months she'd assumed he was happy-go-lucky, impulsive, independent. When they finally surfaced for air and talked as well as kissed, she discovered, a little at a time, how his past had shaped him.

A dad who was enslaved to drink, mostly absent, but quick with his fists when he was around, until the day he walked out to buy a paper and was never around again.

A mum who fell apart, buckling under the pressure of three young children and no money and, she wailed, no future.

The man of the house since he was eleven, Robert had put his best foot forward and never cried; if *he* cried, his mum cried and then his sisters cried. He was, as she put it, her 'little man', her 'best boy'. The apron strings had only been cut when he'd met Marie, and even now he sent Gaynor money, fixed her shelves, dealt with her paperwork.

Robert was programmed to be responsible, to take charge. Providing for his family was at the core of his self-image. If he was suffering genuine fears about his ability to do just that, Marie would have to, unobtrusively, help him find his equilibrium.

Tonight she'd let him have the kitchen. Later in the week she'd make the Victoria sponge for Sunday lunch with Gaynor, and by then Robert's craze would have petered out. The Paul Hollywood book would be relegated to the garage, along with other evidence of past fads: the ski gear, the mountain bike, the taxidermy chemicals.

In the deep dip of the night, midway through a perfectly pleasant dream involving herself, Angus's art teacher and no clothes, Marie was shaken awake by an insistent hand.

'Look!' Robert was gibbering, almost tearful, like a new Miss World. 'Rolls! ROLLS!'

Thrust under her nose was a warm, fragrant, squat and lovely roll that smelled of Cheddar and rosemary and old-fashioned goodness.

'Rolls!' said Robert again.

'Rolls, darling,' agreed Marie, proud of him. And just the teeniest bit envious.

Dear Granny Gaynor,

Thank you for the five pounds. I will put it in the piggy bank. Rose and me are saving up for a cow. Did you like Mum's cake? I think it was the best bit of dinner, apart from when you fell off your chair. Mum had a good time too because she said she will invite you back when hull freezes over and hull is in the north and is cold I think so that will be soon.

lots of love

Iris xxoxoooxoxooo

P.S. And Dad really did make the amazing rolls he wasnt fibbing.

AUGUST

Residents' Association Meeting

Doboz Torte

Dear Aileen and Lynda,

Wish you were here!

Cornwall is beautiful. Long walks. Dazzling sunsets. Remote beaches.

Doing all the conventional family-holiday stuff – built sandcastles/almost split up twice on the drive down/caught crabs (with a net, not by sleeping with a heavy-metal band).

Hope the locum is working out OK. Pleeeease, Aileen, don't do a citizen's arrest on this one.

Lots of love

Marie xxx

'This is the worst picnic ever in the history of the world,' said Iris.

'It's worse than the one where Daddy put the tablecloth down on a horse-poo,' said Rose.

'Don't be harsh,' said Angus. 'It's about the same.'

In sandy swim-things, their damp hair snaking down their necks, eyes creased against the sunshine, Marie's children knelt and pulled towels tight around themselves as they surveyed the spread she'd laid out for them while they splashed in the sea.

'No proper sandwiches?' mewled Iris. 'From the shop?'

'No mini Scotch eggs?' complained Rose.

'Mum,' began Angus, with the voice newsreaders use to announce the death of a president, 'I can't see any crisps.'

Marie, worn out with worry about what her bum looked like in her hastily bought swimsuit (it looked either fat or very fat, she couldn't be sure which), snapped, 'A simple *Thank you, Mum* would suffice, you ungrateful toads.' Angus had been unusually dour this holiday, his manners barely there. 'I agree, it's not our usual crappy supermarket

75

picnic. Just *look* at this fabulous sausage roll your father made.'

'It's not a real sausage roll,' said Iris mutinously.

'It's got stuff in.' Rose shuddered as if Robert had baked a rat's corpse in puff pastry, rather than organic sausage meat and home-made onion chutney. 'And I'm *sick* of Cheddar and rosemary rolls.'

'We were wrong,' said Angus to his sisters. 'It didn't blow over.' He turned to Robert and, training his camera on his father's face, told him sadly, 'We reckoned this was just one of your crazes.' Every Dunwoody summer was caught on film by Angus, before being edited down to high-lights and lowlights in September.

'I don't have crazes,' said Robert defensively.

Marie clamped her lips together. *Best stay out of this*, she thought, marvelling at how people missed the most glaring aspects of their own personalities.

'You do have crazes, Dad,' said Iris in a tone that didn't invite argument. 'And we thought you just wanted to beat Mum.'

'Don't go round at school saying I beat your mother,' warned Robert. 'It sounds wrong. And anyway, me and Mummy aren't in competition. Me and Mummy are a team.'

The twins looked at each other. 'Table tennis,' they harmonised, and everybody recollected that long week at Center Parcs when Robert had faced a terrible truth: his wife was better than him at ping-pong. In her wedge espadrilles. The match on the last day – 'Just one more set, winner takes all,' he'd insisted nine times over – had ended with him on his knees, only conceding when Marie had shouted, 'Robert, you're going to have a heart attack, and it will ruin the children's lives if their father dies in front of them at Center Parcs!'

'This isn't about rivalry,' said Marie, with the air of finality that she sometimes dusted off when the children took an idea and ran with it until they were specks on the horizon. 'It's about living well. It's about teaching you lot the importance of family life. It's about good food, made with love and care, and enjoyed together.'

'Whatever, Mum. It's not a proper picnic without crisps.' Still Dulux-white after a week in the UK's sunniest corner, Angus seemed certain of his facts. 'And by crisps I don't mean . . .' he thought for a moment, then spat contemptuously, '*oven-baked potato slivers with marjoram and cracked pink pepper*. I mean Walkers cheese and onion.'

Eyes meeting across the checkered cloth, Robert and Marie counted to ten in silent, well-rehearsed accord. Spread out among the hummocks of the cloth was a mouthwatering pile of Cheddar and rosemary rolls filled with local ham, a burnished sausage roll and a plump Victoria sponge filled with fresh cream and studded with wild berries, picked that morning in the lane.

'Remember last year,' began Iris, a dreamy look on her freckled face as if recalling a lost era of innocence and plenty, 'when we sat in a car park and ate pasties Daddy got from the petrol station?'

'Happy days,' sighed Angus.

*

Trudging up the track to the cottage, laden like donkeys with windbreaks, hampers, wet cossies and all the paraphernalia of a day at the beach, the Dunwoodys returned to the holiday home they'd rented each year since the twins were two pink commas in a double buggy.

Sitting contentedly on a rough path just above the dunes, the cottage's slate roof and distressed paintwork were in perfect harmony with the beach's soft blues and whites and golds. Marie took a moment to stand and savour it. Later the colours would darken and melt, before being reborn in a peachy dawn. She felt happy, in a straightforward way that seemed elusive back in the suburbs.

By the time she reached the front gate, Iris had kicked the door open, and the kids had dumped their burdens on the floorboards, before disappearing to their favoured nooks and crannies.

In customary holiday garb of T-shirt and truly awful shorts, Robert was stooping to pick up what his children had dropped, with a murmured 'Gee, thanks, guys'. His tan had deepened. His back no longer twinged. He was shedding years with each day of the trip. Perfecting Paul Hollywood's sausage-roll recipe was another reason for the spring in his flip-flops. 'Fire tonight?' he asked as Marie shouldered the big old beach-bag into the hall.

He always asked this, and Marie always said yes. The thickness of the old cottage walls meant the interior felt a touch too cool after the relentless warmth of the day, but the real reason was the cosy romance of crackling driftwood.

Not to mention that Robert loved making a fire and

would sulk if Marie said no. She liked her husband's inner caveman, and its need to make fire to protect his tribe.

Her nose itchy with sunburn, her bottom scritchy-scratchy with sand, Marie gravitated to the small, higgledy-piggledy kitchen. She felt pleasantly sleepy, but roused herself with a strong cup of tea in the misshapen earthenware mugs that lived in the cottage cupboards. There was work to be done.

The minimal kitchen apparatus supplied with the rental cottage had been supplemented by a battalion of kit that Marie, a seasoned over-packer, had decanted from a small suitcase on wheels. Last of all, out came Mary Berry's book, now with a couple of pages turned down and a smear of batter across its cover.

Robert had rolled his eyes, watching Marie unearth her favourite mixing bowl, her lucky wooden spoon and her electric hand whisk. (How, she liked to ask herself, HOW had she *lived* without this item, before Mary showed her the error of her ways?) When Marie had held up Robert's own lucky spoon, saying *I'm sure I didn't pack this*, the eye-rolling had ceased.

Snatching it, Robert had said that maybe, just maybe, he was going to attempt rough-puff.

'Sometimes,' Marie had smiled at him, 'it's like I don't even know you any more.'

'I'm starving, Mum.' Iris was suddenly beside her, filling the small, square, whitewashed space with childish energy and hunger.

'There's all manner of unholy rubbish in the fridge,'

said Marie, knowing this was what Iris wanted to hear. The picnic had been an experiment; she wasn't radical enough to make her kids go cold turkey on processed foods all at once.

And besides, Marie would kill for a late-night Ginsters.

'Yessss!' Iris poked her nose into the fridge and punched the air. 'Cheese triangles!' She greedily ingested half a packet, before turning to notice Marie weighing flour on the scales she'd brought from home. 'Oh, are you cooking?' She sounded flat again. 'We want you to watch *The Sound of Music* with us.'

Her daughters' enthusiasm for Julie Andrews baffled Marie. 'I'm practising a cake to take to the Residents' Association meeting, darling. Daddy will watch with you,' she said evilly, as Robert, in a fresh pair of truly awful shorts, entered the kitchen.

'Why are you suddenly so keen on the Residents' Association?' Robert pilfered a cheese triangle from his daughter. 'You usually make me go on my own and you say, and I'm quoting here, *I'd rather make sweet love to a tramp than listen to speeches about planning permission for sheds*. What's with the sudden enthusiasm?' He didn't wait for Marie to stop cracking eggs, but carried on, 'Oh, hang on. This is about your nemesis, isn't it?'

'What's a nemesis?' asked Iris, own-brand quiche crumbs all down her front.

'I don't know, and Lucy isn't one,' said Marie hurriedly.

'Nice save,' said Robert.

'Shut up and get out!' said Marie, never at her best when separating yolks from whites.

Ignoring her, Robert pulled the Mary Berry book to him and peered at the recipe. 'Doboz Torte?' he read. 'Sounds like a Venezuelan hooker. What is it?'

'You'll find out later.'

Checking that Iris was otherwise engaged with E-numbers, Robert asked, under his breath, 'Is it . . . sexual?'

'I refer my learned friend to my earlier *Shut up and get out.*' Marie was anxious about this cake. It was a level up from a standard sponge, another step on the path to next year's show-stopper, but she'd neglected one of Mary's commandments – *Read the recipe right through before you decide to make it* – and she paid the price.

A Doboz Torte was a daunting, labour-intensive thing of beauty. At heart it was a sponge filled with oozing chocolate buttercream. But when Marie read on, she found that the top layer of sponge had to be cut into triangles, which then sat in the buttercream at an angle, like the blades of a windmill. In between each blade she had to pipe a single immaculate buttercream rosette, before anointing the whole thing with caramel. *Home-made* caramel. It was a whimsical delight, all the more glorious because it had to be eaten quickly, according to Mary, before the caramel seeped into the sponge and the whole thing collapsed.

Marie knew how it felt. 'Good God!' She cast her eye over the page. 'It doesn't even need cake tins. You bake the sponge layers straight onto parchment. And you make six of them!' She looked at Robert and he read the message in her eyes. Within moments there was a glass of wine within reach. 'Now run,' she said to her husband and daughter. 'Save yourselves.'

Every fifteen minutes the face of a twin – or occasionally a Robert – would poke around the kitchen door and plead for her to join them.

'It's the best bit,' cajoled Rose at one point.

The best bits of *The Sound of Music* were indistinguishable from the worst bits in Marie's opinion. 'Later, darling. When I've finished.'

Marie liked the optimism of that *when*. It felt more like an *if* as she peeled the thin, delicate sponge circles from the parchment paper, poking her fingers through them and growling at her own clumsiness.

Lavender dusk deepened to sooty night beyond the small, deep windows as Marie embarked on the caramel. Her new sugar thermometer stood ready and waiting as she gingerly heated sugar and water, aware of the dangerous temperatures these two innocents could reach when they ganged up.

In front of the fire in the sitting room the other Dunwoodys sang 'Climb Every Mountain' as Marie climbed her own personal mountain in the kitchen. It was tough to withstand twinnish pleading; Marie was keenly aware that they wouldn't always crave her company. Few pleasures gave her keener happiness than slouching on a sofa with Rose snuggled up on one side of her and Iris cosied up on the other, but the challenge buried in the pages of the *Baking Bible* couldn't be ignored.

Even a woman who adores her husband, loves her

children, appreciates her career and cares about her workmates can feel that life is a hamster wheel. With Mary,
Marie stepped off the wheel. Learning to bake was a shiny
new venture in a life that threw up the same old problems
day in, day out, like a home-movie version of *Groundhog
Day*.

Yup. *Groundhog Day* on a hamster wheel. That, essen-
tially, was modern woman's lot. A pang at her own disloy-
alty made Marie pause as she stirred the caramel. Was
this passion for baking a way for her subconscious to flag
up some deeper problem, some basic boredom with her
life? Robert, she felt certain, never had such dark thoughts.

Moving her spoon through the sweet, sluggish tar, Marie
shooed away such treason. There was no deep dissatis-
faction with life behind her new-found passion, just the
joy of a few hours in a warm, scented kitchen, busy with
something that was *hers*, all hers.

As she carefully poured golden caramel over one of the
cooled cakes, enjoying the sensual *schlurp* as it sank into
the sponge, Marie felt a connection, right in the centre of
her being, with women who'd stood and done just this
through the centuries. Generation after generation of
women standing stirring by a stove, their wooden spoons
drawing gentle circles in food that would feed the hungry
bellies around them.

It was a proud tradition. All those strong, generous
daughters, sisters and mothers bringing their creativity and
their application to a room as humble and as mighty as
the kitchen. *And what's more*, thought Marie happily, *this
is my choice*. For years, women had no say in whether

they cooked or not, but as a twenty-first-century bird, she could both go out to work *and* cook.

Or not; later Robert would be dispatched to fetch fish and chips.

It took two hours, some freshly minted swear words and a lot of faith in Mary, but the Doboz Torte was ready to serve after the sublime haddock and chips Robert brought back from the village. Nothing like the picture in the book, the cake would need to be prettied up for the meeting of the Residents' Association.

'That,' said Iris, licking her fingers, 'was almost as nice as a Viennetta.'

Tears crowded Marie's eyes. You really couldn't say fairer than that.

'It's lovely,' said Marie, her face raised to the sun, eyes closed, so relaxed that she could barely get it together to form words, 'when we're all together, isn't it?'

'Mm-hmm.' Robert, prostrate on an adjacent towel agreed, his voice heavy with sun-induced apathy. 'But even lovelier when the kids are out at sea.'

Marie propped herself up on one forearm, shaded her eyes and watched the progress of the tiny white boat chugging across the bay. 'That skipper did have safety certificates and everything, didn't he?'

'Yup. And he's been out of jail for *ages* now. Lie down and enjoy the blessed peace before they get back.'

Flat out again, Marie felt the sun kiss her here, there and everywhere like an attentive lover. Like Robert after a few beers. Lying here together, murmuring, the way they chatted late at night in bed, it was as if her husband was inside her head. *I love you*, she thought soppily.

'Listen, love, could you take it easy with the whole cake thing while we're on holiday? It's meant to be family time.'

The soppy mood fetched its coat and left. 'You've been cooking, too!' she tutted. With four attempts at the sausage roll before declaring himself satisfied, Robert was just as guilty as she was of this new crime. Marie had tasted the rejects and would have been perfectly happy with them; Robert was both harder on himself and a more gifted cook.

'True. But my cooking's for a reason. It's to consolidate my position at work.'

'I'm cooking for a reason, too.'

'Yeah, but what is it? A mission? Are you Trying to Have It All? Or are you locked in battle with your nemesis?'

It was all of those things, and none of them. Unable to do justice to the way she felt when it was just her and Mary making merry in the kitchen, Marie dodged the question with some stealthy flattery. 'While we're on the subject, your sausage roll was outstanding.'

'I'm sure there's a rude joke in there somewhere, but I'm too relaxed to winkle it out.'

'Tell me again what Magda said about your rosemary rolls.'

'No, don't be silly. Oh, OK, if I must. She said she'd never had better, even in a swanky restaurant.'

'And tell me again what Caroline's face did.'

'It did a spot-on impression of a bulldog chewing a wasp.'

'You're not really worried about, you know . . .' Marie faltered. She didn't even like to say the words. 'About losing your job, are you?'

'No no no no *no*,' said Robert, as if perfecting how to say 'no' unconvincingly.

When, wondered Marie, had Robert lost his career mojo? Once upon a time he'd have seen off a whipper-snapper like Caroline with one hand tied behind his back. She felt as if she'd missed vital episodes of a favourite serial. Had she not been listening, or had Robert not been talking? Neither possibility pleased her. 'Is the new cutlery still selling strongly?'

'Selling like hot cakes, if you'll pardon the topical pun.'

'Fab.' She reached out her hand to him. The moment was right to ask how he was really feeling. 'Darling—'

And with that they both sat up quickly, as would anybody who'd just had an ice lolly slapped on their bare stomach.

'We're back!' shrieked the twins.

As a Residents' Association-meeting virgin, Marie hadn't grasped that it was actually an opportunity to nose unashamedly around a neighbour's house. All her post-holiday blues fell away as she took in Erika's sitting room, like a forensics expert at a crime scene. A smorgasbord of shag-pile, squashy leather and oversized mirrors, it was a plush room devoted to pleasure, dotted with velvet cushions and cashmere throws and bare-shouldered studio shots of the *femme fatale* lady of the house.

'A cake!' Erika cried. She had only one volume. 'You sweetheart!'

Like a pampered pet, the Doboz Torte had travelled triumphantly across the Close in a new plastic cake-carrier. Erika produced a pretty cake stand and set it in the middle of the spread laid out on the dining table, her chiffon leopard-skin sleeves trailing in the Hula Hoops.

'I think not!' A shrill voice cut in, and Holistic Hattie (as Marie privately called her) was between them, reaching for the cake. 'The feng shui in this space is way out, Erika. The food should be on your right as you enter.'

'Really?' Erika looked just like somebody who couldn't give a toss.

'And, sadly, your buffet doesn't offer the five elements.' Hattie, her hair bursting from her head in electrified curls, snatched up the Doboz Torte, and Marie had to stop herself grabbing it back as if it was a tug-of-love child. Hattie, pint-sized and rotund, free of make-up and wearing plain grey sweats, was a stark counterpoint to their glamorous hostess. 'Do you even know what the five elements are?' she asked, more in sadness than in anger.

Materialising to filch a breadstick, Rose guessed. 'Um, ice cream, potatoes, cheese, Mars Bars and salsa?'

'Metal,' said Hattie. 'Water. Wood. Fire. Earth.'

Not a tempting menu. 'Mmm,' said Marie. 'Wood sandwiches. Lovely.'

Hattie laughed. 'Sorry, I do barge in, don't I? I just want everything to be harmonious.'

'Here.' Erika thrust a glass at her. 'Have a lovely glass of chilled harmony.'

Marie clinked drinks with Hattie. 'To booze – the sixth element. And by far the best.'

Looking askance at the alcohol, Hattie asked earnestly, 'Erika, have you any room-temperature tap water?'

'Sweetheart, the day I answer yes to that question is the day you have my permission to shoot me.' The doorbell rang and Erika wafted off on shoes high enough to double as stilts.

Small talk with Hattie was easy, so long as you asked questions about feng shui, aromatherapy, reiki or any number of worthy topics Marie knew nothing about. Halfway through a long discourse on why yams are good for your spleen, Marie was rescued by Mrs Gnome.

This was not her real name. The Dunwoodys had rechristened their next-door neighbour for the battalion of garden ornaments on her front lawn. There was a fishing gnome, a sunbathing gnome, a ballet-dancing gnome; for all Marie knew, there was a psychopath gnome lurking behind a trellis. Mrs Gnome was small, white-haired, twinkly-eyed; standard-issue cute old lady.

'Load of frigging rubbish, all this Residents' Association bullshit,' she said, by way of hello. 'Nobody never gets nothing done. Every sodding meeting I ask for a new *Slow Down* sign for the end of the road, and what do I get? Bugger all!'

Hattie's brow furrowed. 'I did petition the council on your behalf, and—'

'They won't listen to you, you nutter,' said Mrs Gnome. 'Oh look, here come our new poofs.'

'Keep your voice down, *please*,' begged Hattie, but Graham and Johann, newly moved into the Close, had heard.

'That's OK, we *are* your new poofs, I guess.' Graham, tall and tanned in all sorts of denim, seemed more amused than affronted by Mrs Gnome's rudeness. 'You must be the old bat I've heard so much about.'

Mrs Gnome guffawed. 'Good one,' she cawed, before moving off to scare and humiliate other guests.

Graham, who had lived in Caraway Close for four weeks, was able to introduce Marie to people she'd passed in the street for years. The room filled up, the atmosphere swelled, and Graham summed up Marie's feelings exactly by saying, 'This would be a perfectly nice party if we didn't know it'll turn into a deadly boring meeting at some point.'

Tasked with finding salty snacks for the insatiable Mrs Gnome ('Nothing that'll stick in me dentures'), Marie noticed that, although the buffet was going down a storm with residents, her Doboz Torte still stood on its raised stand, virginal and untouched. One side drooping, as prophesied by Mary, the torte was just another cake to the Residents' Association, but for Marie it represented hours of toil, memories of unrisen sponge flung in the bin, buttercream in her hair at midnight, a pagan dance of joy when the caramel had behaved. It was a frontier, a new skill set, a milestone in her relationship with St Mary of the Cake Tins.

Trying to look at it through a stranger's eyes (and ignoring Mrs Gnome's shouts of 'Oi! Stupid! Where's me nuts?'), Marie saw a different cake altogether. She saw a lopsided dollop, its windmill blades tilting unevenly on brownish icing the colour of . . . She didn't want to pin down what the icing reminded her of.

'Wow,' said Graham at her side. 'What a cake!'

Her heart suddenly weighing nothing, Marie beamed up at him, to see that his gaze skidded over the Doboz Torte's poor wonky head and took in the front door.

'Lucy! Tod! Chloe!' Erika was greeting late arrivals. 'And you've brought a cake! How marvellous!'

Bringing *her* cake to the table, Lucy was mobbed by salivating residents oohing and aahing. It was a modest effort, more petite than Marie's, and a blazing pristine white in comparison to her – ahem – *brownish* effort.

'I just hope it tastes OK,' said Lucy, placing it carefully on the table.

On top of impeccably smooth white fondant, Lucy had iced a map of Caraway Close. Marie saw her house, outlined in electric blue, and wished she was back in it, ignoring the Residents' Association, hunkered down with BBC iPlayer and a bag of Doritos as big as her head.

'That is amazing,' she said with sincerity and a kind of ache that she'd never, ever achieve such perfection, even if she kidnapped Mary Berry and tied her up in the cellar. The cake was not only technically flawless, it was witty and imaginative to boot. 'Well done, Lucy.'

'Oh, you know, I try.' Lucy tucked fronds of sunshine-coloured hair behind her ears.

At Marie's shoulder a grating voice, like a possessed squirrel, wheezed, 'That's the last time I send *you* for nibbles, you dozy mare.' Mrs Gnome glanced down at the cake and her voice changed. 'Aw, look!' she cooed, pointing at the cake. 'Me 'ouse! She's done me 'ouse in icing!'

Chloe had been got at: she was in black, naturally, but

in the sort of black that would pass muster with Lucy. Tidy jeans. A pressed T. Her eyeliner was toned down, more Audrey Hepburn than Courtney Love. She and Tod, flanking Lucy, were perfect accessories for the accomplished home-maker: the pretty young girl with shiny hair; the distinguished man in an impeccable suit and flashing smile. There was something presidential in the way they stood, as if posing for an official photograph.

Slinking away, Marie caught Chloe's eye and winked. The girl looked thoroughly uncomfortable, pulling her sleeves down over her knuckles, shoulders up around ears that were naked of their usual line of silver studs.

Chloe smiled back tightly, her expression taut.

'Oh, you've made a cake, too.' Lucy, looking aghast and biting her lip, caught Marie mid-slink. 'Oh God, I'm sorry. Erika never said. I didn't mean to muscle in.'

'I *did* say,' said Erika, looking not at Lucy but at two of the four reflections of herself offered by her sitting-room walls. 'Didn't I?'

'It doesn't matter a bit,' said Marie, her smile reminiscent of Chloe's. 'Always room for more cake!'

'I suppose.' Lucy wrinkled her nose.

Not a natural nose-wrinkler, Marie wondered if she should take it up.

'Chairs!' yelled Erika incongruously, and the regulars set about creating a semicircle of stools and armchairs and dining chairs around the mantelpiece (and a whopping photograph of Erika looking into the middle distance, in such soft focus that she appeared to have no nostrils). The seats soon filled up, and Marie had to take Iris on her lap. A few chairs along, Erika landed briefly on Tod's lap with a girlish 'Oops!', before squeezing his knee and moving on to a spare seat. Tod caught Marie's eye and pulled a discreet face of alarm.

Coughing to cover her titter, Marie accepted the lozenge that Hattie, on her right, spirited out of a pocket.

'I think your chakras may be closed,' she mused.

'Wouldn't be a bit surprised,' agreed Marie. She shook her head quellingly at Tod, who was inching his chair away from Erika, just for Marie's benefit. Loose and funny and approachable, the man was nothing like his wife.

The minutes, ironically, took hours. Erika took the floor, delighted when Angus crouched, filming, on the edge of the semicircle. This promised to be an interesting set-piece for the summer home movie. Presenting her best profile to the camera involved much twirling, and much leopard-skin chiffon hitting Tod in the face.

'The crazed sex attacker reported by one of our senior members,' Erika gestured to Mrs Gnome, assiduously reading a copy of *heat*, 'turned out to be a badger. And Hattie scored a triumph with the council, who have *finally* replaced our vandalised street sign.'

There was a round of applause for Hattie, who blushed to the roots of her hair. Nobody had relished living in *Carawank Close*.

'I'm very disappointed that there are no takers for the early-morning running club.' Erika lifted her chin to glare at her audience, who all shuffled and mumbled and looked at their feet.

Marie examined her fingernails; only Mary could get her up early.

'Umm, one last thing – what was it?' Erika held her glasses midway between her eyes and her notes. 'Ah yes. Could we please stop leaving rubbish in the right-of-way?' More mumbling. More shuffling. The horseshoe-shaped alley that backed onto all their gardens was a tempting place to dump unwanted paraphernalia. Marie thought of the twins' old trike, which had been in the alley so long it was covered in ivy.

'And before any hands go up, I insist that we do *not* debate yet again whether or not the bottle-recycling station at the corner of the Close is a good idea. It's here and it's staying, and I for one will be throwing all my empty Moëts into it. That's all from me. Here's a word from one of our younger members.'

Chloe stood up and took Erika's place with much less self-assurance than the hostess. 'Um,' she began, managing a smile for Angus's camera just as he switched it off. 'Er . . . I'm . . . kind of raising money?' Chloe's inflection turned her statements into questions. 'For PeTA? So if I could babysit? Or wash cars? Or . . . um . . . I don't know – anything? That'd be great?'

'Bless her,' whispered Hattie, and Marie silently seconded that.

After a brief interjection from Mrs Gnome, along the lines of *Don't any of you bastards park across my drive or I'll come at you with a machete*, the meeting was over. Chit-chat broke out as chairs were replaced, cheeks kissed and Erika extravagantly thanked.

Where once Lucy's cake had stood there was now just a mound of sweet rubble. As Marie contemplated the two large slices of Doboz Torte left on the stand, Tod reached over and scooped them both onto a paper plate. 'This,' he said, 'looks delicious.' Raising his eyebrows at Marie, he shovelled a forkful into his mouth. He had a symmetrical, pleasing face that smiled easily and often, the skin smooth with a golden tinge. 'Yum!'

'Really?' goggled Marie.

'Lucy,' called Tod, 'taste this, darling.' And he forked another chocolatey blob at his wife.

Obediently she opened her mouth. 'Oh *yes*!' she said approvingly, widening her eyes.

'It's bloody gorgeous,' enthused Tod.

He'd saved Marie from a flashback to a sixth-form disco; tonight, thanks to Tod, she was no wallflower. 'Oh, I don't know . . .' Marie was dismissive, unaccustomed to praise for her food. 'It's a bit too crumbly.' It was a typically British self-deprecating comment, so Marie was surprised when Lucy took her up on it.

'Maybe a touch,' she said gravely, screwing up her eyes as she savoured the cake. 'Hmm. Yes.' Zealously she went on, 'Make sure you don't over-beat.' She made a circular motion with one fist. 'Let the mixer do the work. Over-beating can dry out a cake before it even goes in the oven.' She smiled, happy to help.

'I'll do that,' smiled Marie. Unhappy to be helped. *Typical Delia fan*, she thought. *Giving advice before it's asked for.*

Lights came on all over the Close as residents dispersed

back to their homes. Marie could see Robert in their kitchen window, raising a mug to her. She could also see Prinny behind him, standing on the kitchen table, wolfing down whatever Robert had just left unattended. She hoped to God he'd taped the first episode of the new *Great British Bake Off* series, or he'd be wearing that mug he'd so jauntily lifted. 'Come on, kids,' she muttered, speeding up in anticipation of an hour with Mary.

'Angus,' said Iris to her brother as they made their way down Erika's crazy paving. 'Just make Chloe your girl-friend, will you? We want to be bridesmaids.'

'Shut *up*,' said Angus.

'She's really pretty,' said Rose.

'She's not my type.' Angus was adamant.

Marie swung the cake-carrier to catch Angus square on his non-existent boy-arse. 'Ssh!' she hissed.

On the far side of Erika's picket fence, the Grays had reached their front door, with Chloe falling behind and plenty near enough to hear what had just been said. The girl kept her head down and hurried indoors after her parents.

The tiny glass pot, expensive enough to contain unicorn droppings, was full of the latest must-have anti-ageing cream. Regarding her naked, pink, scrubbed-looking face in the unflattering en-suite mirror, Marie wondered if the scented goop would actually *do* anything. The actress 'spokesperson' for the brand was ten years Marie's senior, yet looked ten years younger. Did she even use this stuff? Marie suspected she'd be better off borrowing the woman's plastic surgeon and hiring some digital genius to Photoshop the Dunwoody holiday snaps.

Even after ruthless editing, there were only three photographs of their Cornwall fortnight in which Marie looked human, never mind 'youthful', 'vibrant' or 'glowing', as promised by the jar.

It was just one little jar against a tidal wave of genes. Marie's nana had been officially old by fifty, with flat shoes, a tight perm, comfy cardis and a firm belief that there was no such thing as a lesbian. Recalling her nana's wrinkles, Marie doubted that she could stave off her own lines with goo.

Rubbing the costly stuff into her cheeks, she wandered out to the bedroom, where Robert lay reading a motorbike magazine. Never one to sleep naked, he was in a *Sesame Street* T-shirt and a pair of pyjama bottoms so old they were eligible to vote. 'If you saw me in the street,' she asked him, 'how old would you think I was?'

'Twelve,' said Robert, without looking up.

'Seriously.'

'No way!' Robert shook his head, eyes still on the page. 'Do you think I landed yesterday from the Planet of No Women? I like my testicles exactly where they are, thanks very much.'

'Go on. Be honest – I won't get upset.'

Robert took a deep breath, laid his head back on the pillows and looked at his wife. 'Marie,' he began, 'I don't know what age you look. You look like you look, and you look lovely – like you've always looked.'

Marie was touched.

'To me,' he added, going back to the magazine.

Wishing her husband knew when to stop, Marie peered into the mirror propped on top of the chest of drawers. She leaned in, a fingertip to one eyelid, searching for new lines, but a sudden image stopped her mid-scrutiny.

Superimposed over Marie's bare and shiny face was a much older visage, that of the lady she'd been watching for the past hour. Robert had come good and remembered to tape *The Great British Bake Off*, so Marie had spent a joyous sixty minutes watching her heroine pussy-whip Paul Hollywood and dispense her patented brand of genteel tough love to the stressed-out contestants.

Mary's face, Marie recalled, was a map of the woman's life. Lovely, proper wrinkles marched unashamedly across her brow and from the corners of those iridescent peepers, telling a tale of people loved and people lost, mountains climbed and hills hurtled down on a tea-tray.

There were no apologies in that face. No *Whoops, how did that happen? I got old! Pass the Botox!* And Marie loved that face.

Feeling better about her own countenance, she turned to the window and peeked out through the gap in the curtains. Across the Close a door opened, slapping a rectangle of light onto the Grays' dark path. Tod was manhandling a large bin on wheels out into the street.

'Oh God, it's bin-day tomorrow. Did you . . . ?'

Robert groaned. 'It's always bloody bin-day.'

'Go on,' said Marie. 'They're full.' Of half-baked sponge and misfired sausage roll, mainly.

'Why are the bins my thing?' He swung his legs angrily off the bed.

'Because they are,' said Marie. 'Men do the bins. That's how it is. Look at Tod.' She peered closer. 'My God, he's even taking it to the end of the Close, by the looks of things. What a hero!' She couldn't resist adding, '*And* he's wearing a proper dressing gown.'

'Good for him,' grumbled Robert, pulling on Marie's pink towelling shortie number. A grumpy cross-dresser, he stomped out of the bedroom and down the stairs, shouting, 'This sudden Tod-love would have nothing to do with the fact that he praised your sodding cake, I suppose?'

TO: stargazinggirl247@gmail.com
FROM: geeksrus39@gmail.com
27.08.13
00.11
SUBJECT: OI!

Hi Soulmate

Email me!

Why are you all quiet tonight? I can sense you're there. Have you given up on me because you got brilliant results and you can't hang out with the asshat who got a D in eng lit?

Twins are pairing me up with this Goth Girl Across The Road. Some hope! They don't know about YOU. And they don't know I DO NOT WANT A GIRLFRIEND.

The Clones are quiet at the moment. Maybe they've gone abroad or something. Waiting for it to kick off again is almost as bad as when it's full on. I feel like Sigourney Weaver in Alien being creeped out by all the dark corners on the space ship and wondering when the creature will jump out at her again.

Come on, Soulmate! Email me. Nobody else knows what's going on. And I need to hear what you're thinking and doing and what you hate today and what you love today.

laters

Angus

SEPTEMBER

Angus's Birthday

Bunny-Rabbit Cake

TO: rdunwoody@campbellandcarle.com
FROM: marie.smile!dentist@gmail.com
01.09.13
12.09
SUBJECT: Quickie

Hi Huz

Just a quick one (while I await Mrs Donaldson and her broken front crown) to say GOOD LUCK!!!! with your speech to the department today. Slay 'em with your sausage roll, big boy. Oh I keep meaning to say – ask Magda for a new chair. I was shocked when I visited last week. That chair you sit on should be in a skip, not cradling the (rather nice) buttocks of the UK's foremost cutlery personage.

Love you.

See you at home.

(You're on putting-to-bed duty tonight because I'll be busy making Angus's birthday cake for tomorrow.)

Mxxxxxxxx

P.S. Mary Berry could soooo take Paul Hollywood in a fight.

ANGUS THIS IS MY FOURTH TEXT! R U STILL IN BED???? Get up NOW. Are girls up? Have u walked Prinny? Invite Joe over for tomorrow and we'll make a party of it – you've hardly seen him this hols. GET UP NOW! Love you. Mum. x P.S. GET UP.

'Aileen, don't do that.' Marie shuddered. 'Not in reception.'

'Don't do what?' Aileen turned from the mirror, a forefinger jammed on either side of a particularly magnificent traffic light of a pimple on the end of her nose. 'Squeezing is necessary to maintain me complexion.'

Aileen's complexion could double as a devilishly hard dot-to-dot puzzle; the squeezing wasn't paying off.

'You can . . . *squeeze*,' said Marie squeamishly, 'all you like – just not in front of patients. They expect high levels of hygiene from us.'

'Fair enough.' Marie lowered both hands with an elegant gesture, like a gymnast finishing a routine.

'Seventeen weeks and three days to the wedding!' According to the schedule on the whiteboard, Lynda should have been updating the clinic website, but she was mooching about on her wedding spreadsheet, a document that made *The Da Vinci Code* seem clipped and perfunctory. 'The seating plan's in its final stages.'

'Who am I sitting next to?' asked Aileen belligerently. She only knew how to put questions belligerently: if she asked a stranger the time, they assumed they were being mugged.

'Let's see.' Lynda scanned the rows and columns earnestly. 'Hmm. You're between another bridesmaid and the best man.'

'He'd better keep his hands to himself.'

'He's gay.'

'I have a strange effect on men.'

'Oh, I know you do,' said Lynda.

Aileen tidied the plaque leaflets. 'Is there room for a small canister of pepper spray in those little lacy handbags you're forcing us to carry?'

Ignoring her, Lynda tapped the screen. 'Ah, wedding cake.' She looked over at her boss, who was scowling and ringing her home number. 'Have you researched croquembouche yet?'

'Yes!' Marie nodded enthusiastically, phone to her ear, making a mental note to research croquembouche as soon as Lynda went to lunch.

'Isn't it fab-yoo-*lus*!'

'Oh yes,' said Marie, listening as the phone rang a mile away in Caraway Close.

'D'you think you'll need a ladder?'

Wondering why she'd need a ladder to make a cake, and now far too scared to research croquembouche, Marie was saved from answering by a childish squeak at the other end of the line.

'Good morning. Dunwoody residence.'

'Rose. Is your brother out of his pit yet?'

'No. And his room smells like that circus you made us go to.'

'Tell him I said to get up. It's the second-last day of the

holidays and he shouldn't waste it in bed.' Even as she said this, Marie wondered when she'd started quoting *The Handbook of Dumb Things Mothers Say*; she could think of nothing lovelier than a day-long lie-in. 'Have you two had your cereal?'

'No. We had eggs Benedict.'

Of course you did, thought Marie with a smile, wondering how their no doubt inventive version had tasted. Her resourceful daughters were a constant surprise to her. 'Listen, any ideas for what sort of cake I should make for Angus's birthday?'

'Is this where you ask me a question, but you've already decided and you want me to agree with you?'

'Not at all, darling!'

'Fruitcake. That's his favourite.'

'How about a *shaped* cake?'

'Fruitcake's his favourite.'

'But how about a cake in the shape of' – Marie looked down at Mary's book, open on Lynda's desk, beside a brochure for bridal vajazzling – 'a bunny rabbit.' *That*, she thought, *would stretch me*.

'Fruit cake's his favourite,' said Rose. 'And we don't say bunny rabbit any more. We say rabbit.'

'OK.' Marie gave up. 'Well, don't play with matches or stick your fingers in the light sockets, sweetie pie.'

'You forgot about opening the door to murderers.'

'You can do that, if you want.'

Rose's giggle was like pretty china breaking. 'See you later, Mum.'

The cheerful *ding* of the bell above the door signalled

Mrs Donaldson's arrival, her rueful smile and 'Sorry I'm late!' exposing the craggy stump of a front tooth.

'You look like a tramp,' said Aileen with a smile. 'Or a Victorian prostitute.'

'We'll soon have you back to normal,' said Marie soothingly, as Mrs Donaldson's hand flew to her mouth. 'And then we'll ask for a refund from Aileen's Charm School.'

As Mrs Donaldson handed over her debit card, she flashed her pristine gnashers unnecessarily. 'Did you notice they're doing up the old snack bar across the road?'

All three Smile! folk peered like meerkats over the frosted bottom section of the window behind Lynda's chair. The loss of Baguette Me Not had hit them hard; Aileen still mourned the snack bar's baps.

'Ooh, yes,' said Marie, intrigued. 'Wonder what it's going to be?'

'They're spending a bit of money, whoever they are,' smiled Mrs Donaldson. She would smile all day, now that she had her front tooth back, even if she had to deliver news of a death. 'An army of workmen. Whole place is gutted. Saw lots of chrome and glass going in.'

'Aileen,' said Marie, knowing her assistant was one of the few people in the world who was nosier than her, 'go and find out what's going on.'

'Yeah,' said Lynda, as Aileen shot out of the door like a dog following a thrown ball. 'Use your irresistible charm.'

'Thanks again for fitting me in, Marie,' said Mrs Donaldson, stuffing her purse into her bag. 'I feel human again. You've done a brilliant job, as always.'

'Aw, shucks, it was nothing,' smiled Marie, her face ketchup-coloured. Not very expert at accepting compliments, she felt warmed when a patient thanked her like this. She knew she was good at dentistry and she knew that a healthy smile made a difference. When people made jokes at parties along the lines of *How can you spend all day looking in mouths?*, she wanted to tell them it was a vocation, a calling – a small way to add to the sum of happiness in the world. But that would sound pompous. And she was usually too tiddly to pronounce 'vocation'.

The shrill scream of Aileen's rape alarm brought them all back to the window. Across the road the builders seemed to have locked themselves inside the property, peeping out as Aileen stomped back to her colleagues.

'They were un—'

'We know.' Lynda held up a hand. 'Undressing you with their yada-yada-yada. What's the shop going to be?'

'It's going to be . . .' Aileen paused to maximise the drama. 'It's going to be a state-of-the-art, all bells and whistles, no expense spared . . . dental clinic.'

A happy side-effect of the Residents' Association meeting was that Marie now felt better equipped to greet her neighbours. When she saw Hattie power-walking around the Close that evening she called out, 'Evening!'

Hattie power-walked over, all elbows and knees, the sweatband around her head so Eighties that it could well be in fashion again. 'Can I help you with those?'

'No, I'm fine.' Marie heaved Sainsbury's bag after Sainsbury's bag out of the boot, wondering if they'd mated and reproduced on the short drive home. The welts that the vicious plastic handles left on her fingers were scars of motherhood – part of a matching set that included stretch marks, varicose veins and eye-bags, which, if examined, contained the words *just let me sleep* in microscopic letters.

'Expecting visitors?' Hattie, marching on the spot, eyed the massed bags.

'No,' laughed Marie. 'But I'm baking tonight.' Even with the comprehensive Mary-inspired makeover, Marie's cupboards never held everything she needed for a new cake.

'I bake when I'm out of sorts,' said Hattie. 'It makes me feel very close to the Earth Mother. It balances me.'

'I know what you mean.' Marie never considered her relationship with the Earth Mother, but she did feel a great deal more sane after a kitchen session with Mary, once she'd stopped banging cupboard doors and shouting *Where's the arrowroot – and WHAT is arrowroot?*

'Yoo-hoo!' Erika was clambering out of a taxi, breasts first, on the other side of the Close. 'Anyone fancy a swift G and T?'

Marie fancied one, but the bags cutting into her fingers reminded her she didn't have time. 'Another time!' she shouted, wondering what her younger incarnation would make of this strange middle-aged woman turning down booze in favour of making a cake shaped like a rabbit.

'You know I never touch the stuff!' called Hattie, still marching, her expression a verbal *tut-tut*. For somebody who lived so healthily, Hattie was, thought Marie, rather well upholstered. Perhaps she strayed from the path of holistic righteousness now and again?

'Just have to drink the whole bottle myself then!' yelled Erika as she paid the taxi driver, bending over her handbag and offering him a ringside view of her D-cups.

'Look at the cabbie's face,' laughed Marie, awkwardly slamming the car boot with her elbow. 'He's in seventh heaven. Boobs *and* a tip!'

Robert, ambling down their path in the sort of super-scruffy trackie bottoms that shouldn't be seen by any-body except immediate family, held out his hand to take a bag or two and asked, 'Boobs? Where? What boobs?' with exactly the same expression on his face as Prinny wore when he heard the fridge door opening. He spotted Erika, tottering on her platforms, and said, 'Ah, those boobs.'

Marie dug him in the ribs. 'Eyes front,' she barked.

'Isn't she . . .' began Hattie, forgetting to march for a moment '. . . a little *old* for those clothes she wears?'

So, wholesome Hattie had talons. Having developed a soft spot for their eccentric sexpot neighbour, Marie defended her. 'If that's what makes her happy,' she said.

A car, sleek and low, nosed up, and Erika, with a flick of her bouffant hair, rushed over to greet Tod.

'She's not so old,' said Robert, earning a soft mew of agreement from Marie, who was proud of her gallant husband. 'About, what – ten years older than you, love?'

'At least fifteen,' said Marie, teeth so suddenly clenched they could have shattered. '*At least*,' she repeated warn-ingly, as he half-opened his mouth to speak, then thought better of it.

'Oh God,' said Hattie out of the side of her mouth, 'she's all over poor Tod now.'

Erika put her arm through Tod's and leaned in to whisper in his ear.

'And if I'm not mistaken,' said Robert, 'poor Tod's *loving* it.'

'Men are so obvious.' Perhaps it was the obviousness of men that got Hattie marching on the spot again, as Tod threw back his head and laughed at some saucy comment of Erika's.

'Give us a break,' said Robert genially. 'Men are straight-forward. If a woman hangs on every word we say *and* favours a low neckline, we're happy.'

Erika shouted across. 'A customer for my G and T at last!'

'Tod's just being polite,' said Marie, as they watched Erika abduct him in broad daylight and waltz him to her front door.

'No, he's not. He's enjoying himself,' insisted Robert.

Marie saw Lucy's face pop up at the small round window beside the Grays' front door. A small, wan blob, Lucy strained to see where her husband had gone, before disappearing again. 'Tod's so handsome and suave and *tasteful*. He wouldn't look twice at Erika.'

'I agree,' said Hattie vehemently, as if big-breasted wealthy women were the last thing any man would enjoy.

'Don't get me wrong,' said Marie, uneasy that they might be disparaging a perfectly nice woman. 'Erika's great, but she's not Tod's type.'

'Who is?' asked Robert. 'You, I guess?'

'He's married!' snorted Marie.

'Yeah. And so are you. To *me*.' Robert puffed out his chest, and the egg stain on his Everton shirt expanded.

'It's at times like this,' laughed Hattie, powering off, 'that I thank God I'm single.'

'Should I have plumped for a koala?' Marie looked from the rabbit on the page to the three circular sponges idling on racks. Her stomach lurched in a way that brought to mind art lessons at school. She could never wrestle washing-up-liquid bottles and toilet rolls into rockets; they remained, obstinately, washing-up-liquid bottles and toilet rolls.

'I'll just toast the coconut before I start assembling,' she said airily, as if toasting coconut was a cinch, and assembling a mere bagatelle. After shovelling the third blackened heap of coconut into the bin, she began to appreciate the virtues of a standard fruitcake.

The glass doors to the garden were blank black rectangles, closed after weeks of standing wantonly ajar each warm dusk. September had started as it meant to go on, and the garden furniture huddled, chilly and shocked, out in the dark.

Eyeing the coconut through the oven's glass door (she knew by now that the difference between 'golden' and 'burned to buggery' was but a moment), Marie savoured the peace of the kitchen.

All was calm in her queendom. In the sitting room the twins were welded to the sofa, determined to make the most of the last late night of the holidays. The soft thud of music through Angus's bedroom door was the only evidence that he was in the house. Robert was in the garage and had been for some time, doing whatever it is that men do in garages. He was looking for batteries maybe, or cleaning a hammer. Possibly he was planning an elaborate murder – whatever it was, he was doing it quietly.

Now. *Now!* Marie whipped out the coconut. It looked like a Lilliputian beach, bronze and beautiful. The next step was to cover her largest chopping board with foil, as a (frankly not very convincing) backdrop for her rabbit. Was it, Marie pondered, a space-rabbit? A rabbit from a hi-tech future? Briefly she regretted not buying green crepe paper to make a grassy background, but if foil was good enough for Mary Berry, then it was more than good enough for Marie Dunwoody.

The diagram was clear, but Marie was tired. She nudged her hacked-up sponges this way and that, wondering which were the feet and which the ears. Across the Close, Lucy's kitchen was dark. Lucy never seemed to burn the midnight oil, despite her production line of mouth-watering goodies. For one moment Marie imagined a life married to Tod, with no need to work, no need to worry about the bills, spending every day conjuring up cakes and pastries and pies and . . . rabbits.

'*That's* an ear,' she decided, plonking down a crescent of sponge. 'Or is it?' She snatched it up again. 'Where's his bum?' she whispered desperately.

Time to go back to basics. Again! Marie took a deep breath, a glug of strong tea, shook herself vigorously and reapplied herself to the instructions. It all fell into place and soon the rabbit took shape on the foil. True, he was part Elephant Man, but he had a friendly look in his crooked eye and Marie felt confident he would taste great.

Slowly, methodically, she smeared yellow buttercream all over the rabbit, working carefully and refusing to panic when his tail fell on the floor and she only just beat Prinny to it.

Mary's unchanging advice had worked again.

If only Mary could run the rest of Marie's life. Mary would know how to react to news of a rival dentist on her turf; a rival with deep pockets and, according to Aileen, eight other 'highly successful' dental practices.

Mary wouldn't have huddled with her team all afternoon, alternately bitching and panicking. She wouldn't have broken out the Baileys after the last customer left. And she certainly wouldn't have spent the evening predicting bushweeds drifting across reception, and a conga line of patients snaking out of Smile!'s door to the new dentist. The imagined highlights of Marie's catastrophic future were: falling behind on the lease; sacking Lynda just before her wedding; and Aileen selling her body outside Waitrose.

The door from the garage opened and Robert emerged, wiping his hands with one of the many oily rags that lived in there. 'You were wrong earlier,' he said, one eyebrow cheekily raised. 'My Paul would Chinese-burn your Mary into submission like *that*!' He clicked his fingers. 'She'd have no comeback. Nothing.'

'Come now, Mr Dunwoody. She'd bring him to his knees with a karate-chop. Like so.' Marie laid down her spatula and brought her hand down like a cleaver, stopping just short of Robert's arm. She enjoyed his flinch, and did the same to his groin. 'That's what she does to your little chum just before they saunter in front of the cameras in *The Great British Bake Off* tent.'

'He'd be back, quick as a flash, with his karate-kick.' Robert demonstrated and toppled backwards over Prinny's bowl.

'Mind your back,' said Marie, returning to the rabbit, as Robert fell through the utility room to sprawl on the tiles.

'I meant to do that.' Robert bounded up and converted his wince into a look of nonchalance.

'Does this look like a rabbit to you?' Marie swivelled the board and almost pitied her husband as he searched for an answer. Letting him off, she wondered how the *Bake Off* contestants managed to churn out such quality items with the rain lashing down on the canvas roof and Hollywood stalking the marquee like an irritable badger. Her crumb-structure would surely collapse under his stern eye. 'It'll be better when it's covered in toasted coconut.'

'That's what they all say.' Robert settled against the worktop, hands in tracksuit pockets, ready for a chat.

Marie hesitated to tell him about her new rival. Robert was already worried about his work; she didn't want to burden him with her business woes just now. He would panic, and she needed him to be his usual steady, solid self while she digested the news. Even though he earned the lion's share of their income, it was Marie who balanced the books. It was she who knew how much council tax they paid, the interest rate of their mortgage, how much violin lessons and trainers and rucksacks and school shoes cost. And besides, he was off on another topic, folding his arms and chuckling.

'Caroline put her foot right in it today,' he said, gleefully. 'As usual she was poking her nose in, reading over my shoulder, and she caught that line in your email where you said I should ask for a new chair.'

'That's private!' Marie resolved to be careful about what she wrote in emails to Robert at work. If Caroline had read the one from last week . . . Oh dear God, nobody – *nobody* – must ever know their codeword for sex, or Marie would have to pluck out her own eyes and jump in the river.

'She got her comeuppance because her little mind started working overtime, and of course she couldn't let me get away with having something new, so she said, "Ooh, I need a new bin. Where do we keep the requisition forms?"'

Not riveted by this tale of bins, Marie said, 'So you're getting a new chair then? Good.' She selected two small Liquorice Allsorts for the rabbit's nose.

'Of course I'm not!' Robert was shocked. 'Magda is obsessed with cutting waste. She expects us to use things until they fall apart. She fishes paper clips out of the rubbish and we reuse teabags until they beg for mercy.' He chuckled, enjoying himself. 'Caroline even pointed out in a catalogue the bin she wants. It's state-of-the-bloody-art.'

Marie flinched: that was the second time today she'd heard that expression.

'It's ergodynamic. It's chrome. It's by a designer. It's a *designer bin*.' Robert was enjoying himself hugely. 'Magda's brain will come out of her ears when she sees that requisition form. And then in I come with my sausage roll. Bam!'

'Yes, darling – bam indeed,' said Marie, not listening any more and trying to correct the rabbit's squint.

Peeking in at the sleeping twins later that night, Marie tucked the duvet around Iris, who was doubled up like a prawn, her bottom sticking out of the bedclothes. In the other bed, a foot or two away, Rose's head was thrown back, eyelids moving as her avatar moved through some twinny dream.

Hopefully it was a good one. Marie wanted nothing but sunny dreams for these two. Her skin had thinned perceptibly when she became a parent; she felt their every slight and bruise.

Pausing at Angus's door, she wavered and almost padded past, but instead knocked gently and poked her head around the door, knowing that even this would be an intrusion for the boy who used to leap into her arms the moment he saw her, squealing, 'Mummy! My Mummee!'

'All right, love?' she whispered, as if in a library or an old folks' home. The room was full of sharp shadows thrown by the angled desk lamp.

Long limbs drawn up like a spider, Angus leaned back

on a chair, its two front legs off the floor. Marie assumed that a by-law had been passed stating that all teenage boys must use chairs in this fashion. Not looking up as he tapped on his laptop, cords trailing from his earphones, he took her question literally. 'Why shouldn't I be?'

'No reason.' Marie wavered again, but ploughed on. She hadn't seen him all evening. 'You typing something?'

A huge exhalation, and Angus swivelled to face her with exaggerated patience. 'Yes,' he said, 'I am.'

'Did you invite Joe tomorrow?'

'Yes!' Angus responded as if Marie had asked him this question three times an hour for a year. 'Well,' he frowned. 'I asked him round. I didn't *invite* him. It's not a party. It's just us lot and a cake.'

'You've just described a party.'

'No, it's just hanging.'

'Or chilling,' suggested Marie. 'Could we even be chill-axing?'

She could tell he wanted to laugh, but all she got was a stern 'Mum? I'm emailing?'

'Goodnight, love.'

This was *not* how Mary Berry would buy a birthday present. That coiffed, fragrant lady would never tear around the local shops on the day itself because she'd put so much thought and energy into the cake (a cake the birthday boy would barely notice) that she'd forgotten about the present.

Realising her mistake, as Angus withstood an off-key Dunwoody rendition of 'Happy Birthday to You' at the breakfast table, Marie had manhandled Robert to the utility room for a brief, frantic, whispered argument about who should rush out in their lunch hour.

'Wall-to-wall meetings,' claimed Robert, brazenly stuffing his squash racket into a bag.

'But you're surrounded by present possibilities! You work for a sodding department store!' hissed Marie, glancing neurotically at the door.

'In the buying department. Which is ten minutes from the nearest branch.' Robert added an unconvincing: 'I'd like to help, love, but I can't.'

'Help?' Marie spat out the word. This tactic annoyed her more than any other. 'You're not *helping* me. It's a present for your own son – the product of your ejaculation sixteen years and nine months ago. You were happy to help that night!'

'You could have used my staff discount, if you'd organised yourself earlier,' said Robert. He was offensively cheerful, having spent the whole of breakfast rubbing his hands with glee at Caroline's upcoming bin-based disappointment.

'I know that, thanks very much,' snarled Marie, looking wildly around her and wondering how to kill him using what came to hand. Fabric conditioner? Prinny's towel?

So, as Robert held unimaginably important meetings about the future of . . . well, *forks* or something, Marie herded the twins through the revolving door of Belloc's. They'd insisted on coming, to 'help'.

Belloc's was a local institution, having stood on the same spot (and, Marie suspected, having sold the same stock) since Edwardian days. It was stuffy and dated and naff, and it was all the tiny high street had to offer, apart from charity shops and gifty-wifty emporiums and a mobile-phone shop.

Tearing through the ground-floor departments at full tilt, picking up and putting down possible gifts like a chimp, Marie bombarded the girls with questions. 'Does Angus want a ski mask? Would he like some shears? Has he ever mentioned a wild-bird seedball?'

'Just buy him something *you* want,' suggested Rose, striking a pose by a headless mannequin in a bikini. 'Like you did with the cake.'

Channelling Mary Berry in the middle of Small Electricals, Marie heard her say *Think like a sixteen-year-old,* her voice eerily like a Home Counties Obi-Wan Kenobi. As the twins dragged her, one on each hand, towards Beauty and Toiletries, Marie imagined a life lived in a fog of Lynx, fighting a permanent erection.

'We haven't time, girls,' she said tetchily, as Iris and Rose squealed with excitement at the rainbow rows of cosmetics.

As their faces fell, she heard the tone of her voice and didn't like it one bit. It was too easy to fall into the Cruella de Vil style of mothering. 'Tell you what: you two wait here and look at all the lovely colours, while I go to that counter over there.' She pointed over to Leather Gifts. 'Don't move out of my sight, and don't try on any make-up. Just look at it. OK?'

Marie eventually bought a wallet. She hated the wallet, and Angus would hate it even more. He wouldn't, however, hate the thirty-pound credit note when they returned it to the store; she would take the credit note off his hands, leaving him with thirty pounds in cash and her with a credit note to blow the next time she needed a foot-spa or horrible shoes. Angus, like all teenagers, loved money with a fervour that amounted to lust.

'Okey-dokey, ladies,' she said brightly, returning to her girls. They'd been on the periphery of her vision throughout the transaction, giggling and jumping up and down. Marie wished she still giggled and jumped up and down when she was happy; maybe she'd try it the next time she finished a tricky pulpectomy.

'Look, Mum!'

Iris and Rose turned together to face their mother, who gasped. And not with joy.

'I said don't put on the make-up!' said Marie limply.

'Did you?' Iris bit her lip. Her cherry-red, glossy, outlined-in-purple lip.

'Sorry.' Rose fluttered her stiff, black, lumpy lashes and knotted her glittery brow.

'You're both orange,' said Marie.

'That's the fashion.' Iris turned her face to the left and to the right, so that her mother could admire the full easy-peeler effect.

'I couldn't make my mind up between the pink blusher stuff and the brown blusher glop, so I used them both.' Rose seemed pleased with the results of her experimentation.

'Let's get you home.' With a scant half-hour before her next patient, it would be a race to return the girls to Angus and make it back to Smile! in time. 'And let's just hope we don't meet anybody we know.' Marie flinched as they walked past mirrored pillars reflecting a dishevelled mother and two shrunken WAGs.

Head bent, burning with shame, Marie propelled her pungent charges (they'd gone bananas with the perfume testers) towards the exit. The brass revolving doors slowed as two adults stepped in on the other side. Lucy was chattering away happily to Mr Cassidy, the girls' headmaster, as the door swept Marie and the twins into it. Trapped in the corresponding half, Marie met Lucy's eye.

Really? Marie asked the universe, as she managed a lame hello. *I mean, really? Lucy?* And *the headmaster?*

Marie had never seen Lucy on the high street before. She'd never seen Mr Cassidy in any context except St Ethelred's. Now here they were *together*, their wholesome smiles freezing as they took in the two tiny hookers holding onto Marie's hands.

The door revolved twice with them all in it. All smiling. Especially the tiny hookers. Those tiny hookers thought it was truly hilarious.

With the phone shouldered against her ear, Marie made one last craven apology to the patient she was late for and stooped to pick up the package on her doorstep.

'Is it for me?' asked Iris hopefully.

'Of course not,' snapped Marie, adding with a tut: 'It's not even for me. It's addressed to . . . one of the neighbours.' As the girls lost interest, she followed them into the house, shouting, 'Don't disappear! I'm running a bath right now!'

Once all traces of make-up had been scrubbed away, Marie snatched up the package.

Pausing only to refresh her lipstick, curse her pot-belly and step into her best shoes, she trotted over the road with the parcel. Just as she was about to give up, after three rings at the doorbell brought no response, a shadow appeared beyond the glass door and Chloe, her head wrapped in a towel and her hands black to the wrists, opened the door.

'Oh God!' she said, flustered. 'I'm dyeing my hair.'

'Don't panic.' Marie held out the parcel. 'It's only this.'

Inky palms up, Chloe said, 'Could you take it up for me? They like me to leave deliveries on their bed. But I'll get *murdered* if I drip dye up there.'

'Well . . .' Marie gagged her conscience – good and tight. 'Of course.' This wasn't poking around her nemesis's home. Not at all. This was *helping Chloe*.

'Ta!' Chloe sped off into the house. 'Up the stairs! On your left.'

Stealing across carpet so soft it felt like moss beneath her feet, Marie climbed the staircase, drinking in every detail. Every detail was beautiful. This was a glorious house, with the sunlight stealing along the painted panelling in the hall, and an open door hinting at a sitting room full of velvet. She saw an antique wing-chair in blood-red leather and knew that it must be Tod's.

Hard to believe this house was the same basic design as the Dunwoody homestead opposite. It was exquisitely thought out and well finished, with none of the forgotten corners that she lived with, where skirting board suddenly ran out or a Hoover lurked forlorn and homeless.

Pushing open the door to Lucy and Tod's bedroom, Marie trespassed further.

What is *that colour?* The walls and blinds weren't pink, they were too pale to be pink; yet it was pinky, but not girly . . . Marie realised it was a fleshy, nude colour and thought how she would have shuddered if somebody had suggested it, and yet here it felt sumptuous and right.

A suede headboard in the same shade crawled halfway up the wall. Fitted wardrobes stood discreetly to attention, closed and correct. Marie thought of her own room – the mirror-image to this one. She visualised her discarded tights mating by the overflowing laundry basket, the jumble of toiletries on the chest of drawers, Robert's Y-fronts draped like grimy bunting over the chair.

Nothing in this room was out of place. Marie – the bad part of her, the part that watched *You've Been Framed* and laughed without conscience at old women falling through garden chairs – wanted the room to be stiff and offputting and Lucy-like, but she was too honest to pretend it was anything but sensuous and inviting. She wanted to lie on that bed and nap forever.

She put down the package carefully and backed away, noting that the Grays had two en suites.

Two.

The party that wasn't a party was going well, if you liked note-for-note reconstructions of the latest round of *Britain's Got Talent* performed by identical nine-year-olds.

Marie *did*.

Angus *didn't*.

The only one wearing a party hat, Marie had misjudged things badly and could see now that the catering teetered between kiddiewink and teen in a way that pleased nobody. Peanut-butter sandwiches had been a good idea; cutting them into flower shapes not so much. Angus had asked for burgers, but he hadn't asked for mini ones on pirate-themed paper plates. He and Joe had eaten nothing, muttering about going for a Maccy D later.

When she'd produced two cold bottles of beer, saying 'As you're sixteen now! Just the one each!', there had been a snigger she didn't care to analyse. The boys' body language was almost liquid, their limbs pooling over the sides of their chairs. Communication was by grunts and exhalations, a Neanderthal dialect that Marie couldn't fathom.

Alone in the utility room with her Frankenstein's rabbit, Marie saw it through Angus's eyes and wished with all her heart that she'd made a fruitcake. She was infantilising her son, willing him back to an uncomplicated time when she could protect him.

Birthday parties used to mean a scrum of boys in her kitchen, all squirting each other with juice and rubbing banana sandwiches in their hair. Now there was just Joe, and a clearly marked no-man's-land around the reason for the lack of personnel.

Marie's hand hovered over the cake. Where to put the candles? It seemed disrespectful to put them anywhere near the rabbit's bottom, and plain grotesque to have them poking out of his face. Plonking them on his buttercream chest would have to do.

'Here it comes!' She backed out of the utility room, awkwardly manoeuvring the outsize cake to the table.

There were whoops from the girls, and even Joe sat up, forgetting for a moment that he was a cool sixteen-year-old and looking like a little boy in the glow of the candles. Angus, however, stared past the cake and out through the kitchen window.

'Who invited *her*?' he demanded.

'Happy birthday, darling!' said Marie, rushing to the door to let in Chloe.

And Lucy.

'Hello! Hello!' Lucy was beaming, her sun-kissed cheeks taut like windfall apples. 'You're so kind to let us join in Angus's birthday!'

There was no acceptable way to say 'But I didn't mean *you*!' to a smiling woman holding a prettily wrapped present on your doorstep, so Marie answered her beam with a beam, and her nemesis was over her threshold.

As Lucy, an unexploded bomb in a pastel sundress, moved through the hall and into the kitchen, Marie saw – as if magnified and set to dramatic music – the damp patch on the ceiling, the cracked tiles behind the sink, the shape that her thighs made in her chinos. If she'd known Lucy was coming she'd have spring-cleaned, redecorated, cut Angus's hair, vacuumed the dog, burned the whole house to the ground and started again.

'Hi, guys!' Lucy was a masterclass in understated elegance. Those flashes of brilliance at her ears were real diamonds; those buttery stripes in her hair were not the handiwork of Kool Kutz on the high street. Whatever Tod did when he roared off in that Merc every morning, he was a breadwinner on an impressive scale. 'What a lovely kitchen!' She looked around her. 'So homely.'

Even a novice at suburban bitchery knew that was code for 'messy'.

'You've brought a cake,' said Marie, proud of herself for not shouting this fact.

'Yes. Nothing spesh. Just my weekly bake.' Lucy plonked down a fruitcake. 'Oh, look! A lovely bunny!' She went into raptures about the cake – how delicious it looked, how adorable. Turning to Iris, she asked, 'Did you make it, sweetheart?'

'No, she didn't.' Marie's high-pitched voice startled her children. 'I made it.'

'Oh . . .' Lucy's beam widened, stiffened. 'May I have a slice?'

Marie had to admit that her wincing daughters had a point: it *was* macabre to slice up a bunny. Particularly when Iris asked for an eye on her portion. She appreciated Angus's diplomacy in tasting a sliver of the rabbit cake first; later he'd devour that fruitcake, like Prinny with a torn bin-bag.

Her birdlike head to one side, Lucy asked Angus countless questions about his birthday, his summer, the coming term. Marie felt for her son, struggling to answer Lucy fully enough to qualify as polite, but vaguely enough to protect his privacy. Did Lucy subject Chloe to this kind of interrogation, she wondered? Poor girl. Beside Angus,

Joe sank further into his seat, forking rabbit ear into his mouth, fearful that he'd be next for the middle-aged-woman inquisition.

'We got you this.' Chloe abruptly held out a package.

'Right,' said Angus, accepting it.

'I think the expression you're groping for is *Thank you*,' said Marie tartly, willing her son not to show her up in front of this poor man's Felicity Kendal.

'Thank you,' said Angus obediently, his cheeks pink. His mum knew it was shyness that chased his manners away, but his mum also knew that Lucy would revel in every slip and gaffe. The memory of the revolving-door pile-up of child-sluts, nemeses and headmasters was still fresh enough to induce a whole-body cringe. 'Cool!' Angus's intonation had changed – brightened – as he examined the gift. 'I really, really need an external mic. Thanks. Look, Joe!'

'Cool,' concurred Joe.

'That's so generous, Lucy,' said Marie. 'Thank you.'

'I used *my* money,' said Chloe suddenly, as if vomiting the words.

Angus's face closed down again. A twin nudged another twin. Lucy changed the subject.

Teenagers, Marie concluded as she cleared up around them, freshened drinks and responded to Lucy's genteel chit-chat, *are a non-stop soap opera*. Chloe watched Angus hungrily; Angus ignored her; Joe never took his eyes off Chloe. Why couldn't people want the people who wanted them? She felt for all three of them, each one a brave little boat setting off into the choppy hormonal seas of young adulthood.

Iris had instigated her favourite game of asking, 'What's your favourite . . . ?' She canvassed everybody's favourite colour, smell, cow name, before asking Chloe, 'Who's your favourite boy?'

As Chloe pulled blue-black hair over her face, Marie waded in to save her. 'I've got a better one.' She nodded at Angus. 'As the birthday boy is a film freak, let's all choose our favourite scene from a film.'

'That's easy!' said Lucy. 'The end of *Gone with the Wind*.'

'The end of what?' asked Joe.

'Is it about blowing off?' asked Rose.

'Shut up!' said Angus. 'It's a brilliant old film about the civil war in America. It had Clark Gable and Vivien Leigh in it.'

'You really are a film buff.' Lucy was impressed. Marie hoped her son's film knowledge would go in the file, too. 'It's very romantic. The heroine is trying to convince the hero to stay, but he walks out and leaves her there, sobbing.'

'That doesn't sound romantic,' said Rose.

'Couldn't he just buy her flowers or something?' said Iris.

'Love's not always about flowers,' said Lucy.

'I like the bit in *Toy Story*,' said Rose loudly (that she was a loud child was something the Dunwoodys had learned to live with, although sometimes it still surprised Marie that the child honking her order in Pizza Express was one of her own), 'you know, the bit where thingy does that thing.'

'Yes, that *is* a good scene.' Marie shared an amused look with Angus, grateful that he was warming up a little. 'My favourite scene from a film is when the wedding choir sings "Love Is All Around" in *Love Actually*.' She stared into the middle distance, mourning for the briefest of moments that no man had ever bribed a choir to sing a love-song for her. 'Chloe,' she said, drawing the girl into the conversation, as her stepmother obviously had no intention of doing so, 'what's *your* absolute favouritest scene?'

'Um . . .' said Chloe. Then she said, 'Er . . .' and pulled her hair in front of her face again, like blackout curtains. 'I can't think,' she said in a small voice. 'Not when everybody's looking at me.'

The boys exchanged a look best translated as *Typical girl*.

Lucy licked the fork she'd been using to sample Marie's cake. Marie braced herself for unsolicited advice, but instead her guest winced and put her hand to her cheek.

Oh God! Marie's stomach plummeted. *I dropped something in the cake.*

But no. 'This damn tooth at the back,' said Lucy prettily, 'it twinges every now and then. I really do need to get it seen to.'

'Well, you know where to go.' Iris looked up from the rug where she was kissing Prinny's feet.

'I certainly do,' smiled Lucy. 'That new dentist near the station looks amazing. Might get my teeth whitened while I'm there.'

A car horn beeped a three-note tune outside and Lucy

jumped to her feet, hoicking her bag onto her shoulder. 'Chloe! Up-up-up, darling!'

Chloe, as slothful as Lucy was urgent, unfolded her black-clad limbs. 'Thanks,' she said to the room in general.

'See you at school,' said Joe, trying to toss his hair, but forgetting that it was stiff with gel.

'Thanks so much – been lovely, must-do-it-again, come *on*, Chloe.' Lucy grabbed at the emptied cake tin held out by Marie.

Lingering at the front door, Marie watched Lucy scuttle across the road, scattering endearments and welcomes towards Tod's car. She pulled the door open for him, gazing delightedly on him as he stepped out, kissing him as if he was back from war. 'Darling!' she breathed. 'Welcome home!'

As Chloe caught Marie's eye and mimed puking, Lucy took Tod's briefcase from him, awkwardly cramming the cake tin under her arm, and preceded him into the house, looking behind her as if anxious that Tod might trip and stub a cherished tootsie.

'OK, boys,' Marie released her prisoners as she closed the front door. 'Party's over. You're free to go.'

With insultingly obvious relief, Angus and Joe darted from the kitchen. The twins, too, dissolved into the ether, as people tend to do when there's clearing up to be done. As the woman of the house, Marie couldn't dodge that ball and began the tedious business of scraping plates and loading the dishwasher.

There wasn't a speck of rabbit cake left. She felt a nuclear glow of satisfaction travel to the ends of her limbs.

The squint in his liquorice eye hadn't put them off. She'd baked, if not a show-stopper, then a *crowd-pleaser*.

And part of that crowd had been Lucy, baker *par excellence*, baker *extraordinaire* – and other French terms Marie couldn't recall just now. She paused mid-scrape – Chloe had nibbled one tiny slice; Angus had dived straight into the fruitcake after one fragment; Joe had politely eaten one portion; and the twins had shared an ear.

Which meant that Lucy had demolished the rest of the rabbit. Scraping again, Marie assumed that, along with the pricey jewellery and haircare, her neighbour also had a top-of-the-range tapeworm. There was no other way to consume such quantities of cake and stay so slender.

The scraping took on a savage edge as Marie remembered Lucy's remarks about the new dentist. All these years of living opposite each other and the woman hadn't even bothered to find out that Marie was a dentist!

Comfortable on her high horse – the view was nice from up there – Marie didn't linger on the fact *she* had no idea what *Tod* did for a living.

A car growled to a halt on the gravel outside. As an experiment, Marie trotted out, sweet expression on her face, to give her husband the Lucy treatment.

Seeing her smiling broadly, her head on one side, Robert backed away. When she held out her hand for his bag, he clutched it to his chest like a shield. 'Stop it!' he said, disturbed.

'Have you had a wonderful day, darlingest darling?' she simpered.

'You're scaring me: what have you done with my wife?'

Robert retreated with every step Marie took, until he was flattened against the car. They fought briefly, hand-to-hand, until Marie wrenched the bag away from him.

'I'm being the perfect wife,' she snapped.

'You're being bloody weird.' Robert gave her a wide berth on his way into the house.

'OK, no more geisha, I promise.' She took pity on him, and then, after a second look at her husband's expression as he tugged off his tie, took real pity on him. 'Robert, what's wrong?'

Robert stopped, mid-tug. 'Caroline got her bin.'

The first morning of the new school year wasn't the new leaf Marie had planned.

A Mary Berry breakfast would involve, she felt sure, granola, freshly squeezed juice, calmness. In the spirit of her mentor, she'd combed the Internet (i.e. checked out one BBC food website) to find a granola-bar recipe. The resulting bars did look a little grim, but they didn't deserve to be described as 'like something you'd get in a Middle Earth prison'. Once Robert had said that, Iris and Rose rebelled and bayed for Coco Pops. The juice she'd squeezed before going to bed had been glugged in one go by Robert, during a midnight swoop of the fridge.

'Ang-*us*!' Marie hollered up the stairs and stalked back to the kitchen. 'If I had a pound for every time I have to shout that boy's name . . .'

'And if I had a pound,' said Robert, rubbing at a yoghurt stain on a twin's hairband, 'for every time you say *If I had a pound*.'

'Will you have PE today?' Having cleared a space on the worktop among the slagheap of receipts, buttons, elastic bands, the nude cardboard middle of a kitchen roll, a glittery pen, an iPhone, a Hello Kitty hairclip and a half-eaten Crunchie, Marie wrote out name tags for the girls' kit. *How*, she asked herself, *could I misspell my own child's name?* Apparently the new trainers belonged to somebody called Irsi.

Even Mary Berry would be tempted to walk away and lob a grenade over her shoulder.

'It's rocket-shaped,' said Robert sadly, turning from the twin/yoghurt situation to deal with the burning-toast-trapped-in-toaster situation.

'Eh?' Marie realised he was talking about Caroline's bin. Still. After more than twelve hours he had not exhausted it as a topic. Bundling Aertex shirts into drawstring bags, she said, 'I know, love. And it has a capacity of thirty-six litres. And a hand-operated stainless-steel lid. And if I'm not mistaken, the fire-resistant, galvanised-metal body has a powder-coated exterior.'

'There is also,' said Robert wistfully, 'a plastic bottom ring.'

'Furthermore,' said Marie, keen to get this over with, 'it's the first time in four years Magda has OK-ed a requisition form for office equipment.' As long as he didn't start banging on about the guarantee, she could hold it together, she thought, writing *Iris Wundoody* on a label.

'And then of course you've got a five-year guaran—'

'ANGUS!'

Marie moved to the bottom of the stairs. Dunwoody

tradition decreed that she drove her children to school on the first day of every term: at this rate they'd *all* be late.

'AN-GUS!'

She'd tried calling her son all ways. Cajoling: *Please come down.* Concerned: *Are you all right up there?* Cheerful: *Come on down!* Thanks to Robert's bin-monologue, she'd reached *furious* faster than usual.

'Time for the stomp, d'you think?' whispered Robert to Iris and Rose, who both nodded.

'Right!' yelled Marie, stomping up the stairs. 'That's it!' What *it* was, she was unsure; it was probably illegal to shoot your own child for ignoring you, even if, m'lud, there were sixteen years' worth of similar offences to take into account.

'I'm coming in,' said Marie pompously, well aware that she looked and sounded silly. She hesitated. Storming into boys' bedrooms could be unrewarding for both mother and son alike. She rattled the door knob. 'This is me,' she said, 'very much coming in!'

The room was dark and muggy, a sampler of all the smells you don't want to smell ever again. Tearing open the curtains, her fury redoubled. 'You're not even out of bed!'

Wound up in his duvet, Angus burrowed further down into it. 'I'm not well,' he said.

'What's the matter with you?' Marie delved in, located his forehead and felt it. 'You're fine,' she said, not needing her medical degree to diagnose School-itis when she saw it. 'Please get up, love. I'll be black-balled out of the Mothers' Union if you lot are late on your first day back, and I have an incredibly hard day ahead of me.'

No movement from the larva.

'Angus Dunwoody, if you're not out of that bed in one minute flat I'll—'

'All right! God-uh!' Angus, fit as a flea, was on his feet.

'Good. At last.' Marie was relieved she hadn't had to finish her ultimatum.

Downstairs, eyeing their son as he pushed away a granola bar and reached for a cereal bowl, Marie said to Robert, 'He's never done that before. I suspect Joe pretends to be ill to get out of school, but not Angus.'

'Hmm?' Robert came out of a reverie, plonked down his mug and kissed her. 'Even geeks have their off-days. If only he knew,' he said, holding Marie close to him, his voice in her ear, 'how much we'd give to change places with him.'

It was nice, this clinch. Robert smelled good close up, of soap and bristles and *him*.

'Urrgh, get a room, you two!' Since Rose had heard the phrase, she used it at every opportunity.

Pulling away, Robert said, 'Did I tell you how much the bin cost?'

'For heaven's sake, Robert!' Marie banged the dishwasher shut, as if everything was its fault. 'You told me how much *delivery* cost.'

With mere seconds to go before the neurotic twitter of the bell, Marie had dropped her children off at St Ethelred's gates. Despite the un-Berry nature of the morning, they were all in clean underwear, with full tummies and new pencil cases.

'First round of the day to me!' Marie raised her arms in triumph after slowing at the lights.

A massive poster loomed on the side of a building to her right.

'Everybody deserves a Hollywood smile!' it shouted, above a bewilderingly long list of the wonders on offer at the new practice.

'Ding-ding. Round two,' whispered Marie.

TO: stargazinggirl247@gmail.com
FROM: geeksrus39@gmail.com
02.09.13
19.14
SUBJECT: INGRID BERGMAN

Soulmate

Sometimes you – yes you! Shock horror! – are wrong about things. e.g. my so called party. It didn't turn out fine like you said. It turned out K-E-R-A-P.

Aren't mums supposed to know their kids inside out? How come mine doesn't know I'd rather set fire to my arse than have a party? She even invited The Goth Girl Across The Road. Mum is soooo lame. She's determined to set us up and she thinks she's being dead sly. She's not as lame as the Goth Girl tho. She couldn't even come up with a favourite film scene. Bet if I asked you you'd have like a million. She even said she couldn't think if we all looked at her?!! WTF?

Joe chose a violent scene obviously. We never got round to me which is just as well cos Joe would have been shocked. Theres no way he'd know Cary Grant. Remember we talked about it (OK OK emailed about it)? Ages ago? It's called 'Notorious'.

Cary Grant is rescuing Ingrid Bergman (big bird, hot, Swedish I think) from a house full of nazi baddies. He picks her up and carries her cos they've drugged her. None of the nazis want to make the first move, cos there are members of the public about and he's walking past them with Ingrid in his arms. She's terrified so he says to her 'Keep your eyes on mine. Keep looking at me'. And he keeps going and the tension is frigging unbearable but they stare into each other's eyes the whole time and Cary rescues her right from under the bad guys' noses and they drive away.

Big letters – T H E E N D.

Maybe you had to be there . . .

Remember you said *it'll be cool by the time school starts again*?

You've never been wrong-er.

Running away feels like a good idea. Maybe I could run to Scotland? The Clones don't do running (heels too high) so they wouldn't follow me there.

laters

Angus

P.S. Do you know Mary Berry? Some old woman, right? I think she's started a cult and my Mum's joined it.

P.P.S. What *is* your favourite scene from a movie?

NOVEMBER

Fireworks Night

Bonfire Cake

Dear Granny Gaynor,

How are you? I am fine. We are looking forward to the fireworks and we made a guy using an old dress Mummy doesn't wear any more. Well only for parties and weddings. We stuffed it with paper and put extra in the bum.

In a way its nearly christmas so if youre sitting there crying because you don't know what to buy me I can help! I desperately need a Barbie Dream House. Seriously, I could die if I don't get one and Mum keeps saying that we need to do our belts up tighter which means something about not buying your daughters IMPORTANT THINGS.

When will you visit us? Please come soon and show us your ghost costume. Daddy told us all about your new job haunting houses.

lots of love

Iris xoxoxoxox

With appointments backing up, Marie didn't really have the time to inch through reception holding Jonas Handler's arm as he took the baby-steps of old age. Passing her next patient poring over Victoria Beckham's lack of cellulite in *OK!*, Marie mouthed *Sorry* as she stepped over a baby on the rug.

'Here we go,' she said encouragingly. Jonas's arm felt like a bundle of twigs through his sleeve. He smelled of soap; Marie knew he made an effort for his trips to the surgery and hoped it wasn't the highlight of his month. She hoped there was a kind face and a soft voice waiting at home, but she suspected there wasn't. 'Nearly there.'

She was a woman of urges. Very often these urges involved digging out *Dirty Dancing*, or jumping her husband as he put away the leaf-blower, but today she had an urge to tell this old chap that he was valued, and to tell the bored young mum tapping away on her phone to cherish these years when her child was a tot. She had an urge to go further, to tell Jonas that he was their favourite patient, and to warn the mum that before she knew it, the dimpled cutie-pie at her feet would be keeping secrets and that their shared vocabulary would have at-rophied.

She fought these urges, though, because she was a dentist, not a therapist.

Hesitating at the step, Jonas steadied himself and set off, solo, down the high street. Marie glanced over the road.

Up and running for almost two months, Perfect You didn't look like Marie's idea of a dental practice. On a gigantic flat screen in the window, film stars and TV personalities smiled toothily on an endless loop, their dazzling airbrushed images interspersed with a long menu of the procedures offered.

Inside (she'd sent Lynda to snoop) was a reception area that aped a boutique hotel, with plush purple sofas and a curved chrome desk. The receptionist who opened up each morning wore a white overall – if a mundane word like 'overall' could do justice to such a short, tight, low-cut outfit. With a face full of slap, and teeth so whitened she could guide ships safely home to port, the poor girl was a porn caricature of a dental receptionist.

Nothing about Perfect You suggested it was a place where trained professionals carried out medical proce-dures. The head honcho had yet to be glimpsed, although Marie saw his convertible parked outside most days. She wondered what kind of person starts a rival business bang opposite the competition, before glancing at her own cheerful but low-budget sign and wondering if he took Smile! seriously enough for it to qualify as competition. So far there'd been little impact on her turnover, but Marie was shrewd enough to realise that Perfect You's cosmetic-led approach held enormous appeal for young adults weaned on modern media, who watched their celebrity heroes and heroines alter their features as casually as they changed their underwear. It was only a matter of time before her takings were affected, and Marie, with her habit of meeting trouble halfway, had begun to make small changes in the family's expenditure.

Any cost-cutting had to be discreet. Robert was already engulfed in career confusion: if he spotted financial storm clouds, it might affect the decisions he was already struggling with. As long as she could, Marie would protect her husband's poignant need to be all-powerful Papa Bear and, if push came to shove, she'd sell her car.

Her beloved, beaten-up car.

And when Robert asked why?

Some bridges could be crossed when she came to them.

Waving at Jonas as he reached the crossing, then turning back to her own domain, to the very specific sound of a gyrating toddler falling into a handbag and the resultant fuss, Marie wondered how Jonas might fare in the clinic across the road. And would they charge for steaming baby-sick off the velvet sofa?

Robert had various vague plans in his head for the far-off distant time when he finally retired. Maybe he would take the safari he'd fantasised about since his first *Tarzan* film, or possibly he'd take up scuba-diving. One thing was for sure: he would find out who invented open-plan offices, track him down and slowly torture him to death by forcing him to listen to an endless loop of other people's inconsequential phone conversations.

Robert missed his old office. It had been a happy little hutch: just him, a desk, a chair and a stash of Crunchies. He'd been able to close the door on office babble, to snatch a snooze or have a damned good phone row with Marie. Now he was on show all day, in an arctic tundra dotted with white desks and white chairs and the odd triffid-like pot plant. Thus exposed, he sat up straight, kept personal phone calls to a minimum and couldn't so much as finger the wrapper of a Fun Size without noses twitching all around him and a chorus of 'Ooh, can I have one?'

If he was back in the hutch (he remembered how it smelled – Mr Sheen and central heating), he wouldn't have to listen to Caroline and Magda's conversation about their recent night out. Magda, perched on Caroline's desk, swinging a booted foot, was pulling apart a muffin in that way some women did, tearing little nuggets between manicured fingers. Robert scarfed down muffins whole, and wanted to yell at Magda *Eat it! Just bloody eat the bloody thing!*

It was *his* home-made muffin, however, so he didn't yell. He simply tried to bask in the sunny warmth of his boss enjoying his muffin. (He'd been surprised to find a Paul Hollywood recipe for muffins; surprised and, yes, a little disappointed – that such a bluff, straight-talking northern bloke had used his beefy hands to bake *blueberry muffins*.) Hard to bask, though, when you're trying to create a complex spreadsheet, and two women are cackling about waiters' arses just two feet from your desk.

'And the size of his pepper mill!' groaned Caroline.

Magda, who would never groan in front of her serfs, tore another clod of muffin and included Robert with a casual, 'Where do you go when you go out, Robert? Do you have any hot tips for us?'

Taking in Caroline's thwarted look – she *hated* sharing Magda – Robert leaned back casually, slid down rather too far on his glossy chair, then sat up hastily while pretending that was what he'd meant to do all along and said, 'Staying in is the new going out, Magda.'

He could almost hear Marie's shout of *HORSE SHIT!*

'Really?' Magda swung her body towards him.

'Oh yeah.' Now that he had Magda's attention, Robert had no idea what to do with it; like Prinny that time he'd stolen a sanitary towel. 'We entertain a lot.' That wasn't a lie, if Mrs Gnome popping in for a toasted sandwich counted as entertaining. 'Very casual, very laid-back.' He remembered Mrs Gnome farting as she left. 'Just chillin'.' Thank God Marie was miles away; she would *never* let him live down that dropped 'g'.

'Lovely,' said Magda approvingly. 'Good honest family fun, yeah?'

'Exactly that,' said Robert serenely.

'When's the next glittering occasion?'

'Um . . .' Robert panicked slightly. 'Oh, yes, that would be our famous Fireworks Night party.' It *was* famous, he told his outraged conscience: if you were Robert or Marie or one of the kids, it was famous. 'It's a hell of a night.' Yes, that was true, it *was* hellish. Baked potatoes with hard centres; Marie neurotically screaming for him to *DEAR GOD! GET BACK!* as he approached the fireworks with a match; Prinny fright-pooing extravagantly at each bang. 'Technicolour rockets against a velvet sky.' Maybe he was having a stroke, he thought. He literally couldn't stop. 'The happy laughter of children. And, of course, banging tunes.' Banging tunes. He'd never said that before in his life and had hoped he'd reach his death before ever saying it. 'Everyone's invited.'

'Aw, thanks!' Caroline perked up, as the evil are wont to do when their innocent victims walk slap-bang into a trap. 'I'll be there. How about you, Magda?'

'Wouldn't miss it for the world.' Magda crinkled her eyes and stood up to squeeze Robert's shoulder. She aimed the muffin-wrapper at the bin and shouted, 'Let's do some work, people, *per-lease*!' to nobody in particular.

Staring at the spreadsheet, seeing past it – seeing the face of his wife when he plucked up the courage to tell her – Robert talked himself down. 'It'll be fine,' he told himself. 'Marie will be fine about it.'

'Are you mad? Have you gone mad? You have. You've gone mad, you . . . madman.'

Marie was not fine about it.

'What were you *on*? Magda? Bloody Magda with her Manolos and her high-maintenance hair? In our garden where the fence has half-fallen down and the swingball's been on its side since September?' Marie wished vehemently that they were at home and not at the school parents' evening. She wanted to shout and slam doors, but being in the queue for the headmaster's office meant she had to content herself with a hushed growl. Later, she promised herself, she would twat him with a tea towel or throw a Yakult at him. 'Dear God,' she hissed, 'we'll have to repaper the downstairs loo!'

Another couple emerged from Mr Cassidy's inner sanctum and Robert, Marie and the girls shuffled forward a pace or two. Marie slumped against the wall, seeing her lovely relaxed and shambolic Fireworks Night morph into a very different beast, one requiring catering, planning, extensive hoovering and a dog-nappy.

'Don't worry, Mum,' said Iris, sucking the cuff of her cardigan. 'We'll help.'

'I won't,' said Rose.

'We should . . . um, invite other people too,' said Robert. 'I kind of implied it was a big deal.'

'Lied your stupid head off, you mean,' said Marie, repeating '*Implied!*' in a bitter undertone. She took in Robert's bowed head, the studious way he examined a flyer for after-school bouncercise and knew he was waiting for the storm to blow over. She could already feel her umbrage deflating; it was showy but short-lived. It had been a stroke of genius to tell her at parents' evening; it's hard to murder your husband in front of your children's teachers. Plus he had the advantage that her head was already spinning from their brood's polarised reports.

The twins were, according to their teachers, 'mature', 'capable', 'confident'. Marie sensed that the maths tutor wanted to add *and bloody scary*. In short, the girls were doing fine, hitting their marks, integrating well with their classmates and laying the foundations for the day when they would rule the known world.

Angus, however, had his elders and betters scratching their heads. His grades were down, but not dramatically. He was a little quieter in class – 'Although,' his form master said, 'with Angus that's hard to gauge.' All of them noticed a change in the boy; none could put their finger on it.

'Aha!' Robert waved, looking past Marie. 'Two possibles for the party!'

Her lips mewing to form a no, Marie rearranged them to form a 'Hi!' as Tod and Lucy, arm-in-arm like well-dressed Siamese twins, joined them.

'You look *lovely*,' said Lucy.

Aware that she didn't look lovely, having rushed straight from the clinic with her hair in disarray and livid red marks from her goggles across her nose, Marie said, 'Thanks, so do you,' which was the only possible riposte. Besides, it was true. Lucy's pale face glowed, the end of her nose a dainty pink, her eyes sparkling. She seemed genuinely excited to be in an over-lit school corridor that smelled faintly of Brussels sprouts on a sleety November evening.

'We're hearing great things about our Chloe,' said Lucy happily.

'Well, darling, to be fair, it's not all great.' Tod pulled a wry face.

'It never is,' said Robert sympathetically. He was never drawn into parental boasting/criticising; *they is what they is* was his take on his three. 'But, listen, are you two free on Fireworks Night? We're having a get-together.'

'Have we anything sorted out for Bonfire Night, darling?' Tod looked down at his wife, so much smaller than him, as if she'd been designed to make him look dominant and sexy. And it was working.

'Um . . . nothing – nope.' Lucy smiled. 'We'll be there!' Then, with the inevitability of night following day, she asked, 'Can I bring anything?'

'No,' said Marie a little too fast, tempering it with: 'You're a guest, I'm going to spoil you, not put you to work!'

'Well, I might make a little something, just in case!'

As the talk turned back to the teachers, Marie tuned out, wondering if Robert ever listened to her. Perhaps he just heard a distant quacking when she opened her mouth. Or perhaps it all came out in Flemish and he'd disabled his sub-title option. Because by now he really should know that, if you lined up all the people in the world whom she didn't want to invite to the party – including Hitler and Robert's mother – Lucy would still be right at the very back.

Probably holding a cake. *Just in case.*

At a lull in conversation, Lucy said, over-brightly, 'How *do* you tell your girls apart?'

'Everybody asks that,' said Rose.

'Don't be rude, darling,' said Marie, silently cheering her daughter for outing Lucy as a tedious small-talker. 'It's not that hard . . . You see, Iris has— Angus!' Marie broke off as her son ambled past. Should she kiss him? Best not to, she thought, as he dragged himself over to them. His face displayed that horrible anxiety that children suffer from when their family are on school property, as if his mum and dad were bombs stuffed with embarrassing anecdotes that could go off at any moment.

'Hi. Hi, Mrs Gray, Mr Gray.'

'Tuck your shirt in,' said Marie, suddenly seeing him through the Grays' eyes.

'Mu-um,' grumbled Angus, doing as he was told.

'What's this?' Marie peered at a graze on Angus's forehead, proprietarily sweeping aside his curls as she'd been doing since he first grew them. 'When did that happen?'

'It's nothing.' Angus shook his hair, like a horse refusing a bridle. 'P.E. I fell.'

A girl his age swept up behind him, her one-sided ponytail bobbing, and stuck her arm through his. 'Is this Mummy and Daddy? Aren't you going to introduce us?'

The colour that flooded Angus's face was hard to describe. On a Farrow & Ball chart it might be 'Cheeks of a Devonshire Virgin'. 'Well . . .'

'I'm Lauren,' said the girl, her confidence as high as her hemline. She lifted her chin and smiled at each one in turn. 'Should be interesting hearing what Mr C has to say about Angus here.' She chucked his cheek as he hung his head.

Awww, said Lucy's expression. She winked at Marie, who smiled, but didn't share the sentiment. A thought ricocheted back and forth between her antennae and Robert's: *Is this the unwanted admirer who texted all through the summer?*

'He'll say,' Lauren put on a gruff voice, imitating the headmaster, 'Angus Dunwoody is a young man who gets what he wants. Who won't take no for an answer.'

'Will he?' asked Robert, surprised.

'Oh yeah. Just ask the girls in his year. A right ladykiller, your son,' said Lauren, wiggling so that Angus, wedged against her, wiggled too as he stared at the floor, head hanging like an exhausted tortoise.

'Ladykiller?' Marie reappraised her son rapidly. Angus's private life was just that. He and this Lauren had a history she knew nothing about. She hoped he hadn't led the girl on, or taken advantage . . . Marie immediately chastised herself for even suspecting her boy of such behaviour.

'You bet!' laughed Lauren, planting a kiss on Angus's blazing cheek.

'Ooh!' said Iris, thrilled beyond measure.

'In *school*?' boggled Rose, mirroring her mother's thought exactly.

Lauren disentangled herself and bade them all the kind of full and polite goodbye that Angus could never manage.

As she sauntered off, Lucy broke the silence with a 'Seems like a nice girl', with sufficient edge to her tone to suggest that she found the short skirt and nosestud a little challenging.

Tod nudged Angus and somehow the teenager's embarrassment found an even deeper level to descend to. 'Something you want to tell us, mate?'

'She's just . . .' said Angus. 'She's nobody.'

'A nobody who kisses you goodbye,' said Tod, obviously amused, and obviously unwilling to let it go.

'I'll . . . you know . . .' Angus waved a hand in no particular direction and sloped off.

'Boys will be boys,' said Lucy.

'Hmm,' said Marie.

*

Inserting wrapped instruments into the vacuum steriliser, Marie called out, *'Aileen!'* This was part of Aileen's job description: Marie was, to quote her nana, keeping a dog and barking herself. 'Get in here and take over!'

It was the first empty appointment slot in a week or so. The pessimist in Marie heard a faint alarm bell drawing attention to the damage that Perfect You would eventually do to her business. Her optimistic side (a far more likeable but unreliable beast: it was Optimistic Marie who bought jeggings without trying them on) saw it as an opportunity to do some sterilising.

'Mmn gnf!' shouted Aileen.

She sounded happy. And her mouth sounded full.

'Nooo!' Like a tigress defending her young, Marie tore out to reception in time to see one of the thirty Flakes she'd bought (and hidden) disappearing into Aileen's mouth. 'You're like a truffle-hound!' she groaned, amazed by her assistant's cheek and, it had to be said, *skill*. The Flakes had been in a plain bag, right at the top of the cupboard that housed only the electricity meter and Marie's pristine, unworn gym kit. 'Stop!' she barked, as Aileen reached out a hand to take another Flake. 'Drop it,' she ordered, crouching to take the bag, her eye on Aileen's stubby hand. 'Drop it! Sit!'

Aileen sat, thwarted and unhappy. 'I love a nice Flake,' she said sullenly.

'And I love a nice George Clooney, but I wouldn't just grab him and unwrap him without asking,' said Marie, bundling up her chocolate hoard. 'These are for my bonfire cake. For the party you *have to come to*,' she ended, with a hint of threat absent from most invitations.

'Bonfire cake?' Lynda, who'd been contentedly googling 'how to sue a marquee company', lifted her head. 'You said you're practising my croquembouche this week.'

'Oh, I am,' said Marie. 'I've made . . . ooh, about three now.' She hoped she hadn't gone red.

'Why have you gone red?' asked Aileen, swallowing the last of her contraband.

'Because I'm allergic to *thieves*,' snapped Marie, widening her eyes in warning.

'It's him!' Lynda stood and pointed out of the bay window.

'Who him?' asked Marie.

'"Perfect You" him!' hissed Lynda.

Jumping out of his open-top sports car without recourse to the door, the white-coated man just had to be Perfect You's owner. His whites had little in common with Marie's baggy coverall; his were bespoke, and a touch tight. In his hand he held an extravagant clutch of red roses. With a sweeping look up and down the street, he jogged towards Smile!

'He's coming over!' squeaked Lynda, stowing her half-drunk coffee in a desk drawer.

'Bastard!' said Aileen, her braids quivering in their tight circles.

'Ladies!' The new dentist in town was among them, throwing open the door as if sweeping onto a stage. Removing his mirrored sunglasses with a flourish, he looked at each one in turn. 'You must be my deadly rivals,' he said, adding, with what he evidently meant to be gallantry, 'I had no idea you'd all be so beautiful.'

Wassock, thought Marie, well aware that no woman in the history of the world had been called beautiful while wearing the plastic apron and gloves necessary for instrument sterilisation. 'We didn't give you any thought at all!' she responded with enormous amounts of what she termed 'sass' when the twins used it.

The newcomer bowed and held out the roses. 'A peace offering,' he said. 'For daring to trespass on your turf.'

It would take more than roses to make up for his trespass if the clinic went down the tubes. But, hey, it was a nice gesture, so Marie took the flowers and thanked him, noticing that he was wearing a shade of fake tan best described as 'Dirty Protest'. 'Thank you,' she said, graciously. 'How's it going over there?'

'Amaaaazing!' The dentist widened eyes that were rather small – little more than pinpricks of blue in the sweaty Serengeti of his face. With a snub nose and a selection of chins, he was no oil painting, but an insanely high level of grooming lent him a low-grade glamour. 'Beyond my wildest expectations!' He waggled eyebrows of such strict symmetry that they *had* to be waxed. 'I'm Klay, by the way. Klay with a K!'

'You're what?' Aileen pulled a face. 'What with a what? I thought for a minute there you said "clay".'

'I did,' said Klay. 'I said Klay with a K.'

'Klay Witherkay?' said Aileen.

'Before we go completely Dr Seuss,' said Marie, 'let me introduce my team. I'm Marie.'

'But of course!' Klay clapped his hands together. 'The boss!'

'And this is Lynda, who keeps our show on the road.'

'Lynda, Lynda, Lynda!' Klay misread her completely by blowing her a kiss, and Lynda turned back to her screen with the demeanour of Queen Victoria.

'Last but not least . . .' Marie found herself, just this once, happily anticipating Aileen's apocalyptic reaction to the male sex. 'This is our Aileen.'

'A beautiful name,' said Klay gravely, 'for a beeyootiful woman.'

Hunching her shoulders slightly, Marie braced herself.

'Thank you,' said Aileen.

Un-hunching, Marie felt the world tilt. Not only had Aileen neglected to grapple Klay to the floor, but she was smiling at him. Not an evil smile, not a sinister smile, not the smile of somebody who has stolen a Flake, just a smile. The woman was transformed and, despite the curled sausage plaits and the chocolate on her chin, she was . . . lovely.

Aileen's eyes shone and her lips parted and two rose-coloured smudges budded on her cheeks. 'Have a cup of tea with us,' she said, in a voice that made Lynda look up from her gift list. It was a gentle Irish brogue, lyrical and tender and poetic. 'Please,' she added.

Lynda and Marie locked eyes. They'd assumed Aileen had never learned the word.

Seated with a cup – the *best* cup, Marie noted, although at Smile! that meant a mug proclaiming *World's Best Grandma* – Klay expounded his theory about success in business. Nobody had asked him to – he was simply a natural expounder.

'It's dog eat dog,' he said, tiny eyes a-glow. 'I mean, I could have held back, found another premises when I realised there was a thriving dentist already in the area, but I believe in survival of the fittest. That may sound harsh, but I couldn't turn down the fabuloso deal on the premises. I got it for a song.' Fluttering his dyed lashes, he said earnestly, 'I admire women who make it in business. I'm a feminist, you could say.'

'Oh, Marie's not a woman,' said Aileen, in her new lilt. 'She's all balls. Like a bloke.'

A misguided compliment, but a sweet one, particularly in the wake of Klay's condescending nod to feminism. 'You don't have to explain yourself to us, Klay.'

Raising his mug, Klay toasted her. 'May the best man – or woman – win!'

'How long,' asked Aileen, her eyes travelling up and down Klay as if he were an untended mint Magnum, 'have you been in the old dentisting game? Are you like this fool here?' She jerked a thumb at her boss. 'Wanted to do it since you were a kiddie?'

Left to her own devices, Marie didn't usually share her childhood dream to be a dentist. It was a conversation stopper, as nobody else seemed to have poked around in their teddy's mouth with a cocktail stick or begged their parents to lie on the sofa and say *Oooh, me wisdoms*.

'No.' Klay looked faintly appalled. 'I wanted to be a pop singer. With a name like Klay Keaton, you feel you should be famous. But I grew up and realised there was good money in dentistry, so I qualified and now my ambition is to have a Perfect You franchise in every major conurbation in the UK.'

'Ooh, *conurbation*,' murmured Aileen, as if the word was an aphrodisiac. She dipped her head and looked up through her lashes at Klay.

'It takes a while to build up a patient list,' pointed out Marie. 'It takes time to nurture those relationships.'

'I'm a dentist, not a shrink,' laughed Klay. 'Patients will come if my prices are right and there's a funky vibe in reception.'

'We've never had a funky vibe,' said Lynda frostily. And irrelevantly – the Ribena-stained cushions made the point for her. 'And we do all right.'

'Of course you do,' cooed Klay. 'But I want to do more than all right. I want to go mega.'

'Wow!' said Aileen.

'But you love it, right?' Marie couldn't imagine getting up close and personal with people's gums all day without an evangelical drive to improve their health and relieve their pain.

'Love it?' Klay considered. 'Does anybody?' he laughed.

The door clanged and a woman weighed down with shopping bags waddled in, bringing Marie and Aileen to their feet.

'I must rush. You're busy,' said Klay, banging down his mug. 'Well. Busy-*ish*!'

'Come again,' said Aileen.

'Sure!'

'When?'

'Oh . . . well . . .'

'Tomorrow. Come tomorrow,' said Aileen urgently.

Marie felt the need of a rolled-up newspaper to bop her assistant on the nose, a tactic that always worked when Prinny was over-familiar with guests. 'Thank you for the flowers,' she said.

As the door banged behind him, Lynda said, 'What a creep! Those roses are going in the bin.'

'Feck right off! I'm taking them home.' Normal Aileen service was resumed. She swiped them from Marie and cradled the blooms like a baby. 'In a way, Klay's given them to *me* now.'

Marie pep-talked herself. *You can do this*. She glanced at the book open by the bowl. *Mary has every faith in you*.

Messing with Mary's recipe was playing with fire. For a disciple as adoring as Marie, this was heady stuff.

To fortify herself, she recalled the date-and-nut squares she'd made at the weekend. 'Yeah! They were delicious, if I do say so myself. Thanks for reminding me, Mary,' she said to her invisible mentor. 'Although . . .' Best not to tell Mary that Iris had said, 'Urgh, healthy rubbish!' and that Robert had covered his in Nutella.

The point was that Marie had made huge strides in her quest to be a baker. Four months of her year-long run-up to the next show-stopper had passed, and an awful lot of cake batter had flowed under the bridge. She could cream. She could mix. She was no longer frightened of millilitres. Ergo bastardising a sponge cake into a bonfire cake was within her powers. *You can smash this*, said Mary in cut-glass tones from the cover of the book, her blonde bob dripping with chocolate.

Beating vigorously, Marie wondered where Mary had picked up such language, and called through the hall to Robert, crouched by the shelves in the sitting room. He was alphabetising their CDs. This was a bad sign. Robert only alphabetised when stressed. Time to resume their occasional joke. 'Mary Berry could take Paul-so-called-Hollywood by icing him while he slept.'

'Yeah,' Robert agreed absent-mindedly. 'She probably could.' After a moment he shouted, 'Did you buy Coldplay? I didn't buy Coldplay.' He put Coldplay to one side, irritated with it for being among the Rs. 'Bloody bed-wetting music,' he grumbled.

'R,' he said to himself, trawling the narrow spines. 'R for Robbie Williams. R for Roxy Music.' Robert sat back on his heels. *R for redundancy.*

It had begun. Above his level, a few strata over his head, Campbell & Carle was being restructured, modernised, trimmed. Certain company stalwarts had taken early retirement. There was resistance, and so far the reorganisation was moving with the pace of a glacier, but the speed would pick up and soon the floor beneath his feet would show the cracks.

Robert reapplied himself. R for Red Hot Chili Peppers.

In the kitchen Marie stared at the back of his head for a while. Time to focus on The Husband for a bit. The twins had needed her the past couple of days, but now that their sore throats had cleared up and the searing injustice of missing a school trip to the Natural History

Museum had dimmed, she could get back to the male Dunwoodys.

Nobody had warned Marie about the many skills she'd need when she'd signed up for motherhood. (Not that she'd literally signed up – the process had been far more fun and had involved a long night, a bottle of tequila and a libido that, along with a flat stomach, she'd left behind in the 1990s.) She'd guessed she'd need patience, resourcefulness and funny voices for livening up bedtime stories, but nobody had mentioned the juggling.

One or another of her charges (and Robert was in that category, whether he liked it or not) always needed her. Their levels of need changed, and that's where the juggling came in, as she bobbed and weaved, keeping all her balls in the air, keeping all her loved ones as happy as lay within her power.

Trailing home from parents' evening last week, she'd tried to probe Angus, amiably, about Lauren. 'So,' she'd said in a light, breezy, painfully-bleeding-obvious way, 'is Lauren your girlfriend?'

'What!' He'd reacted as if she'd Tasered him. 'God, Mum! No!'

That was, of course, the only possible way for any teenage boy to answer such a question. 'I wouldn't mind, love.'

'It's not about you minding!' Angus was still high-pitched. He'd coughed himself down to his normal gravelly tone. 'Me and Lauren – it's complicated, OK?'

'OK.' She'd acknowledged the slamming door. 'Romance, Angus,' she'd said gently, 'is supposed to make people happy. Yeah?'

'Mum, please.'

So she was still juggling Angus, but her touch wasn't so sure these days. A thought ambushed her, leaping out from the bags of flour and sugar and the box of eggs. Who would juggle *her*, if it came to it? Did anybody have their eye on her, watching in case she fell? Marie looked again at Robert, supposedly ensuring that Shakira came after the Scissor Sisters, but now rubbing his eyes in a tired way.

Bip-bip!

Marie smiled, lifted a floury hand and waved through the kitchen window at the sound of Tod's car horn. It was a habit now, this nightly salute as he pulled up. She saw Lucy come out of the front door like a greyhound at the start of a race.

'Here you are, Mum.' Iris, hair wet from the bath, all snuggled up in a polka-dot dressing gown, came in and plopped a naked Action Man on the windowsill. 'Why'd you want him?'

'Don't worry, I won't hurt him.'

The pain in Action Man's eyes told Marie that nothing scared him any more. After years of active service being dropped out of windows, thrown onto the roof and drowned in the bath, he'd been filched by the girls when Angus grew out of playing war. Nowadays, Action Man's life was a nightmare whirligig of endless doll games. One day a Dad, next day an Evil Burglar, occasionally a satin-knickerbockered Prince. Today it was his fate to be Guy Fawkes, with a felt-tipped moustache and a jaunty hat, legs splayed on top of the 'bonfire'.

Ah yes. The bonfire.

Marie could see the finished article in her mind's eye, but how she would encourage flat cakes to rearrange themselves into a conical triangle she wasn't sure. Hoping for divine intervention – or more usefully *Berry* intervention – she would then daub the whole thing with chocolate buttercream and cover it with logs, aka the twenty-nine remaining Flakes. A small-hours trawl of the Internet had inspired her to create realistic licking flames from melted boiled sweets. In the light of day, this seemed psychotically ambitious.

The *Bake Off* contestants were to blame. Nursing a cup of tea on the sofa, she'd watched them create cakey wonder within the weekly sixty-minute format and thought *I could do that.* She envied them their relationship with Mary, trembling when the great lady herself nibbled their macaroons, and she sighed with cosy pleasure at the thoughtful, truthful, but warm critique that was Mary's stock-in-trade.

The end of the series – the crowning of another winner (Marie had almost turned inside out with envy) – had left a gap in Marie's week that couldn't be filled with mini-series or romcoms. Here, in the kitchen, was the only place she could commune with her leaderene until next summer.

In the nick of time Marie remembered to add red food colouring to the cake batter. She hoped for a communal intake of breath when the cake was sliced and the interior was revealed to be a fiery red. Marie was frugal with the little bottle of cochineal, wary of ending up with abattoir hands.

Drip. Drip. Drip. That should do it. The colour bled

and swirled through the mix, before it finally gave in to Marie's insistent spoon and turned a deep, consistent red.

Unwrapping twenty-nine Flakes turned out to be surprisingly tedious work – repetitive and fiddly, with no chocolate to compensate her for her time. Mary was clear on the 'No picking!' rule, and Marie took heed.

'Is this a long one?' Robert stuck his head around the door, a CD in each hand.

'As the actress said to the . . .' Marie tailed off. Robert wasn't in the mood. ''Fraid so. Why?'

Robert sighed. A world-weary sigh suggesting that the fate of the Western world lay with him, and she'd just ruined everything. 'Because I have to get my biscotti in the oven tonight. Never mind,' he said irritably, sounding as if he minded very much, and dodging out of the room with a dip of his head.

Raising her voice slightly (not as far as Full On Row levels, just to Hang On There a Cotton-Picking Minute, Mister), Marie called, 'You should have told me you needed the kitchen. We could have worked something out.'

'You get on with your stuff. Never mind about me.'

The stench of burning martyr overwhelmed the lovely buttery smells of the cake. 'If you hadn't upgraded our little gathering to a sodding *soirée*, I wouldn't be baking at all, matey.'

'You're not baking for the party . . .' began Robert, still in the other room.

When he left his sentence hanging, Marie encouraged him with a tart, 'Go on.'

'You're baking,' said Robert, over the noise of a tower of CDs collapsing, 'to show off.'

The juggler of the family often has to swallow their irritation, take the high road, do the decent thing. With this in mind, Marie buttoned her lip and disrobed another Flake. But not before she stuck her tongue out – really far – at the door that divided her from her beloved.

The fifth of November dawned cool and foggy. Up with the lark, or possibly before it, Marie confronted the six piled sponges sandwiched together with chocolate frosting. Shaping them into the beehive profile of a bonfire had been tricky. Not trickier than she'd expected, because Marie expected every aspect of baking to be tricky the first time around. One of Mary's promises was that everything got easier with practice.

For this project, Marie had graduated from basic icing to the more complex American style of filling. Egg whites had been whipped until stiff, and sugar boiled to exactly 115 degrees Centigrade, while the world (except for those show-off larks) slept. Now, working swiftly before it set, she trowelled the resulting chocolate sludge all over her cake.

One last flourish and it was done. Time to smother it with Flake firewood.

'Mummy . . .' Iris, rubbing her eyes, was beside her in a nightie patterned with cats. A nightie that was far too short.

Marie scribbled *Buy nighties (twins)* on the blackboard by the fridge, then bent to kiss her daughter's face, still creased and crumpled with sleep.

'I had a dream. About bad men.' Iris's mouth turned down.

'Oh, sweetie pie.' Marie bent down and hugged her close, folding Iris right up and calling on all her Mum-power to chase the bad men clean away.

'One of them was being mean to Prinny.'

'No!' Marie feigned shock. 'Our Prinny? How dare they?'

'How very dare they?' giggled Iris, who loved a catchphrase.

Plonked on the worktop with a Hobnob (and no sister around to claim half), Iris was content again. Instructed sternly not to touch, she eyed the chocolate beast.

'Can you tell what it is yet?' asked Marie, pressing Flakes around the base.

'Oh yeah, it's obvious.' Iris nibbled the edges of her Hobnob. 'But why are you making a poo-cake, Mum?'

With the whizz-bang of rockets in their ears, the guests turned their faces upwards to watch the dazzling dahlia-shaped explosions in the dark fabric of the sky

'I love the red best!' shouted Iris. 'No! The orange! No! The blue!'

The fireworks made kids of them all; even Caroline lost herself enough to say 'Oooh!' unselfconsciously when a particularly dramatic Roman candle let rip. Marie's ears were cold, but she didn't want to dash indoors and miss the fun and/or horrific accidents. After the finale – 'The biggest damn rocket Caraway Close has ever seen' was Robert's reckless promise – she'd run in and pull on a woolly hat. She had plenty, each of them a shapeless bastard knitted by Granny Gaynor. Surreptitiously she put a hand to her hair and pulled out the hairclip holding up her untidy bun.

She'd tussled with that bun for a full half-hour, while Robert had gone through his own pre-party beauty routine (washed his face, in other words). She'd aimed for artless, sexily dishevelled. She'd probably achieved homeless. Finally turning away from the mirror and bundling her hair up any old how, Marie had asked Robert peevishly, 'Should I cut it?' It was a rhetorical question and she'd beetled out, grumbling, 'I'm too bloody old for long hair. Mutton dressed as lamb.'

Glad now of her long hair's ear-warming qualities, the thought remained. The relentless march of her forties threw up some knotty decisions. Could she keep her long hair? Did the tops of her arms stand up to scrutiny in short sleeves? When had she swapped knees with a Premier League footballer?

'The garden looks wonderful.' Their neighbour Johann was at her side. He was Belgian, and handsome, in a European heavy-glasses-and-brogues kind of way.

'Amazing what a few fairy lights can do.' Every twiggy shrub and exhausted tree in the wintery backyard had been draped with string after string of fairy lights. The twins had urged her on – 'More, Mum, MORE!' – and the wee maniacs had been right. Somewhere between the fairy-light hanging, the lantern lighting, the strategic placing of folded blankets and the construction of a 'bar' (spangly fabric thrown over an old sideboard), Marie had realised she was enjoying herself, and the parched old garden, a stubby winter eyesore, was altered and had become magical.

'It looks like a stage set,' said Johann, his hair so trendy it was possibly already out of date.

'Thanks, by the way, for lending us your garden furniture.' Johann and Graham had donated LA-style slatted wooden loungers, each costing more than all the garden furniture Marie had ever bought put together. All the neighbours had been happy to help: the Gnomes had lent a ripped hammock; Hattie had dragged round a tiled table she'd bought in Morocco (with *Made in Birmingham* clearly stamped on the underside). Marie hadn't canvassed Lucy, citing lack of time to Robert, but knowing the shabbier truth herself: she didn't want to be beholden to her bête noire.

Passing by, Hattie clinked glasses with Marie. 'Great party!'

And it was. Nothing to make the Great Gatsby look to his laurels, but a leap forward for the Dunwoodys. Marie had taken Mary's advice and had put good food and hospitality at the heart of it all: just as Ms Berry had prophesied, the rest took care of itself. Every baker is a secret praise-junkie, but tonight Marie's reward was the buoyantly jolly mood in her garden.

'You made it!' Marie kissed Lynda and her fiancé, straining her neck to look up at Barrington's handsome, serious face. He was a red-hot twenty-two-year-old with the dignified demeanour of a Victorian papa, and Marie always forgot how very tall he was.

'I want to thank you,' he said in a deep, rolling, rather thrilling voice, 'for agreeing to bake our wedding cake. I hear you've already made three or four, in preparation for the real one.' Barrington took both Marie's hands in his, his dark eyes full of gratitude. 'It means a lot to us.'

'Happy to help,' said Marie, feeling as if this righteous man might see right through her smile to her crow-black, lying-about-making-croquembouche soul. 'Help yourself to drinks!'

Moving from firework to firework, wielding the extremely long match Marie had bought for him, Robert kept the crowd happy with ongoing bangs and explosions. To quell her neurotic fears, he'd downloaded a Firework Safety pamphlet and followed its instructions to the letter. He'd laid out a firework zone (the lawn), then allowed for fallout and created a spectator zone (the patio). Marie could tell that he relished being Master of Ceremonies by the touch of showmanship as he reached out to light the blue touchpaper.

Some of the showboating was for his boss. Magda, an overdressed peacock in fedora and cashmere cape among the bobble hats and stripy scarves, had wiped the white plastic chair that Caroline commandeered for her before seating herself as if on a throne.

A husky voice behind Marie drawled, 'I must compliment you on your husband's buns.' This was direct, even for Erika, swathed in furs like Russian royalty. She flourished her gourmet hot dog, and Marie realised it was a compliment on Robert's kitchen skills and not on his buttocks.

'Gourmet' hot dogs had confused Marie when Robert

suggested them. Surely, like Pot Noodles, hot dogs were defiantly lowbrow. But no: add a home-made bun, quality saveloys (Angus had sniggered at this for quite some time) plus home-made relish and the result was worthy of the pretentious title. In deference to Magda, the whole buffet had been upgraded; now that Mary had taught Marie to respect cooking times and to accept that a crowded oven takes longer, the baked potatoes were seductively soft all the way through.

Angus, on serving duty, was doling out potatoes loaded with either chilli con carne or wild-mushroom ragu. Aileen, unable to choose, had both, while Barrington reached for a beer from the ice buckets, where it nestled alongside viognier for Magda and the finest Fanta for the kids.

The ear-numbing explosion of the last, showiest rocket erupting overhead in a fizzing shower of whites and golds coincided with some late arrivals. Tod stepped out onto the patio, flanked by his high priestesses: Lucy looked as if she'd stepped off the 'It's Fireworks Night!' page of a catalogue; Chloe's black wrappings rendered her a disembodied and deathly pale face in the dark.

Immediately pounced upon by the twins, Chloe was detached from her family by two pairs of mittened hands and a determined, 'We need you to fill out a form for us.'

Amused, bemused, Chloe let herself be ambushed. 'What form? What are you two loonies on about?'

'This!' Iris flourished a clipboard, and Marie guessed it was the handwritten questionnaire she'd seen them laboriously create earlier on, the one headed *OPERATION FIND OUR STUPID BROTHER A GIRLFRIEND.*

Wondering why her nemesis was in her house more often than her closest friends, Marie moved towards Lucy, but was waylaid by Robert, fresh from his triumph.

The unexpected kiss was warm-lipped, cold-nosed, *intense* and bounced her right back to their first dates, when he'd turn suddenly and grab her as they walked along the street.

Yanked back to the here and now, Marie heard a male voice say 'My turn, matey' and Tod inserted himself between the couple, replacing Robert's arms with his own, Robert's stubble with his smooth cheek, and the time-travelling smooch with his lips planted just to the side of Marie's mouth, an almost-kiss that was somehow more intimate than the full-on version.

Head swimming at the switcheroo, Marie hoped Robert wouldn't be vexed by it, but as Tod pulled away she saw that Robert was already greeting Lucy, laughing with her and accepting – *seriously?* – a cake from her hands. A simple white cake with a pastel fondant Guy Fawkes, it made Marie's Action Man waiting in the utility room, dressed up to the nines in pantaloons and feathered hat filched from a Disney doll, seem irredeemably gauche. Marie touched the kissed patch of skin to the side of her mouth and felt it tingle.

'Here,' Robert immediately handed Lucy's cake over to Marie, as if it were a baby that needed changing. 'Isn't that thoughtful of Lucy?'

'Very,' said Marie, saved from further pleasantries by Caroline, who was piling high a plate of offerings for the Goddess Magda.

'How many calories in a baked potato?' she asked urgently.

'Um,' said Marie. 'More than three?' Since Magda's arrival, Robert had changed from a man enjoying his own party to an actor playing the part of a man enjoying his own party. Fiercely protective of him, Marie knew she had to be cordial to his colleagues. Magda was easy enough: imperious but friendly. Caroline was an entirely different kettle of fish: chic and sharp, she practically had BITCH tattooed across her forehead.

With Tod in the periphery of her vision – would he kiss *all* the women like that? – Marie brandished a paper plate on Lucy's behalf. 'What can I get you from the buffet?'

'It all looks sooo delicious,' said Lucy, her hand to her throat as she stared at the spread. 'But,' she said decisively, 'I'm not hungry.'

'Okey-dokey.' The paper plate returned to the pile, only to be snatched up by Mrs Gnome.

'I'm having seconds,' she said with the trademark clacketty-clack of her dentures. 'You should 'ave an 'ot dog, madam.' She prodded Lucy in the ribs with a serving spoon. 'Not an ounce of fat on ya. Your poor hubby.' Mrs Gnome shook her head sadly. 'Like shagging a pile of folded deckchairs.' She limped away, leaving Marie and Lucy regarding each other awkwardly.

'Don't take any notice of her,' said Marie, feeling responsible for her disagreeable guest. 'When she arrived, she asked me what was I hiding under my poncho, and said no wonder I eat for two.'

'Deep down she's lovely,' said Lucy.

Wondering how far you'd have to drill to find Mrs Gnome's loveliness, Marie moved on. It was exhausting, this proper hostessing. In the pre-Mary Berry years she would have been huddled with the naughtiest-looking clique, the back-of-the-class crew, snorting at rude jokes and sending the twins for refills. Now she buzzed from guest to guest like a bee, topping up here, taking an empty plate there, directing this person to the loo, that person to a vacant seat, smoothing ruffled feathers in Mrs Gnome's wake and agreeing that, yes, they'd been very lucky with the weather.

'Hey, handsome!' shouted Erika above the polite conversation. 'Where's *my* kiss?'

Tod, who'd been dutifully listening to Hattie talk about her colon, waggled a finger at her. 'Naughty-naughty,' he said, but leaned over to kiss her, rather primly, on the cheek.

'You can do better than that . . .' purred Erika.

'Wifey on the premises!' laughed Tod, slapping Erika's hand playfully. He saw Marie's expression and said, 'Oh dear, we've shocked our hostess.'

'No. Not at all. Not a bit,' said Marie. 'God, no!'

'Shame,' said Tod, moving back to Hattie.

I'm not sophisticated enough for this, thought Marie, hurrying on with a plate of sausages. Erika spoke to all the men in that sex-kitten growl. Tod complimented all the ladies. *I'm just an old married bat who's forgotten that consenting adults can flirt without anybody getting hurt.*

The evening was speeding past. Time to check on Prinny, shut in the master en suite, far from bangs and whooshes and with a wipe-clean floor. Trotting upstairs with a chewy treat, Marie encountered the dog on the landing.

'Prin?' She scratched his chin and watched the animal's eyes half-close with joy. Prinny was anybody's for a tickle; Marie had been a bit like that at uni. 'What are you doing out here?' A rectangle of light from the en suite crawled along the bedroom carpet and out onto the landing. Voices – confident female ones – rang out.

Creeping into her own bedroom like an intruder, one hand on Prinny's collar, Marie stole to the bathroom door, wondering who'd been bold enough to seek out a loo upstairs when there was a perfectly good one (repainted that morning, in fact) on the ground floor.

'Sure it's OK to use Robert's en suite?' The perfectly enunciated voice was loud enough to address a Nuremberg Rally: Magda. 'Feels odd.'

'His wife said it was fine.'

Ooh, Caroline, you fibber, thought Marie, frowning down at Prinny, who was enjoying his chew a little too loudly. It wouldn't do to be caught eavesdropping on your guests.

'Those little girls are fab, aren't they?'

Thank you, Magda. I think so too.

The loo flushed. Prinny jumped.

'Hmm.'

Hmm? Bloody hmm?

'Robert's a genius baker,' said Magda, slightly distracted, as if she was checking herself in the mirror. To a backdrop of what had to be Caroline's tinkling wee, she said, 'Not many people would bother to make hot-dog buns.'

There was a scraping of feet and some rustling. Caroline was pulling up her – no doubt expensive – knickers as she said, 'Although, like you said the other day, perhaps this . . . mania for baking explains why he's taking his eye off the ball at work.'

Marie stiffened. *This* was why she was earwigging; she knew there was something iffy about that Caroline.

Taps ran.

'Did I say that, Caroline?'

'You were dead right, Magda. His heart isn't in silverware, it's in food.'

'When did I say—'

As her vowels became distorted (Marie could imagine Caroline dragging lipstick over her dishonest mouth), Caroline interrupted, 'Mind you, should make your big decision easier!'

Magda's response was sudden and sharp, as if all the air had been sucked out of the shower room and toxic gas piped in. 'A decision that important is never easy. And I don't need any help reaching it. Call me a cab, would you?'

Marie smiled. Magda was no easy touch; Caroline's attempt at stabbing Robert in the back, to his face (as it were), had been foiled. For now. The light went out and the door opened, with Marie stepping neatly behind it.

Tripping over Prinny, Caroline muttered, 'Stupid fucking mongrel.'

'Good dog!' mouthed Marie in the dark, waiting for the carthorse clip-clop of the women's heels to fade on the stairs.

*

It was cake time. 'Sorry,' said Aileen, emerging from the utility room as Marie reached it.

'What for?' Marie looked dubious. It could easily have been for the tartan trousers Aileen was wearing; most of her outfits merited an apology. 'Ah, I see.' A few of the logs had been filched from the chocolate bonfire. She recalled the scribbles she'd found on a treatment form the day before. *Aileen Keaton.* Beneath it: *A. Keaton.* Then: *Mrs Aileen Keaton.* And she forgave her. Any woman who fantasised about Klay with a K had worse problems than gluttony and kleptomania to worry about. 'Give me a hand, Aileen. It's a two-woman job.'

Gingerly lighting a sparkler and setting it between Action Man's legs, Marie nodded to Aileen, and between them they hoisted the crooked pyre and carried it out to the patio.

Graham gave it a roll on the drums by tapping a wrought-iron table, as Johann began to clap. 'Brava!' he shouted.

'Dunnit look lovely!' said Mrs Gnome unexpectedly.

'Now *that's* a cake!' said Tod.

A crowd pressed around Marie as she sliced and served, the delighted reaction to the lava-red interior worth the trouble of scrubbing the red dye from her hands. The party hubbub turned primeval, as everybody scoffed and gorged and let out little sticky groans of pleasure.

A plate hit the floor. Not a paper plate – it smashed and a Rorschach blot of cake disfigured the patio slabs. 'For God's *sake*, Tod!' shouted Lucy, her hands to her head.

Anybody with a feather could have knocked down Marie. Lucy? Teflon Lucy throwing a plate and screaming at her husband? As her nemesis pushed through the silenced crowd into the house, Marie put down her knife and made to follow her, her mind racing as to what she'd say.

'No, no, I'll go.' Tod strode after his wife, adding grimly in an aside, 'God knows, I've had plenty of practice.'

Communal good manners asserted themselves: an animated hum of conversation sprang into life, with only the odd furtive look towards the tantalising muted row within the conservatory.

Somebody turned up the music; Robert cleared up the shards of plate; the party healed over the wound.

Alone on a bench, nibbling her black-varnished nails, sat Chloe. Marie, making her way towards her, followed the girl's line of sight and found, of course, Angus, who was listening to Erika talk about herself as he tried not to stare at her breasts.

'Budge up.' Marie flopped down and plonked a bowl in Chloe's lap. 'Cake. Cures all ills.'

'Not mine.' Chloe picked off a tiny scrap of red sponge and rolled it into a ball before tasting it. 'That's good,' she said. 'Nice to eat something humble for a change.'

Smiling at the backhanded compliment, Marie said, 'Your mum – sorry, *mother* – spoils you and your dad.' She meant that as a good thing, but Chloe obviously didn't agree.

'If only we could just have a croissant on a plate instead of in a gingham basket. Or a paper napkin like *you* use, instead of vintage bloody linen she's sourced at an antiques fair.' Chloe picked up speed: this was evidently a perennial gripe. 'And why does she *source* things anyway? Why can't she just *buy stuff*, like normal people?'

Caroline strolled past, squawking into her mobile. 'Yes, soon as possible . . . address? Oh God, the back of bloody beyond . . .' She saw Marie and handed over the phone. 'Tell this cab firm where we are, would you?'

After Marie had helped out and Caroline stalked back towards the bar, Chloe carried on, impatient to burp it all out. 'And nobody else in my class has starters on a week-night! Tonight she even made some *amuse-bouches*!'

'And were they amusing?' Marie's attempt to lighten the mood was doomed. 'Listen,' she said, feeling the girl's pain, but also eager to introduce some perspective, 'most people would kill to live with a home-maker like Lucy.'

Chloe wasn't listening. She'd leapfrogged ahead in her mind, Marie could tell.

'What?' asked Marie gently. She recognised this pregnant air of something about to break, of a confession or a fear ready to be aired.

'There's a big lie in my life.'

'A lie?' Marie felt the need to tread very, very carefully. She was intensely curious about the Gray house, but she was also immensely fond of this strange, big-eyed girl, who thought she'd disguised all her insecurities by swathing them in black and adding a scowl. 'Am I the right person to talk to?'

'Yes!' Chloe shed ten years as her face crumpled. 'I can't lie any more. It's wearing me down.'

If her own children went to a stranger with their woes,

Marie would want that stranger to turn them round and point them back at their parents. 'Sweetie,' she began, hoping the soft word would help to soften what could sound like a refusal to listen.

'Chloe!' Lucy stood over them. 'You've had cake.' It was, no two ways about it, *accusatory*.

'Yes, I mean, I . . .' Chloe looked down at the empty plate, as if caught stealing. Crumb by crumb, she'd polished off the lot.

'Home!' said Lucy, with a clipped tartness to her tone that was absent when she turned to Marie. 'Thank you so much for a lovely evening.'

'Chloe can stay for a bit. If she wants.' Marie put a finger under Chloe's chin, felt Lucy bridle, and held the girl's gaze. 'Do you want to stay?'

'Nah. I'd better . . . you know?' The upward inflection, the evasive expression – Chloe had closed down again.

Hello Wife

I'm leaving this note by the anti-ageing cream so you'll definitely find it before you go to bed. Listen: NEVER CUT YOUR HAIR. Please. I've always loved your hair. In fact, when I'm old, I intend to live in your hair. So don't cut it. OK?

Your husband x

DECEMBER
Christmas

Yule Log

OPERATION FIND OUR STUPID
BROTHER A GIRLFRIEND

Name: Chloe Gray

QUESTION 1 – Do you like little sisters of boys?
Yes.
QUESTION 2 – Would you be nice to a boy, not shouting?
I wouldn't shout.
QUESTION 3 – Are you pretty?
I don't know! I don't think so.
QUESTION 4 – Are you a big tarty-tart?
No.
QUESTION 5 – Do you like dogs?
I love dogs. Especially Prinny!
QUESTION 6 – Are you a femininist?
Definitely.
QUESTION 7 – Would you sing with us if we arsked?
Yes.
QUESTION 8 – What is your favourite bit of a fun fare?
I find the dodgems v v exiting.
QUESTION 9 – Do you really like Angus lots, almost loving
a bit in a way?
You are very nosy and I'm going now!

TO DO LIST

- Order doll bed online for Rose
- Order doll fridge online for Iris
- Fashionable something (???) for Angus
- Send overseas cards NOW
- Order turkey
- Wash curtains
- Find Mum's tablecloth in attic
- Presents for Aileen/Lynda
- Christmas tip for paper boy
- Send cards to R's family
- Quietly, and when nobody is looking, GO STARK STARING MAD.

Christmas. The working mother's Vietnam.

How, thought Marie as she wrestled with the fold-down steps to the attic, *has it crept up on me again?* Reliably, on the exact same date every year, each Christmas found Marie with her metaphorical pants down. Even without her new-found lust for baking, the festive season was a logistical nightmare.

Weeks of planning, list-compiling and impulse purchases culminated in one frantic day of cooking an ostrich-sized fowl that Robert would pronounce 'a bit dry', an Everest of washing up and a credit-card-bill bottom line that could be mistaken for a telephone number.

Stumbling up the steps, Marie gingerly inserted herself into the gloom of the attic, the swaying bulb rendering the corners ominous. It was an unsettling metaphor for her head up here: a dusty place where anything stored was soon forgotten. She exhaled unhappily and had a classic early-December thought: *Why the hell didn't I put the decorations away carefully last year?* She'd promised herself, in this very spot, in this very mood, twelve months previously that she would never again scrabble around like a rat, tearing open random boxes, only to find the Christmas tree eventually in a box marked 'dining-room miscellaneous'. She had vowed to wrap each bauble in tissue, wind the lights around cardboard tubes, launder and iron the holly-patterned napkins, before stowing them all in boxes plainly labelled in thick black marker pen.

And then, after the big day, she'd impatiently flung everything into black bin-bags and hurled them overarm into the attic, before shutting the trapdoor with a bang and applying herself to the last of the advocaat.

After brief diversions into a box of the twins' old toys, a box of manuals for long-dead household appliances and a massive box that contained one single broken tape measure, Marie struck Christmas gold: a plastic baby Jesus, some torn paper chains and a Polaroid of Robert trying to look pleased with his new slippers.

And another thing, said the Mrs Angry currently managing Marie's thoughts, *why is Christmas women's work?* She hadn't noticed Robert working on a To Do list written in his own blood. He wasn't waking up in the middle of the night shouting *Barbie caravan!* Neither was his mind stuck in a constant loop of *Must order the turkey – but none of us really like turkey – but Christmas isn't Christmas without a turkey – must order the turkey*. If she were to instigate a game of word association and start with 'turkey', Robert would probably answer 'package holiday'.

Yet again her ovaries had determined matters. Marie pulled open a box marked 'things' in Robert's neat hand. Cards, this time. Ancient Christmas cards. She folded the lid down, but not before the handwriting – small and faltering – on the top envelope caught her eye.

It was a red envelope, unopened. Her mother's writing.

Ambushed by the past, Marie let out a small 'Oh Mum!' The last card, never opened. But never thrown away.

When she thought of her mother, she thought of a hundred jostling images. Her mum had been a giggler, a teller-off, a soother, a partner in crime. She'd been intoxicated with her daughter, constantly smelling her hair or gathering Marie to her like an armful of flowers. 'You are my riches,' she used to say when tiny Marie, pink and warm from the bath, had sat on her lap by the fire.

The image Marie hated and fought was the last one, a wretched sparrow-version of her lovely mum making barely a dent in the hospice bed. This card had been written in that place, each letter painfully formed. It could, Marie decided, wait another year to be read.

'What do you think Angus wants?'

'In general? Or for Chris—' Robert thought better of his joke. Something about his wife's face as she leaned back on the pillows, scribbling on a piece of paper that looked like the world's longest bus ticket, suggested this was no time for jokes. He took off his glasses, knowing he mustn't look as if he longed to get back to his new Paul Hollywood book. That – long years a-husbanding told him – would be *wrong*. 'Um . . . money, I suspect. I wanted money at his age.' He still wanted it now. 'He'll need a few quid to get to Scotland.'

'I'm thinking of putting my foot down about Scotland.'

'The whole country or . . .' Again, his wife's face warned him to abandon the joke. 'He's sixteen now, love. If he wants to visit mates in other parts of the country, we should let him. I had a friend in Yorkshire when I was his age, and I used to jump on the train every school holiday.'

'That was you, and that was then.' Marie wrote something furiously, as if she hated the pen and the pen hated the paper. 'He's a young sixteen. And we don't even know this friend he's going to see.'

'I know you raised your eyebrows when he said they met online, but I had a chat with Angus and there's nothing dodgy. It all checks out – it's a girl his own age, and I reckon he's escaping Lauren what's-her-name,' smiled Robert, as if proud of his son's girl trouble.

'So. Your mother.'

'My mother,' repeated Robert, sure that something more was expected of him, but having not a clue as to what. 'Oh, you mean, what should we get her?' Never had words on a page seemed so enticing; Robert felt his eyes stray to a list of ingredients before he shut Paul Hollywood with a bang. 'Let's see. Bath salts? Or, what's that stuff – chalky, whiffy, oh yeah: talc!' he shouted triumphantly.

'I might as well ask Prinny,' muttered Marie, and then, louder: 'Actually, that's a point. What'll we get Prinny?'

'Talc?' suggested Robert.

'Why do I bother?' huffed Marie.

'No idea.' Robert took up his book again.

On the floor, within reach, lay her Mary Berry book. She could simply pick it up and read it, ignore the slavering demands of Christmas, just like her husband. Another option was to pick it up and beat him with it. But Marie did neither. She did what women have always done when faced with Christmas: she soldiered on.

She understood Robert. Christmas-blindness was a reaction to the days when he'd had to organise it all himself while his mother had another attack of the vapours and lay on the sofa with a bottle of Baileys. There would have been no presents under the tree for his sisters if Robert hadn't organised them. In fact, there would have been no tree.

Sneaking a look at him, perving over doughnuts, Marie felt hot shame at her urge to beat him. 'Who's having Gaynor this year?'

'Not us, thank the sweet Lord Baby Jesus. She's going to her neighbours.'

The sigh of relief was not altogether sincere. Marie's ideal Christmas – that elusive creature that flitted within sight each year and then darted off – would involve all the generations, with young and old united by their good cheer and their contempt for turkey. Since the death of Marie's mum, there'd been a job vacancy; if Gaynor had shown any desire to be the family matriarch, Marie would have supported her gleefully. But the woman who embroidered tablecloths with red berries, knitted everybody scarves in their favourite colours and wore comedy antlers on her head *all day* had died, while the woman who pretended to give money to Oxfam instead of presents lived on.

It had taken decades for Marie to understand her mum's

simple, enormous satisfaction in making things. When Marie had been dashing in and out to parties, to college, to her first job, she'd felt sorry for her mother, sitting with a needle or a ball of wool or a washing-up basin of papier mâché. Staying at home while the rest of the world whirled past was like denying life, and Marie thanked her lucky stars that she had choices. She'd always wanted to earn her own money, to be independent, to plant her flag on the world. Nothing flashy: just a pretty flag of her own design on her own little hillock would suffice.

Be careful what you wish for. The writing on her To Do list danced tipsily, and Marie rubbed her temples, like a bad actress in a painkiller advert. Since the overheard mention of Magda's 'big decision' at the bonfire party, Marie had visualised an axe poised over Robert's neck. Caroline was a clever strategist, and Robert seemed to have laid down his weapons. He seemed *resigned* to his impending messy execution. If Caroline won – no other way to think of it: this was a competition – Marie would be the breadwinner. She wondered how men had coped with the pressure of this mantle down the generations.

It had been a long day. She deserved a little bit of Mary. Like a school library book at the rude bits, the book fell open at a well-thumbed page.

Yule log. A staple on the Christmas sideboard since Marie was old enough to drool. This year's would be home-made for the first time since Mum had died. A thought stabbed Marie, an insistent bony finger: *Must ring Dad.*

*

'Whaddyathink of me new high heels?' Aileen did a twirl and fell over.

Helping her up from the reception rug, Marie said, 'They're a bit high for work.' *Unless one's a prostitute.*

'Hmm. And me top?'

'A bit low for work.' Come to think of it, Aileen's whole outfit was rather prostitute-y.

'This is all for Klay, I suppose?' Lynda, who had given up all pretence of work now that the wedding was less than a month away, halted her tireless search for the perfect bridal nail colour to counsel Aileen. 'You should just be yourself around men.'

For most people that was excellent advice. But for Aileen . . . 'Tone it down a bit,' said Marie. 'That much cleavage, this time of day, it gives the wrong impression.'

'But men like boobs!' said Aileen. Never a patient woman, she'd been waiting weeks for Klay to come to his senses and ask her out.

'Judging by his staff, Klay is indeed a boob man, but that doesn't mean you should show that much flesh.' Marie tried to pixelate her employee's décolletage. Impressive but scary, it was the Cheddar Gorge of cleavage: a man could get lost down there. 'Lynda, is our three fifteen late?'

'We don't have a three fifteen.' Lynda tapped a nail painted with 'Pearly Princess' on the diary. 'They cancelled.' She stopped, lips clamped together, as if her mouth was full of ball bearings.

'I know that face. Another defection?'

Lynda nodded. 'Same pattern. Mid-twenties. Said she wanted to take advantage of Klay's Christmas offer.'

'Free whitening with every check-up,' said Marie, peering through the glazed door towards Perfect You's window display, featuring a life-sized Photoshopped Nicole Kidman holding a money-off voucher.

'He's a genius,' breathed Aileen as her top button flew off.

As if conjured up, Klay appeared at the door of Perfect You ushering out a customer, kissing her on both cheeks, small chubby hands flying as he made his hammy goodbyes.

'Look at him!' growled Aileen. 'Now that's a *man*.'

And that's *a nemesis*. Lucy was putting up her umbrella against the hailstones, smiling as she backed away in a barrage of Klay-with-a-'k' compliments. *Typical*, Marie thought. *Even though she now knows I'm a dentist, she still goes to the flashy newcomer*. She heard the thud of another nail in Smile!'s coffin; there were so many nails these days that the noise almost constituted a theme tune.

'Why don't *we* offer—' Lynda was cut off by Marie's firm 'Nope!'.

'But, Marie, free whitening might entice some patients back.' Lynda had a head for business, as the marquee-hire company who'd given her an 80 per cent discount would attest.

'The whole point of being a dentist is to improve dental health.' Marie wondered if she sounded righteous and smug and decided she didn't care. 'I can't offer whitening to people who don't really need it. That sets them on a lifelong journey of paying for the upkeep. Plus we'll end up with a nation of fluorescent-toothed TOWIE types.' She could have gone on, could have bored them again with how, as a dentist, the colour of teeth told her a lot about what was going on beneath the enamel, but she spared them and repeated, 'So nope, it's not for us.'

'Let's invite Klay to our mince-pies-and-sherry day.' Aileen was reapplying jammy lipstick in a pocket mirror.

'Let's not.' Marie tidied the magazines, then mussed them up, then tidied them again.

'You two are supposed to support me.' Aileen snapped the mirror shut, her wound plaits bristling. 'You're me posse, me homies. If you don't help, how will I ever experience the joy of sexual congress with the hottest dentist I've ever laid eyes on?'

That was a mental image Marie could live without. 'Can't you fall for somebody else?' she asked, lining up leaflets on the mantelpiece as fastidiously as if it was the final of a Lining Up Leaflets competition. 'Throw a stone in the most miserable nightclub and you'll hit a better prospect than Klay. Go and have *congress* with a normal bloke.'

'I haven't saved me virginity all these years to waste it on some eejit in a club.' Aileen rearranged in her hair the fourteen sparkling Claire's Accessories accessories that she considered de rigueur these days.

Marie and Lynda exchanged a glance, checking that they'd heard right. Later they'd discuss this in detail, teasing out the nuances, fine-tuning their theories about how a woman could reach her thirties in today's hypersexualised world without having the merest bonk, but for now they had to tread carefully. Aileen was a strange 'un, but she was *their* strange 'un.

'What's so special about Klay?' Marie used a softer voice, the one she'd used to tell the twins about periods, only to be interrupted with an airy 'Oh, we know all about the red weewee thing'.

'His looks, obviously.' Aileen sailed past the baffled expressions. 'And his air of mystery.'

Marie glanced out of the window and saw Klay rolling about with a customer's pug in the window of Perfect You.

'And come *on*, bitches!' Aileen dipped her head and smiled coquettishly, a move that made Marie suddenly want to go to the toilet. 'Don't pretend you haven't noticed the chemistry.'

'You've barely spoken to him.' Lynda, on the threshold of the most expensively romantic day of her life, was brutally honest. 'I shouldn't think he remembers your name – even if you do stagger over there in your stupid shoes and your boobalicious tops to borrow a cup of sugar every other day.'

'He remembers me all roight.' At moments of stress, excitement and, it would appear, disturbingly sexual certainty, Aileen's accent cranked up the Irishness. 'You should have seen what he was doing to me last night in me dreams.'

'No. I shouldn't.' Marie held up a stern hand in case Aileen was in the mood to share.

Sitting in her car outside St Ethelred's, with 'Mistletoe and Wine' on the radio, Marie tried to summon a festive sense of goodwill to all men, but felt only unease.

The Smile! mince-pies-and-sherry day had been a success. A muted success, of course – not like the party across the road, where Klay's muscly, oiled Sexy Santas had handed out shots – but a success nonetheless. The stack of presents on the back seat had surprised and profoundly touched Marie. With a global recession in full swing, housing markets lurching and benefits being slashed as if Freddy Krueger were Chancellor of the Exchequer, she hadn't expected anything from her patients this year, and yet today had brought a steady influx of novelty slippers, bath gel and body lotion: all the staples from the shops catering for People You Don't Know Very Well Yet Feel Compelled to Buy a Present For.

Old Jonas had been first in, of course, bearing a bottle of horrible perfume that Marie had immediately squirted all over herself, sniffing rapturously and trying not to pass out. He'd been settled in the nicest chair, fussed over like a guest of honour as the party waxed and waned around him – Wham!'s 'Last Christmas' underscoring the action, as mums with pushchairs sipped their sherries guiltily, unaccustomed to an afternoon hot blast of alcohol. Marie's least-favourite guests had been greeted with the same gusto as her pets, and everybody left full of cheer, with vivid pink dots (part alcohol, part joy) on their cheeks.

Smile! was a living, breathing creature to Marie. She was proud of it, she worried about it, and on days like today it blew her away with its capacity to enrich life. Who would have thought a dental surgery party would be so well attended? She had been sorry to leave early, but she'd decided to surprise the kids with a lift home on the last day of term. Angus was so reliable, walking his sisters to and from school every day, never complaining, never ducking out of his duties. She suspected that at times he could be less than charming with them – she'd overheard a snapped 'You're doing my head in!' once or twice – but he was solid big-brother material, and today she would whisk them all home in the dubious luxury of her rarely vacuumed Focus.

Stroking the crocheted steering-wheel cover fondly, Marie saw her motor car in dewy soft focus. She usually cursed its inability to start first time on winter mornings; the left windscreen wiper that had a mind of its own; the glove box that fell open when she braked. But since she'd marked it out as the first victim of her austerity drive, she appreciated its good points. She'd laughed a lot in this car; ferried her children from A to B and then on to C; driven to see her friend Jo, generally staying over because she was too sloshed to drive back; made countless supermarket trips; delivered Prinny to the vet's that time a savage kitten mauled him; and made the round trip to Smile! every day for a decade.

It had served her well, despite her neglect. The blankets folded on the back seat smelled more like the dog than the dog did. The floor was a sweet-wrapper cemetery. That empty tissue box in the back window had been there when she'd bought the car.

It was a defeat, of sorts, to have to give it up.

Head back, eyes closed, she reminded herself that it hadn't come to that yet, and let her thoughts roam. Some women, when encountering an unexpected free moment, might find their minds alighting on Channing Tatum's chest, but Marie's went straight to cake-making.

She loved the planning stage, when your masterpiece was still theory, with no washing up to do. Her Yule log would have a twist – not your average log. Mary, she felt certain, would approve.

Second-guessing Ms Berry was second nature now. If only Marie could channel her advice on Angus. Part man, part boy, all conundrum, he was certainly *capable* of travelling north of the border on his own, but Marie was curious as to why he *wanted* to. Why the need to skip town for New Year's Eve? Canny old Mary would know the right words to winkle out the boy's reasons for leaving his mates behind to meet up with a virtual stranger. Mary, that wise elder of the tribe, would probe the inner workings of his mysterious mind with the same elegant economy she brought to her recipes. Angus would open up like a flower, in marked contrast to the clenched face he'd been showing his mother for . . . Good Lord, it was *months* now.

The girl's existence had only been discovered because Angus needed his parents' permission to visit her. He'd given only the scantest details, each one a tooth pulled from his unwilling mouth. The girl was, apparently, his age; into films; funny and, of course, *cool*. He hadn't even shared her name.

What did Angus derive from an email relationship that was missing from his flesh-and-blood relationships? As somebody who'd negotiated her own teenage years without the Internet, Marie struggled to imagine that a true friendship could be forged at such a distance. But, apparently, for the modern teen, it could: Angus was very keen indeed to get to Scotland.

A loud and silvery noise, like cutlery clattering down iron stairs, rolled out through the school gates. The bell had sounded. Term was over and a tide of maroon blazers flooded the road.

There they were, her three. Ponytails bobbing, Iris and Rose chatted intensely about some twinny subject – might be cow names; might be theorising who would win a race between an emu and a man on a scooter; might be how best to split an atom. Her big-footed son walked behind them, rucksack halfway down his arms and . . . Marie squinted. Were those leaves in his hair?

'Mum!' Iris saw her first and quite literally jumped for joy. Nice to provoke such a reaction, thought Marie, beaming. The little ones ran towards the car; the larger one sped up only minutely.

'Surprise!'

'Oh Mum you're brilliant we made you a card look no don't look it's for Christmas the car smells of bananas are these presents for us?'

'Angus, darling,' said Marie, as he bent himself into the passenger seat. 'Are you aware you have most of a tree in your hair?'

'What?' Angus ruffled his hair and a twig hit the dashboard.

'And look at your knees!' She noticed the spreading dark mud-stain on his trousers. 'What goes on in that school?'

'He's been helping clear the waste ground round the back of the gym,' said Iris.

'Yeah. The big boys are making an adventure playground for us,' said Rose, trying on earmuffs in the back seat.

'My hero,' said Marie approvingly.

Why did I bother to theme the wrapping? Marie asked herself. The family had fallen on their presents like hyenas on a wildebeest. Nobody had commented on the pleasing tonality of the red-patterned papers as they tore impatiently through them. Stubbing her toe as she stuffed screwed-up tissue into a bin-bag, she consoled herself that real-life Christmas Day never resembles the movies.

Except, that is, at number twenty-three Caraway Close, where the curtains were obligingly pulled back so that Marie, elbow-deep in kitchen-sink suds, could enjoy the blazing tree and the three figures around it, decorously handing round gifts as they sipped what Marie was pretty damned sure was hot chocolate topped with cream. (She'd planned to serve hot chocolate topped with cream, but she'd forgotten the cream. And the chocolate.)

There was no scuffling in that idyllic scenario, no twin knocking over the tree during a desperate Barbie-centric struggle. Nor was there a teenager feigning delight with a camera flashgun that didn't fit his camera. The man of the house at twenty-three hadn't stayed in his (seen better days) dressing gown until noon, having failed to thank his wife for his present. Marie could hardly blame Robert – how could a jumper she'd spent so long pondering and pawing, and holding up to the light and asking the assistant would he call it *heather* or *lilac*, look so damned ordinary the moment Robert unwrapped it?

Lucy's Guy Fawkes outburst had proved to be a one-off. Tod had intimated, during a chat over the gate one evening, that his wife had difficult 'times of the month'. 'Amazing what a foot rub can do,' he'd said, as Marie wondered if Robert would ever suggest rubbing her feet, even if she held a gun to his head. 'A little spoiling goes a long way,' Tod had carried on. 'That's why I'm taking us all off to Claridge's for lunch on Christmas Day.'

'If you ever write a handbook for husbands,' Marie had laughed, 'I'll be first in the queue to buy one for Robert.'

'Robert,' Tod had said, suddenly very serious, 'is a lucky man, and he knows it.'

The lucky man, who'd spent the preceding six months competing with her for worktop and oven space, had become kitchen-phobic on the most notable culinary day of the year; presently peeling potatoes in the utility room with a general air of huffy put-upon-ness, Robert was maintaining his hardline attitude towards Christmas. For the first few years of family life he'd tried to ignore it, but had eventually conceded to Marie's insistence that Christmas, like the sun or Jeremy Clarkson, is a constant in our lives and cannot be ignored. His opting out simply made more work for *her*. So Robert endured it instead, which wasn't pretty, but at least meant he peeled the potatoes.

Wondering which god she'd offended enough for him/her to nobble the dishwasher on the twenty-fifth of December, Marie swirled soapy water around the champagne flutes. She regretted her Martha Stewart-style decision to serve Bucks Fizz with the presents; she had a mini-hangover already, *and* Robert hadn't commented on the use of their best glasses or her careful staging of the tray with artfully arranged tinsel. It was Lucy-style presentation without the Tod-style appreciation.

'Can we put on the telly yet? asked Iris, a new Ken clutched to her chest.

'At Christmas when I was your age,' began Marie, as her anecdotes queued up, wondering which of them would be dusted off first: *we weren't allowed telly until the evening; we were happy with what we got; we helped with the lunch; we didn't threaten to murder our beloved sibling over who got to read out the joke in the cracker*. At the sight of Iris's little face settling into an expression that could only mean *withstanding Mum's childhood anecdotes*, Marie relented. 'Oh, go on then.'

'Yay!' Iris reacted as if this was the best news ever: the *true* Christmas miracle. 'Rose! TELLY!' she screamed.

Robert held a pan out to her through the utility-room door. 'That enough?' he asked hopefully.

'Yes,' smiled Marie, 'if you're peeling potatoes for a solitary pensioner who doesn't like potatoes. If you're peeling them for the Dunwoody Christmas lunch, then *obviously not*.' She relented. 'A few more, please, or you'll be all grumpy. You know how you like your roasties.'

'I don't like them,' Robert corrected her, 'I love them. I think about them all year. I may leave them all my money when I go.'

'And here was me planning a world cruise with Antonio Banderas.'

Plying his peeler once more, Robert said, 'Hasn't Antonio gone off a bit? He's getting on.'

'Even a gone-off-a-bit Antonio will do me.' Marie rather loved the way Robert managed to be insanely jealous of her film-star crushes. 'When you start that far ahead, you can afford to lose a bit of ground.'

'He's got a funny accent.'

'If by "funny" you mean mind-bogglingly sexy, then yes, he does.' Marie craned her neck to check on his technique. 'Get *all* the skin off.'

'I am.'

'You're not. You're really not.'

Robert held a potato up to his eyes, like a jeweller examining a diamond. '*That* is a perfectly peeled potato. It could win awards.'

Opening her mouth to dispute this, Marie changed tack. 'You know what?' she said, drying her hands on a tea towel. 'Let's not waste our Christmas Day row on a potato. Let's save it up for – ooh, the affair you're having with Magda, or the moment I crack and put the kids out with the rubbish.'

'Aw,' complained Robert, 'I'd rather like to argue about a potato. I could get really worked up; somehow bring your friends into it; say *bloody typical* a lot.' He paused and seemed to be considering his next words, before saying, 'Rung your Dad yet?'

'I'm run off my feet,' muttered Marie. *Ring Dad* had been the first comprehensible thought in her head when she awoke, and it had reappeared hourly since.

Ring Dad.

*

'Do you need any help?' asked Angus from the doorway, surveying the boiling pans, the beeping microwave, the overheated middle-aged woman.

'All under control!' Marie smiled at him, shooed him away. She felt as if she'd been in this kitchen since she was born.

The stuffing was burning. The table was yet to be laid. (Mary would have laid that table the night before. But then Mary wouldn't have sat up wrapping until 2 a.m.) The carrots were staring accusingly at her, still unpeeled and in no way cut into cute flower shapes.

Mobile to her ear, Marie stirred gravy (which was steadfastly, sarcastically refusing to thicken) as a phone rang in a distant hallway. A woman picked up. Marie recognised the voice and could picture the care worker's checkered overall and trainers.

'He's asleep right now,' the voice told her, warm, measured. This woman, Marie could tell, *understood*.

'Oh.' Marie wished a futile wish for the thousandth time: that her father had agreed to move nearer to them, that she'd fought him on his stubborn wish to stay near the sea when it became clear he'd need to sell the house. 'Did he . . . like his present?' The need in her voice was raw: she was a child again, sitting in the dark while her parents chatted downstairs.

'He loved it!'

'Did he know it was from me?'

The slightest of pauses and then: 'Don has good days and bad days.'

That'll be a no, then.

'Would you remind him I'll be up in a week's time?'

'It's marked on his calendar.'

'I'll bring him a cake.'

'He'll love that!'

Somebody in the sitting room whacked up the volume, and the crashing soundtrack of a blockbuster movie, all bombs and bombast, invaded the kitchen.

The pan lids danced, the gravy sulked, the turkey loomed, the smoke alarm woke up and began its raucous song.

A car horn cut through the rattling, damp kitchen noise as Marie fanned the alarm with a filthy tea towel.

The Grays' Mercedes was turning outside, Tod's hand raised in salute. Beside him, Lucy pulled her seatbelt across a white, surely new, fur-collared coat.

Marie waved back, then stopped, stock still, as the beeps and the explosions and the shouts of 'HANDS OFF MY SPIROGYRO!' reached a crescendo.

This, she thought with surprising clarity, *is the moment the juggler drops the balls.*

TO: stargazinggirl247@gmail.com
FROM: geeksrus39@gmail.com
25.12.13
12.34
SUBJECT: Santa's Little Helper

HO HO CRAPPING HO!

Happy thingmas, Soulmate!

Don't be jealous of Chloe. And don't bother saying you're not. You so are. I can tell.

I'd be jealous if a guy on your street fancied you. But Chloe's boring. She always says the obvious thing if she says anything at all. Can't think if boys are looking at her apparently. Derp.

Christmas is balls when you're not a kid but we can save New Year, if you'll just let me come and see you.

PLEEEEEEEASE!

Just give me your address and I'll be there. Your theory is wrong. This wouldn't fall apart if we met.

Sheeeeit. Bashing about from downstairs. Mum's always stressed on Christmas Day but this year there's something else. Why can't Dad see it? Mum's a volcano and we'll all be covered in lava by the time the Queen's speech is on. (Thank God Granddad's not here this year or we'd have to be quiet while her madge drones on and on.)

Watched Taxi Driver last night. Well, this morning. Another all nighter. That makes it 17 times I've seen that film. Epic.

I downloaded Officer and a Gentleman. I tried to watch it. Honest! Why why why why why why is it your favourite

film? You usually like the HIPSTER stuff. You're a Juno/
Reservoir Dogs/Lost in Translation girl. Sorry. *Woman*. Officer
and a Gentleman is slushy mushy romantic rubbish, innit?

If we met face to face you could explain what you see
in it.

And you could also help me work out what the f*@k
I should do about my so called life.

Everything nearly blew apart the other day.

Mum turned up out of the blue to take us home. There
I was happily sitting in the cafe when I noticed her rubbish
car. Have you ever bunked *into* school? Of course not.
You're normal.

Ish.

Climbed over the hundred foot wall and dropped into
bushes on the other side then sneaked through the playground to find my sisters. If a teacher spotted me my
whole plan would have been ruined. (And there's no need
to tell me agen – I know you think it's a dumb plan.)

Luckily Mum believed my excuse for having leaves in my
hair. All those years of nerdy good behaviour paying off!
Just like my teacher believing the forged note about my
'shingles'. (Never google shingles by the way.)

I felt bad about lying to Mum. She explodes now and then
but most of the time she puts up with my moods. The
other day she said all sad, 'Where did my lovely little boy
go?' because I shouted at one of the twins. She'd understand if she knew about the Clones.

The twins helped me out with the cover story, then they
cut a deal with me. They're worse than the mafia. Said
they'd tell the Olds about the bunking off unless I explain

to them why I'm doing it. Had to confess all or the shit would hit the fan. And the fan is right by my face.

I gave them the PG version.

Once upon a time there was an evil Queen called Lauren. She ruled the kingdom of St Ethelred's with black magic and short skirts. All her serfs were desperate to go to Queen Lauren's fantabulous ball at her uncle the school governor's amazing house but only the aristocrats were invited.

And a lowly dork named Angus.

Gasp!

The dork is embarrassed to admit that he punched the air and shouted YESSS! when the text arrived.

But the ball sucked big time. Clones in stripper shoes trying to get off with the trendy knob heads he couldn't stand at school. The evil Queen made a beeline for the dork and he was mightily confused. Was Lauren (who all the knob heads madly fancied) *flirting* with him?

Angus wasn't flattered.

Angus was SCARED.

Scared like a rhino was charging him.

Angus the Dork tried to avoid the evil Queen. Thanks to the Goth Girl Across The Road he has skills in this area. But nothing worked. Even when he shut himself away with the Queen's dad's vinyl collection (you'd have loved it – he had BOWIE) she sent a minion to summon him.

'Come, O Dorkish one,' said the minion. 'Queen Lauren is screening your favourite movie in the home cinema.'

You know this Dork well so you know he couldn't resist a HOME CINEMA.

Plus he was drunk. (This wasn't included in the twin version.)

Angus assumed there'd be other people there.

Duh!

The Queen was alone in a dark room with an amazing Bose Acoustimass system and a big squashy sofa. Twilight was on the screen.

Twilight!

Yes. The Queen thought TWILIGHT aka Lamest Film EVER was the Dork's favourite film.

The Queen was kind of odd. Eyes shining. Skin clammy. (No need for the twins to know that this was cos the Queen was off her freaking head on the tablets being passed around like Smarties.)

The Dork sussed out what was happening a minute too late. He genuinely hadn't realised he was a sacrificial offering.

The Dork tried to act normal when the Queen sat on him and squirmed about like a lap-dancer. He moved his head when she tried to snog him.

This is hard to believe but the Dork felt sorry for the Queen, i.e. the world had officially turned upside down. He felt sorry for her cos she was wasting her best moves on the wrong guy.

The Dork is a romantic.

The Dork wouldn't admit this to anybody except you.

When the Queen wrapped her legs around the Dork, he tried to get her off without hurting her or groping her. Not easy when one of you is smashed and the other one is high. The Evil Queen morphed into an Evil Octopus.

She was sticking her tongue down his throat and grabbing at his fly.

So the Dork held her shoulders and said, 'Look! Any of those guys upstairs would kill to be with you but I'm into somebody else.'

(He didn't add that this someone else wouldn't even *give him her address* cough cough.)

The Queen's face changed. (The twins liked this bit best.) She went from super sexy to screaming monster, with lipstick all over her chin. She said 'Don't you get who I am?'

The Queen shouted, 'Help!'

The Dork heard heavy pissed feet thump along the corridor. The Queen – who was turning out to be less nice than the Dork had expected, and he'd expected her to be an almighty bitch – said 'You're nobody and you should thank me for even noticing you. You. Are. Dead.' With a full stop after each word like in American sitcoms. The Clones arrived and things got very loud. The Dork shouted they shouted the Queen shouted.

She said I'd jumped her and forced myself on her. She shouted 'Throw him out but don't beat him up!' Nice touch your majesty. But then she said, 'Spread the word.'

The Dork is a perv!

The Dork is a sicko!

The Dork is a rapist!

The Dork is a poof! (Confusing, I know.)

The Queen's subjects carried out her bidding. On Facebook. On Twitter. By text. By phone. In notes. In whispers. In graffiti in the bogs. The Clones are very obedient.

And the Dork lived unhappily ever after.
The End.

My little sisters had no idea. Even tho we go to the same school, primary and secondary are different worlds. I thought they'd tease me but they cuddled me. After all the ess aitch one tee *that's* what made me cry!!! Iris and Rose are too young to really understand. They don't realise it's not the rejection that makes Lauren hate me, it's the fact that I *know*.

Me, the dorkiest dork in our year, *I* know she's a virgin. In Lauren's fucked-up world being a virgin is embarrassing. Sex and love aren't tied up together. She just wants to 'do it'.

Plus she's a virgin with a crush on somebody who doesn't fancy her back.

She assumed I'd tell everybody. She thinks boys are a different species with willies where their hearts should be. She could have trusted me. I'd never tell. Instead she tried to destroy me so nobody would believe me.

The twins promised to 'sort her out'. Sure.

Right. I'll go now. That was a long one! Not exactly Christmas cheer. Sorry.

And listen, I get it. You don't want me to come to Scotland. I'll stop nagging.

laters

Angus

P.S. It's very very quiet downstairs. The traditional Christmas Day row should start any . . . minute . . . now . . .

How Marie came to be on the sofa, she had no idea. A cushion was propped up behind her, her shoes were off – she always cooked Christmas lunch in 'good' shoes – and there was a glass of halfway-decent wine (i.e. more than £6.99 a bottle) in her hand.

She remembered the smoke alarm going off. She remembered somebody who sounded a lot like herself saying loud things about 'this bloody family' and 'Who am I? Superwoman?' She remembered Robert entering the kitchen with a determined but wary air, like a vet about to sedate a skittish llama. She remembered him saying, 'Step away from the smoke alarm. I repeat: Step away from the smoke alarm.'

And then, somehow, she was on the sofa, with a Terry's Chocolate Orange.

On the rug the twins were absorbed in a complex doll game. They were silent. Robert had used 'Daddy's Remote' on them. Marie had never fathomed how it worked, but every now and then, when things got out of hand, Robert aimed an imaginary handset at them and pretended to press a button. 'Mute,' he'd say. And they would. They'd mute.

Angus came downstairs with his trademark half-stumble, half-lope. 'All right?' he said, head round the door. That wary look, just like his father.

'More than all right.' Marie popped a dark segment into her mouth, this being the only date in the calendar when a Terry's Chocolate Orange was acceptable as a pre-lunch snack.

Twenty minutes later there was a Dunwoody bottom on every seat around the dining table. The candles on Marie's mother's embroidered tablecloth were lit. The gravy steamed in its boat. (Where on Earth had Robert found the gravy boat? It had been AWOL since last Christmas.) Slabs of luscious white meat lay stacked on their plates, cosying up to roast potatoes all golden and crisp and come-hither.

His sleeves rolled up, a sheen of sweat across his brow, Robert held up his glass. 'To Mum,' he said.

'To Mum,' three voices echoed.

'To us,' said Marie, properly, stupidly happy.

The Yule log lay devastated, as if run over by a tank. The family, already full of turkey and 'all the trimmings', had somehow found a second wind when confronted by the magnificent cake.

The 'twist' had gone down very well.

'It's *white*!' Rose had breathed.

'That's meant to be snow!' Iris had melted with the romance of it, and the prospect of so much white chocolate. 'Awesome, Mum,' Angus had said.

There were only streaks of white left, and a tiny traumatised plastic robin on its side.

The sitting room – its untidiness a testament to the long, cheerful day – was flattered by the cherry-and-emerald glow of the lights on the tree. Head on her mum's lap, Iris slept, mouth open, eyelids flickering. On the opposite sofa Rose was propped against Robert, quietly debating Father Christmas's existence.

Angus, from where he lay flat on his back on the rug, was firmly anti-Santa, but Robert allowed Rose space to prolong her faith in him by saying, 'If you believe in Santa, he exists. And I do believe in him.' He was wearing the lilac/heather jumper: despite his protestations, Marie could see it was too snug under the arms.

Iris snored a tiny snore, like a fairy coughing. Feeling sleepy and safe and *ready*, Marie slid a Christmas card from its red envelope.

Robert heard the rustle. 'I thought we opened them all.'

'Just one left,' said Marie.

Best girl,

I know how hard you've worked to make this Christmas special, but really all I need is you and Daddy and Robert and little Angus. No talk of 'last this' or 'last that', please! I'll always be with you at Christmas, and every other day of the year for that matter, watching Angus grow, and laughing at the antics of those two little girls growing in your tummy. Say hello to them for me, and remind them how much their grandma loved them, even when they were just two little pipsqueaks inside her own darling daughter.

Marie, listen. This is important. Your mother has a promise for you and it's this: Love changes, but it can't die.

Merry Christmas

Mum x

DECEMBER

New Year's Eve

*Croquembouche
Wedding Cake*

NEW YEAR RESOLUTIONS

1 Lose 7 lb by March (i.e. ½ lb per week – easy!)
2 Go to gym 2 3 2 times a week
3 Get up half-hour early
4 Look after feet
5 Read more
6 Walk everywhere and take stairs
7 Swear less
8 Stop making bloody stupid resolutions I can't pissing well keep.

The P.S. to every year, New Year's Eve brought the usual automatic, no-need-for-an-invitation invitation to the yearly bash thrown by Marie's oldest friend. She and Jo had met at university, and although they lived just an hour's drive from each other, life conspired to keep them apart for much of the time. New Year was sacrosanct. Just as Jo didn't need to invite them, the Dunwoodys didn't need to say they'd be there: attendance was mandatory.

'I hope there's a magician again this year,' said Iris as she helped her mother fill the (thankfully fully recovered) dishwasher after a lunch of festive leftovers.

'I hope there *isn't*,' said Robert. Magicians came a close second to clowns in his nightmares. 'Mar, are you driving tonight, or am I?'

'Dad means,' said Angus, tipping his sprout-'n'-stilton soup dregs into the yucca, 'is he drinking or are you?'

'I'll drive. You drove last year.' Marie fell on her sword, sacrificing the vodka luge for the sake of marital harmony. 'If Dad's drunk,' she said to the twins, 'he might dance.'

'Oh, please dance, Daddy!' Rose clasped her hands

219

together, a Dickensian orphan begging for gruel. 'You're hilarious when you dance!'

'Must be some other daddy you're thinking of,' huffed Robert. 'I'm suave, lithe. Sensual even.'

Angus shuddered and left the room.

'Jump in the shower, Angus!' shouted Marie, adding: '*now*!' She turned her gaze on the twins, both in dire need of a general going-over with a sponge. 'I must throw you two in the bath, too.' Hygiene standards had slipped over that cosy, nameless period between Christmas and the New Year. She looked at her watch. 'What time are we expected?'

'Nine. As usual.' Robert tucked what was left of his latest loaf into the bread bin as tenderly as if it were a newborn. 'Seven hours should give you just about enough time to get ready.'

'Ooh, how I love your gender-joshing,' deadpanned Marie, handing out slabs of Victoria sponge (now an oft-requested family favourite) to Iris and Rose. '*I'm* not the one fannying about with scruffing lotion and anti-fatigue eye gel before bed.'

'They were a present. It'd be rude not to use them.' Robert patted the skin beneath his eyes surreptitiously; he hadn't realised they looked fatigued until Magda's present spelled it out.

'Before we know it, you'll be wearing guy-liner.' Marie enjoyed the twins' snigger. 'Which you'll keep in your *manbag*.'

'It's not a manbag, it's a perfectly ordinary, if – admittedly – rather small briefcase that . . .' Robert ran out of steam. He was tired of defending his leather goods.

'. . . looks like a handbag.' Marie was anything but tired of the subject. 'Now shoo, everybody. I need the kitchen to myself.'

'Oh no, you don't.' Robert lowered his head, treating his wife to a penetrating stare. 'There isn't time for you and Ms Berry to get down and dirty with a new recipe.'

'There's plenty of time,' said Marie blithely. Or as blithely as she could with her top lip stuck to her teeth. The thought of what she had to achieve before leaving the house, made-up and perfumed, at 8 p.m. made her mouth go dry.

'This isn't Lynda's wedding cake, is it? Bloody hell, Marie! That thing has to be two feet high! I assumed you'd told her you couldn't do it.'

'It'll be fine. I'm good at this stuff now.' She wanted to lie down and cry, and run up and down the Close with her hair on fire, all at the same time; the feeling opened a wormhole in time and whisked her right back to adolescent Sunday evenings and the prospect of doing a week's homework in the half-hour before bed.

The week since Christmas Day had been so relaxed that Marie hadn't squared up to the dreaded croquembouche. Robert had taken leave from work – a risky manoeuvre, leaving Magda in Caroline's clutches during a notoriously non-productive and relaxed time for buying offices – and the bitter weather had kept all five Dunwoodys indoors with the heat whacked up, tasty goodies emerging daily from the oven, and much mooching-about in onesies to a backdrop of indie and pop and Radio 2.

Looking for a pastime to unify the family, Marie had

stumbled on a most unlikely one. Slumped, happy and idle, on the sofa, she'd been channel-hopping one afternoon, but could find nothing she wanted to watch. Marie's TV habit was an open secret. In public she would admit only to taking in documentaries and the news, with the odd box set for variety, but Robert and the children, nodding loyally, knew she craved frequent doses of pointless reality TV, inane quiz shows and repeats. There were times when only bona-fide rubbish would hit the spot: dark days when she would emerge drained from a Jeremy Kyle marathon, to check that Robert was there for her 100 per cent and talking in bleeps. She'd been saved from resorting to such a binge by an obscure channel rerunning *MasterChef*. Lots and lots and *lots* of *MasterChef*.

No matter how often she turned the TV on, there was a heat she hadn't yet watched. Never having enjoyed the show – *cooking? in my downtime?* she'd always thought, contemptuously pushing buttons until she found an *Antiques Roadshow* that was itself an antique by now – these days she understood the contestants' fervour for food.

One by one, the others had crept to her side, attracted perhaps by the demented commentary. Even Angus had corkscrewed his behind into the mound of cushions: *MasterChef* was unlikely family cement. Phrases from the show wove themselves into daily life. 'Cooking doesn't get TOUGHER than this,' Angus had shouted that morning as he made toast. When he'd added jam, Iris had declared, 'There's too much going on that plate.'

When Robert queried Marie's no-show at the sales – usually she stormed them, cutting a swathe down Oxford

Street like Paris Hilton on steroids, returning home exhausted with eight new outfits that didn't fit – it was easily explained away by the weather. 'I don't blame you, love,' Robert had said, putting the kettle on yet again, as his wife gave thanks for his lack of curiosity. The real reason would have spoiled his cuppa: sale-surfing at a time when both their financial futures were so imperilled was out of the question.

So the Dunwoodys had been on cushy house-arrest, apart from Marie's dashes back to Smile! to open up for emergency patients.

One had been a screaming seven-year-old with an abscess; the other Jonas, complaining of inexplicable jaw pain. The problem had palpably been loneliness and not ill health, and Jonas had been sent home with a Tupper-ware box full of cake.

Tearing her thoughts from Jonas – it wasn't easy – Marie took down her Berry bible. She did a few knee-bends. She stretched her arms, cracked her knuckles. Said a speedy prayer.

In many respects she was completely ready for tomor-row's wedding. Her outfit, compulsively colour-coordi-nated, right down to her knickers (it wasn't out of the question for Lynda to carry out a spot-check at the church), hung on the outside of the wardrobe. New shoes stood to attention. A fascinator sat like a winged alien creature on a shelf. She'd even had her lipstick OK-ed by Lynda, who had been speaking in a noticeably higher pitch for the last fortnight and seemed to be surviving on cup-a-soup and adrenaline.

There was, however, one box on her wedding checklist that was resolutely unticked.

Time and again Marie had set aside a couple of hours to practise making the cake; time and again she'd been sidelined into messing about with the twins, hunkering down for a black-and-white movie with Robert, stalking Angus with a sandwich.

Now she could look back – with much gnashing of teeth – and admit it had been plain old fear keeping her from the kitchen – the white-hot dread of cooking something you can't pronounce.

At ten the next morning Marie was expected to deliver a croquembouche to a four-star boutique manor-house hotel with a discount marquee squatting on its lawn. It couldn't be an adequate croquembouche; it had to be a magnificent croquembouche. She needed to create a croquembouche that would make Gregg Wallace cry.

Steeling herself, she turned the page and faced the photograph head-on. No blinking. Like a jury member taking in a crime scene, she forced herself to linger on the details. She saw a densely packed, unthinkably calorific golden pyramid of soft pastry globes, piled on top of one another, *stuck* (how, in God's name, *how?*) to one another, all beneath a veil of gilded spun sugar.

Deciding hastily that the spun sugar was a step too far – Lynda would have to make do with a naked croquembouche – Marie girded her loins and read through the recipe. Each ball was made with choux pastry ('It's pronounced *shoo*,' said Iris loftily, pausing in her unstoppable consumption of Quality Street to look over her mother's shoulder) and was piped full of sweetened cream.

The list of necessary equipment was a roll call of the usual suspects, except for one item that reared up in letters of flame. 'A croquembouche cone?' said Marie, horror-struck. 'Angus!' she shouted, 'google something for me!'

Angus brought her a printout of an anodised aluminium wizard's hat. The idea was to turn it upside down and use it as a mould, pressing the choux globes down into it, bound together with freshly made caramel (here she paused for an efficiently brief panic attack, before moving on) until it was full, whereupon it would be inverted and the stunning structure would emerge, proud, sticky and tall.

Mary suggested improvising a cone from cardboard. But then Mary would. Mary was a Girl Guide at heart, never daunted. Marie had been thrown out of the Guides for customising her uniform: 'Are you trying for the trollop badge?' Brown Owl had asked, eyeing the hemline. Today, more than ever before, Marie would have to channel Mary.

Because John and Gregg were right. Cooking *didn't* get tougher than this.

It was a classic rookie mistake, one that was by now beneath her. Robert, disgruntled at going to Jo's party without his wife, didn't let her off the hook. 'You were crazy,' he said as he shrugged on his best jacket, 'to think you could accomplish something like this in an afternoon.'

Every surface in the kitchen and the utility room and the sitting room was covered with trays of cooling choux balls. Marie had been astonished to find that choux pastry was made in a saucepan, not a bowl: she'd washed and rewashed her pan countless times before she'd even embarked on the task of requisitioning every tray, plate, board and large book in the house to accommodate the resultant spheres.

'So many balls,' murmured Marie, wiping shaking hands on her second apron of the day. 'So little time.'

'You'll follow us later, yeah?'

'Of course.' For Marie this was a fairy tale: there was no longer a 'later'. Her entire future revolved around pastry balls. The twins looked edibly cute in matching pastel dresses – her two little macaroons. Angus had changed his jeans – Marie was moved to tears by such extravagant effort. 'Have fun without me,' she said bravely.

'We will!' sang Iris, skipping to the car.

'I won't.' Robert leaned in for a kiss and Marie smelled the aftershave she'd given him. It was the wrong moment to be ambushed with lust for your husband, but he always scrubbed up well. Their kiss wasn't perfunctory, and was accompanied by a soundtrack of Rose's '*Uuuuuuuurgh!*' 'Don't be long,' whispered Robert, with one final squeeze.

'Just you and me now, Prinny,' said Marie as the car pulled away.

Out on the Close, New Year's Eve revved up.

The Gnomes' joint was jumping, every window lit and a 'Birdie Song' singalong leaking out into the cul-de-sac. The Grays' house was dark, but the crooked path to Graham and Johann's house was lined with LED lanterns, their partly drawn curtains offering a candlelit glimpse of a genteel supper party. Marie could almost smell the canapés as she stood at her window, wine in hand, cream in hair, suicide options taking shape.

She longed to be at her friend's party, watching her tipsy husband dance, ruffling her children's hair, gorging on food she hadn't prepared, wishing she'd worn lower heels, winking at Jo across the dance floor, making memories.

She rubbed her hand, the red mark there still sparking and tender. The caramel-making, at least, was over. Luckily she'd heeded Mary's pessimistic advice to have a bowl of cold water within reach, for the dunking of burns. Now it was time to *construct*.

Sidestepping the splats of dropped batter on the floorboards, Marie surveyed her improvised cone. The cockeyed cardboard spire jammed together with Sellotape had a whiff of last-minute art homework about it. 'Wish me luck, Prinny.'

The dog, a notorious mood-sponge, looked in need of a stiff drink, cowering under the table, baleful eyes following Marie. His mistress, usually a soft touch for a titbit, was strange this evening, wired and tense.

It was almost 10 p.m. There had been various texts from the party-goers.

Have you finished yet, wifey?

Mum, we miss u!

Jo's friend is trying to get off with me. She might succeed if you don't COME QUICK!

Mum, u hav 2 get here! We got dad 2 dance!!!!!!!!!!!

Mum, for Christ's sake hurry up and stop Dad dancing.

Marie jabbed out a message she didn't want to send.

Darlings, have fun without me, still baking. Sorry. Love you!
I'll text you at midnight.

The silence that provoked was deafening: Marie could just imagine Robert pausing halfway through getting down with his bad self to 'YMCA' (or perhaps he was in Boogie Wonderland – hell, by this stage of the party he might well be Walking On Sunshine).

The dainty golden orbs, all 150 of them, had been piped full of cream scented with limoncello liqueur. Never confident around a piping bag, Marie had suffered a near-terminal case of clenched buttock throughout. Her choux balls wouldn't win any beauty contests, but she knew from a few test-licks of her spoon that they tasted dreamy.

The mobile jerked. The message wasn't from Robert. It was Jo, the hostess.

Seriously? You're blowing out my party for a CAKE?

She'd placate Jo tomorrow. If tomorrow ever came. If there was a life beyond this kitchen.

As instructed, Marie propped the cone, point first, into a vase. This made it all too high to work with, so she put the vase on the floor. That was better, if awkward.

Raucous laughter and shouts that might or might not denote a fight drifted over from the Gnome homestead. Right now even that party felt preferable to crouching on her kitchen floor, a choux ball in one hand and a teaspoon dripping with caramel in the other.

'Cover me, Prinny,' she said. 'I'm going in.'

A discreet stress-wee escaped her sous-chef.

Leaning in – the cone was *enormous* – Marie bedded down the first ball in the cardboard nose. Then a dab of caramel, inside the echoey cardboard burrow. Another bun, pressed gently into place. Dab. Press. Dab. Press. Dab. Press.

And so on.

And so forth.

Time ceased to mean anything, as bun after bun followed its brave comrades into the cone's hungry belly. At one point Marie, high on croquembouche fumes, hallucinated John and Gregg egging her on.

'She's juggling huge flavours!' bellowed John.

'She's flicking my switches!' howled Gregg.

It was tricky to find a rhythm in such gooey, hot work. Like a coal-miner down a patisserie quarry, Marie carried doggedly on, caramel in her fringe and a tiny flicker of hope in her heart that this might work, and Lynda might be pleased, and Marie might not start the New Year in a witness protection scheme.

The moment of truth came. She wasn't mad about moments of truth, and this one – lonely and fraught – had the potential to go horribly wrong.

Prinny was asleep by now, trembling his way through

doggy dreams. His legs quivered, much as his owner's did as she placed the white cake-board on top of the filled cone and gingerly turned the whole thing upside down.

The weight of it took her by surprise. She hadn't thought that bit through. She wondered if Mary, far away at some dignified gathering, could feel a disturbance in the force as the board tilted, the cone's Sellotape flaps fluttered open and choux balls bounced all over the kitchen.

Prinny came to and lunged, all his maddest fantasies come true, as cake rained from the skies. With a shameful impulse to save and reuse what she could, Marie lunged too, and her heel skidded on a glob of the cream mixture that she'd made so lovingly an hour earlier. Down she went, as if a sniper had picked her off.

Head versus cupboard door is an uneven contest. Marie's skull throbbed as, groaning on all fours, she took in her kitchen to a soundtrack of Prinny's hysterical slobbering.

Only a small clot of buns adhered to Lynda's painstakingly chosen board: a godforsaken parody of a croquembouche. The rest – the sum total of Marie's toil, the reason she'd pissed off her oldest friend and packed off her family without her – dotted the kitchen as if shot from a scattergun.

Her *MasterChef* boyfriends evaporated: this was too gigantic a disaster even for their hysterical vocabularies. With no Plan B, just the prospect of calling the bride at dawn to say there'd be no wedding cake, Marie sat and wept.

The tears came thick, fast and noisy. She cried with the unselfconsciousness of a child, slumped on the cream-flecked floor, jammed up against the fridge-freezer, legs splayed out in front of her. When Prinny, with a gentle doggy harrumph, nosed his head under her hand in empathy, Marie just cried harder. This wasn't the Mary Berry way – she'd been bested by a fancy bake.

Weary, spent and riddled with feelings of worthlessness, she sank even further into her bespoke pit of despair when a tap at the window announced Lucy. That symmetrically pretty face was creased with photogenic concern. *You all right?* it mouthed from the darkness.

As stupid questions go, it was a doozy. Marie had never felt less right. From the very end of her toes she dredged up sufficient stamina to smile – ghoulishly – at Lucy, as she jerked to her feet like a puppet on sadistically yanked strings.

Going to the window, she pushed it open, its creak echoing her own joints. Marie felt older than the moon. 'Hiya!' she said jauntily, as the frigid night air rushed in. *Nothing to see here – move along* was what she wanted to say, but politeness forced her to wipe her eyes with the backs of her hands and turn the state of her kitchen (not to mention the state of her mental health) into an anecdote. 'Having a teensy bit of a problem-o, as you can see!'

Evidently the desperate gurn didn't convince. 'Let me in,' said Lucy, tugging down the hood of her Barbour.

'Honestly, I'm fine.' Marie shrugged, as if the devastation around her and her conspicuous anguish were neither here nor there.

'Go to the door,' said Lucy clearly, as if addressing a mass audience of village idiots, 'and let me in.'

Marie sleepwalked to the hall. Her immediate future – clearing up, crying, telling Lynda, crying forever – was so horrible that adding her adversary to the mix made little difference. The person she needed to see on the doorstep was Mary Berry, fragrant and crisp in a clean apron exuding *eau-de-can-do*. She would sob in Mary's arms for a while, and then Mary would snap her wrinkled fingers and all would be well.

What actually stood on the doorstep was the person she liked least, dripping with sympathy-lite; *all the better to nose around my misery*, thought Marie.

A tiny thing by Lucy's foot, a scrap of beige fluff, jumped and growled and startled Marie.

'That's Cookie,' said Lucy briskly. 'New chihuahua. Present from Tod.' She was talking in clipped snatches, a housewife sergeant-major. 'Ignore her.'

It was tricky to ignore a bad-tempered dustball, but Marie tuned out the self-important yaps as best she could.

'Just popping New Year cards through doors.'

Well, of course you are.

'You look terrible.' Lucy stepped into the hall, unasked, uninvited. 'What on Earth's happened?'

Too weak to resist this house invasion, Marie shuffled to the kitchen and gestured with a *what-am-I-like?* shrug at the defeated huddle on the cake-board. 'That,' she said, 'is meant to be a croquembouche.'

'Croquembouche?' Lucy lit up. 'I made one for my wedding.'

Only a minute under her roof and Lucy had prompted

her second *Of course you did*. 'I'm guessing it was nicer than this one,' said Marie.

'A little.' Lucy's voice softened and the Pathé-news diction fell away. 'Has it been a nightmare?'

The question flicked a switch in Marie's frozen brain and, with Cookie goose-stepping about their feet, licking greedily at microscopic full stops of cream missed by Prinny, the story poured out. Compulsively she spilled every sad and sorry bean, holding nothing back. It felt good to purge, even if Lucy would surely file tonight as further proof of her own superiority.

'It's Lynda . . .' Marie ran her fingers through her matted hair. 'I keep imagining her face. I mean, she's going to go ballistic of course, but I can take that. I can even just about take facing her at work every day, when I know she'll be thinking *wedding-ruiner* every time she looks at me. What I can't take is . . .' Flinching, she approached the summit of her unhappiness. 'She's been driving us mad for months, planning this wedding. She's thought of nothing else. At times I've wanted to hang myself with a lace garter rather than hear one more newsflash about the top-table centrepiece, but I've indulged her because she's been my receptionist for almost ten years and she's got a huge heart and her mum died and . . .' Marie was gabbling. Time to sum up. 'I love the girl. I just love her, and I can't bear to let her down.'

Lucy looked down at the chihuahua. 'Sit!' she said. 'Stay!' To Marie she said, 'I'll be back in two minutes with my croquembouche cone.'

*

Accustomed to the slacker help that a woman gets from a husband or the people she gave birth to, Marie was astonished at how quickly the kitchen was put to rights with both of them on the case. As Cookie effortlessly manoeuvred Prinny under whatever it is that chihuahuas have in lieu of a thumb, her owner did much the same with the epic mess. Dog and woman had different methods: Cookie sat on Prinny's face; Lucy behaved as if the kitchen belonged to her.

'Right.' She slapped down a weighty book on the newly gleaming worktop. 'We'll use Delia's recipe.'

'Oh.' Marie stiffened. The anti-Berry cook right here at the heart of number nineteen, her Mona Lisa features on the cover promising *Everything will be fine, as long as you never ever dare to disagree with me.* 'I used a Mary Berry one . . .'

'Ah.' The air thickened. The books sat side by side, seeming to throb. 'Mary Berry?'

Too tired to analyse Lucy's tone of voice, Marie nodded. 'Mary,' she said and then, with what she hoped was a *don't mess with me* intonation, but might have been a frazzled squeak, '*Berry.*'

'Okey-doke.' Lucy's capitulation was both immediate and sunny. 'Ooh, limoncello!' she murmured approvingly, scanning the recipe. 'How are you for plain flour?'

'Almost out.' The shame of it! The hot, burning shame of it.

'Eggs?'

'Down to my last two.'

'Righty-ho. Back in a min. I've got loads of *everything*

at my place.' She pointed at Cookie, farting contentedly in Prinny's bed. 'No widdling, you,' she said, and Marie could have sworn that Cookie nodded. Half-turning, Lucy stopped and reached up to Marie and wiped a gobbet of cream from her forehead. 'There,' she said, 'that's better.'

And it was.

The tender touch with a damp cloth was the pivot on which the night turned. Plus a lot more besides.

When Lucy returned, laden with eggs and flour and a giant vat of double cream, the kitchen began to hum again, with the expectant, contained buzz of backstage an hour before curtain up. Watching Lucy move deftly, with the assurance of an expert and the focus of a zealot, Marie dared to believe that she could come good on her promise to Lynda.

'I'll do the pastry, you do the filling,' said Lucy, colonising the kitchen with the same Napoleonic ease with which her minuscule animal had occupied the dog-bed.

She paused, as if remembering where she was. 'Unless . . .' she held out the pan, '*you* want to do the pastry?'

'I have choux post-traumatic stress disorder. I'm on cream. And music.' Marie turned on the radio and a moronic dance tune spurred them on with its insistent *sss-sss* bass-line. 'I'd assumed you'd be off somewhere fancy-pants tonight,' she said over the music and the mixer.

'Tod doesn't do New Year.' Lucy was weighing flour, stooping to check the digital readout. 'And Chloe is off out somewhere – you know teenagers.'

'I do.' The remark triggered surprise – belated surprise:

how come she hadn't noticed this earlier? – that Angus *wasn't* off out somewhere. He was with his embarrassing dad and his annoying sisters at Jo's party. With the briefest of emotional detours for a rapid *Wish I was there*, Marie wondered why her own teenager hadn't been invited to run wild with his own kind, half-blind on WKD.

An assembly line of sorts was soon purring. Things cooled as other things were whipped while yet more things were baking. A chihuahua yawned; Daft Punk chugged on; Marie's fear receded, but couldn't fade completely: she'd witnessed Lynda's verbal take-down of the wedding singer who didn't know 'Wind Beneath My Wings' and was in no doubt about her fate if croquembouche number two failed.

'You'll laugh,' said Lucy, dipping and piping, dipping and piping, as comfortable with an icing bag as a seasoned midwife with a tricky C-section, 'but sometimes, when I'm panicking about something, I think to myself *What would Delia do?*'

Flabber-efficiently-gasted, Marie's concrete ideas about her neighbour crumbled a little more. 'Only ten minutes to twelve,' she reported, stirring the caramel, with cold water to hand. This would be the first New Year's Eve since meeting Robert that she wouldn't kiss him at midnight. After so many accumulated New Year kisses, it shouldn't really matter.

But it did matter.

'What's Tod got against New Year?' she asked, scrutinising her caramel. Was it amber yet?

'Sentimental tosh, he says.' Lucy smiled indulgently. 'I'm the same,' she said. 'Yes. I am. The same. I am.'

'Got it, Yoda.'

Lucy laughed. Another chip of concrete fell to the (spotless) floor.

With a concise lesson from Lucy and a no-nonsense 'You can do it', Marie piped a neat queue of choux balls. 'Aw*right*!' said Marie. 'If I had a smidgen less personal dignity, I'd high-five you, Lu.'

Lu. Had she just nicknamed her nemesis?

Big Ben kicked off on the radio. 'The bongs!' shouted Marie. It was rude to ignore the turn of the year altogether. Swiping a bottle of unchilled champagne from the wine rack, she barked 'Lucy! Prinny! What's your name . . . um, Cookie! Outside!'

As they hit the front garden, a conga line snaked out of the Gnomes' house, hooting and high-kicking, headed for the central green.

'Ten!' shouted the conga line. 'Nine!'

Marie had always wanted to shake a bottle of 'poo and then crack it open, à la Grand Prix winners, and now was her opportunity. Lucy pulled a face, but seemed game about being drenched in alcohol. Cookie sheltered under a dead rose bush. Marie guzzled, then passed the bottle to Lucy. 'Happy New Year!' she shouted over the roars of 'Eight! Seven!'

'Ooh, cripes.' Lucy was in full *Mallory Towers* mode as her lips met possibly the first bottle-neck of her life.

A front door crashed open. Graham and Johann's supper guests invaded the green. 'Six! Five!' Prada eyewear and ironic jeans mingled with elasticated waistbands as fireworks burst over the Close, making rainbows in Prinny's sudden and extravagant wee.

A text arrived on Marie's phone. Robert had evidently been at Jo's infamous Hogmanay punch.

HAPPY NEW YEAR bESTest wif in world LOVE YOU hatlips! X CWn%

The children made more sense, with a *Happy midniht Mummyxxx* from the girls, and Angus's *I AM NEVER COMING TO JO'S PARTy AGAIN AND I NEVER WANT TO SEE DAD AGAIN HE SHOULD BE ASHAMED OF HIMSELF HAPPY NEW YEAR X*.

'Happy New Year, Delia!' Marie waved the bottle, swept away by bonhomie.

'And Mary!' laughed Lucy, sparkling with the spirit of the moment, her beam a goofy eye-crinkler that utterly lacked the elegance of her usual composure. 'And us!' She grabbed the bottle and drank too fast, bending double to cough in the New Year as Mrs Gnome screeched, 'Three! Two! One! HAPPY NEW YEAR YOU SHOWER OF BASTARDS!'

'Join us!' called Johann, his hair an asymmetric wonder, even when drunk.

'Nope. Sorry!' Lucy straightened up. 'We have work to do.'

One hour into a new year, Marie realised she wasn't fretting. She had faith that the croquembouche they were glueing carefully and slowly together, in the slightly fetishy cone supplied by Lucy, would work out.

Lack of fear freed up her mind for enjoyment of the timeless satisfaction of creativity. She felt generous; she felt plugged in; she felt useful and happy.

She realised something else, castigating herself for taking so long about it. There had been neither a call nor a text for Lucy at midnight. Not so much as a shout across the Close. Marie watched her reach into the cavernous cone, and wondered about that for a while. The small discordant note sounded by the smashed plate back on Bonfire Night chimed louder in the calm.

They'd promised themselves it would be done by two. As the hands of the retro clock inched towards three, they repromised that three was the deadline. The two women, like First World War tommies in a trench, were worn out from battle, but grimly determined to see it through to the end.

Without Lucy's encouragement – or was it more of a command? – Marie would never have attempted spun sugar. Now here she was spinning a gleaming spider's web, as Lucy stood at her elbow, her instructions composed and concise.

Upstairs the party-goers snored, having arrived home in a whirlwind of slammed minicab doors and a snatch of 'Auld Lang Syne'. Later today, at the wedding, she'd ask Robert about the lipstick stain on his collar, but his hangover would be punishment enough without recourse to cold-shouldering. The Gnomes' party had deteriorated into a marvellous brawl, which Marie was, unfortunately, too busy to enjoy. Graham and Johann's house was dark, like every other one in the cul-de-sac, except for the Dunwoody hive of activity.

'Lovely, lovely,' murmured Lucy, intent on Marie's sugary sorcery. 'Keep a steady hand. That's it.'

After a stuttering start, Marie and Lucy had found common ground. Acres of it. They made each other laugh. Marie could never have guessed, when she'd woken up that morning, that by the time she saw her bed again (and, dear God, how she *longed* to see her bed again) she would know her arch-enemy to be generous, kind, *fun*.

Perhaps it was the bonding properties of a shared goal, or the enchantment of the first dawn of the New Year, but Marie and Lucy leapfrogged a couple of stages in the getting-to-know-you process. Neighbours for years, they'd never considered each other friendship material until tonight; if anything, they'd been anti-magnetic, repelling each other.

When Marie was less tired – in, say, six months' time – she might force herself to reappraise that and face an awkward, humiliating fact. Was the antipathy between them a fabrication? *Did I*, thought Marie, guilt battling exhaustion for the upper hand, *wilfully misconstrue Lucy all this time?*

The woman squeezing her arm and saying 'Well done!' was transparently happy to help, with no airs or graces, no claims to superiority. *Their wires had been crossed*, thought Marie, *and now they're uncrossed*.

'Stand back,' said Lucy, wiping her hands on a tea towel,

shoulders drooping with fatigue, 'and take a look at what you've achieved.'

It *towered*, that croquembouche. It stood tall and proud, a gleaming white-and-gold colossus that would grace any feast, would delight Lynda and Barrington, and would fill many tummies and spread the wedding love.

For the first time in a long time, New Year's Eve hadn't involved loud music, poor-quality dancing and an inkling that Marie would pay for the drunken merriment in the morning. Instead, she'd revisited a mistake made long ago – one she'd doggedly stuck with, viewing all evidence through the prism of her own prejudice.

The turn of the year had brought a revelation: Lucy. She was a revelation so total and so welcome that it boded well for the coming twelve months. Fizzing without recourse to champagne, Marie chose to see Lucy's rehabilitation – from fiend to friend in one mighty bound – as an omen. *No need*, she told herself, *to be frightened of the future. You never know what's around the corner. It may all work out tickety-boo.*

'Thank you.' The two words were memorably inadequate.

'I enjoyed myself.' Lucy shook her head, as if to ward off praise or gratitude.

Marie took Lucy by the shoulders, noticing how narrow they were, how tiny she was. 'I mean it. Thank you, Lu.'

'Thank *you*,' said Lucy. 'For rescuing me from yet another deadly-dull New Year.'

From the corner came the small, wet snap of a chihuahua yawn.

THANK YOU

Dear Boss Lady,

I've saved this card until last, because I'm still wondering how to thank you properly for the amazing croquembouche. My family is still talking about it, and I can still taste the delicious lemony cream. I said to Barrington, 'Marie probably spent at least an hour making that.'

Did you enjoy the day? You looked as if you did, right up to the moment you fell into the fountain. I said to Barrington, 'I hope I'm that relaxed about strangers seeing my knickers when I'm Marie's age.' As you know, that champagne was twenty pounds a bottle (inc. discount for bulk), so I'm glad you liked the taste of it so much.

Were you as surprised as me when Aileen stood up to make a speech? I have to admit I was a *little* peeved, but I just bit down on Barrington's hand and got through it. I didn't mind the whole bit about marriage being a fairytale told by Satan, but my aunties are still getting over the (rather long) section about how awful sex is and how, if Barrington and I have any sense, we'll take up a hobby instead. By the end, though, when she said I was like the horrible big sister she'd never had, there was a tear in my eye.

I said to Barrington, 'Marie and Robert's marriage is an inspiration' – and after he'd remembered who you were, he agreed. When he and I are past it, I want to be just like you and Robert, still together, still in love. All in all, a huge THANK YOU from me and my husband (can't get used to calling him that!) for the amazing cake, which truly made our day.

And just from me, another thank you. For being more than a boss lady when my mum passed away. You understood and gave me space and then, when I needed it, you held me close.

I said to Barrington, 'Marie is my other mother.'

L xxx

FEBRUARY

St Valentine's Day

Heart-Shaped Cake

TO: stargazinggirl247@gmail.com
FROM: geeksrus39@gmail.com
13.02.14
07.52
SUBJECT: Cupid is dead

HAPPY ALMOST VALENTINE'S DAY SOULMATE!
OK come down from the ceiling. I know you hate mush. Even you have to admit it's weard that I have to spend the official most romantic day of the year with The Goth Girl Across The Road. Thanks Mum for roping me and her in to helping with some stupid party. If you were here I'd give you hmm let's see obviously not roses or you'd shoot me in the balls but maybe one small daisy? Would that be alowed?
School's rough. Surprise surprise! Wish I could fake another illness but you're right (as usual) it's too risky. One teacher is kind of suspicious and asked me if everything's cool. I said yeah.
Things sound freaking CRAP at your place. Jump on a train and come here. Mum would LOVE you. She'd give you cake and talk to you about spots and periods and all the other things you gals chat about. Dad would make you taste quiche and ask if it was too salty or too herby or too eggy. And the twins would go full-on apeshit to meet my girl friend.
Stop having a fit and re-read that sentence. The two words are not joined up. 'girl' and 'friend'. Totally different thing.
laters
Angus
P.S. Found spelling mistake in your last email. Your first! Ha! You can NEVER lord it over me agen!

On tiptoe at the door's glass porthole, the twins spied on the school secretary.

Mrs Ardizzone was famously formidable, a throwback to the days when children were irritants. She scorned the right-on approach of modern teachers who referred to their charges as 'students' and were aware of their 'needs'. To Mrs Ardizzone, they were all 'kids' and their most pressing 'need' was to be told off, on the hour, every hour.

'Her bosoms!' whispered Iris.

'I know!' whispered Rose.

A sturdy 40GG, Mrs Ardizzone's breasts were encased in a bulletproof bra beneath one of her myriad itchy twinsets. The breasts hypnotised the twins, who found it hard it concentrate around them.

'The plan!' hissed Iris. They were on borrowed time: it had been risky to ask to go to the loo together, and they mustn't arouse suspicion by taking too long. They both thought of the exercise book crammed with pencilled scribbles, diagrams, drawings and stickers of kittens. *The Plan*, it said on the cover, each letter felt-tipped with a different pattern. *Keep Out Or Else!!!*

Dipping beneath the porthole, her eyes sweeping the long hall, Rose whispered, the words ripped from her, 'I'm scared, Iris.'

Until Rose said so, Iris had been scared, too. But now the twin seesaw creaked into action: Rose shed her fear in order to buoy up her sister. 'If we just stick to the plan, it'll be fine. Don't be scared, Rosie-Posie. You've already done something almost as scary.'

True. Pity she couldn't boast to Mum about yesterday's triumph, thought Rose. She'd displayed Dench-level acting skills by faking a convincing tummy ache when the other secretary had been on duty. That lady, known for her kindness, always kept suffering students by her side, rather than imprisoning them in the sickroom. Emitting the odd groan from a hard plastic chair, Rose had watched the secretary go about her business, her nut-brown eyes taking in the labels on each file drawer until, information gleaned, she'd declared, 'I feel a lot better now, Miss,' and had trotted back to class.

'Ready?' Iris's steady gaze locked onto Rose's and they both nodded. They were more than the sum of their parts. They were two to the power of twin. They pounded on the door. 'Mrs Ardizzone! Mrs Ardizzone!'

'Keep it down!' A menopause on legs, Mrs Ardizzone tugged open the door. 'Noisy articles! What d'you want?'

'There's a boy!' shouted Iris. In Mrs A's world, boys were like velociraptors. Iris paused for a vital beat before the killer detail. 'In your roses!'

The small corner of the school grounds dedicated to roses was off-limits, *verboten*. If Mrs Ardizzone could have got away with electrified wire, she would have installed it. She loved roses the way other people loved other people. 'What?' she shrieked, making the girls jump: they'd unleashed a Valkyrie.

'I'll show you.' Iris ran ahead, adrenaline pumping, knowing that her twin had already slipped through the door before it swung shut.

After propping the door slightly open (it locked automatically; pupils were buzzed in by office staff), Rose made straight for a tall grey filing cabinet and pulled out the middle drawer. As she flicked through the clacking folders, the relevant one seemed to jump into her fingers. With a sibilant Y*esss!* – just like her dad's when some muffin-baking went to plan – Rose pulled it out and laid it flat across the shoulders of its hanging brethren. Scanning the form within, she scribbled on her palm, glancing neurotic-ally at the door all the while. A seasoned *what if*-er – just like her mum – she tried to subdue thoughts of the repercussions if an adult walked in.

As she was replacing the file, it hooked itself onto another. Rose tussled, sweat breaking on her brow beneath her impeccably brushed fringe. 'Get *in*,' she begged and the file complied. Slipping out of the room like a ghost, she was halfway down the corridor when Mrs Ardizzone clattered back into the building, Iris close behind.

'Next time,' she was saying darkly. 'Next time I'll get 'im.' She turned to her apple-cheeked companion. 'Want a Werther's Original, dear?'

'Ooh, yes please, Mrs Ardizzone!' simpered Iris.

*

'That's taking things a little *too* far,' winced Lucy.

'I don't regret a minute of it.' Nowadays Marie felt at home in Lucy's kitchen, but it had taken a while. So much gloss, so much Smeg, Bulthaup and other hard-to-pronounce, bordering-on-comical brand names. She'd coached herself and practised hard until she could fearlessly put down a mug on the Corian, and these days she appreciated the steam rotisserie, the hissing adjustable breakfast-bar stools, the swan-necked tap that spewed boiling water.

'What happened? No! Don't tell me!' Lucy's small hands, glittering with rings, flew to her face with an idiosyncratic movement that always made Marie smile: sometimes she shocked Lucy just for that silent-film reaction.

'I can't be the first woman to have a rude dream about *MasterChef*.' Marie sipped her coffee; it truly did taste better out of bone china. 'Ooh, the things they did to me!' She relished Lucy's *No, no, no*. 'John smeared me in mango, and Gregg took me right there in the *MasterChef* kitchen, among the makings of a paella. The man's an *animal*.' She was laughing now, too. 'When he came, he shouted *It's a taste explosion!*'

'Please stop.' Lucy's eyes were squeezed tight. 'What would Mary Berry say?'

'Oh, she's probably had them both.' Marie enjoyed Lucy's peal of appalled laughter. It was the real deal, not the polite noise Lucy generally made. She was so carefully polite, so genteel and inoffensive that at times she could seem like a constructed *thing* rather than the flesh-and-blood, interesting woman she truly was. For so long Marie hadn't looked beyond Lucy's facade, blinkered by prejudice and – she could admit it now – envy. Daily she gave thanks that she'd finally broken through; the Close was a better place with a chum across the road. 'I can just see Mary, John and Gregg in a hot tub with Delia.'

'No.' Lucy held up a stern forefinger. 'Delia's a good girl.'

'She's a bore,' said Marie. 'She probably stands a safe distance away, shouting *You can catch verrucas in hot tubs, you know!* and *Put Gregg down, Mary, you don't know where he's been.*'

'But we do know where he's been.' Lucy refilled Marie's cup, adding a tiny pastel macaroon to the saucer. 'In the paella. With you.'

Marie shuddered. 'Where's the gang?' she asked, noting the quiet, churchy ambience of the house. 'All out?' She looked through to the sitting room, an inviting place of deep cushions and dense rugs.

'Yup. We'll eat later. And then maybe a movie.'

Lucy would, Marie knew, make popcorn, and serve it in striped tubs she'd tracked down online. And Chloe would curl her lip. There was probably an inoffensive way to report Chloe's outburst about Lucy's over-styling of family life, but Marie hadn't hit on it yet.

'Ah!' Lucy jumped down from her stool as if she'd just remembered something. 'You may as well take this.' She reached into a spotless cupboard – did nobody in this house leave fingerprints? – and retrieved a magnificent Dundee cake. 'Made it last night. Delia's recipe, of course.'

Marie was drooling so hard she had to clamp her lips together. Although nobody – *nobody* – could challenge

Queen Mary's crown, she had to admit that Delia's creations were special. 'When I die, bury me in that,' she said. 'Why are we getting it? I mean, thank you and everything, but there's only a couple of slices missing so far.'

'It's you or the bin.' Lucy's eyes flickered over Marie before she carried on. 'Truth is, most of my baking is thrown away.'

Marie sat up straight. This was shocking stuff. She could understand murder (under the right circumstances) and accepted that there must always be war, but *throwing away home-made foodstuffs*? 'Come OFF it!' she hollered, in the vulgar tone of voice that usually only escaped her lips during the voting segment of the Eurovision Song Contest.

'Really.' Lucy shrugged. 'Tod doesn't care for cake.'

He ate my *cake*, thought Marie, not smug, just puzzled. And a tiny bit smug.

'He watches his weight, you see.'

'That's good, though.' Marie valiantly attempted to half-fill her friend's metaphorical glass. 'It's you who gets to see him in the nuddy, after all.'

'True.' Before New Year, Lucy's combined blush/giggle would have made Marie want to put her head through the nearest Smeg appliance, but now it charmed her. 'And of course Chloe's a typical girl – always on a fad diet.'

She ate my *cake*, thought Marie again, not at all smug, even more puzzled. 'But what about you? If they don't want any, surely there's more left for you?' To Marie, who had to fight off husband and children like feral cats for the last slice, this could be construed as a positive.

'I have to be careful.' Lucy patted her midriff, flat

beneath a plain T-shirt that was so simple it just had to be designer. 'I don't want to balloon.'

Marie winced. She detested the self-hating talk, promoted in every glossy, that referred to 'ballooning' (often 'overnight') or 'piling on the pounds'. 'You won't *balloon*,' she used the word with distaste, 'by having the odd slice of gateau. Women have to eat, you know. Only LA A-listers can survive on coconut water and Botox. Besides' – time to point out the obvious – 'you're a skinny minnie, Lu. If they cut me up, they could make two of you.' Marie felt her own warm, gently tubby midriff. 'Hmm. Possibly two and a half.'

'Obviously Tod doesn't say anything about *me*.' Lucy smiled at the idea of her gallant husband being so crass. 'But he does, now and then, mutter about women getting to a certain age and letting themselves go.'

'Good luck to them!' Marie saluted these heroines with her coffee. 'They're living it large, cramming themselves with jammy doughnuts, instead of sweating to death in a spinning class.' Marie had a sudden unwelcome thought. 'Has he said that about me?' She wasn't sure what a 'certain age' meant, and suspected she'd been letting herself go since she could walk.

'God, no, he loves you.' Lucy fiddled with a macaroon. 'But he does, occasionally . . .'

'What? Go on.' Marie was avid.

'He's a bit mean about lovely Hattie.' Lucy said it all in a rush, then winced. 'About her . . . well . . . her *bottom* and that.'

'Hattie does carry a lot of junk in her trunk,' mused Marie. 'And I speak as one with enough junk in my own trunk for a lucrative car-boot sale. I suspect,' she said sagely, 'that Hattie wouldn't give a hoot what Tod thinks of her.' She went further. 'It's not really his business what a grown woman wants to eat, is it?'

'No,' said Lucy uncertainly, replacing the macaroon among its compatriots.

Getting to know Lucy, with the speed and gusto of compatible women, Marie had chatted about pretty much everything with her, from Simon Cowell to gingham and religion, but they'd never touched on Tod's domination of her. It was too fundamental, too big, to broach. Many of the character traits she'd mistakenly attributed to Lucy were the direct result of Lucy's desire to please her husband: she hadn't been showing off, she'd been meeting Tod's astronomically high standards. Lucy's immaculate grooming, the glossy sheen of their home, her tight rein on Chloe were all orchestrated in order to reflect well on the man of the house.

Thank Gawd, thought Marie, *for my own silly husband, who loves my podgy bits and wouldn't dream – or dare – to comment on how much I do or don't eat.*

As if on cue, her own silly husband rapped on the window. 'Your timer's going off!' he mouthed, his unwashed hair and stubbly face incongruous above the set-square lines of the evergreens in Lucy's windowbox. 'TI-MER!' he repeated, as if Marie might have become senile since leaving the house.

'Come with me,' said Marie, clambering off the stool. 'Let's have coffee, take two, at mine.' Now that she had a pal on tap, she liked to abuse the privilege.

And so did the pal. 'Great idea.' Lucy threw their cups into the dishwasher – unthinkable to leave a stained cup at large – and they left the house together.

Meandering around the curve, instead of crossing straight over the green, Lucy said in a small, confiding voice, 'Chloe's in therapy. Did she tell you?'

'Nope.' Marie's heart swelled a little, to make room for this. 'Why? She's so loved. Ah.' She stopped short, embarrassed by her own insensitivity. 'Her mum, right?'

'I think so.' Lucy, a rookie at sharing, proceeded slowly, carefully, as if walking over a spot where broken glass has been dropped. 'They never see each other. The most recent photo we have of her is . . .' Lucy shrugged. 'I don't even know. I send pictures regularly to her last address, but for all we know she's moved on. She's a bit of a gypsy, apparently.' As somebody whose children were densely woven into the fabric of every day, Chloe's mother's behaviour was incomprehensible to Marie. She wondered if therapy was the secret to which Chloe had alluded on Bonfire Night, but quickly rubbished that theory; Chloe's generation were more matter-of-fact about these matters than their elders. The secret, whatever it was, was still just that. 'She has *you*,' said Marie emphatically, taking Lucy's arm, feeling how fragile it was in her robust grip. 'It can't have been easy marrying into the Grays – a daddy's girl and her daddy – but you're on Chloe's side, and if she doesn't know it now, she'll realise it soon.' Pointless to whitewash over the uneasiness between Lucy and Chloe. Their disconnect was too obvious to ignore.

'I don't want to replace her mum. She *has* a mum.' Lucy

had clearly had this conversation with herself many times. 'And one day they might repair their bond. I just want to have some kind of relationship with her.' They were at Marie's doorstep and they both stalled, looking at each other. 'I don't,' said Lucy as if it was news, 'have any children of my own, after all.'

'No.' Although Marie had friends who exulted in this fact, she knew that for Lucy this small truth was a sadness, an enduring emotional wound that would never quite heal over. 'But you're a good mum . . . stepmum – whatever we end up calling it – to that girl. You never lose patience. You're always there. Chloe'll come round. When she's older and can see the bigger picture.'

'I don't know.' It sounded as if Lucy *did* know, but what she knew wasn't good. She folded her arms and looked back over the Close, as if the stylish tidy, empty house was her stepdaughter. 'She barely talks to me. If I could have an insight into her mind for just one minute . . . perhaps I'd know how to approach her. Everything,' she finished, 'I do is wrong.'

'Welcome to the club.' Marie blew out her lips in a horsey expression of defeat. 'Angus can go days without speaking to me or Robert. If I breathe, I embarrass him. All my advice is redundant. He seems to believe that if I touch him, he'll break out in boils. And as for a kiss . . .' She tapered off, remembering small Angus arms about her neck every morning at the school gates. 'A kiss would spark the Apocalypse. So, you see, you're doing better than you think. It's not that you're a stepmum; it's that Chloe's a teenager.' She pushed the front door. 'And luckily that's curable. Turning twenty puts an end to it.'

Lucy stayed on the wrong side of the step, despite the brisk nip in the air, and despite Marie holding the door wide.

'If Tod and I had a child of our own . . .' she said, and Marie could tell these words had never before been put together like this out loud. She stayed perfectly still, allowing Lucy to finish. 'If we had,' she repeated, 'maybe things would be different.'

'Maybe,' agreed Marie gently. 'I didn't realise you'd tried, Lu.'

Outside, in the cold, her pretty nose a raw red, Lucy said, 'We tried and tried. It's not in my story. That's how *my* therapist puts it.' She tried an anaemic smile. 'My fault, obviously. As Tod has Chloe.'

'Come in.' Time to break the moment, thought Marie, hating the vocabulary Lucy had lapsed into, and eager to sit her down somewhere warm. 'It's not about fault. I bet Tod doesn't use that word. It's nobody's *fault*. He married you for *you*, and he was damned lucky to get you.' She stopped, not trusting herself to say the right thing, pulsing with empathy, needing to help, but uncertain how to go about it. 'I'm glad you told me,' she said at last as they stared at each other in the hall.

'So am I.' Lucy coughed, shook herself like a wet dog and altered the mood. 'That timer,' she cocked her head, 'is still going.'

A tinny peep-peep escaped from the kitchen.

'Robert!' barked Marie, striding in and stabbing the

gizmo clinging to the oven door. 'You could have switched it off.'

'I suppose,' said Robert, at the kitchen table poring over scandals in one of the grubbier Sunday papers. 'But where's the fun in that?'

The comparison between chez Gray and chez Dunwoody was stark. The bin was so full that a secondary bin had sprung up beside it – a sad plastic carrier bag slumped against the wall, full of milk cartons, chewed-to-death gum and used teabags. Perhaps the empty dog-food tub now stuck to Prinny's head had once been in it, too.

'If you weren't here so often, I'd say *It's not always like this*,' said Marie, clearing a place on the worktop by pushing aside comics, dolls, headphones, DVDs and a Smurf key ring. 'But you are, so you know this is actually pretty tidy, considering.'

'Robert,' said Lucy, sitting beside him (having first moved a *Dandy* annual and a framed, defaced photo of Marie and Robert's wedding day). 'This is a strange question. But I have to ask or it'll be too late to bring it up, and I'll never know.'

'I'm intrigued.' Robert tore his attention away from a four-page story highlighting the rapport between footballers and lap-dancers.

'What is it,' said Lucy, 'that you *do*?'

'Haven't I ever said?' Marie spoke over her husband. She considered all Robert's conversations to be her conversations. 'Really?'

'Nope.' Lucy, chin on her hand, leaned in to hear all.

'I'm a silverware buyer,' said Robert.

'Which means . . . ?' prompted Lucy.

'It means I seek out the best possible silver products at the best possible price, so the man or woman on the street can stroll into Campbell & Carle and buy silver photo frames, silver knives, silver forks, silver spoons, silver rattles, silver—'

'Pens,' interjected Marie, opening the oven.

'*Pens*,' said Robert, with all the scorn of a man who's made this clear many, many times, 'are dealt with by the pen buyer. As I was saying . . .' He held up his hand and ticked off the list on his fingers. 'Silver salt-and-pepper sets. Silver napkin rings. Silver ice buckets. Silver . . .' He slowed. He exhaled showily. 'Bloody hell, Lucy, I'm boring *myself*. God knows how you feel.'

'I'm fascinated,' said Lucy with sincerity.

'Then, after ensuring I've made as much profit as possible for my bosses, while meekly accepting that in the current financial meltdown I can't expect a rise, I come home,' said Robert. 'I kiss my wife, I roll my eyes at my children, I trip over the dog and I make something like this.' He reached over for a plate. 'This is Paul Hollywood's marzipan and apricot twist,' he said, happier now. 'And it tastes like heaven might, if it was a comestible.'

'It does!' agreed Lucy, after her customary one bite. 'Chewy. Crammed with fruit. Rather like Stollen, but lighter.'

The smile cranked up a notch. Robert was accustomed to the kids' simpler critiques of 'Yeah, lovely, shut up, Dad'.

Looking past him, Lucy said with a dewy sigh, 'Oh,

look! Your wife's baked you a heart-shaped cake for Valentine's Day tomorrow! You're a lucky, lucky man, Robert.'

'Darling!' Robert was moved.

'Is it Valentine's Day tomorrow?' Marie froze with surprise as the last of four heart-shaped sponges fell from its tin onto the cooling rack. 'Oh, shit!'

Robert rolled up his newspaper and left the room.

'Say cheese!' said the photographer from the local paper.

'Cheese!' said everybody, huddled under the *HAPPY 10TH ANNIVERSARY, SMILE!* banner, except Aileen who shouted, 'Willies!'

Aileen was drunk. Not falling-over drunk, but slurring drunk. Shouting 'Willies!' in a room peppered with children and old-age pensioners drunk.

'I've never seen her like this before,' murmured Marie, disconcerted, as she and Lynda handed out paper plates and nibbly bits, and plucked rogue Wotsits from the Quavers bowl. She looked around for her son: tonight these activities were in his job description. Chloe, keen to earn her modest fee, was hanging up coats, wiping spills, shyly making conversation. Sternly ordered to pull together with his co-waiter, Angus had lapsed into sullen silence and eyes-on-the-ground introversion, which had ruined any chance of teamwork.

'Aileen's on a mission to get smashed,' Lynda whispered back, directing a mother and child to the toilet. 'She never usually drinks, because she has to stay sharp for that inevitable moment when a rogue pervert undresses her with his eyes.' Tonight a pervert would have to mentally extract her from a skin-tight emerald-green dress, which – along with the glittery eyeshadow and heels sharp enough to take out an eye – outglammed her associates, both of whom were tidy and groomed rather than va-va-voomed.

'Keep an eye on her.' A pointless request: like asking Lynda to keep an eye on a buffalo stampede or a tidal wave. 'Jonas!' Marie greeted him, waving over the throng. 'Come in!' She spirited up an empty chair, and Jonas, so stooped by his years on Earth that he was barely taller than a nine-year-old he passed, made his slow progress towards her. 'Do you remember,' she said, bending to his ear, 'you were the first customer through the door ten years ago?'

'Was I?' Jonas's jittery voice was chalky, the accent local, but dressed up. 'Doesn't feel that long ago.'

He had been sprightly then. No stains on his tie in those days. 'It certainly doesn't,' agreed Marie. 'It feels like half an hour.'

'Ho-ho-ho,' said Jonas, enunciating his laugh – his way, Marie suspected, of papering over the fact that he hadn't quite caught what she'd said. 'Nice turnout,' he went on.

'Everybody's here!' laughed Marie. When Lynda had suggested a party, Marie was dubious. The expense. The fuss. What if nobody came?

Lynda, itching to take up the graph paper and highlighters lying idle since the wedding of the decade, had insisted. 'This place is part of the community. You'll see. It'll be just the boost we need.' They never discussed Perfect You's poaching of their custom; they didn't need to. The evidence was there in black-and-white in the appointments book.

'Angus! More wine over here,' Marie called to her son over the Kylie compilation that had incited some of the guests to their feet. *Extraordinary*, she thought, *what some people will do after half a glass of sparkling wine and a vol-au-vent*. She was grateful for their lack of inhibition: a party's not a party until the dodgy dancing kicks off.

'Look at these!' A middle-aged woman, jigging epileptically to 'Can't Get You Out of My Head', bared her teeth at Marie. Tapping them, she shouted, 'That's you, that is!'

'If it wasn't for that brace you put on my Chantelle, she'd be goofy,' said a small, intense man who seemed to have forgotten the day that Aileen locked him in a cupboard for 'having erotic thoughts' about her.

'It was my pleasure,' said Marie. And it *was* her pleasure. She loved saving, straightening, replacing teeth and didn't care that dentists weren't heroes; that no romcom ever featured a dentist in the lead; that there are no famous dentists. She found her job both challenging and rewarding. And when her patients smiled at her and thanked her, she could see the fruits of her labour right there in their mouths.

'Shall I put the candles on the cake?' In a white apron over her customary black, Chloe looked cute, like one of the dressed-up dolls Marie constantly found underfoot in the twins' room. She was a good worker, enthusiastic and full of initiative, overshadowing her colleague, who skulked on the fringes of the chattering crowd, carefully avoiding any eye contact that might lead to him having to do something.

'Good idea.' Marie was grasped by another long-time patron, her hand pumped and back slapped. Out of the corner of her eye, as she said, 'Of course I remember your root canal!' she saw the clinic door open and deliver Klay to the fray.

No need to wonder what the hell he was doing here; Aileen galloped to the door, gushing, 'You got my invitation!' Taking him coquettishly by the arm – a move that owed more to ju-jitsu than romance – she steered him through the party. Klay was politely confused. Aileen glowed, her green dress blazing as she dragged him past Lynda, who was leading a small, anti-Kylie splinter group in a spontaneous hokey-cokey. The sight of her beautiful receptionist shaking it all about with a gaggle of old-age pensioners made Marie's chest swell.

'Who made this magnificent cake?' Mrs Aiken touched Marie's elbow.

'Me!' *With Mary Berry's help*. Marie, flush with bakey pride, assumed that her mentor wouldn't mind being left off the credits. Mary had decades of compliments in the bank, whereas she was new to this.

'No!'

The gasp was music to her ears, as was Mrs Aiken's broad smile. Marie had seen her patient through the misery of losing eight teeth during her chemotherapy. Mrs Aiken had seemed to shrink, all her juice extracted, and Marie remembered how Lynda had always sent the woman home in a taxi after each long session in the chair. The cancer had slunk away, whupped by modern medicine, and the implants in Mrs Aiken's mouth matched her original teeth so closely that nobody would know this chatty, vivacious woman had ever had a day's illness.

'It's so big!' said Mrs Aiken.

'I don't seem able to make small cakes,' laughed Marie. She hadn't realised just how tall four heart-shaped sponges with filling between each layer would stand.

'And so professional-looking.'

That, Marie suspected, was kindness triumphing over honesty. The icing was smoother than she'd ever achieved before, but it was far from 'professional'. She had accepted that her creations would always betray their homely origins. She would never be Lucy.

A tut at her shoulder made her turn. Aileen's face was folded into an expression of disgust. 'He's teetotal!' she spat. 'He doesn't feckin' drink!'

'Who? Klay?' Marie saw him on the far side of the room. Hard to miss, in a blingy leather blouson that must have cost as much as her first flat, he was throwing back his head in a theatrical laugh. Aileen had invited the fox into the hen house: Klay was obviously touting for work. 'So what?'

'It's wrecked me Valentine's Day!' One of Aileen's coiled Princess Leia plaits was working itself undone. 'I was going to get him sozzled and force a date out of him.' She burped. 'Pardon me.' She burped again. 'Ooh, I could taste Wotsits then.'

And this is Aileen in seductress mode, thought Marie. She couldn't help but admire the woman's gung-ho attitude to the chase. Aileen was no wallflower. She was sure of her charms, despite her deviation from the strict and constricting guidelines for feminine beauty laid down by the media. Stating her needs clearly, with no fear of rejection, on paper she was the kind of self-possessed feminist Marie hoped her daughters would grow into. Shame, then, that she exhibited the sensitivity of a runaway bulldozer. 'You have to allow Klay a say in all this. You can't *make* him go out with you – that's not fair.'

'Fair?' Aileen puffed out her chest. 'I'm offering him *this*. Fifteen stone of prime female real estate' (or, as she pronounced it, *eshtate*). 'I'll give him a glass of punch. That'll put a tiger in his tank.' She moved off purposefully, a guided missile in a push-up bra.

Camera phones popped and, as Marie posed good-naturedly with a baby whose full nappy gave him the density of a bowling ball, she realised *We didn't make any punch*.

Busting some moves to 'I Should Be So Lucky', she remembered the hackneyed advice she'd read on many, many fridge magnets: dance as if nobody's watching. *If only*, she thought, *nobody* was *watching*. Marie liked to dance, but she was under no illusions about how it looked – 'as if you're shaking off a burning boiler suit' was Robert's best stab at capturing her style.

Beyond the fascinated onlookers, Chloe nudged Angus and said something behind her hand that made his face crumple with laughter. It was worth being the butt of the joke (the joke possibly *was* Marie's butt) to see her son's carefully maintained battlements crack. She had noticed a slight thaw in Angus's antipathy towards Chloe, but had refused to read any kind of progress into it. Tonight she revised that refusal. *Perhaps Chloe's winning him over*, she thought, watching them as she gyrated. She'd always felt Angus's attitude was a knee-jerk reaction to the twins' enthusiasm for a Girl Next Door romance; perhaps he was really looking at Chloe at last.

A knot of people had drifted greedily towards the cake. Lynda found her eye and winked. It was time for the speech.

'I've never really made a speech before,' began Marie, surprised to find that talking to forty people in a smallish room was as daunting as addressing Wembley Stadium. 'But here goes.' She thanked Lynda. She thanked Aileen. She stopped short of thanking her family, in case she sounded like an Oscar winner, but she thanked all the patients who'd come through the door in the past decade. She told them she was grateful, and she told them she loved her job, and she said she was looking forward to the next ten years. And then she really grabbed their attention by saying, 'And now let's cut the cake!'

The irony of sharing a heart-shaped cake with her customers on St Valentine's Day while her husband sat neglected at home wasn't lost on Marie.

She'd explained it to him as best she could. 'I wanted the party to be on Smile!'s exact anniversary, and it just didn't register that it was Valentine's Day,' she'd said, wringing her hands, wondering at her own date-blindness. Robert's wry acceptance hadn't fooled her. He was disappointed. At a time when his beliefs about himself as a provider – as a man – were being challenged, she had demoted him as a lover. Tight-lipped about changes at Campbell & Carle, he had told her enough to worry her. Along with redundancies at all levels, he and his workmates had been horrified to learn they would have to reapply for their own jobs.

The powers-that-be were underrating her husband. Later, his wife would show him how she really felt. Hanging up with her trenchcoat was a carrier bag from a lingerie shop Marie had never been into before today. A quick dash along the racks before coming in to set up for the party had bagged her the most lurid, trashy, roaring red bra, thong and suspenders in the place.

They were nylon. They were held together with cheap lace more dangerous than a nettle-bed. They were the last thing Marie ever wanted to clamber into (particularly after a long day), but, although he'd never ever admit it – although he insisted he preferred her *au naturel* – she knew her husband would secretly adore the sleazy undies.

And, she decided, carving a hefty slice, she'd bring him home some cake, too.

'Ta.' A fleshy hand, white as a baby's, reached out and took the cake before Marie could put it to one side. Klay leaned in to whisper, 'Where can we go for a private word?'

In the kitchenette, door closed against the shindig, he alternated mouthfuls of cake with a proposition. He was sweaty, loose, with an air of mischief very different from his usual focus. He was, Marie realised, a little drunk, thanks no doubt to Aileen's mysterious punch, mixed for him – and him alone.

'Look at this figure.'

For a dreadful millisecond Marie thought he was going to pull up his shirt and show off his torso, but no, he'd scribbled a number on a Perfect You compliments slip.

'What is it?' Marie's hostess bonhomie evaporated.

'It's what I'm prepared to pay you for your business. The lease. The goodwill. The contents. Lock, stock and barrel.'

The paper crumpled in Marie's fist. 'I'm not for sale.' She made to push past Klay, but he stayed put and, faced with such a bulky hurdle, she had no choice but to hear him out.

'Don't be hasty!' He was smiling, his cherubic mouth wet. 'Do yourself a favour and at least think about it.'

'Even if Smile! was for sale – and it isn't, it *is not* . . .' Marie flinched at the naked gluttony in Klay's eyes at the words *for sale*. 'Even if it was, that would be an insultingly low offer. Did you look around you out there?' She gestured at the closed door, wishing passionately she was on the other side of it. 'You can't buy that kind of patient satisfaction.'

'I don't have to look out there for your customers.' Klay trowelled in the last blob of Robert's cake as if slinging rubbish down a chute. 'I see them every day at my place.'

The door opened a crack, and a small hand identifiable as Aileen's by the chipped nail varnish offered up a glass of punch, before the door closed on them once again.

As he raised it to his lips, Marie almost warned him that it was alcoholic. Almost. If he was a big enough boy to barge about, stamping Godzilla-style on other people's hard-won livelihoods . . . well, he was a big enough boy to withstand the attentions of a randy dental assistant.

'I can't sell to you, Klay,' said Marie. 'Our ethics are too different.'

'Ethics don't pay the bills.' He drained the glass and put it down with a touch too much force before wiping his mouth with the back of his hand.

'I want my patients to have a lifetime of healthy teeth. I want them to come to me as seldom as possible. I can still make a good living that way, and they have a smile they can be proud of. Not,' she said with an emphasis possibly lost on the increasingly tiddly Klay, 'a *perfect* smile, but a healthy one. Being able to smile happily and freely is a gift that illuminates everybody's life – the smiler and the . . . er . . . smilee.' *Christ*, she thought, *I'm coining words*. 'No, no!' She shushed Klay. 'It's still my go. My kind of dentistry is about helping people with good advice and affordable treatment based on their needs, not about . . .' Marie, flustered by the passion she felt, waved her hands around. 'It's not about luring them in with flashy advertising that makes them feel bad about themselves, because they don't have teeth like Tom-bloody-Cruise.' She spoke over him again, enjoying this, feeling as if she could take down the government with a teeth-oriented coup. 'Persuading people to have veneers they don't need, and implants and all the rest of it, turns them into cash-cows that you can milk for the rest of their lives.'

'Yes!' Klay accepted another cup from the mysterious hand. 'You get it! They're happy with their fabulous teeth, and I'm happy with my open-top car. Everybody's happy. It's good business.'

At the mention of his flashy car, Marie flinched. Her own little runaround was trembling under the execution-er's axe because of Klay. 'Good business maybe, but bad dentistry.' She felt she should rein things in before she became some sort of parody – a dentist hell bent on healing the world, one cavity at a time. 'And what about my staff in this brave new world of yours? They've been with me for ten years!' It struck her how long that was: she'd been higher of buttock, smaller of waist and firmer of chin when she'd met them. 'I can't see Lynda or Aileen fitting in with your *Hollyoaks* set-up.'

'You're wearing . . .' Klay looked to the ceiling for inspiration. Aileen's punch had scored a direct hit on his vocabulary. 'Little square leather things – horses wear them . . .'

'Blinkers.' Marie's arms were folded. Her foot was tapping. Robert could have warned Klay to stop, step away, possibly hold a mattress or similar item in front of him, but Klay didn't know the signs and blundered on.

'That's them!' He pointed and clapped. 'You're wearing . . .' He'd forgotten again.

'*Blinkers!*' shouted Marie. He had got, as the twins put it, right up her goat. 'I'm wearing blinkers, man, blinkers! Can we please get this over with?'

His confidence undented, Klay continued, 'This is a sweet deal I'm offering you. Accept it now and walk away with a few grand in your pocket, or I'll simply wait a year and snap up your empty premises for buttons.' He raised two slug-shaped eyebrows.

Bundling past the mound of his gut, Marie tugged open the door, startling the eavesdroppers outside. Lynda, Aileen and Angus all coughed and straightened up, looking away and humming. 'Tell this *businessman*,' said Marie imperiously to them, 'that some businesses are built with love and are not for sale to the highest bidder.'

As ever, in times of distress, Marie made for the cake. Lynda came up close and rubbed her arm. 'Don't let him get to you,' she said in an undertone, as a cork popped. 'This is your party and you deserve to enjoy it.'

'But what next?' said Marie. She rarely showed this face to Lynda – the one with doubt written all over it.

'We'll be all right.' Lynda didn't seem fazed. 'We always are, aren't we?'

'We are,' smiled Marie.

'Mum,' said Angus, coming up to her. 'You are *sick*.'

'Eh?' Marie pulled her chin down to her collarbone.

'He means,' said Lynda, with a soupçon of superiority at being down with the kids, 'you're an impressive lady.'

'Yeah. That – what she said.' Angus jerked suddenly and Marie realised that Chloe, sneaking up behind him with a platter of cocktail sausages, had goosed him. She winced, knowing the girl had misjudged, but her wince was redundant. Angus looked amazed. Flattered. And amused. He didn't look, as she'd expected him to, disgusted. *Go, girl*, thought Marie. *At least one woman's getting through to my son.*

The party was dwindling. Klay had disappeared, and the other revellers weren't party animals, but people for whom nine o'clock was crazily late to be out. Marie eyed a pyramid of baby-vomit by the fax machine as she let Jonas make his courtly, complex farewells.

'Excellent spread. Most delicious. That cake reminded

me of the tip-top Swiss roll my dear mother used to bake.'

'My pleasure. No problem. See you soon,' she smiled as she slowly, regretfully closed the door on him. 'Safe home.' She leaned back against it, glad to discard her party face. 'Leave it, Lynda,' she said as the woman stooped, bin-bag in hand. 'The kids and I will take care of it.'

'You sure?' Lynda looked around her. 'Where's Aileen? Never here when she's needed.'

The door to the treatment room opened and a large man half-fell out. He had the dazed look of a person locked in a ghost train for a month.

'So that's sorted then?' Aileen followed Klay out, businesslike and precise, despite the lipstick smeared all round her mouth.

'Shorted?' Klay gazed around him, evidently unsure who'd spoken, and in what language. Blotchy marks all over his face matched Aileen's lipstick. He lurched towards the reception desk, stopped dead, swivelled daintily and lumbered a few feet backwards.

'Next Thursday. You're picking me up here at six.' Aileen herded him to the door as if he were a wayward heifer. 'I wrote the date on your arm. In indelible ink. So, no nonsense about washing it off by accident.' She opened the door and Klay put on a sudden spurt of speed and, head down, raced through it. 'Don't be late, or I'll tie your tackle in a reef knot!' she shouted as he pirouetted from lamp post to lamp post. Slamming the door, she turned to the others. 'I love that man,' she said.

Refusing the proffered high-five, Marie said, 'How could you even let him . . . urrgh.' She shook herself, like Prinny that time Robert accidentally threw a bowl of washing-up water over him. 'He's a monster.'

Looking into the middle distance, Aileen said in a husky, emotional voice, 'My heart is in charge.' She recovered and added, 'And me knickers are pretty bossy, too.'

'How did you get him to say yes?' Marie didn't really want to know, but this development had the same macabre allure as a car crash.

Talking over Aileen, Lynda said, 'He didn't say yes . . . He said *yesh*. The man's blind drunk. Plus he's probably never before met anybody quite as forceful as our Aileen.'

'Irresistible force,' said Chloe in her little-girl voice, 'meets immovable object.'

'Yeah,' mumbled Angus, looking at her sideways. The only way he ever looked at anything.

'I'm off,' said Aileen. 'Seducing men is exhausting. See youse.'

'Thanks for all your help, Helen of Troy!' shouted Lynda as her triumphant co-worker swanned off.

'Look,' said Chloe, 'why don't you both go home, and Angus and I can finish off here. You're paying us, after all.'

Ignoring Angus's shell shock, Marie took Chloe up on her offer, deciding to pop an extra couple of coins in with her fee. As she shrugged on her coat and picked up her carrier bag of lacy contraband, she heard Chloe say, as if the idea had just occurred to her, 'You know what, Angus, we could go back to mine. Have hot chocolate. Listen to some stuff.'

Angus froze, as if the question held life-or-death

implications. Eventually, after more consideration than most people give to buying a house, he said, 'OK.'

St Valentine is a tyrant.

There are rules attached to his special day. Nobody knows who made them, but they must be obeyed.

All over the country nonplussed men had struggled to choose between a teddy holding a satin heart embroidered with *I luv u* and one with a heart that said *Be my Valentine*. Women had honed their acting skills, ready to jump with nymphomaniac joy at a bunch of supermarket flowers.

On Caraway Close a flagging dentist attempted to get herself in the mood for romance, candlelight and memorable hanky-panky, as demanded by the rules.

Changing into the squeaking underwear at the clinic had been a masterstroke. Yes, it had felt peculiar driving home with just her coat over her undies and she already had a rash on her inner thigh, but it meant she could dash in, rugby-tackle her husband, make the beast with two backs, share a slice of cake and then turn over and fall asleep – all before her teenage son put his key in the door. Robert wouldn't know what had hit him, and St Valentine would be appeased.

Usually keen on 'kissing+', as Robert had been known to call it, Marie felt decidedly unamorous. She was tired, her feet hurt and she couldn't evict from her thoughts Klay's insulting offer.

A scuffling, snuffling noise from the porch stopped her in her tracks as she approached, key out, stomach in, pout on standby. Her first thought was 'Fox!' and her lip curled;

in common with most townies, she considered the handsome, red-coated creatures to be noisy sex addicts with a nice sideline in toxic crap. Then she thought 'Rat!' and took a hasty step back. But then a small four-legged beast dashed out and she thought 'Cookie!' and scooped her up.

'Are you looking for Prinny? Are you? Are you?' Marie never used baby-talk on babies, but chihuahuas brought it out in her. She was fond of Cookie, even though the yapping and the snapping and the talent for finding 'amusing' places to leave a meringue-like shit tested her goodwill. 'Prinny-winny's indoors, Cookie.' And Prinny-winny would rather eat his own pawsy-wawsies than play with Cookie: Cookie always won their tug o' wars.

'Come on. Let's pop you home.' Marie cradled Cookie, marvelling at how light the little dog was. 'Your mummy will be ever so glad to see—' Marie's cutesy monologue stopped short as she put her hand on the latch of Lucy's gate.

Vaulting the fence that separated the Gray front garden from Erika's, Tod landed squarely and silently in front of Marie with the ease of a seasoned cat burglar. 'Hi,' he said, as suave as if he'd sauntered into view with a martini. 'I see you found our little runaway.' He took in Marie's freeze-framed confusion. 'I was in Erika's garden,' he said. 'Looking for Cookie,' he enlarged. With an amused ghost of a smile he added, in a low voice, 'Why? What did you think I was doing, Marie?'

Suddenly hyper-aware of the trollop knickers beneath her trenchcoat, Marie handed the chihuahua over the gate. 'Nothing! It was just . . .' Two sets of curtains twitched.

Lucy looked down from one window, Erika from another. Both curtains were closed with a vehement *swish*, as if synchronised. 'I'd better . . .' She shrugged, unsure why or how the atmosphere was so awkward. Or, to be precise, why *she* was so awkward. Tod seemed fine.

'Goodnight. Sleep tight.'

Marie looked back from her own door to see that Tod was still watching her. She waved and let herself in, less keen than ever to make like a slut.

'I'm home!' she shouted. Downstairs was dark, light leaking down the stairs. Robert was already in bed, which saved some time. 'Ready or not!' she shouted up, removing a shoe and massaging a weary foot. 'Brace yourself!' She regarded herself in the full-length mirror at the foot of the stairs: she'd never realised how much she resembled her grandmother. 'Ooh, the things I'm gonna do to you!' she called, heaving off her coat and dragging herself up the stairs with the battered slice of cake in her hand, nylon knicks almost a-flame. At the door of the bedroom she pasted on a sultry look. 'Hello, big boy!' Marie hoped she didn't look like she felt, and threw open the door.

The room was empty, the bed unruffled. The note on her pillow read: *Gone to Mum's. Strange noises in the roof, apparently. She thinks it's a murderer, I think it's a transparent ruse to separate us on Valentine's Day. Don't wait up. R x*

'Yessss!' The temptress in the scarlet peephole bra threw back her head in ecstasy and fell on the bed.

TO MY VALENTINE

Roses are red,
Violets are blue.
If I *have* to find a snoring, scantily clad woman
　　who's rolled in cake on my bed
I'm glad it's YOU.

Here's to another romantic year.
xxx

APRIL

Easter

Lemon Meringue Eggs

EASTER-EGG HUNT

Clue No. 3

Q: The smallest Dunwoody
    Is no goody-goody.
    He's covered in hair
    And he sleeps . . . where?
A: In Prinny's bed.

Before Lynda had fallen pregnant, all Marie knew about broccoli was that it was green and she didn't like it.

Lynda ate broccoli every day: broccoli is an excellent source of calcium and folate, packed with fibre and full of disease-battling antioxidants. Lynda avoided swordfish. She brandished a crucifix when confronted with soft cheese. She was doing pregnancy strictly by the book, and she took her colleagues with her every tedious step of the way.

'Week nine,' she announced as they awaited their first patient on the day before the Easter weekend. She squinted at the pregnancy timeline on her favourite mothers-to-be website. 'It has a face!' she said triumphantly.

'All babies have faces.' Immune to the lure of motherhood, Aileen could work up not one single coochy-coo at the thought of a Smile! bundle of joy. 'If it *didn't* have a face, that would be worth telling us.' She watched Marie pull out patient index cards for the day ahead – a task that officially fell to Aileen – and popped another Tunnock's Teacake.

Undaunted, Lynda carried on. 'It's twenty-two milli-metres long!'

'Lots of things,' said Aileen, 'are twenty-two millimetres long.'

'My uterus,' said Lynda, 'is a wondrous domain.'

'Mine,' said Aileen, 'is closed to the public.' She aimed a Tunnock's wrapper at the bin, missed and went to the treatment room. Possibly to prepare it, possibly for a snooze.

'Aileen's in a good mood today.' Marie's method of gauging her assistant's state of mind was a simple swear-word-per-hour system. Thus far she'd unleashed only a 'Feck that!' on the broken hand-dryer and a 'Holy shite!' when she'd burned her tongue on a dunked Garibaldi. Since her one date with Klay, two months earlier, such calm days were rare. 'Did you hide the flowers?'

'In here.' Lynda tapped the bottom drawer of a filing cabinet. Straightening up, she shouted, 'Eliza!' Then, after a beat, 'Luke!'

'Nice.' It was best to say *nice* or *pretty* or *great* when Lynda punctuated the conversation with another possible name for her twenty-two-millimetre tenant. Engaging with her on the subject was fruitless and dangerous. When Marie had said she'd never liked the name Jessica, because she'd sat next to a girl in school called Jessica who picked her nose and ate it, there had been a *froideur* in reception for hours.

Aileen barged back and leaned, bored, against the wall. 'Where is everybody?' she griped. 'We should be busy. The whole world has fecking teeth, after all.' Her face was free of make-up, her overall defiantly done up to the top button. Her brief foray into sexiness had been short-lived. 'We'd better hope for some emergencies. A nice agonising wisdom tooth. Or maybe some kid'll knock out his front teeth falling off his skateboard. If we're lucky.'

Although too compassionate to wish for emergencies, Marie also deplored the snowy whiteness of the appointment book.

'Matilda!' said Lynda.

A full and frank discussion with Robert about the future was long overdue. Marie could sense the bold move that her husband had up his sleeve. She could always sense what he wanted, whether it was mash instead of chips, or a quickie during the *Coronation Street* omnibus. She'd hinted at the effect Perfect You was having on her business, but the ESP didn't work both ways; Robert was infamously impervious to hints. Mentioning a perfume forty-three times in the fortnight before her birthday more or less guaranteed she'd unwrap a three-pack of pastel tights on the day.

Scratching her scalp with a sterile dental probe, Aileen shared her Easter plans. '*Hunger Games*. A giant Easter egg. I'll take the hard skin off me feet. Another giant Easter egg.'

'My, how the other half live,' said Marie, turning the pages of the appointment book and wincing.

'We're sorting out the nursery,' said Lynda. 'Six months will fly by. I'll mark out where the cot will go. And we're trying out paint colours. Barrington is very traditional about this. As soon as we find out the sex, it'll be blue for a boy and a nice soft pink for a girl.'

'Men are such sexist pigs,' said Aileen.

'Cameron!' said Lynda.

The door opened and all three perked up, only to de-perk as the postman slapped a pile of envelopes and a dental-equipment catalogue on the desk.

'Where's the Sellotape?' Aileen threw open random drawers, finding the bouquet, lying flat like a corpse in a morgue drawer. She snatched it up, the cellophane crackling and rustling around the now-bedraggled roses and gypsophila. 'Why didn't you tell me?' She thrust them head-first into the bin with a booming 'Jaysus Christ!'

'Because you'd do this,' said Marie.

'Bastard!' Aileen wrenched the handwritten note from the roses and ripped it to shreds. 'When will it end? When will he stop?' She stomped out to buy a restorative Walnut Whip.

'Did you read the note, Lynda?'

'Do bears you know what in the woods?' Lynda had given up bad language in case it harmed the baby. '*Darling A, I'm begging you for another chance. Tell me what I did wrong. It could be so good between us. I dream every night of your magnificent white body.*' Lynda pulled a face. 'I pity the poor florist having to take this stuff down every other day. There are twelve kisses – I counted.'

'Poor Klay with a K,' said Marie.

'Greta!' shouted Lynda.

'Remember the night of the date?'

'Who,' asked Lynda, 'could forget?'

Aileen had looked great. Not conventionally great, not Aileen. But Marie was raising two girls in a society bombarded with porny ideas of female beauty, so she didn't believe in narrow definitions of 'looking great'. Aileen's hair, brushed out of those Cumberland-sausage plaits, had hung dark and shiny around her shoulders. Marie and Lynda had manhandled her into the loo and hectored her into removing the garish eye make-up and scarlet lipstick. A slick of gloss, some peachy blush, and Aileen was a fresher, prettier, less terrifying version of her usual self. Marie zipped her into a full-skirted dress the colour of dried blood and stood back to survey their handiwork.

'You look lovely,' she'd said. The glow on Aileen's face lit the room and made Marie almost tearful; this was a big step for Aileen. A date with a man was a tiny bridge between her and the rest of the human race.

'No swearing,' Lynda had commanded.

'No jumping on him,' said Marie.

'No accusing him of undressing you with his eyes.'

'No accusing anybody else of undressing you with his eyes.'

'No swiping the food from his plate while he's looking the other way.'

'No talk of your verruca.' They all knew far, far more than they wanted to about Aileen's verruca.

Lynda had tweaked Aileen's hair one last time and whispered, 'Here he comes!'

The three women had watched Klay cross the road from Perfect You. Feet dragging, shoulders sloped, he'd looked like a man approaching his own gallows.

'Jaysus, he's gorgeous.' From Aileen, compliments sounded like threats.

'Hmm,' Marie had said. *If you like oversized baby-men*

dressed in white suits one size too small. 'Remember, Ail, don't let him pressure you into sex.'

'Ooh, he won't have to pressure me.' Aileen had hopped from foot to foot.

Wearing his dread like a cloak, Klay had taken a deep breath and entered the clinic.

'Hiya!' Aileen waved enthusiastically, as if from a departing ocean liner.

His face slack, Klay had taken her in. And Marie had seen a change creep over his features, like summer sun creeping up a cold wall. She checked later with Lynda and found that she, too, had noticed the metamorphosis from condemned to cheerful. Maybe it was the guileless glee in Aileen's face, or the undeniable ecstasy his presence provoked in her, but Klay had grown six inches and returned her smile.

'M'lady.' He had bowed.

'Jaysus!' Aileen had shrieked, and curtsied. 'He's mental! I love him!'

'I reckon,' Marie had said, watching them make their way to Klay's sports car, Aileen tottering a little on her heels, 'that man might be experiencing genuine desire for the first time in his life. He's bought into such a silly fake version of what's sexy – you know, big silicone boobs on tiny frames, pillow faces, everything a kind of pooey-orange – that perhaps he's never stopped to think about what *he* actually fancies. Cos we're all individual, aren't we? We fancy people for their quirks, really.'

The car had roared off. Marie and Lynda had crossed their fingers. Evidently they hadn't crossed them tightly enough: the date was now out of bounds as a conversational topic.

Last to arrive the following morning, Aileen strode straight to the coffee machine. Lynda switched off the radio and she and Marie had stared at Aileen, expectantly.

'Youse might have warned me!' Aileen had been loud and disgusted. '*That*'s what all the fuss is about?' She'd downed her coffee in one. 'Sex is not half as interesting as Carrie Bradshaw makes out.' Rooting about in the biscuit barrel, she'd come up with half a Bourbon. 'Jaysus, the fuss!' Aileen's top lip had turned up in scorn. 'He was *touching* me, and *nuzzling* me, and *stroking* me and telling me *Oh Aileen you're beautiful you're a goddess you're blowing me mind* yada-yada-yada. So I screamed at him *Get on with it, ya halfwit baboon*.' She'd pointed accusingly at Marie. 'Do *you* like that – oh, what's it called – *foreplay*?'

'Well,' Marie had stalled. 'Umm . . .'

'Waste of time, more like.' The brief, horrible mime Aileen did with her hands would stay with Lynda and Marie forever. 'It's like sitting through the ads when you're waiting for the movie to start. So, I whipped off me dress and you'd think he'd never seen bosoms before. He turned into a simpleton before me eyes. *You're a divinity*, sez he. *Get your willy out*, sez I.'

Marie had exchanged a look of alarm with Lynda. Feeling sorry for Klay was something she wouldn't previously have believed possible.

'Have you ever,' Aileen had challenged Marie, with the indignant tone of a woman returning a faulty cardi to Marks & Spencer, '*seen* a willy?'

'Well, yes.' At her age and after three kids, Marie had been surprised to find she could still blush that hard.

Aileen had shaken her head, slowly, the way Marie did when she wanted to communicate to the kids that she was both disappointed and appalled. 'They're horrible!' She'd sketched Klay's member in the air, and Lynda had shrunk back in her swivel chair. 'They're long. And bendy. And a sort of mauvy-bluey red! What sort of colour scheme does *that* fit in with? Imagine carrying one about all day. Like having a stick of rhubarb down your knickers. No wonder men are weird. And, yuk, the feel of it.'

Here both Marie and Lynda had protested, but there'd been no stopping Aileen. Her verdict? 'Basically a Hoover attachment covered in sweaty velvet.' She'd gone further, 'And the yelps of him! I thought he was dying.' Eventually, after a lot more in the same vein, she'd summed up her first sexual experience as 'twenty minutes of bouncy nonsense' and bemoaned the mess it made on her best BHS duvet. 'Never,' she'd finished darkly, 'again.'

The box marked 'sex' had been ticked and Aileen moved on, content with her life of box sets and endless biscuits and starting arguments. Taking in the rejected roses, Marie thought *But Klay thinks differently.*

Early-morning calls never bring good news. In Marie's experience, they meant death or the imminent arrival of a seldom-seen (and for a damned good reason) relative. When the Dunwoody Good Friday lie-in was interrupted by the needy trill of Robert's mobile, she opened one eye and listened suspiciously to the one-sided dialogue being carried out in the hushed tones reserved for grave tidings.

'What?' Robert sat on the side of the bed, head hanging, phone to his ear. 'No! Oh God, the poor woman . . . That's terrible . . . Of course. Of course. Don't worry . . . I'll be right there.'

'What is it?' Marie braced herself.

On his feet, quivering with joy, Robert shouted, 'Caroline's kitchen is flooded!' as if this was news they'd been yearning to hear. He did an impromptu jig. Marie looked away. Even after decades of intimacy, no wife should be confronted with her husband's dancing rude bits before breakfast.

'You realise you're dancing with happiness because a woman's home is ruined?'

'Oh, come on!' Robert skipped into the en suite like a goat. 'She'd do the same if it was me. This is an act of God. A sign from on high. The inter-departmental bank-holiday brainstorming was Caroline's idea, *and* she insisted on doing all the catering. Magda's high and dry – unlike Caroline – so *who* comes in like the cavalry at the eleventh hour?' Robert's head bobbed around the door, toothbrush poised. '*Moi!*'

'You told Magda you couldn't make the brainstorming. You told her we needed you for our Good Friday treasure hunt. You said you've been slaving over the clues for weeks. You said you're a family man and this treasure hunt has been a tradition since Angus was little more than a dot.'

Spitting foam, Robert shouted from the sink. 'What I didn't tell you was Magda's response. She was very put out. *Very.*'

'Well, tough!' shouted Marie, a vision of the thwarted twins in her mind's eye. 'And it's too late to bake now, anyway.'

'That's the beauty of it!' Robert was back, ramming a leg into his trousers with a gleam in his eye that Marie rarely saw outside of *Top Gear* marathons. 'There's a whole pile of fabulous goodies all ready and waiting in the kitchen.'

'But they're for us!' Marie sat up, her hair a tipsy haystack that would never qualify as sexy bed-hair.

'Don't look at me as if I'm the Devil, darling. I'll make some more.'

TO: stargazinggirl247@gmail.com
FROM: geeksrus39@gmail.com
18.04.14
11.05
SUBJECT: Eggstraordinary

HAPPY EASTER, SOULMATE!

Just eaten 4 creme eggs. Feel barfy.

Soz I haven't emailed for a few days. Not ignoring you. Honest. I could say that I'm busy revising but that's a bit of a lie. I *am* revising but hey it's still April. I'm not you with your rotas and your schedules. I've been quiet cos my Mum's right (not often I type that) I DO think about stuff too much and recently the Clones've been getting to me. I know I shouldn't let them in my head but sometimes I can't tune them out. Even tho they're off on some stupid school trip I'm still getting texts. Too bad to show you.

FFS why's it still going on?!! It'll be the first anniversary soon. Mum can bake a black cake with poisonous candles. Whose idea was it to have a virtual sofa afternoon? It was probably you. Me on my sofa, you on yours, both of us watching a brilliant film and messaging the shit out of it. I can't today, tho. I'm seeing a mate. Soz.

laters

Angus

A sign sat above the front door of the semi-detached house. *Colinanna*, it said, presumably a clunky marriage of the inhabitants' first names. Despite their tender years, the twins knew they had journeyed to the heartland of kitsch.

Each pair of ruffled curtains, like matching sets of frilly drawers, offered a peek at an ornament. A clown leaning on a lamp post winked from the sitting room, while upstairs a porcelain shepherdess looked forlornly for her sheep out in the small concrete front garden, colonised by a stone donkey dragging a stone barrow full of tulips.

Iris and Rose had been disappointed about the treasure hunt, but not as disappointed as their mum evidently expected. She'd seemed insulted *and* relieved by their chorused 'Never mind' and the turning of their attention to the ever-vexed question of Coco Pops or Rice Krispies. Mum had, of course, waved a home-made granola bar under their noses, but by now it was little more than a token effort.

The sudden cancellation had freed up the whole day and they'd looked at each other with one of those *Village of the Damned* flashes of empathy that so spooked their parents: time for phase two of the plan.

A hasty tick in the exercise book and they'd set off on their bikes, promising their mum that they wouldn't go beyond the park.

They were beyond the park. They were significantly beyond the park, outside the address Rose had written on her palm in Mrs Ardizzone's office, and they were about to add more fibs to the day's balance sheet.

'You do it,' said Iris.

'No, you do it,' said Rose.

'Just do it, Rose!' said Iris.

'Why should I?' said Rose.

'God!' snorted Iris. She knew that Rose was scared, and Rose knew that Iris was scared, but admitting such things would contravene the twins' code. 'I'll do it. As usual.'

The bell's shrill 'Edelweiss' brought a woman to the door.

'Hello!' The twins said it together, sunny and toothy and *adorable*. They knew no middle-aged woman in her right mind could be anything other than delighted to find two charming identical girls in matching hand-knits on her doorstep.

'Well, hello to you!'

Getting inside was almost too easy. Within three minutes they were on a floridly patterned sofa, clutching glasses of room-temperature squash and trying not to gawp at the collection of flamenco dolls displayed on every surface.

'So,' said the woman, settling herself on a leatherette pouffe. 'You need my help, do you?' She was be-permed, tan-tighted, flat-shoed: a perfect example of blameless normality. 'Obviously I'll help all I can. St Ethelred's is a fine, fine school and very close to my heart. What *is* this project you're working on, my loves?'

'It's about family celebrations through the ages,' began Iris.

Rose tagged her effortlessly. 'We need photos showing people dressed up for parties.'

'If you could let us use some of your family photos, we'd copy them.'

'And bring them right back.'

'We'd take great care of them.'

'Because we know your daughter so well, and we really admire her.'

'Do you?' Their hostess smiled, flattered. 'How sweet.' She heaved herself laboriously off the pouffe. 'Just wait there. I've got *stacks* of piccies.'

Later, with the ten precious images stowed in Iris's saddlebag, the twins stopped by the canal for a quick Fruit Shoot. They watched the regal progress of a supermarket trolley floating past. They didn't catch each other's eye.

'She'll get them back tomorrow,' said Rose, sensing her sister's unease.

'She'll never know what we're really going to use them for,' said Iris. 'She won't be *hurt* by it.'

'And it's for a good cause.' Rose cheered up at this. 'A really good cause.' She stood up on her pedals. 'Race you home!'

That, too, was strictly forbidden, but this was a day for sinning, it would seem.

*

'I'm faintly shocked to hear myself say something so . . . *blasphemous*,' confided Marie, easing herself onto one of Lucy's chrome stools with all the elegance of a carthorse in labour, 'but I'm sick of chocolate.'

'Easter will do that to a girl.' Lucy waved a dog-eared recipe. 'That's where this secret weapon comes in. I am about to out-Mary Mary.'

'Don't make me strike you.' Marie took a sip of Lucy's home-made elderflower cordial. It was like drinking from an angel's slipper. No matter how much she emulated Ms Berry, Marie would never be the kind of woman who made her own cordial. But now that she had a friend who *was* that kind of woman, she didn't need to be. 'What are you making?'

'Lemon meringue eggs.' Lucy handed her a white duck egg. 'Blow that.'

'I beg your pardon? I'm a married woman.'

Lucy showed her how, incredulous that Marie had never blown an egg before. 'Look. You stick a pin in both ends to make two little holes. Make sure you twiddle the pin and prick the yoke so that it's broken. Make one end slightly bigger, then put your lips to one end and blow.' She watched her protégée. 'No. Really blow! As if you're playing the sax. The white and the yolk will be forced out of the other end. Oh, give it here!'

Even blowing an egg didn't dent Lucy's poise; she was the Grace Kelly of egg-blowing. Marie got the hang of it, but she was red-faced and gasping when Angus appeared at Lucy's front door.

'Hi,' he said, in the self-conscious way resulting from

the belief that everybody in the world was looking at him. He hesitated. 'Um. Chloe in?'

It took extreme willpower for Marie not to look at Lucy, and she appreciated the effort Lucy put into not looking at her. The pairing of Angus and Chloe – a kind of suburban royal marriage of the ancient houses of Dunwoody and Gray – was a cherished mutual fantasy. They discussed it in such detail that they'd already had a verging-on-ratty conversation about beef or chicken for the reception.

'Yes. Upstairs.' Lucy helpfully pointed upwards, as if Angus might not know about stairs. 'Revising. Or working on her health and social care portfolio. Nose stuck in a book anyway, that's for sure.'

'I'm taking Prinny for a walk.' Angus flicked his head towards where the dog stood, with his customary shame-faced demeanour, on Lucy's front lawn. 'I thought Chloe might like to bring Cookie along.'

Not only seeking out Chloe, but taking Prinny for a walk? Aliens had replaced Marie's son with a cunning counterfeit. The women watched the two youngsters dawdle away, a dog apiece, a careful distance of three feet maintained between them at all times.

'Doesn't mean anything,' said Marie, already planning a hat.

'Chloe's been *singing* around the house,' said Lucy. 'Has he had a change of heart?'

'It would seem so.' Marie didn't feel equipped to speak for Angus. 'But, boys . . . I just hope they don't hurt each other.' She didn't trust this new rapport. It was too sudden.

'You know there's this other girl in the mix, this pen-friend.'

'Or email-friend?' Neither women knew the correct term. 'Maybe he has room for both of them in his life.'

'Yeah.' If Angus was anything like his dad, he was a one-woman chap. And Angus *was* like his dad.

Back to business. Lucy began to saw gently around the top of an empty eggshell with a serrated knife. All the while she worried at the front of her mouth with her tongue.

'Tooth trouble!' Marie knew the signs.

'Yeah, this one.' Lucy rolled back her lip. 'It's a veneer, but it doesn't feel right.'

'That's cos you didn't need a veneer,' said Marie.

'I didn't? But Klay said—'

'Klay says a lot, but mainly he says *ker-ching*! I'll sort it out. Mate's rates.'

'Really?' Lucy looked grateful, amazed. 'That's kind.' She turned shifty suddenly – it didn't suit her. 'I've been meaning to say. Sorry about not coming to you in the first place. I never thought how that would look. Were you pissed off?'

'Yes,' said Marie with bald honesty. 'But to be honest, back then . . . it was all misunderstandings and misconceptions between us two.'

'It was like we spoke different dialects of the same language. Everything I said came out wrong,' said Lucy. 'I went to Klay because it was simpler, somehow.'

'I'll fit you in tomorrow,' said Marie, rueful that she could offer this so readily.

'I heard you and Robert having a . . . *debate* this morning.'

'You heard our screaming match? Blimey! You were up early.'

'Power-walking with Hattie. I feel sorry for her. Going round and round the Close like a trapped bluebottle.'

'You're too nice, that's your trouble.' Marie took the knife and an empty eggshell and gingerly beheaded it. It wasn't as neat as Lucy's, but it would do. 'I hope our *debate* didn't put you off your stride.' She took up another egg. 'The headline reason for the row was missing the treasure hunt to ponce about with Magda, but if I'm honest, it was the nastiness that got to me. He's *pleased* Caroline's kitchen is knee-deep in sewage. The row staggered on to other topics, of course. Whatever we start to row about, it always seems to come down to his mother and the bins.'

'Wish Tod and I could argue like that.' Lucy sounded winsome, as if wishing for world peace. She was becoming more real by the day, able to let rip with the odd 'Bullshit!' and to pout if she was feeling down, instead of wearing the perma-grin that had once alienated Marie.

'What would *you* argue about?' Marie was curious. Lucy found it so hard to criticise her husband.

'That's just it!' laughed Lucy, unable to bear the carnage any longer and taking egg and knife out of Marie's hands. 'Tod's bloody perfect.'

'Nobody is.' Marie was adamant. 'If Tod's perfect, why did you throw one of my plates at him on Bonfire Night?'

A flush crept up Lucy's neck. 'Oh, *that*,' she laughed. 'I was being silly.'

'You're *never* silly.'

Lucy laughed fondly at her new friend's automatic defence of her. 'It was the inevitability of it, I guess. The hitting on you. The always hitting on any women in my orbit. There's no harm in it, obviously. Your virtue was safe. No worries on that front with Tod. None at all. None. Oh.' She held up the shattered shell. 'Whoops!'

Spirited denials like this had convinced Marie that Lucy suspected her husband of infidelity. She watched as Lucy assembled lemons and sugar and unblown eggs. 'This is Delia's curd recipe, I guess?' she queried.

'Of course,' said Lucy, with the serene certainty that Marie used to mistake for smugness.

Since seeing Tod throwing his leg over Erika's fence on St Valentine's Day, Marie had seen him do it again. Only once more, admittedly. Not enough to build a court case. *I put it to you, ladies and gentlemen of the jury, that the accused has been getting his leg over, in all senses of the word*. And yet, how often did Cookie escape? The pygmy creature was a furry Elastoplast, its days and nights spent glued to Lucy's side.

The leg-overs were too flimsy to bring to Lucy's attention. But Marie's memory of Tod's expression on St Valentine's night – a cocksure, calm *You know, and I know, but you can't prove a thing* – made her uneasy about keeping it from her.

The hot cross buns were *Great British Bake Off* quality. Robert arranged them just so on the gold platter he'd borrowed from Lucy's vast stash of decorative bits and pieces. After some initial uncertainty about Lucy – how could a nemesis become a BFF overnight? – Robert had welcomed her homely, comforting presence and never baulked at finding her, yet again, in his kitchen with his wife. She was a constant, quiet sort of person, who crinkled her eyes at his jokes and gave thoughtful praise to his baking.

Tod, though . . . Robert couldn't get a handle on the man. His instinct was to dislike Tod with a sort of low-level antipathy, possibly because Marie obviously fancied him rotten. There had been rebuttals and many an incredulous *Oh, for God's sake!*, but a husband can tell.

Robert rearranged the buns one last time. The brainstorming had been stormy, but not particularly brainy. There had been showing-off, there had been scribbling on whiteboards, there had been excruciating animal role-play, but there had been no good ideas.

Possibly – and this was heresy – that was because good ideas happen when you sit down and think hard, not when some berk from Accounts is pretending to be a cat.

Hoisting the platter aloft, Robert walked back to the boardroom, his soles slapping with a noisy echo in the almost-empty building. *Magda*, he thought, *will die at my simnel cupcakes*.

Robert was insanely proud of his simnel cupcakes; he suspected they were his own invention. Pity they were 'cupcakes' – he felt faintly Julian Clary for making such a thing – but perhaps they could be renamed? Mancakes? Hmm. He couldn't see it catching on.

His hand on the handle of the boardroom door, Robert

suddenly saw himself as if through a long-distance lens. He saw a man who had memorised Hello Kitty! wall-clock sales figures for the period 2011–12. A man who had rehearsed a short speech casually dissing a co-worker for 'playing hooky' in her sub-aquatic kitchen. A man who'd baked (nay, *invented*) goodies for his family, but was sharing them with the people he usually avoided at work.

Robert preferred the bloke who let his assistant take the rest of the day off when she was stricken with period pains; who told Geoff to cry it all out when his budgie died; who bought the Christmas tinsel out of his own pocket.

'I'm a monster,' he thought, turning the handle and returning to a world where bank holidays meant team-building exercises instead of lie-ins. 'I'm a monster who knows a hell of a lot about clocks.'

By the end of Easter Saturday, every Dunwoody was full of chocolate, sick of the stuff and desperate for more. Lazy and inert, they lay around the house like abandoned mattresses.

Peeling herself off the sofa, Marie shut herself into the conservatory to ring her dad, a call she preferred to make on her feet, so that she could walk off her jittery anxieties as she loudly repeated herself over and over, trying to gauge his state of health by his muttered, fractured conversation.

'Bye, Dad!' she said.

'Bye, Margaret,' he said.

Margaret was Marie's mother's name. Marie stared at

the phone's little screen for a while, aware she was holding it too hard. Her father was the same age as Mary Berry, an extraordinary fact, given that lady's energy and sparkle. Marie fervently hoped that when she was of their generation she'd still be part of the action like Mary, and not tidied away like a once-loved toy at the back of a cupboard.

In their mother's absence from the sitting room, Angus dumped his revision as if it was hot.

The twins stood between Angus and the television.

'What?' he said, suspiciously.

'Will you help us with a school project?' said Iris.

'No.'

'Please,' said Rose. 'Pretty please.'

'No. Get out of the way. This is the bit where he says "I'm Spartacus".'

Iris turned off the television. Rose goggled at her, shocked and thrilled at such daring. 'We need you to make a short film. Like those brilliant ones you make of the holidays and stuff.'

'Put the telly back on. Don't make me turn you upside down.'

On a nod from Iris, Rose laid photocopied images on the carpet at Angus's feet. 'We want you to make a montage of these. Animate them, or something.'

Fanning out the images, Iris said, 'You need to put it to music. "Who's That Girl?" by . . .' She faltered.

'The Eurythmics,' said Angus. He leaned down to inspect the photos. 'What are you two up to?'

'It's for school,' said Iris.

'That's all you need to know,' said Rose.

'Are you being evil?'

'A bit,' said Iris.

'I hate it when you bring the laptop to bed.' Marie turned grouchily away from her husband. The screen's harsh bluish light sucked all the gentle tones from the low-lit room and destroyed its sanctuary vibe.

'Talking of computers, do you remember when we—'

Marie cut him off. 'Yes, I remember. And that subject's off-limits.' She cringed. The inspiration for their bedroom home-movie had been found at the bottom of a fourth bottle of wine, and Marie still suffered flashbacks that stopped her in her tracks in the chilled-goods aisle. It was barbaric to witness one's own arse from that angle, and the soundtrack – not unlike a Wimbledon final, with all its grunts and exclamations – was seared into her brain. 'What are you doing, anyway?'

'Brushing up on clock facts.'

'And here was me thinking it might be something dull.'

'*And*,' added Robert loftily, 'working on a document about how to merge the departments without doing away with either me or Caroline.'

'But then you'd have to work even more closely with her.'

'Yeah, well, if it saves my job . . .' Robert tailed off. He tapped a key, then another, lost in his task, oblivious to the relief surging through his wife. Bracing herself for an announcement from Robert that he was giving in, taking voluntary redundancy, starting afresh, she had been barely able to breathe these past weeks. A feminist to her fingertips, Marie would be happy to be the breadwinner, but, realising that she'd misjudged his mood – that what she'd taken to be a mid-life crisis was just a blip – she allowed herself to unclench a little, to unfurl and admit how relieved she was not to have to take the wheel.

There could be no avoiding the plain truth that the ground was shifting in the teeny-tiny empire Marie had built. (And that's how it felt; as if she'd laid every brick herself.) The clinic was tottering, the familiar landscape shuddering, as if a marauding giant was stomping nearer and nearer. One clumsy step and Smile! would collapse into rubble.

Having an empire, no matter how tiny and insignificant, was exhausting, and there were days when Marie would like to lie down and give it all up. These were the days when she almost – *almost*, mind – envied the lady of leisure across the Close.

Lucy didn't have employees relying on her for their livelihoods, nor did she have a dozen red bills stapled together in her handbag. *Another thing she doesn't have*, Marie reminded herself as she watched Robert's intent profile, *is him – this man right here.* She couldn't let Robert down, lose her business and plunge the family into financial dire straits, just when he needed her to be strong.

How was it all so delicately balanced? She and Robert had always worked hard, had never been wildly extravagant, saved when they could, spent when it felt right. It felt unjust that they should spend their forties worrying that the family bandwagon might career off the road.

But life is unjust, thought Marie. *People you need die,*

others lose their marbles, and the babies you fussed over go off into the big bad world without their vests on.

Propelled out of bed by such maudlin navel-gazing, Marie escaped the reach of the laptop's dazzle and crossed to the window. The Close was in a chocolate coma, all the gardens colourless and still.

A trundling noise at the side of the Grays' focused Marie's lazy sweep of the street. Tod emerged, with a wheelie bin of bottles that jostled and clanked. 'Tod's doing the recycling,' said Marie.

'Unh,' said Robert, lost to her down a rabbit hole of statistics.

'He gave Lucy an egg-shaped emerald pendant for Easter.'

That got Robert's attention. 'Is he crazy? Easter's chocolate time – everybody knows that.' The laptop closed with a faint *snap*. 'Is he wearing his poncey dressing-gown-'n'-leather-slippers combo?'

'Dunno. I'll tell you when he comes back.' Marie could hear bottles dropping and crashing into the recycling station at the end of the street, out of view. Tod's feet of clay had been exposed, but she had to give him his due: not many men bought their wives emeralds and dressed like a 1940s movie star to take the rubbish out. 'Come on, Toddy boy,' she encouraged him as the Close regained its stillness without any sign of him coming back along the curve.

A base thought struck: did he buy Lucy jewellery because emeralds aren't fattening? Marie recalled Lucy's pleasure with her sparkling new ornament and hoped the same thought hadn't struck her. 'Where is he?' Marie scanned the street. 'Strange . . .' she began, but was distracted by Robert's hands around her waist and his lips on her neck.

'Hello, you,' she said.

'Fancy a quick merger?' said Robert.

The Easter leg of lamb, meltingly soft, delicate yet hearty, was fallen upon and devoured. 'I hope you left room,' said Marie, standing to clear their plates, 'for my *pièce de résistance.*'

'Yum-yum,' said Lucy.

'Eh?' said Iris.

'That's French,' said her father. 'For *Your mum took ages making this, so pretend you want some, even though you think your jeans are about to burst.*'

'I don't really do dessert.' Chloe nibbled a fingernail. She'd barely done lunch; the twins had noted this and pitied her.

'Maybe if you did do dessert,' suggested Iris, 'you might grow boobs.'

'Iris!' Robert chastised her. 'Sorry, Chloe.'

'S'all right.' Chloe sank a little lower in her chair, glancing at Angus, who was looking at the salt cellar as if it were the most fascinating salt cellar he'd ever come across in a long history of dealing with salt cellars: there was *no way* he could engage with a girl regarding a boobs-based comment in front of his parents.

'Where's Tod today?' asked Robert.

'Dad's working.' Chloe moved on to another fingernail with a hunger she didn't bring to her food. 'He works really hard.'

'He does!' agreed Lucy fondly, fingering the green egg at her throat.

'My dad works hard too,' said Rose.

'He makes spoons,' said Iris.

'Well . . . kind of.' Robert rather enjoyed his daughter's slippery grasp of the adult world.

'Ta-daa!' Marie had never *ta-daa*-ed before, but felt that the clever, witty lemon meringue eggs deserved one.

'They're eggs,' said Angus suspiciously. 'For afters? You sure about this, Mum?'

Eggcups of differing sizes – some striped, some plain – sat on a bleached wooden tray, pilfered, of course, from Lucy's stylish-homeware stockpile. Each eggcup held a white duck egg, its crown removed and replaced with a fluffy beret of meringue.

'Take a spoon and dip in,' said Marie.

They all chose an egg, and their cagey caution was replaced with glee as their spoons dived through a layer of warm, sweet meringue to reach buttery-smooth lemon curd beneath.

'It's like a real egg. But not really!' shouted Iris. 'In a real eggshell!'

'Like I said,' said Marie. 'Ta-daa!'

Chloe ate two.

Last at the table, presiding over a wasteland of screwed-up napkins and stains on the good tablecloth, the women validated their decision to open yet another bottle of wine with Lucy's *It's a bank-holiday weekend, after all* and Marie's *I tidy up better when I'm sloshed*.

Ruddy-cheeked and slapping the table to punctuate her rambling stories, Lucy was more tipsy than Marie. With the attention span of the inebriated, she skidded from topic to topic, her mood following suit. One moment they were giggling uncontrollably at Marie's impression of the Gnomes having sex, and the next Marie was cackling alone as Lucy announced, stony-faced, 'I don't believe Tod's at work, you know.' She slapped the table, and an eggcup with legs fell over. 'There. Call me an ungrateful bitch. But I've said it. I don't believe my husband.'

Catching up, Marie stopped laughing. 'I'd never call you any sort of bitch, Lu.'

'I feel like one. Tod's so good to me. He's so generous and caring, and just lovely. Why can't I get a grip on the stupid jealousy?'

The time to tell her about the fence-vaulting and the longest-recorded trip to the bottle bank was now. Marie hesitated, as if on the edge of a mine-laden field, and Lucy rushed to fill the pause.

'I have to remind myself that our marriage isn't like his first. He wouldn't do that to me – we're different.'

'Hang on. She left *him*, I thought.'

'No, no. Tod had . . .' Lucy slowed down, but a sip of Dutch courage helped her push it out. 'He had an affair.' Perhaps in response to Marie's look of shock, she rushed on, almost gabbling. 'She pushed him into it – neglecting him, letting herself go.'

Beneath the table Marie sensed Lucy pull in her stomach. 'Listen.' Time to step onto the minefield.

Robert materialised behind Lucy, drawing his finger across his throat, mouthing *No! No!* at his wife.

Ignoring him, Marie said, 'Maybe I shouldn't bring this up now, but . . .'

'Go on.' Lucy was straight-backed, braced.

Robert put his hands to his head and left the room.

'It just struck me as strange.' Marie looked down into her wine. She might be about to upset Lucy for no good reason. And yet. And yet. 'Last night – and this could be nothing, really it could, but – Tod went off up the road with your recycling bin and . . .' Suddenly she lost faith in her tale. *I'm drunker than I realised*, she thought. 'He didn't come back.' She groaned at how silly it sounded. 'Oh, ignore me, please. Christ, what is the poor man supposed to have done? Jumped in a taxi in his dressing gown and gone to a hotel for some quick how's-your-father while you warmed the cocoa? Forget I spoke.'

Scowling with concentration, Lucy disobeyed this request. The cogs of the mind turn more slowly when lubricated with rioja, but at last she said, 'The right-of-way!'

'Oh, of *course*.' There'd been a perfectly innocent explanation all along. 'Tod got back to yours by going through the back gardens.'

'No.' Lucy leapt up. 'He got back to *Erika's* by going through the back gardens.'

'No. Yours,' insisted Marie, scrabbling to hang on to her cosier interpretation, unwilling to accept that Lucy's explanation also neatly answered the question of Tod's excursions into Erika's front garden. Wincing at her unwitting double entendre, she had to accept that Lucy could be right.

'He's there now! The bastard isn't working this late on a bank holiday!' Lucy was zealous, bristling with the urge to right wrongs, a Boden Boadicea.

Feeling it was her duty to neutralise the tension a little, Marie said, 'You don't know that,' even though she trusted her own wifely intuition utterly. She could usually tell from the way Robert said 'Good morning' whether he'd used the last of the milk or had yet another rude dream about Fern Britton. Some terrible mornings he'd done both.

'I do know it.' Lucy drained her glass, then slammed it down. 'And so do you.'

Robert stood across the hall doorway, *über*-calm and very butch. 'Now, Lucy, hang on. Think about—'

'GET OUT OF MY WAY!' she bayed, and Robert did exactly that.

Feeling responsible, Marie tailed her out into the twilight. Lights were on in half the houses, as their neighbours' Easter dribbled on in a haze of television, chocolate and naps. *Lucky them*, she thought, suddenly caught up in a drama that couldn't end well. 'Lu, listen . . .' she began, suddenly sober.

'I'm done with listening.' Lucy didn't look drunk, either. She was wired, as if all the seething, simmering energy she'd bottled up, in order to play the perfect helpmate to her perfect partner, had suddenly popped its cork and was powering her across the Close.

At the top of the cul-de-sac they rounded the corner

and confronted the high wooden door that led to the public right-of-way, a route that sliced eccentrically through the Close's back gardens. Anybody could push this door open and walk through the gardens, but in reality the neighbours were far too polite and British to take advantage of this quirk in the design of their circular street. If they forged ahead, Marie and Lucy would have to cross the gardens of two families they knew only by sight, before reaching Erika's garden, via Hattie's.

Palms splayed on the rickety wood, Lucy said, 'Right. OK. If he's not there, then I owe him an apology. But if he is – well, there'll be some changes.' She looked at Marie and whispered, as if it was a terrible secret, 'I love my husband, Marie.'

The first garden was modern, a Zen landscape of pebbles and bonsai and wind chimes. Creeping through it in Lucy's wake, Marie felt like an intruder and hoped they weren't freaking out the householders.

Garden two's door stuck, before giving and introducing them to a Provençal dream of grey-green lavender and strict, knee-high hedging. Laughter, the jangle of cutlery and the theme from *Mad Men* floated out of the house as the trespassers made their furtive way through.

Cottagey and quaint, Hattie's garden was familiar to them both. Marie breathed more easily. The conservatory was lit; Hattie was home.

Lucy slowed. 'Maybe we should say hi – explain ourselves. It seems rude to tramp through Hattie's flower-beds without saying something.'

'Good idea.' Gregarious, lonely Hattie would probably

invite them in for a coffee, and the situation would be defused organically. Lucy could regroup and plan a more civilised way to confront Tod. Marie intuited that, now they were in the last garden before Erika's, Lucy secretly hoped this, too.

Following the brick path, they approached the glass extension bolted to the back of Hattie's house. Dotted with rattan furniture, the room doubled as solarium and treatment space.

'I've been kneaded and pummelled many a time in there,' whispered Lucy over her shoulder, and Marie was relieved to hear something like her friend's usual tone reassert itself.

The conservatory stood still and empty before them, like a stage before curtain up. Lucy raised a hand to knock on a pane, then the door from the kitchen slammed open and Hattie dashed out to the glass room in a pinkish all-in-one.

'Nooo!' hissed Lucy, ducking down.

Catching up and bobbing down, Marie saw what Lucy already knew: Hattie was naked.

Squawking, thighs a-wobble, belly flopping, Hattie easily outran Tod – also in his birthday suit – as he emerged to chase her on, around and over the rattan three-piece suite. Huffing, puffing, trying for a good shot at her dimply buttocks with a rolled-up yoga mat, he skidded to a halt at the sound of laughter.

Lucy was hooting. She straightened up, to point and guffaw, and then bent double again, still helpless with laughter.

With an animal sound, Hattie grabbed a fake-fur throw

to cover her nakedness and shot back into the house, like a Bronze Age woman fleeing a woolly mammoth.

As for Tod, his handsome features sank into blankness, as if he couldn't compute what was happening. When Lucy's laughter subsided with a satisfied sigh, his face rearranged itself into an angry mask. 'What the hell is this?' he shouted out to her. 'Are you spying on me?'

Lucy wiped her eyes with the backs of her hands, shaking her head, the odd giggle still escaping. 'Yes, darling,' she said. 'I am.'

Not the response he'd expected, perhaps, as Tod seemed lost for a reply. Self-doubt was not a good colour on him. He held the yoga mat carefully in front of him. 'This isn't . . .' he began.

'No, please, don't!' Lucy held up her hand, shoulders shaking again, trying to rein in her smile. 'Don't say *This isn't what it looks like*, or you'll start me off again.'

At her side Marie watched her friend closely, distrusting this mirth. Tense and ready, she awaited some kind of collapse, but it didn't come.

'Tod – to use a Chloe kind of phrase – you're busted, darling.' Lucy turned to Marie. 'Come on,' she said. 'Let's leave them to it. I don't know what my husband's wearing, but it needs ironing.'

Robert's advice – 'Don't give advice' – was Marie's motto through the rest of Sunday. So long suppressed, Lucy's emotions held a fiesta, and Marie was on hand for mood swings, from self-righteous elation to naked fear and back again, via tears and silence. But Lucy was fastidious about holding back. This interlude would shape the Gray family's future; such soul-searching was too important and too personal for Marie to barge in with her tuppence-worth.

The exquisite Gray house was the wrong setting for high drama. It sat, cool and patient, impossible to disorder, as if waiting for the rightful monarch to return and reclaim his rule over the tranquil acres of seagrass. Tod had left half an hour after the nudie show, holdall in hand and leaving a vapour trail of fury in his wake. Next door but one was dark and quiet; no Easter Monday power-walk for Hattie.

'I'm sorry,' said Lucy for the umpteenth time. 'About all this.'

'Shuddup already.' Marie refilled the cafetiere, and the rolling conversation moved with them to the mile-long sofa, then the marble-topped dining table, then the stools in the kitchen.

'I've been waiting for this,' admitted Lucy. Outside, clouds, as if they knew her mood, dimmed the kitchen. 'If I'm honest, my marriage has always felt . . . flimsy. Not airtight, like you and Robert.'

'No marriage,' said Marie, 'is airtight,' hoping/believing that hers was. This close to the disintegration of a partnership she could see all the damage, the twisted body parts, the blood. 'What if he said he's willing to change?'

'He'd be lying.' Lucy was implacable. She saw no chink of light. It was over, she said: 'And my only job now is to work out what to do next.' She looked smaller than ever in the context of her all-mod-cons kitchen.

At noon Robert dropped in to deposit a marzipan and

apricot twist, plus a report of strange goings-on back at the ranch. 'The girls and Angus have been together all morning.'

'Have they tied him up or something?' Marie cut a large wodge of twist for herself and, as custom dictated, a more genteel portion for Lucy, who was living from coffee to coffee with few solids in between.

'No. They seem to be collaborating on something on the computer. They're really quiet. Then every so often there's a shout of laughter.'

'Well, obviously, Robert, those are not our children. Look into it.'

The twist had disappeared in moments. Witnessing Lucy's sudden, unabashed appetite, Marie thought *Perhaps Tod's long reign is well and truly over.*

The Gnomes pootled off in their camper van. Graham and Johann touched up their paintwork. The family at the end, whom nobody knew, had a loud row about an omelette. And Erika turned up, bearing a bottle of brandy and a long, contrite speech.

'I knew,' she said, leaving a scarlet lip-print on her glass and leaning back in an armchair. 'I bloody knew, and I should have said something.'

Lucy absolved her. 'Such as what?' she laughed. 'It can backfire horribly when you interfere. I don't blame you for keeping schtum. Not one jot. I'm just sorry you were put in that position by my arrogant arsehole of a husband.' Lucy noted Marie's and Erika's slight start; Erika's bangles clinked. 'Yes. Even I use bad language when I'm upset.'

'About time you called Tod a few names,' said Marie. 'He deserves them.'

'Bastard!' said Lucy. 'Bugger!' She thought hard. 'Swine!'

'Our very own Gordon Ramsay,' said Marie.

'She's up.' Lucy stiffened, and plumped cushions that didn't need plumping. Above their heads they heard the creak of boards beneath Chloe's feet. 'She just disappeared yesterday when Tod started shouting. Melted away into her bedroom.' Lucy stood up, her hands trembling so much that she clasped them together. The detail touched Marie's heart – Lucy hadn't trembled in front of Tod.

Utterly un-goth in a pink nightie, Chloe looked all of twelve without her face-paint. Without acknowledging Marie or Erika, she stood square in the middle of the cream rug, chin down, mouth set, holding up her phone like a warrant. 'Dad says you threw him out!'

'Darling . . .' began Lucy.

'This is his house!' shouted Chloe. Her eyes were raw. 'We—'

'You told my dad to go!'

'There was—'

'Why can't *you* go? He's my daddy!' The word surprised Chloe. She disowned it as it slipped out.

'Chloe, you're a big girl now.' Lucy held her palms up, trying to clear a path through the girl's noise and blather. 'Your dad and I have some problems and . . .'

'What problems? Does he buy you too much stuff?'

Lucy closed her eyes for a moment. 'Chloe, I've tried to make my life with you and your dad work. But sometimes you have to walk away. And I know how much you love your dad, and how much he loves and adores you, but the truth is . . .' She hesitated.

'The truth is, Chloe,' said Erika, crossing one leopard-skin leg over the other, 'your lovely stepmum can't bear to say it, but I *can*. Tod's been having an affair with Hattie next door for six months. There!' She responded to Lucy's gasp with a firm: 'The girl needs to hear the truth. She's growing up. You can't protect her from this.'

'Bullshit!' barked Chloe, taking advantage of the licence to swear granted her by this extraordinary day.

Marie watched Lucy put her hands to her face. She felt for both the women in Tod's life, each in a personal hell, each straitjacketed by love for a man they had good reason to hate. She remained mute. Erika's interjection notwithstanding, this was between Lucy and Chloe.

'It's true,' said Lucy. 'However much we wish it wasn't, it's true. And you have to try and be as grown-up as you can. The next few days will be hard, but if we look after each other we'll get through it.'

'I hate you!'

Stomping as much as is possible in bare feet on plush carpet, Chloe retreated up the stairs.

'Should I . . . ?' Marie motioned to the stairs.

'I don't think so. She's very private.' Lucy dropped to the sofa. 'She's made me think, though. This house is Tod's. Maybe I should go to a hotel or something.'

'Are you mad?' Erika was shocked to anger. 'Good God, woman! Where's your backbone? Let Tod rough it. He's been boffing the arse off that self-righteous little tofu-guzzler while you've been cleaning his house and bringing up his daughter! You're staying put.'

Marie liked Erika more and more, and was glad that Lucy responded positively to her well-meant tyranny.

As Erika left in a cloud of cigarette smoke and Chanel No. 5, she said to Marie in an undertone, 'Keep an eye on that kid.'

'The custody battle,' said Lucy, as Marie returned to the tasteful-beyond-words sitting room. 'You know, Tod's famous custody battle?' She gave a sarcastic half-laugh, and Cookie looked up from sniffing her own unmentionables and whined. 'Not what it seemed, you know.' Lucy played with her wedding band, scooting it round and round her finger so that its diamonds flashed an SOS. 'It wasn't about . . .' Lucy pointed up at the ceiling, to where loud music now crashed from Chloe's room. 'It was about spite. About getting one over on his wife. He told me his legal team battered her into the ground like a tent peg. That's the expression he used. She'd tried to kill herself, you see, when she was younger, so it was easy for his highly paid lawyers to make out she was – that bloody awful phrase – *an unfit mother*. Had a history of depression. Addicted to medication. A very sad story. But only if you have a heart.'

'Why didn't you run a mile when he told you this?' Marie couldn't see the logic in making a life with somebody who'd abused his previous partner. 'Didn't it tell you something about him, that Tod could separate a child and her mother just because he wanted rid of his marriage?'

'Who's logical when they're in love?' Lucy shrugged,

absolving herself with the same good nature she'd shown Erika. 'When Tod focuses on you, when he's besotted with you . . .' She struggled to find a way to describe it, flapping her hands pointlessly. 'It's like being in the middle of the sun. Everything's bright and new, and you feel that life is opening out. I suppose I followed his lead and I blamed *her*, Chloe's mum.' Lucy looked hard at her hands, then said, each word bitten down on, 'I've never been able to admit this, but I suspect . . .' She faltered again. 'No, damn it, I *know* there've been letters and cards that never got passed on to Chloe from her mum.'

Carefully preserving her expression, Marie said, 'That's unforgivable.'

'You're right. I accepted it when he said the envelopes with foreign stamps were from pen-friends he disapproved of. I stood and watched as he binned them. I chose to believe – the way a kid chooses to believe in Santa Claus – because not believing would put me out in the cold, just like his ex. She thinks her own daughter is ignoring her! Good God, Marie, that poor woman . . .'

They were quiet for a while. Marie asked herself a question as she regarded the battlefield of Lucy's life, calm now, but scarred and treeless: *What would Mary Berry do?*

'Come on.' She slapped her knees and stood up. She held out her hands to Lucy, marooned on the over-large, over-priced, utterly-Tod sofa. 'Time to bake.'

It helped.

With the radio oozing cheesy tracks, the two women weighed and sifted and stirred. The familiarity of it was soothing, the certainty of the outcome was comforting. If you mixed together eggs, flour and sugar, you got a cake.

As they put it in the oven, Chloe slammed the front door and took off on her bike. Families were a more complicated recipe.

.

Sent over with a message from Robert – 'What cloth am I allowed to use to wipe the worktops?' – Angus mumbled, 'Is, you know, everything OK over here?'

'Nah, love. Far from it.' Marie put out her hand to ruffle his hair, then remembered she was forbidden to and dropped her hand. 'But it'll work out. Everything does in the end.' Did she believe that? On balance she did, and felt comfortable encouraging her son to believe the same. 'Oh!' She looked beyond him, to the drive. 'Hi, Chloe.'

Without answering, the girl walked her bike to a stop and stood, holding the handlebar. Her head hanging, black hair obscuring her face, Chloe stayed on the pavement, keeping her distance from the house. Her slender, colt-legged frame looked bone-weary, as if an old, old woman had somehow found herself in a sixteen-year-old's body.

Angus, hands rammed into his pockets, stared at her. He seemed to vibrate, as if pulled by a powerful magnet and doing all he could to withstand it.

'She looks,' said Marie, 'as if she could do with a friend.'

That was evidently the permission he needed. Angus darted out to Chloe, his mother watching as she half-closed the Gray front door. His father, Marie noted, was also watching from their kitchen window.

A brief conflab, presumably in muttered half-sentences,

and then Chloe gestured helplessly to the flat tyre on her front wheel. In a move that reminded Marie poignantly of Robert, Angus squatted, concentrating on the tyre, clearly relieved that matters had taken a practical turn. A flat tyre, his body language said, was a problem he could solve.

A phrase floated over to the eavesdropper.

'No worries!' said Angus, his long fingers tapping the tyre.

Above him, Chloe's shoulders began to shake, and Marie saw Angus's eyes turn to her and glaze with panic. The boy seemed frozen into his squat.

Chloe drooped under the weight of her misery, sobbing into her hands.

Angus stood, suddenly upright and a foot taller than her. He held out an awkward arm and Chloe clung to his middle like a koala, bawling.

Marie shut the door, intensely proud of her unpolished, unrefined, big-hearted boy.

It was late when Tod turned up.

Chloe was in bed, and Lucy was newly bathed, pink as a baby in a towelling dressing gown, about to embark on a medicinal *Midsomer Murders* and a large gin, both prescribed by Marie, who was finally going off-duty.

'I should leave,' said Marie as Tod let himself in and appeared in their midst, tie askew, by far the most dishevelled thing in the room.

'I think you should,' agreed Tod. 'You've done more than enough.'

The stubble, thought Marie, was a theatrical step too far. Nothing, but *nothing*, would keep Tod from his shaver. She moved towards the door, but Lucy said, 'No. Marie's my friend, and I want her to stay.'

'She's not your friend,' said Tod. 'She's a witch, and she's come between us.'

'Hattie,' said Lucy, 'came between us, Tod. Please leave. Call next time, before you come, and I'll have a suitcase packed for you.' She returned her gaze to the television screen and pressed a button on the remote control.

Sitting beside Lucy, following her lead and feigning interest in the conversation between a policeman and an actress whose name she should know but didn't, Marie marvelled at Lucy's composure. Marie's sarcasm knob turned up to eleven if Robert left the toilet seat up; if he'd shagged a neighbour, she'd cry, shout, throw things, chuck him out, then beg him to stay.

Competing with a fictional policeman checking out alibis, Tod addressed his wife's dispassionate profile. 'Hattie's moving away. We can start again. It was a glitch, darling.' He turned neurotically at a soft noise behind him. 'Chloe!'

She ran to him and they swayed together, his arms about her.

'Dad,' she said, more a snuffle than a word.

'All this,' said Tod to Lucy, above Chloe's untidy head. 'You're wrecking all this.'

She didn't wreck it! Marie had to visualise screaming at Tod to stop herself doing it. *You did!*

'And for what?' He kept tight hold of Chloe. They

looked like shipwreck survivors somehow transported to a domestic interior. 'For one tiny slip-up!'

'But not the first slip-up.' Lucy turned off the television and looked up at him. 'Now that my blindfold's come off, I see things very clearly.' She nodded at Chloe, whose face was screwed up, eyes tight closed, against her father's chest. 'No need to go into it here. I'm talking to my lawyer tomorrow.'

'*My* lawyer, you mean.' Tod peeled Chloe away from him, but kept a proprietary arm about her narrow shoulders. 'You don't have anything of your own. It's all what I've given you. Even your so-called daughter is mine, you barren bitch.'

'Hey!' The word was jolted out of Marie.

'It's OK,' said Lucy. 'Tod's just leaving. Seriously, Tod, we're done here. All that's left is to mop up the mess as best we can.' Again, the merest inclination of her head towards Chloe: a typical co-parent secret message, which Robert would instantly have recognised as code for *Not in front of the child*.

'I can practically see the pound signs in your eyes. Good luck with that! You'll walk away barefoot, I promise you.' Tod looked down at Chloe, his face animated, over-happy, the way childminders gee kiddies up for a visit to the swings. 'Chop-chop, Chlo! Pack a bag!'

Chloe danced over to the door, then turned and leaned against the wall, surveying the adults. Marie stole a hand onto Lucy's lap and took her trembling fingers, closing her own over them. Lucy was barely breathing, as if awaiting the lop of the executioner's axe.

'Where d'you want to go?' asked Tod playfully. 'The Ivy? Somewhere funkier? I think,' he turned his gaze on Lucy, still talking to Chloe, 'we should plan a trip somewhere hot.' His face was supercilious, a sadistic mask that Marie berated herself for ever finding attractive. 'Ibiza maybe. By the time we get back, your stepmother will have come to her senses.'

Nibbling her fingers, Chloe said, 'Ibiza, Dad? Really?'

Lucy spoke, in a voice that teetered in tone between defiant, sensible and broken-hearted. 'She has work experience at Robert's office next week.'

'All the more reason to go to Ibiza!' Tod clapped his hands. 'Hurry up, Chlo. Come on.'

Still nibbling, Chloe said quietly, 'You need to start caring about the things that matter, Dad.'

'I do, darling. I do. I care about you. Now move yourself, gorgeous.'

'Dad, I don't want to go to Ibiza.' Her chin went up and a tear rolled off it. 'I want to do my work experience.' She looked straight at her stepmother. 'Any cake left?'

TO: stargazinggirl247@gmail.com
FROM: geeksrus39@gmail.com
22.04.14
06.03
SUBJECT: Wakey-wakey

Hi Soulmate

Wake up!

This is an early one.

I've been awake all night and I have to write this down. I can't stop thinking. About you and about me which is about *us* I guess.

If there is an us?

I don't want to push you. I'm not that guy. I'm really not. But I have to ask.

Do we have a future?

I know you feel something. (This is really really hard to write down.) Don't ask me how I know but I do. & listen I get it that it's your 'thing' to be mysterious but right now I need some words from you. Just summat straightforward like where you live e.g.??!!

There's something else. Maybe you won't even care. But listen I might (MIGHT JUST MIGHT YEAH?) have feelings for somebody else. Ive been trying not to, Ive done my best to ignore her but recently things have changed a bit.

I'm not trying to make you jealous, honest. (Altho that'd be nice.) I'm not forcing you into saying stuff you don't feel. I'm telling you because I tell you everything like I used to tell my mum everything but I'm too old for that now. Parents live in another universe. She'd make all the crap at school worse. So it's you I talk to. Lucky old you! Not.

I think the girl likes me too. A bit. Something could happen. Except I can't stop thinking about YOU.

I need more from you. Just a bit more. To see if there's a point to this hanging around.

I'm waving my heart at you Soulmate. Please wave back.

laters

Angus

MAY

Funeral Tea

Swiss Roll

FOR SALE

Ford Focus 2002 / Hatchback / 1.6L / 96,000 miles
Manual / Petrol

£750 ONO

07779 342401
(Please be kind to it)

'You really don't get this whole employer/employee thing, do you, Aileen?' Marie loomed over her assistant, who was lounging across three seats in reception. 'I tell you to do something, and you do it – that's how it works.'

'What if you asked me to set my knickers on fire?' Aileen pulled a smug face, proud of her nuanced debating skills. 'Or strangle the Queen?'

Marie gritted her teeth.

'Heidi!' shouted Lynda, setting down mugs on the coffee table.

'Obviously I'd never ask you to do either of those things,' said Marie. 'A long-standing patient who lives three streets away is late for his appointment and he's usually bang on time, so all I'm asking is that you pop round and make sure everything's OK.'

'When I finish me tea.' Aileen held the mug in front of her like a shield. 'You wouldn't come between an Irishwoman and her tea, would you?'

Settling back behind her desk, with the limbo-style leaning and groaning that her growing bump necessitated, Lynda said, 'He's at it again.'

In the window of Perfect You, Klay was waving and bouncing on the soles of his feet. Not so much hit by Cupid's arrow as mown down by Cupid's tank, he was infatuated with the 'feisty goddess' (his description) that he'd taken out on just one date.

Presents arrived daily. Little tributes in the shape of bonbon selections, and bigger ones of Swarovski jewellery. Marie had only ever seen giant heart-shaped boxes of chocolates in Doris Day movies before Klay had come a-wooing.

Aileen ate the chocolates, pawned the jewellery and necked the vintage champagne with her lunchtime burger. Klay assumed she was playing hard to get, unaware that Aileen never played and was impossible to get.

Aileen was rude to him. She cut him dead in the street. The less interest she showed, the keener Klay became. Eurostar tickets arrived and were torn up in the window as he watched forlornly from Perfect You, a dejected Romeo and his whatevs Juliet.

'Where's me sign?' Aileen heaved herself up and crossed to the window, holding up a piece of white cardboard bearing a marker-pen message: *YOU MEAN NOTHING TO ME.*

Klay rolled his eyes indulgently.

Retrieving today's roses from the bin, Marie said as firmly as she dared, 'You're not being fair to Klay.'

Lynda butted in. 'He wasn't fair to *you*.'

'Not the point.' Marie knew all about Klay's sizeable dark side; his snide offer still rankled. Yet she couldn't stand by and watch him being tortured any longer. 'You have to put him out of his misery. Tell him how you feel, in person. Not *exactly* how you feel, mind you. No man needs to hear that sex with him doesn't hold a candle to a tub of mint choc chip. But he should know where he stands, once and for all.'

'All this stress,' said Lynda, cradling the faint curve of her tum, 'is bad for the baby.'

'Do I have to?' Aileen was surly.

'Yes,' said Marie.

'I had another drunken phone message last night,' she said, turning her back on Klay, who was now miming hearty laughter at his beloved's cute little handwritten signs.

'What was it this time?' Lynda, like Marie, had her favourites. 'Was it *You can't fight this, sexy lady,* or *I'm Caesar to your Cleopatra, Richard to your Judy*?'

'Or,' asked Marie, momentarily forgetting to be annoyed with Aileen, 'was it *Damn it, you owe me! That meal came to two hundred and forty-three pounds!*'

'We must be due a *please please please please please please* soon,' said Lynda.

'Remember the night it was just the extended version of "Total Eclipse of the Heart"?'

'For a change,' said Aileen, replaiting one of her buns, 'it was interesting. He reckons he—'

'I know what you're doing, and it won't work. I don't care what Klay said from the depths of his poor heart-broken soul. Get yourself round to Jonas. Now!'

Twenty minutes later Aileen returned, almost falling through the door.

'Tatiana!' said Lynda.

'Is Jonas with you?' asked Marie.

'He's not coming,' said Aileen.

Sayings are passed down through families. One of Marie's mum's expressions that still got bandied about was *Have the name of an early riser and you can sleep all day*. The twins had puzzled over the meaning until Marie had explained: 'Once you have a good name, you can do bad things and nobody will suspect you.'

Their grandmother's opinion of human nature was borne out that morning by Mr Wilson's immediate 'yes' to the twins' request. He would never normally dream of allowing pupils to use the ICT suite unchaperoned during the lunch break, but those two had a stain-free record of high test-scores, perfect attendance, enthusiastic involvement in after-school clubs and general sucky-upness.

'We need to practise a presentation for assembly,' said Iris, as Mr Wilson, one of the last proponents of the Fair Isle and tweed tie as teacher-wear, flicked on the overhead fluorescent lights. The dead air of the blank white basement room began to hum.

'Tidy up when you're finished,' he said, leaving them to it.

'I'll set up,' said Rose. 'You go get her.'

'Roger,' said Iris and laughed. Rose laughed too, and then they both stopped laughing, because they were secret agents on a mission and that sort of person wouldn't laugh at the word 'Roger'.

Out in the neither-here-nor-there sunshine of a watery

May day, Iris dodged through the 'big' playground. The two halves of St Ethelred's were segregated, but she'd gained admission to the more glamorous secondary-school stretch of tarmac by claiming to carry a message from the headmaster.

Spotting her target, Iris felt her first twinge of doubt about the plan. Those girls were scary. Short skirts. Bitchy faces. They'd probably kissed boys and everything. Swallowing hard, she went over to where Lauren's coven huddled around her, a carefully cultivated air of bored languor hanging over them.

Lauren scowled. 'Mr Cassidy wants me?' She turned to her crew. 'Being a governor's niece sucks!'

This *bon mot* provoked a blizzard of laughter.

'He's waiting in the ICT suite,' said Iris, and bolted.

The scrupulous nonchalance of Lauren's gait ensured that Iris got to the computer room minutes before her.

'All set?' she whispered.

'Yes. Get down here.' Rose yanked her sister down below one of the Formica desks that dotted the room. Down here, through the tangle of cables and chair legs, they could see the huge pull-down screen on the end wall, currently on standby. The lights were out and the anonymous room was lit only by the screen's gentle fuzzy glow.

'This,' said Iris, 'is like something they'd do at Mallory Towers, isn't it?'

'Shush!'

The door opened.

'Mr Cassidy?' Lauren's default voice was a pissed-off whine. 'Mr C?'

Iris and Rose watched her carefully from their knee-level vantage point. As they'd anticipated, Lauren groped for the light switch. And, as they'd anticipated, when she found it to be taped over, she just swore lightly and made no attempt to pick the tape off, preferring to ask the air, 'What the fuck's going on?'

A swear, mouthed the twins, wide-eyed with disapproval. Rose pressed a button on her control.

The screen jumped to life. Lauren twitched, looking around her, as WHO'S THAT GIRL? appeared in scarlet capitals and the Eurythmics track of the same name boomed from the speakers.

Huddled together and high on the drama they'd created, the twins could see Lauren's head and shoulders silhouetted against the screen. She was stiff. They had her attention.

An image spiralled onto the screen and sat square in the middle for a few moments, before another twirled in to take its place.

'Who's that girl?' Annie Lennox sang her soulful question over the pictures. A young child, about the twins' age, was dressed as Minnie Mouse, a tearful third in a fancy-dress contest. The same girl, slightly older, walked hand-in-hand with two cheerful elderly people, her flowery dress unwittingly tucked into her knickers.

'What's going on!' Lauren spun on her heel, but couldn't keep her gaze from the pictures for more than a second or two.

Larger than life, the girl's spotty face heralded puberty, her puppy fat spilling over a checkered bikini. Thrilled with her princess birthday cake, she showcased the braces on her teeth.

'This is fucking crazy shit!' shouted Lauren over the music.

Snap after snap filled the screen, documenting the mundane horrors of Lauren's 'difficult years'. Iris and Rose were not the sort of children to laugh at pimples or braces or double chins, but Lauren *was* that sort, and she nurtured it in her disciples. Bullying is so much easier when everybody agrees that the normal facts of life are humiliating. The twins were smart enough to know that where they saw a cute photo of a little girl hanging out with her beloved grandparents, Lauren would see an opportunity for the creatures she'd created to mock her.

'Here comes the last one!' whispered Iris.

'The *best* one!' said Rose.

A wedding party, lined up outside a country church, appeared.

Lauren let out a guttural sound.

No detail had been left out by the careful bride. She'd kitted out her young bridesmaid in floor-length satin the colour of egg yolk. She'd added a floppy hat. She'd added a crocheted bag. She'd added fingerless gloves. She'd added – and the twins would always be grateful to her for this – a cummerbund.

For Lauren, being outed as a psychopath would be preferable to being outed as a naff bridesmaid.

The credits rolled. This was the only part of the film the twins had made without Angus's knowledge and they were proud of the ransom-note style, using letters and words painstakingly cut from newspapers and magazines.

Arms folded, foot tapping maniacally, Lauren took in the words that Iris and Rose had drafted and redrafted, before committing them to paper.

This short film was brought to you by the freinds of ANGUS DUNWOODY.

No more HORRID TEXTS.

No more MEAN PHONE CALLS.

No more EVIL NOTES in his locker.

Tell your stupid followers that Angus is a cool dude.

Stop the bullying right now or this film will go to every person on our list.

If you agree text YES to 07793438483

The email addresses of Lauren's entire class scrolled past.

A petulant yowl from their audience, then a stamp of her foot. Lauren was an oversized toddler having a tantrum. She kicked a chair, slammed the Formica work surface with the flat of her hand. 'You bastards!' she spat, as her tormentors, slitty-eyed with mirth, put a hand over each other's mouths as they crouched in the darkness.

Lauren bent over her phone and then the borrowed mobile tucked inside Rose's blazer pocket flared in the darkness.

YES.

'What's Swiss,' asked Marie, peering through the glass door of her oven, 'about a Swiss roll?'

'No idea.' Lucy was dipping grapes in melted chocolate at the kitchen table, then dropping them into her mouth. 'Doesn't the marvellous Mary explain in the recipe?'

'She could if she wanted to.' Marie reached over and popped a grape. Dipped in chocolate, the jade globule was a cunning synthesis of her five-a-day and a naughty treat. 'She just doesn't want to.'

'Are you making a plain roll? Delia does a coffee version.'

'Jonas would prefer plain,' said Marie confidently. 'I think he'd be old-fashioned about it, and see coffee Swiss roll as the work of the Devil.'

'I look at elderly people in the street sometimes and wonder what they make of the world now. Everything changes so fast.'

'God knows what sort of OAPs we'll make. People used to just accept ageing. Sort of *I am sixty, therefore it's time to have a terrible haircut and wear elasticated slacks.* Our generation won't accept it. The drop-in centres will be full of old dears with tattoos and giant silicone breasts.'

'Did he,' asked Lucy, 'die alone?'

'I wish I could say he didn't, but he did. Poor Jonas!' Surreptitiously Marie took Lucy's emotional temperature. Lucy repulsed anything that could be described as fussing, so direct enquiries were out, but her compassionate question was telling. 'His neighbour noticed two newspapers sticking out of his letter box. The police broke down the door and Jonas was . . .' She sidestepped *dead*, power-walking past the dreaded word. 'He was lying in the hall. Heart attack, they think.'

'I hope when I'm dead somebody bakes a cake for me, just like you're doing for Jonas.'

No need for Marie to consult her amateur-psychology

handbook to conclude that this was one of Lucy's bad days. 'How about I make you a cake while you're still alive?'

'Ha!'

The snorted laugh was welcome.

'Whose idea was it to dip grapes in chocolate?' Marie threw one in the air and caught it in her mouth, trying to hide how proud she was of this skill. 'It's so yummy. Not Delia, surely. It's too decadent.'

Not rising to the bait, Lucy said, 'Chloe suggested it.'

'Our anti-chocolate, eternally dieting Chloe?' Marie smiled. 'How times change.' She thought back to the Fireworks Night party; the night the cracks in the Gray family had first showed. 'God, I feel so bad for suspecting you of being jealous when Chloe ate my bonfire cake.'

'You weren't to know.' They'd long ago drawn a line beneath the past and declared an amnesty. 'I so badly wanted to be your friend back then, but outside the house I was a paranoid mess, believing Tod's commentary about how worthless I was. It was the same with poor Chloe. She's so young and impressionable, and the man of the house – her hero – subjected her to a constant drip-drip-drip of snide remarks about fatties. She constantly denied her appetite, pushing away a half-emptied plate, as if she was a fairy who could survive on air. I tried to intervene, to balance out Tod's influence with positive stuff, but . . .' Here Lucy faltered. 'Well, let's say I haven't been the best role-model . . . So I wasn't jealous when she ate your cake. I was flabbergasted. I couldn't believe she'd actually gobbled up actual cake out in the open. I had to say something, but I was a nervous wreck and it came out wrong.' She ended, more quietly, with: 'It often did. Tod gave me hell about that little scene. Silent treatment for days, then counterfeit concern and the suggestion that I see a shrink.'

Chloe had been eating more. There was less talk of 'bad' food and 'good' food, more proper meals, no binges; she'd unselfconsciously wolfed down the endless bakes Robert had taken into Campbell & Carle during her work experience.

Her post-Tod appetite was only part of a wider-ranging rebellion. It was the mildest revolution in history. No gunshots, no bloodshed, just an un-hoovered rug here, a soapy footprint on the bathroom floor there. Mrs and Ms Gray watched their favourite rubbish on the television without being judged; had seconds at dinner if they fancied it; and dirtied mugs for the sheer joy of leaving them in the sink.

'I left a *Radio Times* crosswise on the sofa today,' said Lucy proudly.

'Bet you're itching to get home and put it away, though.'

'I am a bit, yeah.' Lucy licked her chocolatey fingers daintily as Cookie stared up at her, shaking with violent desire. 'Chloe's visiting Tod after school today.'

'Really?' Marie was taken aback. Tod had been calling his family incessantly – one call nice, the next nasty. He pitted them against each other (*This is all your stepmother/ your stepdaughter blowing things out of proportion*) while showering them with gifts. As Lucy wryly told Marie, she had a blingy new iPad cover, but no cash to buy groceries;

Tod had cut the purse-strings the moment he received the letter from Lucy's divorce lawyer.

'Yesterday Chloe deleted his number from her phone.'

The final straw had been Tod's confession that yes, he and Hattie had been in the Maldives for a week.

'When she did that, actually got rid of his number,' said Lucy, 'I felt it had all gone too damned far.'

'But whose fault is that?' A staunch defender of family solidarity, Marie still managed to sympathise with Chloe's drastic step. Tod had threatened to 'seize' her, as if she was a household fixture and fitting. 'She's my daughter,' he'd thundered. Lucy's response – 'And she's sixteen, Tod, she can stay here, if that's what she wants' – had been more polite than he deserved.

Turning a grape between her fingers, Lucy said, 'But whatever his faults, Tod's still her dad. I sat Chloe down and we had a talk about it. Well, to be honest, *I* talked. She's not exactly a chatterbox. I persuaded her to think hard, because Tod's the only father she'll ever have and he loves her. She is, let's be honest, the only person he truly does love.'

'We don't know that,' said Marie. 'Maybe he loves you as much as a man like that is capable of loving a woman.' Lucy was adamant about facing the ugly truths that Tod had left blinking in the light, but sometimes Marie tried to ease the sting a little. Without any further details, she knew that Lucy's heart-to-heart with Chloe had been patient, gentle, respectful. None of these adjectives could be applied to what Tod might say about Lucy to Chloe.

Since his abdication, a truer view of life at Casa Gray

had slowly emerged. Lucy was no tattletale, but sharing seemed to help her come to terms with her new reality. Marie had sat open-mouthed at tales of Tod shouting at Chloe for eating too much; shouting at Chloe for eating too little; raging about her school report, then sneering that she'd better find some sucker to pay her way for the rest of her life. A pointed look at his wife would ensure the parallel was neatly drawn.

The matching en suites that Marie so coveted had been installed because Tod 'couldn't bear' to be in the same room as his wife as she brushed her teeth or used the toilet. A soiled cotton-wool ball left out in the open could trigger a day-long bad mood in her Lord and Master.

Those Fired Earth tiles and glass sinks weren't so enviable now. Marie recalled how she'd weed on a stick in their own scrappy shower room, shrieking when the line appeared. Robert, covered in suds, had dragged her into the shower and kissed her and cried, and her hair had been ruined.

Taking pains to be fair, even while Tod enjoyed five-star tropical luxury with his mistress, Lucy emphasised how 'good' he'd been to them. 'It wasn't all moods and drama,' she said. 'We had lovely holidays and lots of treats, and on the whole we got on and life was calm.'

Tod's brand of calm was laced with dread, like the sticky hours before a storm. The atmosphere would tighten and strain until *kaboom*! Then Tod would loudly speculate on whether Lucy had gained a pound or two, or snipe that Chloe had left a ring around the bath tub.

The poignant truth was obvious: Lucy's apparent

hauteur was only a symptom of the deep emotional distress that her husband carefully cultivated in her. She'd walked on eggshells twenty-four hours a day, and that can make a woman twitchy.

'Chloe's very lucky to have you, Lu. Don't pooh-pooh me – she is. And she obviously agrees with me, or she would have scarpered with Tod. She stayed put, and *that* speaks volumes.' Marie admired the girl for emerging from her shipwreck of a childhood to recognise a good and wise woman when she saw one. The secret that Chloe had desperately hinted at during the bonfire party – the hidden unhappiness at the heart of the Gray marriage – had been outed. 'You worry about what sort of a role-model you were during . . . let's call them *The Tod Years*. But now you're showing her how a strong and independent woman copes on her own.' Lucy's qualms about going back to work (Marie had been amazed to hear she'd once been a big noise in PR) were a frequent theme. Marie had resolved to cheerlead as Lucy retraced her steps to relocate her long-lost chutzpah. 'Chloe and you are a team now.'

'She doesn't call me "Stepmother" any more.' Lucy said it shyly, like a timid child daring to boast of some tiny triumph.

'Yay! Does she call you—' Marie stopped short. The word in her head felt too loaded.

'No, not "Mum". Which is fine,' said Lucy. 'I'm not her mum. She calls me "Lum".' She sighed/laughed, or maybe laughed/sighed. 'I adore that girl's mind. Half-Lucy, half-Mum. Lum!'

'I love it.'

The two women shared the moment, acknowledging the progress the silly word represented.

Quickly, as if she wanted to force it out before changing her mind, Lucy said, 'Do you remember you asked me once why I went ahead and married Tod after I found out how he treated his first wife?'

'Mmm-hmm.' Marie tugged on the novelty fish-shaped oven gloves that she hated and kept meaning to replace.

'I think I said something like I was already in love and it was too late . . . Or something along those lines. Which was true. But not the whole truth.'

The large tin, liberated from the oven, sat on the rack between them and Marie pulled off the gloves. 'Yeah?'

'I was pregnant.'

Marie kept her gaze on the cake's golden pockmarked surface.

Lucy continued. 'He didn't survive.'

He. Lucy and Tod had made a boy.

'I'm sorry.' Marie looked up to see the struggling, crumpled expression Lucy always used to fend off tears.

'Daniel.' She coughed to cover the break in her voice. 'Danny.'

'Danny,' repeated Marie, gently and with wonder. 'Danny Gray.'

They sat in silence for a while.

A key turned in the front door and Robert shouted, 'Halloo!'

As Lucy rearranged her features, dredging up a banal expression, Marie called, 'What're you doing home at lunchtime?'

'Could ask you the same thing. Oh, hang on. The old boy's funeral. Sorry, love, you did say you were baking.' Robert bent and hugged Lucy. Since Tod's desertion he'd treated her gently, as if she'd been bereaved. At some point it would have to stop, but for now they both enjoyed it. 'I've come back for my tennis racket. Magda's drawn up a league, and it starts tonight.'

'Hang on, Andy Murray. You've forgotten we need you at home tonight. Angus is doing some after-school thing and we're hosting Jonas's funeral tea at the clinic.'

'You never said that.'

'I did. I said that. I said it loudly.'

'No, you didn't. Because – guess what – if you had, I'd remember.'

'The twins,' said Lucy, rising from the table, 'can come to me.' She'd caught the Dunwoody habit of fond sarcasm and added, 'I'll get out of here, so you two can have the row you're both obviously dying for.' *I'm fine*, she mouthed to Marie as she backed out of the room.

'I don't want a row,' said Marie, as the front door closed behind Lucy.

'Nor me.'

They kissed lightly, chummily, but as Marie turned to attend to her cake, Robert held her back, clasping her by the elbows. 'I can't go on like this for much longer.'

'Very dramatic for a Thursday.'

'Seriously.'

I know damned well you're serious, but I can't give you the permission you want, thought Marie.

'Just before I left the office,' said Robert, relinquishing

her to the Swiss roll, 'I heard myself say to Magda that Caroline's ginger snaps are too brittle. And I added that her clocks-and-watches quarterly forecast is fundamentally flawed.'

'And? Your point?'

His voice a hiss, Robert said, 'Caroline's ginger snaps are mouth-watering! Her forecast is masterly! Christ, can that girl ever forecast! I've got to get out of that place before I turn into a prize git.'

'Don't do anything rash.'

'Rash?' Robert almost shouted the word as he reached into the garage for his racket. 'I've worked there since the dawn of bloody time!'

'Exactly. So you shouldn't waste all the effort you've put in. For all we know, you're worrying about nothing. Magda might not even amalgamate the departments; and, if she does, she might sack Caroline, not you.'

'You're right – I *have* made an effort. I'm now an expert on clocks, and an expert on vaguely shitty comments about my colleague when she's not there.'

'That's not all you've been doing. You've been running your department at a profit, looking after your staff and coming up with a bestselling new line.'

Robert leaned back against the fridge-freezer and loosened his tie. 'But I've been doing that day in, day out, for the past fifteen years. So why, suddenly, isn't it enough? Why do I have to bake sodding muffins to prove myself?'

'Now don't abuse the muffins, Robert,' said Marie sternly. 'This isn't the muffins' fault. And besides,' she said, head on one side, 'you love the muffins.'

'Yes, I do,' admitted Robert, tormented. 'I love the muffins. But . . .' He slammed the racket against his thigh, punctuating each word. 'But! But! But!'

'Calm down.' Marie would hate it if anybody said that to her: *calm down* is possibly the least calming thing to say in any situation. Every couple knows that *calm down* = *shut up*, and she didn't want to shut Robert up, but neither did she want to broadcast the facts she'd suppressed during their numerous late-night tête-à-têtes on this topic.

They were harsh and pointy, these facts: Smile!'s takings were down by a quarter, and one-tenth of their patients had already defected to Perfect You. The road ahead was a slippery slope.

Lynda had taken her usual no-nonsense approach. 'When life gives you lemons,' she'd insisted, 'chuck them out and make champagne.' She'd suggested new, cheaper premises beyond Klay's reach, but Marie was only two years into a ten-year lease. She'd suggested expanding, but Marie had no capital: 'I seem to have accidentally spent my life savings on Barbies, pencil cases and food.' Lynda had jogged relentlessly through a number of options until she'd arrived at 'Murder Klay in his sleep'. Marie had thought for a moment. 'Sounds like fun, but nope.'

'Calm down?' Robert took it badly. 'Bloody-calm-bloody-down? Do you realise that every morning I drag myself to work, only to have my balls neatly snipped off at reception? Apart from the absurd pressure of only being as good as my last scone, I hate how the company is run. I remember when personalities were important, when our idiosyncrasies were valued. Now you move up by brown-nosing the boss and making flowcharts and multicoloured analyses. I have nightmares that statistics are crawling on my body like ants. Just because I put people first, I'm made to feel out of step, like an old, old man. Like poor what's-his-name – poor Jonas.'

Robert gathered his things together cantankerously, as if all this were his sports bag's doing. 'I'm not ready for the scrapheap. But neither am I up for another decade of competing for the boss's favours.' He snatched up his car keys. 'I have to jump before I'm pushed, Marie.'

'Maybe,' said Marie, 'it'll be Caroline who's pushed.'

'And then what? Elbow another younger contender out of the way, this time next year? What if she has a killer Bakewell-tart recipe? I want to take control of my own life. I want out!'

'Don't do anything hasty.'

Robert made for the door. 'Thanks for the support.'

'Seriously. We have to talk before you do anything.' Marie tailed him to the hall, calling down the path after him. 'Promise?' She knew him well enough to take his seething silence as a 'yes'.

Rolling a Swiss roll isn't easy at the best of times. When you've just had words with your other half and you can't shake off the feeling you've mishandled something fundamental, it's uphill work.

The instructions, as Marie had come to expect from Mary, were clear-cut. With her sharpest knife (gone were the days when the kids could juggle with Marie's knives in complete safety) she began to trim the edges.

In her determination to achieve the uniformity of Mary's illustration, she trimmed and retrimmed until she took herself aside and gave herself a good talking to: any more trimming and the Swiss roll would have to come complete with its own magnifying glass.

Then, following the instructions of her guru, she scored a small indent in one of the shorter edges. With no notion of why she needed an indent, Marie did this completely on trust, believing in Mary utterly, the way pagan people used to believe in the sun.

The jam, a glistening goo the colour of spilled blood, was spread. Robert had made it, in response to Caroline's much-praised chutney. Marie judged the amount carefully: too little and it would be stingy; too much and it would leak out.

It was important to get this right for Jonas.

'Right,' said Marie to the empty kitchen. 'Let's roll.' She flexed her fingers. 'Right.' She flexed them again. 'Here I go.' She shook her shoulders. 'This is me. Rolling.'

I should be able to do this by now. Marie took up the edge of the jammy sponge and whimpered with dismay as it cracked and fractured. Her instinct was to call for Lucy, but she took a few deep breaths and reapplied herself.

The cake folded a little creakily, but didn't split.

Tonight, she thought, *I'll do what I should have done a long time ago*. She would lay the dental-practice books in front of Robert. She'd show him the bank statements. She'd flatten out the long credit-card bill she'd screwed into a ball.

With tiny persuasive flutters of her fingers, Marie cajoled

the cake into a coil, centimetre by centimetre. Her confidence grew, and her pace quickened.

It would be hard to climb down in front of her husband and admit she wasn't a superhero. Marie had always believed that women could be breadwinners: one of the reasons she'd trained in dentistry was the solid career it more or less guaranteed. Seeing Lucy scrabble and scrimp, penniless because she'd put her faith in a man, was chilling. Marie's aim – even within a happy and sound marriage – had always been to be able to take care of them all if something happened to Robert.

Another gentle push and the cake rocked to a halt. There it sat: fat, squat, delicious. A perfect Swiss roll.

Jonas's perfect Swiss roll.

Now, something *had* happened to Robert. *And I'm not sure we can cope without his income*. The comfortable and modest kitchen, her favourite place in the world, shifted – as in a horror film – into a shadowy place full of greedy gullets, all ready to gobble money.

The dishwasher, reprieved at Christmas but now on its last legs, would chomp up £200. The damp patch on the ceiling would devour another £200, while ninety quid or so might satisfy the cracked pane in the conservatory.

We'll work it out tonight. Icing sugar drifted over the Swiss roll. *We'll talk it through*. Marie mustered her resolve. There was a funeral to get through, and then she'd have to tell her husband that there was no escape – not yet – from his misery.

*

The head-count came to eight, and that included Marie, Lynda and Aileen. Eight mourners hovered around the sandwiches set out as prettily as possible on the reception desk.

Five other people had turned out to celebrate Jonas's long life. There was no wife: the delightfully named Editha had died long ago. According to the baseball-capped neighbour who'd found Jonas, he'd gone to her grave every Sunday with a big bunch of flowers.

'Imagine him,' murmured Lynda, her lovely features solemn, 'just sitting there by her headstone.'

'Arranging Editha's flowers.' Marie had been startled by her torrent of emotions in the church. The short, spare service had seemed horribly inadequate. *Say he was lovely*, she'd wanted to shout at the vicar. *Say what a gent he was*. She was shaky now, not quite herself, as she moved among the paltry crowd, offering glasses of the unspeakable wine that Aileen had 'sourced' at Lidl.

'Uncle Jonas was a lovely old bloke.' The great-nephew counted on his fingers and admitted that he hadn't seen his great-uncle for almost a decade. 'Time flies,' he muttered, embarrassed, but not too embarrassed for a refill.

'Lovely spread!' The meals-on-wheels lady tucked in enthusiastically, saying through a mouthful of egg mayonnaise on brown that she liked to attend the funerals of 'her' people – an admission Marie found both heartwarming and creepy.

Nobody present had really known Jonas. The great-nephew knew of a son, but there had been an estrangement over 'Ooh, what was it now? An inheritance, I think. Or was it something to do with a mobile home? They haven't spoken since the late 1980s.'

It was hard, very hard, for Marie to imagine a world where an altercation over a caravan could estrange her from Angus for twenty-five years.

'Cut the feckin' cake,' advised Aileen. 'This mob is getting restless.'

While disputing that eight people constituted a mob, Marie accepted that the 'do' had peaked. The Swiss roll sat patiently in the kitchenette, a relic of old England on its floral-patterned plate.

The red-and-gold spiral was a throwback to when treats were modest – *Hey, kids, it's fatless sponge and jam for high tea today!* – and was therefore a perfect tribute to Jonas, also a throwback to the days when gentlemen lifted their hats on passing a lady in the street.

'This,' said Marie quietly, 'is for you, Jonas.'

Everyone fell on the cake, drained their glasses and left. They'd have forgotten the Swiss roll by the time they got home, but they might recall Jonas once in a while, until he too faded from their memories, just a little old chap in a carefully belted raincoat.

Closing the door on the last guest, Lynda leaned back against it and cradled her tummy. Thanks to regular news-flashes, Marie knew that at fifteen weeks the baby was the size of a pea pod and had fingerprints.

More than that, though, the baby was a promise. It was the future. Marie, rendered super soppy by the funeral, caught Lynda's eye and they smiled – a weary, happy smile that only happens around the big stuff, the important stuff.

'Life's strange, isn't it?' said Lynda.

'Yup,' said Marie. 'And wonderful.' She swept the paper plates into a bin-bag with one hand and texted with the other: *No more talk. DO IT! DO IT NOW! Jack in the stoopid job that's making you so unhappy! Onwards and upwards to our next adventure. xxxx*

After all, she thought, *bankruptcy is a kind of adventure.*

The tiny bubble-shaped car, a bright candy-pink, made its new owner so happy that Aileen was atypically generous and offered Marie a lift home. 'Where's your car these days?' she asked as they buckled up.

'Sold,' said Marie succinctly, glad that Aileen's limited attention span with other people's lives meant there'd be no follow-up questions; she didn't want to break into a rant about rainy bus stops and struggling home with bulging carrier bags biting into her fingers.

The car smelled of newness. Where Aileen saw gleaming bodywork and white leather seats with modish black trim, Marie could only see a hire-purchase agreement. There were other practices, plenty of jobs for a skilled assistant, but who else would employ a woman who had arrived on time only once (they celebrated the anniversary every year) and referred to her boss as Droopy Drawers?

Ready to jump out when the car slowed, Marie stayed put when Aileen yanked on the handbrake and turned the key in the ignition. Relaxing, Marie said, 'Makes you think, a funeral.'

'Makes me think I hate feckin' funerals.'

One of Aileen's unexpected virtues was her ability to

sit in companionable silence without the need to rush in and fill the conversational void.

Dusk had fallen over Caraway Close. The Gnomes were already hunkered down for the night, their television flashing silver around the edges of their drawn curtains. Graham and Johann's lights were on, but nobody was home; while they mooched around the art galleries of Amsterdam, a timer operated their lamps and uplighters. Erika's house was lit as if for a ball, but the next-door house was dark and empty and a *For Sale* sign had sprouted in the front garden where Hattie had once practised her tai chi.

Offering Marie a Rolo from the glove compartment, Aileen said, 'Klay's given up.'

'At last!' In the wing-mirror Marie saw Chloe turn into the Close, dragging her feet, swinging her school bag, mired in thought. Fresh, no doubt, from visiting her dad.

'I tried to tell you the day Jonas died, when I said he'd finally left something interesting on me answerphone.'

'Oh, yes. Jonas's death kind of took over, didn't it?'

The garage door yawned open and Angus shot out on Rose's tiny bike, arms and legs preposterously long for his child-sized transport.

'Klay was sobbing and yelling. The usual owld guff. *This is goodbye*, he yowls, like a big pansy. *You've broken me heart and trampled it into the ground.*' Aileen tutted. 'All this fuss over a little bit of sex! Sure, people have sex every day.'

Angus's knees sliced wildly up and down as he swooped down the short drive and past the pink car, pedalling frantically.

'But people really like sex.' Marie stuck up for poor old sex. 'Some people like it more than . . .' She thought and took another sweet. 'More than Rolos.'

Angus circled Chloe, who'd paused, keeping her eyes cast down, only peeking up now and then at the loon veering around her in erratic loops.

'He said I'd ruined his life.'

Finally giving in, Chloe bent at the waist and belly-laughed. Candy-striped streamers flapping from his handle-bars, Angus cycled harder on the minuscule bike, in ever-decreasing circles.

In a flash, Marie saw the sort of man he'd be.

Able to laugh at himself. Male, but not macho. Just like his dad, he'd do anything to cheer up his favourite girl. Marie watched Chloe trail slowly up Lucy's path, peeking over her shoulder as Angus trundled over the Dunwoody gravel and was swallowed by the dark interior of the garage. Could people find each other, so young? Angus would have to act, because Chloe didn't have the confidence to make a move, but she'd make things easy for Angus if he only had the courage to take that first step.

'. . . so he'll be gone by the end of the month.'

'Sorry? What?' Marie turned to Aileen again. 'Who'll be gone?'

'Am I wasting me breath or what? Klay, Droopy Drawers, *Klay*. According to the message, he can't cope with seeing me every day and not being able to touch my – what was it now? – oh yes, me alabaster breasts. It's a living hell, apparently, and there was a lot more about me boobs, which you don't need to hear, but the bottom line is he's fecking off.'

Loath to take this too seriously, Marie said, 'But he's usually drunk when he leaves messages. Is it a trick to get you back?'

'He's given the staff notice. I checked on the Internet and the lease is for sale. Reckons he's going to Spain.'

'Spain!' Alongside growing glee at the magic wand that was returning the landscape to a pre-Klay era, Marie found time to respect Aileen's technique: when that woman broke a heart, it stayed broke. 'That's an awfully long way to go after just one night of passion.'

'What can I say?' Aileen was complacent as she lovingly twiddled a moustache hair. 'He did mention something else, about some woman suing him. He took out all her teeth and there was nothing wrong with them, and he replaced them with implants and her gums exploded or something. But mainly he's closing down his business because of my irrepressible sexuality.'

TO: stargazinggirl247@gmail.com
FROM: geeksrus39@gmail.com
12.05.14
11.23
SUBJECT: It's over

Hi Soulmate
Thanks for the email.
I think.
It was v long.
And confusing.
Lots of words I didn't understand but that's normal.
Before we get into that I have to tell you about today at school. The Evil Queen sat beside me at lunch. She friended me on Facebook. At home time she shouted 'Bye Angus!' in that dumb voice she puts on and all the dumb Clones shouted 'Bye Angus!' too. One of them blew me a KISS.
It's over.
I wouldn't tell anybody else in the whole world but I cried (proper tears and everything) on the way home. It's over! It's really over.
Deep breath. Back to you and me. Daren't call it us.
I agreed with some of the stuff in your email.
1 Yes we *can* trust each other with secrets
2 Yes we *are* ourselves with each other
3 Yes you *don't* have to act dumb with me (I LOVE you being smarter)
4 Yes talking about our schtupid families helps
Here's what I disagree with.

1 No it *wouldn't* spoil everything if we met

2 No I *wouldn't* be disappointed if I met you. Not possible. Not even if you have a bum where your face should be or something.

3 No I *shouldn't* give it a go with The Goth Girl Across The Road. Why can't you just be jealus like normal people? We promised to be honest so I can tell you this. I DO like her. I like her sort of a lot.

But she's not you.

And I love you Soulmate.

So I'll wait.

Goodbye Goth Girl Across The Road.

laters

Angus

x

JUNE

Just Because

Rainbow Layer Cake

TO: tod.gray@lpsco.com
FROM: luckymrsgray@btinternet.com
15.06.14
22.44
SUBJECT: Unfinished business

Dear Tod,

Thanks for your email. I'll call my solicitor first thing tomorrow and let him know we've finally hammered out the settlement. Perhaps you'll finally accept, after all the accusations, that I never wanted maintenance? Now that you've signed over the house, you are free of me, Tod. I intend to return to the job market and earn my own living, just like I did before I met you. You've been very quick to accuse me of freeloading during our marriage, but if you remember it was *you* who insisted I stay at home. I was too weak and too besotted to argue.

I want to say this, loud and clear – thank you a thousand times for agreeing to let me keep this house, so it can continue to be a home for me and for your daughter. I'll be able to sleep at night again. Thank you.

Thank you.

But while we're saying things loud and clear I'd like to clarify something else. I'm not 'nuts'. I'm not a 'silly moo' and I'm not a 'psycho bitch from hell'. I'd appreciate it if you could stop calling me names. This is a fresh start for us all and, in the spirit of that, why not drop the pretence that Hattie isn't living with you? Chloe's spotted her more than once in the background when you Skype, and if you really think your daughter hasn't found the locked room where Hattie dumps all her stuff when Chloe visits, then you're mistaken.

You texted to ask if I miss you. That text came while I was dumping at Oxfam all the diet books you bought me.

As I type I look over at Cookie. *She* misses you. She misses the way you aimed a kick at her if she dared to cross your path. She misses the way you'd scream at her if she hopped up onto 'your' chair. Much as you'd scream at me if I did the same, or boiled your egg thirty seconds too long, or didn't wear full make-up to bed. Cookie misses you so much she sits in your chair all the time. Bless her, she's just farted into 'your' cushion.

Tod, the truth is I howl with pain at times. Love isn't a tap I can turn off. No doubt I'll die regretting the mess of our marriage and wishing it had been different. I'll die loving you, but I *could not* let you humiliate me for one moment longer.

I've done some research since you left. Thanks to some judicious diary cross-referencing, some questionable email-hacking (were you aware I know your passwords?) and a few tense phone calls to various 'ladies', I now know that I wasn't 'in need of serious fucking therapy' when I accused you of cheating. I was right. Every time. Plus a few more for luck.

You and I don't really matter. When it comes down to it, I'm just some woman you met in a wine bar. Our sob stories, our damaged pride and damaged hearts are our own fault. What *does* matter is Chloe.

Please, please stop using her as a weapon. Stop asking her to carry nasty messages to me. Stop telling her lies about me. Despite what you clearly think, I DO NOT influence her against you. Quite the opposite. I believe a healthy relationship with her father is vital. So, Tod, please turn up when you say you will, don't cancel at the last minute, keep your promises. (And don't, for Christ's sake, dump her for a night at the theatre with Hattie, like you did last Wednesday.)

Cherish Chloe. Be proud of her. I've been boasting my head off about how she managed to revise for and sit her GCSEs, despite the uncertainty and upheaval you and I caused her. Chloe is an AMAZING young woman. She represents the very best of you, the Tod I fell for so hard.

I know how hurtful it is for you to come to terms with her decision to live with me. I know you're doing your best.

There's one other thing I have to ask. It's the last request I'll ever make of you. Please respect her other big decision, the one she told you about last night. She told me you shouted, and assumed it was all my doing. Well, you're damn right: it is. I knew it would upset you, but that's irrelevant. This time it isn't about you. It's about Chloe. And her mother.

Goodnight.

And of course I miss you.

Lucy

'Still not sure about this colour on the walls.' Aileen scowled at the refurbished reception area. New white shutters gave Lynda some privacy at her desk, and a conker-coloured sofa sat cheek-by-jowl with a lacquered coffee table. 'What's it called again?'

'Eau-de-nil.' Marie attempted a French accent.

'Eau-de-feck, more like.' Aileen put her feet up on the coffee table. 'Jaysus, I'm shagged out. Remember the good old days when Klay stole all our customers and we had loads of time to chat?'

Good, bad, whatever – those days were gone. Across the road Perfect You stood empty, a hillock of mail rising on the other side of the glass door, the plasma screen in the window a dark blank. Klay's sudden flit had left quite a stink: unpaid bills; disgruntled staff locked out on the pavement; confused patients with half-whitened teeth and temporary veneers. The lost sheep had wandered back into Marie's fold, bringing more with them, and the appointment book was plump once more. Marie felt sufficient faith in the future to gussy up their workplace, even splashing out on a few new magazine subscriptions. The latest

Vogue lay open, crayon scribbles all over the super-models. *Toddlers have been at it*, thought Marie in-dulgently, before wondering, less indulgently, *Or maybe Aileen has?*

'I'm starving,' said Lynda. 'Any of those biscuits left?'

'No,' said Aileen. 'You ate them all. Just like you ate all the crisps this morning.' She sounded hurt, as if amazed anew by the cruelties of man. 'And all the chips at lunchtime.'

'I'm twenty-four weeks pregnant,' said Lynda. 'I'm eating for two.'

'Two *what*?' said Aileen. 'Two hippos?'

'Millicent!' shouted Lynda and then, more quietly, 'We need a good sandwich place round here. I could murder a BLT. And an egg-and-cress. And a ploughman's.'

The music of the trampoline – boing-boing-shriek – drifted through from the garden as Marie weighed and sifted and mixed. The sun was dialled up to eleven, and it was impos-sible to resist its good cheer. Humming to herself, merrily 'in the zone', Marie watched Angus and Joe out on the patio.

She had to admire their pluck, filming a zombie epic on a sweltering summer's day. Joe was chalky-faced with talcum powder, raspberry conserve smeared on his chest, his eyes hollowed with Marie's kohl. He stumbled, groaning, arms outstretched, towards Prinny.

'Cut!' shouted Angus. 'Prinny! Act scared, you stupid mutt!'

'She can't. She loves Joe!' shouted Marie, as the dog jumped up ecstatically, trying to lick Joe's jammy guts.

'Don't be mean to Prinny!' shouted Rose, mid-bounce, ever alert for dog-dissing.

There had been a definite shift in the family ether. Angus was lighter these days: more a meringue than a Dundee. Marie daren't ask why, in case that visor of teenage reserve slammed down over his eyes, so she simply enjoyed it. 'No red food colouring?' she tutted, opening and slamming cupboard doors. 'I had a whole . . .' She realised. 'Angus! Have you used my red food colouring for gore?'

'Maybe.' Angus squinted through his viewfinder as Prinny made sweet love to Joe's leg. 'Yes.'

A Woman Who Runs Out of Things needs to know A Woman Who Always Has Loads of Everything; Lucy was out at an appointment in W1, but a brief text brought Chloe across the Close with a tiny bottle.

'Thanks, love.' Marie slowly upended the dye, ekeing out a drip or two into the bowl. 'I hope Lucy's OK.'

'Of course she is,' said Chloe. 'Lum can do anything.'

'How's the napkin campaign?'

'We're making progress.' Chloe, on a crusade to loosen up her stepmother, reported regularly to Marie. 'I've managed to get her to agree to linen napkins on Sundays only. The rest of the time we use paper ones!' She quelled Marie's whoop with a dark, 'Posh ones, though.'

'Every little helps.'

'What you making?' Chloe leaned over the two bowls, one a vivid red, the other growing bluer by the moment, as Marie splashed colouring into the creamy batter.

'A rainbow layer cake.' Marie nodded at the photo in the book and smiled at Chloe's soft 'Wow!'

Only a *wow!* did justice to the majestic, five-tiered beauty. Each band was a different vibrant colour, the stripes of red, blue, yellow, green and pink all outlined with soft, thick white icing. 'For your mum. To say *well done*. And for Robert, too. To say *it'll all be all right.*'

'It'll just say *eat me* to me,' said Chloe. She hadn't once looked out to the patio, where Angus could be heard coaxing his star to perform. 'Up!' he shouted, then, 'Down! Down, Prinny! Stop, Prinny, *stop!*'

A banging on the glass forced Chloe to give the film crew her attention. Joe had noticed her and was gesticulating and smiling and waving, and being about as uncool as a boy can be without actually wearing a tutu.

'I hope Joe's wearing zombie make-up,' murmured Chloe, waving back, 'or he's too ill to be out.'

Joe was yearning to get indoors now that Chloe was on the premises. He reminded Marie of the way Prinny scrabbled at the glass during Sunday lunch. Joe stopped short of howling and jumping at the handle, but he did take Angus's camera out of his hands and shove him indoors. 'Any more of that lemonade going?' he asked Marie, staring – hungrily, obviously – at Chloe, who was faking extreme indifference to Angus, who wasn't faking it. His indifference was the real deal.

Something had happened in Teen World. Marie didn't know why or how, but life had contrived to plant a full stop on the promising harmony between Angus and Chloe.

'Your wish is my command.' Marie poured out her own-recipe lemonade, as the twins materialised, excited by Chloe and her trendy jeans *and* the drink. Marie had successfully weaned them off canned fizzy tooth-rot. A small maternal triumph perhaps, but one that Marie would like on her tombstone. Along with *I owe it all to Mary Berry*.

'Mate!' Joe thumped Angus on the arm. 'I've had a genius idea! Chloe should be in our film.' Joe was as fizzy as the pop with his idea.

'We don't have a part for a girl,' said Angus, firing up his laptop.

'But we could—'

Chloe cut Joe off with: 'I'm busy, actually. As it goes.'

'But . . .' Hormones firmly in charge, Joe couldn't give up.

'Honestly,' said Chloe, firmly. 'I can't. OK?'

'*Awk-ward*,' sang Rose.

'Sshh, you,' said Marie, seeing Chloe's chin sink, her lips compress. The girl was determined to look nonchalant, but her feelings were evidently bruised by Angus's coolness. The hopes that Marie had nurtured during the brief thaw in their Cold War seemed ludicrous now that normal frosty service was resumed. She considered tackling Angus: she couldn't force him to like the girl, but she could damned well drum some manners into him.

'A boy in my class,' said Iris, 'thinks lemonade is made from lemmings.'

Beneath Joe's bark of a laugh, Marie heard her son inhale sharply, his eyes on the laptop screen.

Angus slammed the computer shut. Marie knew to leave well alone, but Chloe didn't have her years of experience at Angus-wrangling.

'Bad news?' she asked.

'Why,' said Angus, a nasty spin on each word, 'are you always here?'

'Hey, bro,' protested Joe, but Angus shoved past him, making for the stairs as if zombies were after him. Or as if, thought Marie, he was about to cry.

'Angus is horrid,' said Rose, putting a hand on Chloe's slender arm. 'Come out to the trampoline with us, Chloe, and forget all about our meanie brother.'

'Only if Marie comes,' said Chloe.

'But I . . .' Marie looked down at her apron, at the bowls brimming with jewel-coloured slop, at the flour-spattered worktop. She was on a tight schedule if the cake was to be ready for Robert's homecoming. 'I have to—' She stopped. Mary Berry would *not* condone such priorities. 'Only if Joe comes.' She nudged the confused boy, who had half-stood, uncertain whether blokey etiquette decreed that he should follow Angus or leave him alone.

'You're on!'

The twins were right. You *can't* be miserable on a trampoline.

TO: geeksrus39@gmail.com
FROM: stargazinggirl247@gmail.com
17.06.14
17.41
SUBJECT: Zombies etc etc

Hey Angus

Your Zombie movie idea is dingdongtastic. Love the script. Bit like that Japanese movie you made me watch, *Bio Zombie*. And a bit like – Warning! Huge compliment alert! – your beloved *Shaun of the Dead*.

Supposed to be clearing out my room – arrrrrrgh – but yeah you guessed it, I'm watching *An Officer and a Gentleman*. That scene. Over and over. Can't believe you don't get it. Only the best constructed most romantic scene EVAH. Duh.

Picture it . . .

Richard Gere on a motorbike. As if that isn't exiting enough for the laydeez, he's wearing an AMERICAN NAVY UNIFORM.

We're talking bright white tailored shit. With those thingies on his shoulders, can't remember what they're called. And Richard has such broooooooad shoulders.

So. Basically we're all swooning.

And yes feminists are allowed to swoon.

Just remembered. The shoulder things are called 'epaulettes'.

The song starts. 'Up Where We Belong'. TBH I hate it. Far too schmaltzy. But it's perfect for the scene.

Cut to Debra Winger. Pretty, brown hair and (obviously)

skinny. Working in the factory along with her mates. She's wearing the worst tweed cap thing you ever saw. Not dolled up.

Richard G walks in. He heads straight for her. He looks really out of place in a factory. Like an angel (SHUT UP, HE DOES) in his white kit.

He goes to Debra. She has her back to him. He kisses the back of her neck. Debra jumps and turns round and recognises him.

She knows then that it's going to be all right.

Everything.

Her life is solved.

Richard puts his hands on her neck and kisses her.

Then he twirls her around.

Then he lifts her into his arms like she's a baby and walks off through the manky noisy factory holding her.

I'm usually crying by this point (yeah, ME, I know, the one who just laughed when they took Dumbo away from his mummy) and I cry harder when her friend shouts, 'Way to go Paula! Way to go!'

All the workers clap. They're all laughing and crying and wanting to kill themselves with jealousy because it's not them Richard Gere is rescuing.

Debra's hat falls off. She grabs his cap and plonks it on her head. They're outlined in the light flooding through the doors and that's it.

Slushy. Commercial. Mainstream. All those other bad words you've thrown at it. But FANTASTIC.

End of rant!!!

Dead flattered you want my help with the zombie title

sequence but you don't need me, you idiot. Your artwork and design is way, way better than my pathetic efforts. Make them really retro and old-fashioned.

I like it when films have THE END in big letters at the end because then you know it's time to have a stretch and a yawn and go off and get on with something else.

That's what I'm doing now, actually.

I'm writing THE END in big letters so we both know where we stand.

Angus, I can't do this any more. I can't take the pressure. You can't come to see me but if I told you why you'd hate me. These emails are getting in the way for both of us. You're not the only one with feelings for somebody else. I do too. It's crazy for us to ignore them.

What if The Goth Girl Across The Road is the one for you?

What if you're missing out because of me?

Which is why I'm going to type in big letters

THE END

'Why are my children so clean?' Robert paused as he hung up his jacket in the hall. 'Urgh!' He backed away from his family, arranged as if for a portrait, all beaming at him – even Angus, whose smile had a hint of rigor mortis. 'Stop that! Ignore me, like you always do.'

'Oh, right? *That* you will obey?' Marie flicked at her brood with a tea towel as they fled, relieved. 'Welcome home, love.' The kiss she tried to give her husband missed his lips, thanks to his startled jerk at the insertion of Prinny's wet nose into his privates. 'Ow!' Marie retreated, her eye smarting from its sudden introduction to Robert's chin. 'That went well,' she said, her Berry-esque tableau ruined.

'I don't want any fuss,' said Robert, the last word dying on his lips as he saw the cake standing proudly on the kitchen table. 'Ah!' He turned to Marie, folded her into his arms. 'I do want fuss. It's lovely. I love it.'

'It's not for you,' she said, allowing herself to be folded. 'It's . . . just because.'

'It *is* for me,' insisted Robert, 'isn't it?'

'How did it go? Seriously?'

'Fine. It went fine.' Robert felt his wife fidget, but he didn't let her go as he remembered all the mundane things he'd done today, which had felt anything but mundane because it was the last time he'd do them: dropping his correspondence in the big mesh box; switching his phone to 'out of office'; winking goodbye at his assistant; blotting out the muzak in the lift; hearing the groan of the sticky main door as it closed behind him.

'How do you feel?' asked Marie, quieter now, cheek-to-cheek.

'I feel . . .' Robert didn't want to pick apart how his last day at work had made him feel. Since his meeting a month ago with Magda, time had speeded up, delivering him to this threshold so fast he was breathless. The past, back behind that sticky door, was busy, purposeful and, from his current perspective, *safe*. When he'd asked for a redundancy package, Magda's dismay had alarmed him. She'd repeated *You're sure about this?* before acquiescing: was he, Robert had wondered, front runner for the new position after all? His second thoughts had been only momentary. *I'm sure,* he'd said, with a certainty he couldn't match today.

'If I'm honest, love, I feel a bit numb.'

Marie shifted: now she was the hugger and Robert the huggee. Their heads bent over each other's necks like swans, they summoned up the marital forcefield, an iridescent bubble that kept the outside world at bay. Surprised by the scale of the redundancy money – she'd resisted, so far, the temptation of working out how many spa mini-breaks it represented – Marie knew that Robert couldn't be 'redundant' for long. Early retirement was not an option for him, any more than it had been for her dad, who'd still been running his building business when Alzheimer's had whispered in his ear and taken the files out of his hands.

'This is nice,' said Robert, his voice indistinct from inside Marie's hair.

'Not numb any more?' she asked gently.

The mobile in her pocket buzzed and broke the moment. Reluctantly they pulled apart. 'Can't I have you to myself for a minute or two?' Robert was woebegone. 'That's Lu, I guess.'

'Yes,' admitted Marie. The contents of the message prompted her brows to knit together. 'Listen, I need to pop over to hers.' She saw the sigh he repressed. 'Just for a minute or two,' she lied. 'Be nice.'

'I am,' said Robert tersely, 'very nice.'

That was true. He was far nicer than most men would be about an omnipresent third party in their marriage and in their kitchen.

Trotting over with a slice of cake, Marie found Lucy breaking and entering the drinks cabinet with a screwdriver, as Cookie danced at her feet. 'Tod took the keys with him when he left,' she said, reaching into the innards of the mahogany colossus. 'Let's have a dram of his oh-so-precious whisky!' She gingerly picked up two heavy, glittering tumblers. 'This feels naughty. Tod was so pretentious about his malts and his crystal.' She paused. 'I talk about him as if he's dead.'

'Cake!' said Marie, swapping a slice for a glass. She was trying to assess Lucy's mood; skittery, evasive, her friend was full of a dark energy.

'The colours!' Lucy gasped at the rainbow cake, as Cookie stood to attention, watchful for crumbs. 'Breathtaking.' She washed down a huge mouthful with a slurp of whisky, which made her eyes swim. 'It tastes divine. I could never produce anything so heavenly.'

For the first time Marie didn't swat away the compliment. Perhaps she'd finally caught up with Lucy in terms of skill. Perhaps, one day, she'd catch up with Mary. If she lived to be a thousand and one. 'The cake is to say *Well done*.'

'Well done for not getting the job?' Lucy snorted. 'It's more of a *Sorry you're past it*, in that case. I was the oldest candidate by about – ooh, let's see, twenty years.'

'Ouch!'

'I felt like a museum piece.' Lucy drained her glass and ignored Marie's concerned look as she refilled it. 'How can everything have changed in PR in so short a time? It's all bloody digital now. We used carrier pigeons in my day.' She wheeled around. 'I've got *bras* that are older than the other candidates!'

'Sit down. Tell all.' Marie dropped to the sofa and patted a cushion. 'Did they give you *any* encouraging feedback?'

'Well . . .' Lucy looked as if she didn't know whether to laugh or cry. 'The managing director asked me out for a drink.' She grimaced. 'Does that count as feedback?'

Ever the romantic, Marie bounced at this news. 'Get you!' she said admiringly. 'Was he handsome?'

The 'no' was unconvincing when backed up by lowered eyes.

'You fancied him!' Marie embraced this swerve to lighter fare: they could discuss the interview in more detail when Lucy had recovered from the initial sting.

'Maybe I should have said yes.' Lucy necked another two fingers of fire-water. 'Maybe Tod's right, and it's my only talent: netting a man.'

'That's the booze talking.' Marie rose and took the glass out of Lucy's hand. 'And the booze is, as usual, a moron. You have plenty of attributes. Charm. Intelligence. Dab hand with a spatula. And you can learn about the digital whatsits.' Marie, who had tweeted just once (*helo is this on*) had every confidence in clever Lucy: enough, she hoped, for both of them. 'You can *net* a man in the future, when you're in the mood. When,' she added softly, seeing the air of dejection that dulled Lucy's pearly skin, 'you're ready.'

'I don't think I'll ever be ready, but God, it's scary being alone. Especially when it's becoming obvious I can't make a living. I can't keep me and Chloe fed and clothed and . . .'

'You're panicking, Lu. You'll manage. We'll help, you know that.'

'I do. I do know that. You and Robert have been amazing.' Suddenly, vehemently, Lucy said, 'I'm nostalgic for what you have with him,' before slowing down to say wonderingly, 'even though I've never had it.'

'We're not special,' said Marie. She reconsidered. That was both disloyal and untrue. She and Robert were super special. But in an ordinary way. 'Everybody in love is special. Does that make sense? It's not some weird skill, or fate. It just . . . happens.'

'Not to me,' said Lucy. The sentiment was morose, but she had rebooted her expression so that it was wry rather than unhappy.

'Run a bath,' advised Marie. 'Have a quiet evening – just you and Chloe. Put the interview behind you, yeah?'

'Yeah. Except Chloe's out tonight. Little gadabout,' added Lucy, pleased at her stepdaughter's new freedoms.

'Oh, so . . .' Marie put her head on one side. 'Ours for supper then?'

'No, no, I'm always there. In your way.' Lucy did her best, but her reluctance was unconvincing.

'Rubbish. Fancy a takeaway?'

'For me? Please?' Marie looped the silk around her husband's neck as he pawed her away. 'Humour me!' She stood back and surveyed her handiwork.

Tucking the knotted scarf into his dressing gown, Robert said sceptically, 'Is it supposed to be a cravat?'

'It *is* a cravat.'

'It's the bloody horrible headscarf my mother bought you last Christmas.'

'It's a cravat now.' Marie handed him a cigar and pushed him down onto the conservatory sofa. The wicker groaned, and so did Robert. 'You're a man of leisure. You should dress the part.' She sat beside him, leaning in, making herself small – or as small as Marie could manage. 'Although, in Mills & Boon, international playboys don't boast about the crust on their multiseed bloomer.'

'Reminds me.' Robert checked his watch over her head. 'I should get those buns out of the oven.'

'Leave them a minute. I'm comfy.' Marie burrowed into his side, enjoying the way his arm tightened automatically around her. 'Remember just a few months ago when it was too cold to venture into the conservatory? We left the wine out here to chill. And now look at us. Luxuriating.'

'Are you trying to illustrate that everything changes, in a poetic – if somewhat wanky – way?'

'Yes,' laughed Marie, hoping he grasped her point. Returning, thoughtful and preoccupied, from Lucy's, the scene she'd found in the kitchen had dismayed her. Radio blaring, Robert had been gyrating in a cyclone of self-raising flour, slinging tins in and out of the oven, pummel-ling dough, playing drums on a biscuit tin with his set of measuring spoons. Such classic displacement activity had moved her, and she needed to find a way to tell him that he was no more out to grass than Lucy: they both simply had to regroup and launch themselves back into the fray. 'I'm saying that everything is circular. It changes, but it stays the same. Like the seasons. Like the Earth revolving around the Sun.'

They stared up through the glass roof at the purple starless sky, until Robert twitched and sat forward.

'Is that a gun in your pocket,' asked Marie, dragging him back to her. 'Or are you pleased to see me?'

'It's a timer in my pocket,' said Robert, taking out a small chrome stopwatch. He pressed the button, and put his face close to hers. 'But, since you mention it, I *am* pleased to see you.'

The doorbell interrupted quite a quality kiss.

'Let me guess . . .' said Robert, relinquishing his wife and heading for the door, where she heard him say, 'Lu! Come in!'

After an inauspicious start, the evening relaxed into the usual blend of low-key jokes and comfortingly banal chatter. Robert, perhaps regretting his earlier churlishness, was attentive to Lucy as they lingered over the last few poppadoms in the darkening garden, and soon the humiliating interview had been reduced to an anecdote they could quote and return to again and again, all its venom neutralised.

When Robert dashed back to the oven, heeding the siren call of yet another timer, Lucy asked, 'What's he making?'

'What *isn't* he making?' In the bright kitchen Robert seemed to be beating something small to death, but Marie knew he was kneading. 'He's baking like the Pillsbury Doughboy's got a gun to his head.'

'D'you think he'll let me help?'

'Um . . . yeah.' Marie hoped this wouldn't test Robert's mood. He, too, had had a long, emotional day. She watched Lucy tentatively go back into the house, saw her husband nod, watched them put their heads together over a recipe and smiled to herself.

Watching Robert, tuning into something she vaguely perceived but couldn't quite pin down, Marie knew something else was cooking, along with the bread.

*

Even, strong, white: Chloe's teeth were like Tod's. 'If all my patients were like you,' said Marie, lowering the chair, 'I'd be broke in no time.'

'I don't need any fillings? None at all?' Chloe looked puzzled. 'That other dentist – the funny little fat one across the road – told me I'd need loads of stuff done.'

'He was fibbing,' said Marie, leading her out to reception. 'Lynda here will send you a reminder to come back in six months' time, but until then, keep flossing.'

'Here.' Lynda handed Chloe a paper bag. 'Free today to every patient.'

'Rolls,' said Chloe, peeping into the bag. Then, puzzled, 'Rolls?'

'Yes, rolls,' said Aileen. 'Her mentalist husband can't stop making them. We've got them coming out of our arses.'

'Beautifully put,' said Marie. Walking Chloe to the door, she asked, 'How's the Loosen-Up Lum campaign going?'

'Not bad, not bad. She went a bit finicky after that interview, but she's fine now, most of the time. During the day.' Chloe screwed up her dainty nose. 'But late at night she kind of deflates. As if somebody's pulled out her plug. That's when we sit down and watch a *Seinfeld* or an old *MasterChef*. If she's very miz, I make her a hot chocolate. Lum loves my hot chocolate. I do it all posh, with chocolate on top and everything.'

'That's so sweet.' Marie hurriedly rearranged the face she was making. It was the face she made at YouTube kittens or the twins' baby photos, and Chloe would not welcome it. 'I know Lucy's doing her best to help you through this horrible period, but actually it's mutual. You're looking after each other, aren't you?'

'S'pose.' Chloe's rocky family life hadn't embittered her: instead it had strengthened her compassion. Freed from Tod's mind games and his crazily high standards, she was less anxious, more herself. 'Lum spent so much of her time running around after my dad, like some freaky robot housewife, that now he's vamoosed there's a big gap in her life. That's partly why I said yes to her big idea.' Chloe clocked Marie hurriedly, as if to ensure she was in the loop, before going on. 'I mean I want to do it, of course I do, but it's bloody – sorry, I mean *very* – frightening.' Chloe put her hand on the latch.

'I think it's a good idea. A brave one. Just take it one day at a time,' advised Marie, passing on her own mother's words. 'Or one luxury hot chocolate at a time.'

'I'll do an extra-spesh one tonight,' said Chloe. 'Unless she's at yours again, like last night.'

'Was she at . . .' Marie frowned, the gentlest of dips in her brow. 'I was at a seminar. Advanced Endodontics.' She looked sideways at Chloe. 'I can tell you're jealous.' As Chloe tittered, Marie wondered why Robert hadn't mentioned Lucy's visit. The state of the kitchen – as if terrorists had been training, using baking ingredients – told her he'd been cooking: had Lucy come over to help again? The two of them bent over a recipe, conspiring over brown-sugar levels and icing consistency. Like the evening before. And the one before that.

And, come to think of it, the one before that. Chloe sprang back as the door began to open. Angus and the twins were abruptly there, spilling through the door like a human 3-for-2 offer.

'Chloe Chloe Chloe!' Rose was overcome to see her favourite big girl out of the blue.

'Ladies.' Chloe bowed gravely. The twins giggled like hamsters on Ecstasy. They couldn't love Chloe any more if she came with a free *Beano* annual.

'Maximilian!' shouted Lynda.

'What a lovely name!' Iris and Rose surged towards the receptionist. 'Can we touch your bump?' Reverently they caressed the taut arc of Lynda's sundress. 'Does it have teeth yet?' asked Rose. 'Imagine if it came out and it was a teeny horse!'

'Oh!' Iris clasped her hands together and screwed up her freckly face in supplication to the Lord. 'I do hope it's gay!'

'What are you lot doing here?' Although always glad to see the faces of those she'd given birth to, Marie was in the middle of a busy afternoon.

'Something you have to sign, for school.' Rose turned her backpack upside down on the coffee table and began to sift through the primary-school sediment of pens and pencils and erasers, and gonks and highlighters and key rings, and pebbles and sweet wrappers. 'A permission for the visit to the owl sanctuary. It should have been brought in today and I really, really want to go. I love owls so much, I really do, and Iris handed hers in, so Angus said he'll take me back with it, if you sign it now.'

His face a slab of granite, Angus squatted and helped his sister root through the debris, as stern and unapproachable as a Victorian papa.

Marie, bending to rifle, stole a glance at Chloe. One hand on the door handle, she was patiently itemising the rings on her fingers for Iris, who gazed at each cheap silver skull-and-heart as if they were sacred relics. Chloe glanced at Angus, but her expression was impenetrable to Marie. It stood to reason that the girl must be shocked by his retreat into rude standoffishness after their short period of harmony, but Chloe was, Marie realised, much more mature than Angus. She'd been tested in ways that, *thank God*, Angus hadn't.

'Gotta go,' said Chloe, gently removing Iris's fingers from her own. 'Don't want to be accused of *always being here*. Laters.'

'Ooh, laters,' said Iris. 'Yeah! Laters, Chlo!'

A tall man, self-conscious in shorts, caught the door as Chloe left.

'Hi, Mr Kinney,' said Lynda from her desk, gesturing to a seat with the grace of a prima ballerina. 'Marie won't be a moment.'

'Come on, kids,' muttered Marie. 'Find this thing and I'll sign it, and you can all disappear.'

'Remember this?' said Rose nostalgically, holding a crumpled form under Iris's nose. She didn't seem to have caught the *Get out!* subtext in her mother's tone.

'Oh yeah!' Iris examined the piece of paper. 'Angus, we were going to interview all the girls in the neighbourhood to find out who you should go out with.' With a look of irritation that converted to intrigue, Angus looked over her shoulder, drawn in by the sloping rows of questions and answers.

'We only interviewed Chloe, in the end,' said Iris. 'We didn't bother with anybody else because she's perfect.'

'Found it!' Rose's permission slip was so creased that Marie could barely scribble her name over the paper's peaks and chasms. 'Hurray! I'm going to meet loads of owls, and maybe buy one!'

'Bitch!' blurted Angus, reaching over Iris to snatch up the girlfriend questionnaire and aim it at the bin.

'Hey! That's ours!' Iris was outraged.

It was time for Marie to unleash her sternest look. The biggie. The one she rarely used, under wraps since a tiny Angus had shouted 'Tits' in front of his grandparents. It worked. It always worked; it was the atomic bomb of maternal looks.

'Sorry!' said Angus. He turned to Lynda, shame-faced. 'Sorry, Lynda. Aileen.'

'I don't give a fuck, Angus love,' said Aileen kindly.

'But she is, Mum,' said Angus, a glower ageing his features. 'Chloe is . . . that thing I said.'

It regularly slipped Marie's mind that she didn't have a lifestyle, just a life, and she fell anew for the big fat lies peddled by glossy magazines. She'd got through a strenuous afternoon of drilling into teeth by imagining an al-fresco feast with her loving family. There was a bowl of blowsy peonies in her fantasy, and a trailing lace cloth. Her family had been replaced by models, their personalities rinsed clean of kinks.

It wasn't like that at 8 p.m., with Rose screaming if a wasp entered British air space, and Iris mulishly insisting she'd gone off chicken. Angus winced as if his family's conversation hurt his ears, and when Marie had rooted out her only lace tablecloth, she'd discovered that Prinny had thrown up onto it a mutilated Star Wars action figure.

'You *do* like chicken, darling,' said Marie patiently. 'You had it yesterday and asked for seconds. Have some Greek salad, or have you gone off that as well?'

'I love Greek salad,' said Iris, insulted that her mother should imply otherwise. 'But Daddy took all the feta.'

'And Daddy's keeping it,' said Daddy. The family knew better than to come between him and his feta. 'Isn't Lucy joining us?'

'I didn't mention it to her,' said Marie, hoping Robert was too bewitched by the nearness of the cheese to catch the twitchy look his question had provoked. 'She doesn't come over *every* night.' She added, more slowly, knowing it to be beneath her, 'She doesn't *live* here.'

'She might as well,' said Angus genially.

The horrible thing about the scenario Marie had pieced together was that she didn't really blame her husband.

For months, until recently, Marie had been tense, pre-occupied, ever-ready with a sarky barb. Whereas Lucy was soft, sympathetic, forgiving; she was a totally feminine being. If Robert and Lucy had bonded over fear of the future, over feelings of loss, over insidious sensations of worthlessness, then she understood. She didn't like it – in fact, it made her heart feel as if it was deep-frozen – but she understood.

'Where's the salt?' Marie studied the spread, before jumping up to get it.

'While you're there,' shouted Rose, 'bring me a knife, Mum!'

'Please!' Marie yelled, yanking at the cutlery drawer. 'What?'

'Nothing,' she murmured, mourning her Provençal-style dinner that never was. Robert had been tasked with laying the table, but he had saved her neither time nor trouble. Every other minute she'd had to dash back into the house for glasses, plates, cutlery and other esoteric equipment that he'd left off. 'Right.' She plonked the knife and the salt down on the clothless table. 'I'm not getting up from my seat again, for any reason.'

'WAAAAASP!' shrieked Rose.

'I bet this chicken had a name,' said Iris.

The abandoned table was as messy as if the children had danced on it, rather than just eaten dinner.

Robert stacked one plate on top of another, then paused, looking expectantly at Marie. 'This is where you say *Leave it, I'll do it – you never do it properly anyway*.'

'Not tonight, mate.' Marie sat back, her bones aching; the emergency gin hadn't worked. Maybe it wasn't ginny enough. She topped up her glass. 'You're a house-husband now. You can't expect me to work all day, then come home and clear up.' She sipped her gin. No need to dig deeper and mention that she'd shopped for dinner on the way home, cooked it and served it. 'Plus I bought it, cooked it, served it.' Oh. Apparently there *was* a need to mention it.

Why doesn't he ask me what's the matter? thought

Marie mutinously. She had questions of her own, but was afraid to put them to him.

'Actually,' began Robert, lifting the plates in a way that made Marie itch to stop him, 'there's something we need to discuss.'

'What?' Marie clutched her glass harder. '*What*, Robert?' Life was ambushing her. Yesterday a perfect evening needed only her kids on the premises, her husband within touching distance and her best friend to hand. Tonight she was fearful of hearing that friend's name in his next sentence.

'It's probably best,' said Robert gravely, balancing a jug precariously on top of his pile, 'if I call Lucy over and we break it to you together.'

Three minutes after Robert's text, Lucy was in the Dunwoody garden, sipping a cold drink, with Prinny and Cookie at her feet and Robert opposite her. Marie watched them. She had often watched them, but never before had she watched them for clues.

'Chloe's welcome, too.' Marie joined them with the cafetiere. She needed a clear head for this. 'Angus is safely in his room, working furiously on something. The zombie film, probably.'

'Chloe went to bed.' Lucy hesitated, bent down to dissuade Cookie from licking Prinny's face and said, 'We've had a long day. She made a big decision, made some calls . . .'

'You mean . . .'

'Yup.'

'Ohmygod,' said Marie, briefly distracted from her own unfolding drama. 'So she's really going to . . . ?'

Robert looked from one to another. 'Please end a sentence, girls, or I'll never catch on.'

'Yup,' repeated Lucy.

'Yup what?' asked Robert impatiently.

'Next month some time, she'll . . .' Lucy spread her hands out, the international gesture for *you know what.*

'She'll bloody what?' Robert was almost shouting. 'Turn into a man? Cover herself in marmalade?'

Marie didn't laugh at that. She couldn't find Robert amusing right now. 'You'll find out,' she said briskly. 'I'm the one who needs to be brought up to speed, aren't I?'

'Before Robert says a thing,' Lucy butted in as Robert's lips framed a word, 'I just want to say . . .' She leaned forward, focusing on Marie. 'I'm sorry.'

'We both are,' said Robert.

Marie listened for a good ten minutes. She knew all. She was stunned.

'Why,' she asked, 'did you say sorry?'

'For keeping it from you,' said Lucy.

'Felt all wrong,' said Robert.

'Like we were – I don't know – having an affair or something!' Lucy snorted at the ridiculousness of this and so did Marie, deftly filing away all her suspicions and misgivings.

'As if!' laughed Robert, spoiling it a little with: 'She'd kill me.'

The idea that had been proving, along with the loaves,

was a risky one. It was also glorious and had ignited Marie's imagination. Robert and Lucy had stood up, sat down, banged the table and all but turned cartwheels as they'd explained it. Marie had instantly visualised their concept. The shop opposite Smile!, charmingly refurbished, no longer a fly-blown dental bordello, but a funky, welcoming parlour. Robert had sketched it for her, down to the (rather badly drawn) little round tables with dainty chairs. The walls would be panelled, Lucy had said, and painted the palest pistachio. A marble-topped counter along one side would groan under the weight of the cakes sitting proudly beneath glass domes, *begging* to be eaten. All kinds. All sizes. All denominations. The sandwich fillings in a chilled trough would range from the standard to the *what now?* Shelves would buckle beneath pyramids of freshly baked breads and rolls and pastries. And standing behind the counter, pleased as Punch in their pistachio aprons with chocolate piping, would be Master Baker Robert Dunwoody and Patissière Lucy Gray.

In just forty-eight hours Robert had already booked himself on a Small Business Start-Up course, and his negotiations with the disgruntled landlord who had been left in the lurch by Klay had resulted in a bargain price for the lease. They'd canvassed people in the street, and most had shared Lynda's heartfelt opinion that the high street was crying out for a decent sandwich shop. Lucy had asked for three estimates from local tradesmen for the panelling and had found cut-price marble online.

'All this behind my back?' Marie wasn't annoyed. She was impressed.

'We wanted to bring it to you as a fait accompli,' said Lucy.

'Lay it at your feet,' said Robert.

'So?' Lucy slapped her knees. 'Do you like it?'

'I love it,' said Marie.

She did. She loved it all. A family business of usefulness and beauty that also meant free baguettes in the middle of her working day. She loved the thought of looking out of Smile!'s window and seeing a pistachio palace devoted to the glory of cake, which was not only filling tummies but paying bills. 'I really love it.'

But the bit she loved the best? The restoration of balance. The lovely shimmering threads that bound them all together were strong again.

'You have to name it,' said Robert.

'Me?' Marie was startled. And touched.

'Yes. First thing that comes into your head!' Lucy clapped once.

'Life Is Sweet,' said Marie.

'Life Is Sweet!' yelled Robert, delighted.

'Life Is Sweet,' repeated Marie, her whole body a-wiggle. 'Because it bloody well is!'

It was at that moment that Marie realised she'd done it again. She'd signed the slip a month ago, but now it was only a few days till the end-of-term fete. As Robert and Lucy hugged, and Lucy cried, and the dogs bounced and the twins appeared at their bedroom window, Marie thought *What the blue blazes am I going to bake for this year's show-stopper?*

*

Later, alone with her cookbook, Marie turned the pages slowly. She fought a growing sense of dread, a stealthy unease sauntering up behind her, whistling, ready to slip a hood over her head and bundle her into a waiting van.

You'll know it when you see it, she told herself.

The vivid photographs of Mary's cakes blurred before her eyes as she flicked faster through the book. *Sugared Pretzels?* Tricky to make, but unimpressive to look at. *Gateau Saint-Honoré?* Wouldn't survive a ride in a car. *Marbled Chocolate Ring?* Not challenging enough.

Somewhere in here was *the* cake, the one that met all her criteria. It had to be challenging to make, awe-inspiring to behold, exquisite to eat. No room here for modesty. Marie wanted to show the world that she'd changed since the debacle of the battered Mr Kipling French Fancies. She needed everybody to know how far she'd come. She'd altered, deep down in her DNA. She'd become a baker. She was a member of that magical club. Her life was enriched – the colour turned up to the max.

Banana and Honey Teabread? Too homely. *Raspberry Meringue Roulade?* She was sick of meringue. *Nusskuchen?* Best not to cook something she couldn't pronounce with confidence.

Inspiration hit. In fact, it flattened her.

The kitchen was dark. Every Dunwoody was asleep. Even Prinny snored, more bathmat-like than ever, stretched out beneath the table. On top of the table, their gorgeous reds dulled by the night, sat a bunch of red roses, hand-tied, with a note attached.

M

You were right. The Earth revolves around the Sun.
Which makes you the Sun.
And me the Earth.

R

JULY

School Fete

Show-Stopper

Dear Iris and Rose's mum

Thank you so much for agreeing to bake the show-stopper for the school fete. Every penny made by the fete will go to the PSA and will directly benefit our pupils.

Best regards

The PSA

P.S. I hope you don't mind me adding that we do expect the show-stopper to be *home-made* – i.e. *not bought in a shop*.

It was a secret.

Marie was not great with secrets. The twins, on the other hand, were expert secret-keepers, but even better at winkling them out. So, in order to keep the exact nature of the show-stopper under wraps, Marie kept the kitchen door firmly shut. Access to the garden (and therefore the glass patio doors) was denied. Wandering through the front garden to peer through the kitchen window was punishable by . . . Well, Marie hadn't got that far, but the punishment would be *unthinkable*, she implied.

Up in his room Angus was unaware of the police cordon thrown around the kitchen. Downstairs, the other Dunwoody male took it badly.

'Stop being all huffy,' Marie told her husband, handing him out a tray of tea and ginger biscuits at the border, or, as they generally called it, the kitchen door.

'I'm not,' said Robert huffily.

'You are, Dad,' said Iris from the sitting-room sofa, where she'd paused the interminable mermaid film to which they were subjecting their father.

'Come back, Dad,' whined Rose. 'So I can lie on you.'

Settling himself huffily down, Robert acquiesced as the twins sprawled over him like tired Labradors. 'You haven't kept anything from me since we married.'

'Except,' Marie shouted through the now-closed kitchen door, 'my long affair with Russell Crowe.'

'I know about that!' shouted Robert. Huffily.

This time last year Marie had been . . . She wondered what on Earth she *had* done with her time before she discovered the joys and woes of baking? She'd probably been on the sofa, glugging wine, critiquing newsreaders' dress sense, trying to engage Robert in footsie, happily unaware that she was expected to supply a fuck-off-fabulous gateau the next morning.

This year was very different. Marie looked around her, content with her massed armies of spatulas, palette knives, bowls. Mary's recipe lay on the worktop. The oven was on. She cracked her knuckles. *Bring it on!* she told nobody in particular.

Weighing. Sifting. Beating. The rituals began. Marie was in her comfort zone. The show-stopper was her Holy Grail, her *Strictly Come Dancing* glitterball, her Olympic gold.

It was Marie and Mary – alone together, the way they both preferred. When inspiration had struck for this latest, most important cake of all, Marie had assumed that Mary wouldn't deliver a recipe for such a left-field idea, but a quick Internet search told her she'd underestimated her guru. Sage old dame that she was, Mary was there ahead of her: as if she'd known all along where this year of cakey self-improvement would lead.

Marie imagined Mary's purred approval as her

apprentice sidestepped the old pitfalls. Tonight there was no cockeyed optimism; Marie didn't expect to finish in a couple of hours. She didn't rush, she didn't get sidetracked, she stuck to her plan.

Batter dropped from the bowl. The oven closed on its charges, Marie peering in at them through the glass with the same tender scrutiny as when she checked on the sleeping twins. She wiped down her surfaces (a phrase she remembered from Home Economics) and dosed herself with hot, sugary tea.

The icing was a tricky customer: Marie had had triumphs with it; and it had brought her, gibbering, to her knees. Tonight she added water, drip by careful drip, and some lemon juice too. When she was satisfied with the texture she divided the mixture into three, and tinted them all differently. The colour had to be perfect, with not a streak in sight. This was a show-stopper, after all.

Brought to the border, the twins hugged their mother and she drank deep of their pyjamas' fabric-conditioner perfume. 'Night-night!' She kissed each nose in turn, and then kissed each nose again, because nose-kissing is very moreish. 'Robert,' she said over their mussed heads, 'why don't you go up as well? You look shattered.'

'I might,' said Robert. 'Especially as my own wife is denying me access to my own kitchen.'

'Bring out the violins, whydontcha?' Marie kissed him too. His bristles tickled her and she lingered a while. 'Now sod off!' she said.

Robert had been a blur the past few days, hardly pausing to eat. He'd wielded a pickaxe at the new premises, tearing down Klay's tasteless decor; he'd briefed a designer for the new logo; he'd carried on a genteel civil war with Lucy about whether or not to gild the edges of the new shelves; he'd requisitioned his wife's bottom to test various chairs. As soon as he'd toppled onto the mattress at night he'd lapsed into sleep so deep it was a coma. When Marie awoke in the mornings her husband was missing, only a dent in the pillow to prove he'd been there at all. But it was a happy dent, at least.

Beyond the kitchen window, Caraway Close ticked over. Erika, watering her geraniums, waved coyly at Johann and Graham's Smart car as it reversed and then whizzed off, to somewhere ritzy by the cut of their jib. *Mind you*, thought Marie, *their jib is always pretty ritzy*. Across the way she saw Lucy in her kitchen and moved her hand towards her mobile to invite her over, but decided against it. This time of the evening had once been dangerous – the time when Lucy's mood dipped and her optimism slipped out the back way – but now Lucy's head was bent over her online book-keeping course.

The same rigorous focus that Lucy brought to housekeeping, cooking or tending Tod's tie drawer was now fixed on the cafe. Her strong opinions had surprised Robert, and delighted him; no Tod-style tyrant, he valued Lucy's input. As he'd told her, 'I don't want a silent partner. I want a gobby one. Like my dear lady wife.' Even he, however, seemed taken aback at how vehement Lucy could be, once she shrugged off the diffidence that Tod had demanded of her.

The house across the way was looking rather tossed

(although still ten times tidier than Marie's), and the PSA had reached for smelling salts on hearing that Lucy was unable to contribute to the baked-goods stall this year. Lucy seemed to relish being too busy with work to perform her usual RoboMum duties, and even mused that she might cold-shoulder the fete completely. Chloe's obvious disappointment, although carefully cloaked, made her stepmother turn a fetching pink and reconsider immediately. As she later told Marie over one of Robert's still-warm caramel-banana shortbreads, to be promoted from 'barely tolerated' to 'necessary' was an emotional milestone.

'Good,' Marie had said, stealing the last biscuit. 'Chloe's not the only one who needs you at the fete. You must witness my triumph.'

Prinny stood up abruptly, ears pricked, eyes a-boggle, and a moment later Chloe knocked at the front door, sending Prinny into full whirling-dervish mode, chasing his tail, barking hoarsely, so desperate for Marie to put his lead on that he knocked it out of her hands.

'Here, he's all yours.' Chloe handed over Prinny, who was immediately assaulted by Cookie and the Gnomes' feisty mongrel.

'Ta.' Despite the recent downturn in Chloe and Lucy's financial situation – the Easter emerald had been sold, the antiques were on eBay, a stack of store-cards had been cancelled – the girl still insisted on giving all the dog-walking money to PeTA.

'An extra two quid today,' said Marie, with a *Don't argue* look. 'On condition that you keep it for yourself.'

'Thanks.' Chloe struggled comically off down the path

Claire Sandy

with her unruly charges, neither asking after Angus nor looking beyond Marie to see if she could spot him inside the house.

Just as well. Angus's ire hadn't cooled. He had careered through the days since his outburst over the girlfriend questionnaire, working up a head of steam about Chloe that dismayed his mother.

The royal marriage was not to be.

The cakes were golden, billowy, perfect. Marie eased the trays out of the oven and allowed herself an abbreviated gloat.

Across the way Lucy looked up from her studies and waved.

Waving back, one of Marie's mum's oft-used phrases spoke to her across the years. 'Winter and summer them, before you call them friend.' She'd wintered Lucy, and summered her.

She could call her friend.

Last to bed, Marie was the first up. While feeling the injustice of this, she also relished the solitude: just her and the dawn chorus, supplemented by Mrs Gnome's thunderous first-fag-of-the-day coughing fit from her front step.

'Hello, beautiful.' Marie greeted her show-stopper. Time to carefully shepherd it into its carrying case.

It was faultless. Tears stood to attention in her eyes, unexpected and bringing with them a rush of feeling more usually associated with weddings or funerals than school fetes.

The enormous satisfaction of a small job, lovingly done,

claimed her. Standing in her past-its-best dressing gown, her hair a fright-wig, Marie felt the essence of Mary Berry all around her. And there were others with her, too. Countless warm arms enfolded her, congratulating her and recognising her as one of their own; Marie was the latest in a long line of wise and kind women, the sort who make the world go round.

The year was over. It had been a year of change and upheaval, but mainly one of discovery. Of skills and truths and friends.

The stabilisers were off.

'Manfred!' Lynda, unable to decide between a Big Mac and a quinoa salad, was eating both at her desk. 'Barrington's panicking,' she told Marie, who was running her hands over the walls, still in awe of the clinic's chic new look. 'Thinks we're not ready to be parents.'

'Well, you're not,' said Aileen, inhaling a Lion Bar over a fashion magazine. She liked to belittle the models and laugh at how thin their arms were.

'He's worried he doesn't know how to be a father.' Lynda drank long and deep of her milkshake. 'And that I don't know how to be a mum.'

'Not a problem I'll ever have,' said Aileen, tearing out an article about a life in the day of Alexa Chung to savour later. 'Thank the sweet Lord Baby Jaysus.'

Marie scanned the appointments book, checking she was still free to get to the fete. 'Who taught Barrington how to be a husband? He's pretty good at that.'

'He's brilliant at it.' Lynda was complacent; Barrington

looked like a movie star *and* he rubbed her feet every night.

'Exactamundo.' Marie folded her arms, relishing the chance to be the wise old broad. 'If you wait until you're *ready*, you'll never do it. I've had three kids, and I'm still not ready for the constant commotion, the fights about nothing, the refusal to eat cauliflower because it looks like a brain. But I *am* ready for the hugs, the absurd way of looking at life, the new door that opens in your heart when each of them is born.'

'Oh, my gosh, that's so lovely.' Her milkshake pausing in mid-air, Lynda put her hand to her mouth. Pregnancy had brought out a sentimental side to her character.

Marie thought of her own children at the breakfast table that morning. (She persisted in thinking of the chaotic food fight that took place in her kitchen every morning as 'the breakfast table'.) All three had been edgy, excited. They'd explained it away by their anticipation of the show-stopper, but she knew them better than to swallow that. Something was afoot.

'You're a brilliant mum,' said Aileen.

'Pardon?' Unaccustomed to praise, or even civility, from her assistant, Marie looked puzzled.

'You're a complete natural.' Aileen licked the Lion Bar wrapper. 'Them kids are lucky to have you.'

'Um . . .' Marie was lost for words.

'I mean, all the feckin' effort you've put into them cakes this past year.' Aileen shook her head, as if awestruck. 'I don't love *anybody* enough to do that for them. But you did that for your children, just to be a better ma to them.'

'Well . . .' Marie felt a fraud for accepting that without demur. The impetus for her 'journey' (a notion she scoffed at on *The X Factor*, but which perfectly described her odyssey with Mary) had initially been the lesser Dunwoodys, but that had changed. She was a baker in her bones these days. She did it for the pure joy of the thing, which of course included the happiness it brought her family, but also gave her confidence and solace.

'Nathaniel!' said Lynda, and then: 'Show us your showstopper then.'

'Ooh, yes!' Aileen was on her feet and hovering around the big cardboard box on the coffee table. 'Come on!'

Carefully pulling back the lid, Marie exposed her pride and joy.

'You're joking, right?' said Aileen, hands flying to her hips.

'Is that it?' Lynda pulled a face. 'Seriously?'

'Isn't it perfect?' Nothing they said could dent Marie's pride.

'I take it all back,' said Aileen, closing the lid with a pudgy, decisive hand. 'You're a terrible mother.'

'I love the smell of fresh plaster.'

Marie's voice echoed in the gutted shop. Robert and Lucy were formidable project managers: Life Is Sweet was coming together faster than Marie would have believed possible. Timber stacked along one wall hinted at shelves and cupboards to come. The chill of a long rectangle of marble seeped out through its protective wrapping. 'It's all just . . . *waiting*.' It reminded her of her pregnancies.

That feeling of potential, of something big around the corner.

'The chairs are arriving later today.' Robert studied some paperwork in his hand. He was energised, as if Red Bull ran through his veins.

'You look good in a hard hat.' Marie waggled her eyebrows. 'Kind of porny.'

'Gee, thanks. Christ, nearly forgot! I have to meet the guy from Planning to go through the cellar details again.'

'You can make it to the fete, though, right?'

'Of course.' Robert picked up a folder, clutched it to his chest. 'I'll be handing out leaflets to our gala opening.'

'You're a workaholic.' Marie said it approvingly. She preferred motivated Robert to the demotivated model. He was funnier, sharper and the sex was better. 'Oh, look. Here's your other woman.'

'Hi-hi-hi.' Lucy, too, had had the Red Bull transfusion. 'Listen, Robert, there's a problem with the ovens.' She and Robert fell into a huddle, and Marie gravitated to Chloe, who had followed Lucy in and was running her fingers along the stacked timber.

'Careful!' Marie smiled. 'Splinters.'

'Least of my worries,' said Chloe.

Should she ask? Marie hesitated. The girl might not want to talk about where she'd been that morning. Then again, not to enquire might seem callous. But then again . . . *Oh, shut up and ask, you fool.* 'So?'

'So.'

'How did it go? This morning?'

'Fine.'

'I'm glad.' *Chloe doesn't want to talk.*

'Although . . .'

Oh. She does. 'Yes?'

'I don't know why I said that. It wasn't fine.' Chloe peered closely at the grain of the wood, following the looping ovals with her forefinger. 'It was odd.'

'Bound to be.' Marie moved nearer, glancing at Robert and Lucy, arguing politely about where to site a fridge.

'She cried. And she talked a lot. Like, a *lot* lot.'

'That could be nerves. If I didn't see my girls for ten years . . .' Even to say it felt taboo. 'Mothering's hard, even when you share a house. To miss out on so many years and then meet your daughter, as an almost grown woman, must have been incredibly tough for your mother.'

'She looks like me. Or I look like her, I guess. My nose makes sense all of a sudden.'

'It's a very nice nose.'

Chloe giggled reluctantly. Up and down, round and round went her finger on the timber. 'I didn't like her house.'

'You don't have to like it.'

'It's really messy.'

It would be wrong, quite wrong, to smile at the irony of Chloe disapproving of mess. 'Does she live alone?'

'She's got a great big stinky cat. And . . .'

'And?'

'A little boy. Fabian. He's, like, two or something.'

A brother. Marie tried to imagine discovering a brother she hadn't known about. 'Bit of a surprise.'

'Just a bit.'

'It *will* get easier, you know.'

'You don't know, though.' Chloe pulled her attention away from the eddies and whirls in the wood. 'Not being rude. Sorry.'

'Ah, but I do know.' Marie shifted the box in her arms; show-stoppers are, by their very nature, heavy. 'I'm not pretending I've ever been in your exact situation, but I've been around a bit and I can promise you that, if you bring honesty and love to it, it'll get better. Maybe she'll be the mum you went looking for, and maybe she won't, but she's yours and that's that.' Marie hesitated. 'And you've always got Lum.'

'I know.' Chloe nodded. Didn't dissemble, or roll her eyes. 'I couldn't do it without my Lum.'

It wouldn't do to cry. This wasn't Marie's story, it was Chloe's and Lucy's. So instead she tapped her watch and said, to all and sundry, 'Time to go!'

'Remember,' said Robert as the car pulled away from the parking space behind what would soon be Life Is Sweet Bakery and Cafe, 'I lent the twins my phone. You're under strict instructions from them to text them when we're on our way.'

Obediently whipping out her mobile – nobody wants to be on the business end of twinny wrath – Marie mused aloud, 'Why have I got to warn them we're coming?'

'Because they love us so,' said Robert.

'They're up to something, you mean.'

'Yes,' nodded Robert. 'That's exactly what I mean.'

*

The grounds of St Ethelred's were once again crawling with people, just like the same day twelve months ago. But Marie was nothing like the woman who'd passed through the gates back then. She didn't cringe or hyperventilate or contemplate faking a heart attack; today she was proud of the show-stopper under wraps in her arms.

'Oops. 'Scuse me.' Marie negotiated the crush of parents and students and teachers, leading her little band towards her appointment with baking glory in the main hall. *If only Mary could be here*, she thought, with shameless whimsy.

In her handbag her mobile announced a text. 'Robert!' She backed towards him, shoulder-bag first. 'Dig out my phone and read that, would you?'

'The twins want us to meet them,' said Robert, eyes on the tiny screen, 'in the Design and Technology block.' His face was a question mark.

'But . . .' Marie looked down at her box. 'Why? Do we have time?'

'I told you,' said Robert, 'those two are plotting.'

'Let's indulge them.' Today of all days Marie had the softest of spots for her little doppelgängers. She collared a passing sixth-former for directions and they headed for a low-built brick and glass cabin on the other side of the football pitch.

'Mum!' From the far end of the noisy, teeming barn of a room the twins waved their hello.

'What are they wearing on their heads?' Marie *excuse me*'d her way through adoring/bored parents watching lathes fly up and down, saws whirr and hammers hammer at the parallel rows of work benches.

'Headscarves?' Lucy, too, was puzzled by the twins' headgear, tied not beneath their chins but at the back of their heads.

'They look like factory workers,' said Chloe.

As they neared the girls, Marie saw Rose tap out a text with a surreptitious air that she knew only too well. Speeding up, she noticed how Rose nodded to Iris, who pressed, with some gravity, a button on the pink ghetto-blaster usually kept between their beds at home, blaring out David Walliams audio books.

Heads turned as music blasted out, the volume whacked right up.

'I know that song, I think.' Marie reached the girls and stared at them sceptically, looking for answers.

'So do I,' said Chloe. She bit her lip and joined Marie in staring at the girls, who refused to meet their eyes and stoically ignored them both.

A romantic female voice, at odds with the mechanical uproar of the Design and Technology block, sang a couple of lines, before a meaty male growl took over.

'Yes!' smiled Lucy, realising. 'It's – ooh, what's it called? – "Up Where We Belong".'

'From that film . . .' said Marie. She turned to Chloe. 'You'll know. What film is it from?'

But Chloe was riveted by the view through the large window that took up the side wall of the block. 'Oh my God!' she whispered.

Following her line of sight, Marie's eyes widened.

Pedalling furiously on Rose's pink, aged 9–11 bike, Angus parted the sea of people out on the football pitch. Knees scissoring up and down to his ears, shoulders hunched, effort distorting his face, he was nearer and larger with every millisecond. Atop his head, hiding his curls, sat the white peaked cap of a US naval officer.

Flashing past the window, the bike screeched to a halt by the open doors at the far end of the room.

'What in the name of . . . ?' Marie almost dropped her precious box as Angus unfurled and shook out his limbs to stand tall in a crisp, white tailored uniform, the jacket studded with brass buttons, epaulettes on the shoulders and the trousers sharply creased. She and Robert offered each other the same bewildered expression. *This is something epic*, thought Marie; her gauche, loner son would never expose himself in this way for anything less.

Striding in, Angus had the attention of much of the room. The hammering subsided; the soaring music was in charge as he strode through the crowd. Heads turned and Marie thought *He's not really that tall, is he?* The uniform made a strapping man of her boy.

Mums and dads darted out of his way as Angus marched, with a purpose he'd never before exhibited, between the work benches. People stared, not sure what was happening, but aware that *something* was happening.

Chloe, Marie noticed, was trembling. The girl's hands came slowly up to her mouth.

'Mum . . .' Iris tugged at Marie's sleeve, asking her to step away, to recede. She did as she was told, Robert and

Lucy following suit, leaving Chloe alone, a slender sapling in a forest clearing.

The girl watched Angus close the space between them; aware of the magic in the air, Marie held her breath as she watched them both.

According to the lyrics, there were mountains in the way, there were eagles crying; no words passed between the teenagers, but any fool could see they were having an intense conversation.

We've all just disappeared, thought Marie. It was another letting-go, yet she felt nothing but elation. The air was charged, filled with the change that had come over Chloe and Angus. They were electric with love and longing and youth.

As the song swelled, Angus drew Chloe's fingers away from her mouth. With greater tenderness than his mother would have believed him capable of, he touched her slender neck with both his hands. Chloe was calm now and she lifted her face to his.

'Hello, Soulmate,' he breathed.

So sweet, so heartfelt, Angus's first kiss was a public one. Slightly clumsy, completely earnest, it held the room spellbound.

Even the twins.

The Design and Technology master lifted his welding goggles to wipe his eye.

With a megawatt smile, Angus pulled away to wrap his arms around Chloe, sweep her off her feet and whirl her round. 'I'm sorry,' he whispered into her neck. 'I've been such an idiot. I'm sorry.'

A mother behind Marie, an obvious devotee of *An Officer and a Gentleman*, murmured, 'I love Richard Gere!'

The spinning and laughing broke the spell. Clapping broke out, slow at first, then wild. Somebody whooped as Angus scooped up Chloe, tucking one arm under her knees so that her hands flew about his neck. He bore her away, as if carrying her over a threshold.

'Now!' whispered Rose.

'Way to go, Paula!' hollered Iris. 'Way to go!'

'What the hell is going on?' Robert's head turned like an owl on speed.

'Just clap!' ordered his wife.

He clapped and so did everybody else, as Angus – his lips glued to Chloe's – made off with his prize.

'The hat, Chloe!' shouted Rose, over the cheering.

Chloe swiped Angus's cap and rammed it on her own head, as they moved out through the door to become a silhouette in the bright sunshine.

'Amazing!' said a man holding a clamp.

'That,' said a woman in a hijab, 'was the most romantic thing I've ever seen.'

'Our boy . . .' said Robert.

'And my girl . . .' said Lucy.

They blinked, struggling to join the dots.

'I think,' said Marie slowly, 'we just watched two people falling in love.'

It fell to Lucy to cut through the pink haze surrounding them all. 'The show-stopper!' she yelped. 'We're late!'

Marie led the charge as her little clan fled the Design

and Technology block, with Angus and Chloe, hand firmly in hand, joining them outside.

'This way, Mum,' shouted Angus, darting in front.

'So, you . . .' puffed Marie, hoping the show-stopper would emerge unscathed from this mercy dash, '. . . and Chloe . . .' She wasn't sure what to ask.

'She's my soulmate,' he said over his shoulder. Just like that. Unembarrassed.

'How did you know?' giggled Chloe, who looked far too happy to be a goth.

Heaving open the double doors of the hall, Angus gasped, 'The girlfriend questionnaire.' He held them open for the others, his lips to Chloe's ear. 'You only ever make one spelling mistake.'

'You mean *exciting*?'

'Yup. You always leave out the C.' Angus let the door bang and they all trotted past the raffle and the bric-a-brac and the Guess the Weight of the PE Teacher. 'I've never known anybody else do that, and it was the only typo Soulmate ever made in her emails. Suddenly everything made sense. Why I could never meet Soulmate. Why she encouraged me to give the crazy goth across the road a chance. Why I was secretly so drawn to the crazy goth across the road.' He hung back from the others and bent his head to Chloe's. 'Why I thought you were so gorgeous.'

'I would never have said a thing, you know,' said Chloe, through his kiss.

'I know. I was furious at first. You lied to me. All that time. But then I remembered. She's complicated, dude.'

Angus kissed her again. Perhaps they would kiss forever. 'But she's good complicated.'

There is a limit to how long a mother can witness her son snogging, so Marie was glad to see the sponges, the fruit breads, the Battenberg, the inevitable cupcakes, the plaited loaf, something odd covered with buttercream, and an empty stand awaiting the head honcho, the big cheese, the top banana.

The show-stopper.

'Come *on*!' The Chair of the PSA – *How can a person be a chair?* thought Marie, amused – was gesticulating wildly, perpetually irritated with the ne'er-do-well parents she had to deal with. 'You're late!' she shouted above the buzz of the browsing crowd.

'I know.' Marie was imperturbable. This was her moment. It would take more than a power-crazed mum of five in a sensible court shoe to rain on her parade.

As she peeled off the brown packing tape, a small knot of people gathered. This was the high spot of the school calendar for St Ethelred's baking fraternity, and last year's epic fail had made Marie's second chance the subject of controversy. A photographer was on hand, and beyond the tombola Mr Cassidy downed a miniature whisky.

'Come on, Mum, the tension's killing us,' laughed Angus. He was beaming from ear to ear, like a Cheshire cat with popstar hair. His arm was clamped around Chloe as if she might blow away, and she in turn was superglued to his middle, arms wrapped around him, rucking up his white fancy-dress uniform.

Iris nudged Chloe as their mother reached into the box.

'Look at Lauren!' They chuckled at the girl's cartoonish dismay on the fringes of the crowd as she took in the school's newest lovebirds, and Marie chided them with a 'Don't be mean'.

'Mum,' said Iris loftily, 'you don't know the half of it.'

The air around Marie thickened as she lifted the show-stopper out of the box. She remembered this from last year: the pregnant feeling of an expectant gaggle, waiting to be wowed. The ghost of a gasp hung in the air, and then – just like last year – the gasp fell back on itself, mutating into a communal, perplexed *Eh?*

'No, Mum . . .' Angus's mouth fell open.

'Omigod,' breathed Chloe.

'Holy sh—' began Robert, before Rose kicked him in the shin.

'Ta-daa!' sang Marie.

The Chair of the PSA looked unhappy. Very unhappy. A-bird-shat-on-her-hat unhappy. 'Mr Kipling French Fancies?' she said slowly, disbelievingly.

'Yes!' Marie took out the four bright boxes with their unmistakable branding, the cheerful illustrations of the delights that lay within, the helpful analysis of each fancy's calorie- and fat-content. 'Good old Mr Kipling.' She undid the first carton and slid out the inner packaging, its cellophane crackling, and arranged the neon yellow, pink and brown cakelets on the show-stopper glass stand. 'Could you give me a hand, Lu?'

'Um . . . sure.' Lucy blinked away her expression of frozen stupefaction and manoeuvred the other boxes open.

Together she and Marie made as appealing a display as they could.

The number of onlookers had swelled. Word had spread that history was repeating itself at the cake stall.

'I don't get this,' said Robert, looking from the colourful cubes to his wife and back again.

'Me neither,' said Iris. 'But I don't care, because I love French Fancies.'

'Everybody loves French Fancies,' said Marie.

'For a woman who's lost her mind,' said Robert, 'you seem remarkably relaxed.'

'One last detail to take care of.' Marie reached into her handbag and produced a small wooden rolling pin. She brought it down gently on the cakes a couple of times. 'There,' she said, before battering them a little more. 'Perfect!' She held out a punch-drunk, slightly squashed fancy to the Chair. 'Try one.'

'If I must.' Her face a rigid mask of disapproval, the Chair bit into the cake. 'Oh,' she said, and what Marie thought of as 'the Mary Berry Effect' happened on her face. The lines softened, the furrows between her brows disappeared, the eyes grew wide and a dozen or so years dropped away. 'It's delicious!' she breathed.

Hands reached out. Fancies were scooped up and torn apart and shared out. Showering her mother with crumbs, Rose laughed. 'You made these yourself, Mum!'

'Yes, sweetie-pie, I did.' Marie winked at her husband, enjoying his enjoyment. The horror-struck silence had segued into *tee-hees* and *mmms*.

'They're fabulous!' Mr Cassidy managed, mid-devour.

'I've never tasted anything so scrummy!' said Lauren, proving that even the most hardened of characters can be reached by cake.

'How . . .' began Robert, leaning in.

'I bought a whole load of the real thing,' said Marie, guessing the question. 'I carefully opened the boxes and I sliced open the cellophane and saved it all. Mary had a recipe, of course. I bought little white paper cases and then I laid out the fancies in the inner sleeve, glued the cellophane back together, put it all back in the outer box and stuck the flaps down.'

'Why? You could have made a massive gateau-type thing. You could have made a bloody crocky-whatsit. You could have wiped the floor with the PSA.'

'I didn't need to.' Marie peeled off some icing and popped it into his mouth, enjoying the contact of her fingers with his lips. 'I don't have to impress anybody. I know what I can do. I do it for you and the kids and my mates and . . . well, *me*. It's a joy, not something I need to show off about.' She endured Robert's eye-roll and said, seriously, 'I've come a long way this year, but it's all in here.' She touched where her heart must be beneath her T-shirt. 'And here.' She touched Robert's chest, and he grabbed her hand.

'So is it goodbye Mary?' he whispered, staring at her mouth the way he did before he kissed it.

'Absolutely n—'

'Yuk!' screamed Rose. 'Get a room, you two!'

Dear Marie Dunwoody,

Thank you for your application to take part in *THE GREAT BRITISH BAKE OFF* 2015. We are delighted to let you know that you have been selected to take part in a regional heat for the Surrey area. Details are below.

Congratulations!

Yours sincerely,

Eleanor Rackham

extracts reading groups
competitions books new
discounts extracts
competitions
books
new
events books
extracts
new titles reading groups
interviews
events extracts
discounts
new books events
events new events
discounts extracts discounts
www.panmacmillan.com
extracts events reading groups
competitions books extracts new
reading groups
books
discounts
events
extracts
reading groups
books
interviews new books extracts